Best Of
YOU SAY WHICH WAY

- DEADLINE DELIVERY
- STRANDED STARSHIP
- MYSTIC PORTAL
- DANGER ON DOLPHIN ISLAND
- IN THE MAGICIAN'S HOUSE

Published by:
The Fairytale Factory Ltd.
Wellington, New Zealand.

YouSayWhichWay.com

ISBN-13: 978-1540740892
ISBN-10: 1540740897

How These Books Work

In these books, YOU are the main character. At the end of each chapter, you make a decision, and then turn to the page that matches your choice.

There are many possible paths through each story, and many different endings. Some paths lead you into trouble, others to discovery and adventure. Once you get to an ending, you can go back to the beginning and try other paths, or you can go to the Big List of Choices for many more options and easy navigation around the book.

Your first decision is which book to read. After that, it gets trickier.

List of Books

It's time for your first decision. Which of these five books would you like to read first?

Deadline Delivery — You're just a poor kid living in the flooded under-city after the waters rose. Life is hard, especially for a courier like you, delivering packages to the under-city's most dangerous neighborhoods, while dodging pirate gangs, wild animals and security robots. But today is no normal day—today, you might end up as an explorer, or a froggy, or a trainee manager. Or dead. **P1**

Stranded Starship — On your first trip out into space, you and your crew are attacked by mutant space pugs. Will your decisions save the unusual cargo? Will your detective skills help catch a thief? Will you and your crew be stranded forever? Or will you save the ship? **P95**

Mystic Portal — is no ordinary bike trail. They say each new jump leads to another world. You and your friends can't wait to try it! Will you ride a camel? Fight bandits? Meet Bog the ogre? Or end up in an underwater city? Whatever you choose, watch out for mad genies, suspicious merchants and one-eyed creatures with orange fur. **P201**

Danger on Dolphin Island — While on Dolphin Island your vacation takes a dangerous turn. Will you and your friends outsmart the smugglers or will you wind up trapped? Oh ... and watch out for the volcano! **P365**

In the Magician's House — Watch your step, this book doesn't play straight! Neither does the Magician's house. Rooms move around. If you're the sort of person who needs predictability then pick up another book, curl up and enjoy it. This book won't mind. But if you'd like to take an active part in a book then stick around. You might be just the reader it's been waiting for. **P465**

Or you can go to the Big List of Choices and choose another place to start. **P531**

DEADLINE DELIVERY

by Peter Friend

Dispatch Office

Out of breath from climbing stairs, you finally reach Level 8 of Ivory Tower. Down the hallway, past a tattoo parlor, Deadline Delivery's neon sign glows red. The word Dead flickers as you approach.

It's two minutes past seven in the morning—is Deadline Delivery's dispatch office open yet? Yes, through the mesh-covered window in the steel door, Miss Betty is slouched behind her cluttered desk. You knock and smile as if you want to be here.

Miss Betty turns and scowls at you. Nothing personal—she scowls at everyone. She presses a button and the steel door squeaks and squeals open.

"Good morning, ma'am. Got any work for me today?" you ask.

She sighs, scratches her left armpit, and taps at her computer. Then she rummages through a long shelf of packages and hands you a plastic-wrapped box and two grimy dollar coins. "Urgent delivery," she says. "Pays ten bucks, plus toll fees."

Ten dollars is more than usual. Suspicious, you check the box's delivery label. "390 Brine Street? That's in the middle of pirate territory!"

She shrugs. "If you're too scared, there are plenty of other kids who'll do it."

Scared? You're terrified. But you both know she's right—if you don't take this job, someone else will. And you really need the money—you have exactly three dollars in the whole world, and your last meal was lunch yesterday. "Thank you, Miss Betty."

"Uniform," she says, pointing to the box of Deadline Delivery caps.

You pick up the least dirty cap. What's that stink? Has something died in it? You swap it for the second-least dirty one and put that on. You'd rather not wear any kind of uniform—sometimes it's better to not attract attention in public—but Miss Betty insists.

The steel door squeaks and starts to close, and you hurry out. Miss Betty doesn't say goodbye. She never does.

After stashing the package in your backpack and the toll coins in your pocket, you hurry down the stairs to the food court on Level 5. Time to grab a quick breakfast. This might be your last meal ever, and there's no sense in dying hungry. This early in the morning, only Deep-Fried Stuff and Mac's Greasy Spoon are open, so there's not a lot of choice.

In Mac's Greasy Spoon, Mac himself cuts you a nice thick slice of meatloaf for a dollar, and you smile and thank him, even though his meatloaf is always terrible. If there's any meat in it, you don't want to know what kind. At least it's cheap and filling. After a few bites, you wrap the rest in a plastic bag and put it in your pocket for lunch.

You walk back down the stairs to Ivory Tower's main entrance on Level 3. Levels 1 and 2 are somewhere further down, underwater, but you've never seen them. The polar ice caps melted and flooded the city before you were born.

From beside the bulletproof glass doors, a bored-looking guard looks up. "It's been quiet out there so far this morning," she tells you, as she checks a security camera screen. "But there was pirate trouble a few blocks north of the Wall last night. And those wild dogs are roaming around again too. Be careful, kid."

The doors grind open, just a crack, enough for you to squeeze through and out onto Nori Road. Well, everyone calls it a road, although the actual road surface is twenty feet under the murky water. Both sides of the so-called road have sidewalks of rusty girders and planks and bricks and other junk, bolted or welded or nailed to the buildings—none of it's too safe to walk on, but you know your way around.

Just below the worn steel plate at your feet, the water's calm. Everything looks quiet. No boats in sight. A few people are fishing out their windows. Fish for breakfast? Probably better than meatloaf.

Far over your head, a mag-lev train hums past on a rail bridge. Brine Street's only a few minutes away by train—for rich people living up in the over-city. Not you. Mac once told you that most over-city people never leave the sunny upper levels, and some of them don't even don't know the city's streets are flooded down here. Or don't care, anyway. Maybe that's why there are so many security fences between up there and down here, so that over-city people can pretend that under-city people like you don't exist.

There are fences down here too. To your left, in the distance, is Big Pig's Wall—a heavy steel mesh fence, decorated with spikes and barbed wire and the occasional skeleton. The same Wall surrounds you in every direction, blocking access above and below the waterline—and Brine Street's on the other side. The extra-dangerous side.

Big Pig's Wall wasn't built to keep people in—no, it's to keep pirates out.

The heavily guarded Tollgates are the only way in or out, and to go through them, everyone has to pay a toll to Big Pig's guards. A dollar per person, more for boats, all paid into big steel-bound boxes marked Donations. Big Pig has grown rich on those "donations". Not as rich as over-city people, but still richer than anyone else in this neighborhood. Some people grumble that Big Pig and his guards are really no better than the pirate gangs, but most locals think the tolls are a small price to pay for some peace and security.

Then again, you happen to know the Tollgates *aren't* the only way in and out—last week, you found a secret tunnel that leads through the

4

Wall. No toll fees if you go that way—two dollars saved. You finger the coins in your pocket.

It's time to make a decision. How will you get to Brine Street? Do you:

Go the longer and safer route through a Tollgate? **P5**

Or

Save time and money, and try the secret tunnel? **P36**

Tollgate

You jog the four blocks to the nearest Tollgate. A surly Gate guard rattles a "donation" box, and you hand over a dollar toll fee.

The gate opens for a boat you know well—the *Rusty Rhino*, an ironclad cargo steamboat with a dozen crew. Looking out over its armored sides is Captain Abdu McCall, wearing his favorite battered red top hat. He waves at you. "Morning, kid. Want a ride? We're headed for Blemmish Market."

The market's only three blocks south of Brine Street—that will save you a lot of walking, and there's no safer way to travel the under-city than on an ironclad.

"Thanks, captain. Great hat."

He smiles, showing all five of his gold teeth. "Another pair of sharp young eyes will be welcome. Pirate trouble's been simmering this last week. Probably just the Kannibal Krew and the Piranhas fighting over their borders, but my left knee's been aching since I woke up this morning, and that's never a good sign."

You don't trust the captain's knee, but you do trust his instincts—he's captained the *Rhino* for years. Maybe this won't be such a safe journey after all. Any pirate gang would love to get their hands on an ironclad.

The *Rhino*'s steam engine chuffs into action, and a sailor hands you a long spear, the same as most of the crew carry. You've never used a spear, and aren't sure whether you could, even to save your own life. Anyway, the spears and other weapons are mostly to scare pirates away. So you stand at the *Rhino*'s side, peer between two armor plates, and try to look fierce.

"How is dear Miss Betty?" Captain Abdu asks. "Still as lovely as ever?"

"Lovely as ever," you agree, trying hard not to giggle. According to rumor, Captain Abdu fell madly in love with Miss Betty twenty years ago. Maybe back then she didn't scowl all the time.

6

Five minutes later, the *Rhino* passes under a bridge. The crew scan the bridge suspiciously—bridges are a favorite ambush spot for pirates.

Nothing.

"Eyes to port," warns Captain Abdu.

You can never remember the difference between port and starboard, but a red speedboat is approaching at low speed. The driver is a pirate in a skull mask—no, as the boat gets closer, you realize it's a skull tattoo covering his whole head. Next to him is a woman with a Mohawk haircut and a necklace of human teeth. No weapons—well, none in sight.

The speedboat passes the *Rhino*. The pirates wave, grinning unpleasantly.

"A good morning to you," calls Captain Abdu. "You slime-sucking Kannibal Krew scurvy maggots," he adds under his breath.

Surely this can't be an attack—even the Kannibal Krew aren't crazy enough to attack an ironclad with just two pirates—but these two could be scouting before attacking later with bigger numbers. Or maybe they're just going grocery shopping. Either way, the *Rhino*'s crew aren't taking any chances.

The pirate speedboat disappears down a side street. "Good riddance," Captain Abdu mutters.

Half an hour and seven bridges later, just as the *Rhino* turns a corner, the captain kills the engine and sighs.

More pirates? No, a couple of blocks ahead are the flashing blue lights of over-city police hovercraft and jet-skis. Must be something serious—the police never pay much attention to anything happening down here, not unless it affects the over-city too. News drones are buzzing around above crowds of people watching a grey building, as if waiting for something to happen.

"Danger. Please stand back," repeats a voice every few seconds, over a dozen loudspeakers.

The grey building trembles, sways, then collapses in slow motion, and the surrounding block disappears under a huge roaring cloud of dust. The crowd cheer and yell. Some, especially those who were a bit too close, scream and run.

"Wow," says Captain Abdu.

Wow is right. City buildings fall down every year or so—they weren't designed to be up to their ankles in water permanently—but you've never seen it happen before.

"Very entertaining, but now the street will be blocked for weeks while they clear the mess," the captain grumbles. He turns the Rhino and heads south, but the streets are already crowded with boats, barges, canoes and jet skis, some heading towards the blocked street and others headed away, and everyone getting in each other's way. He tries turning east, then west, and shouts and toots the Rhino's steam whistle, but everyone else is shouting and tooting too.

"Can't say when we'll reach Blemmish Market." He looks over at you. "Might be faster to walk to Brine Street. It's up to you."

He's right. It's time to make a decision. Do you:

Stay on the Rhino, even though it might be slower? **P8**

Or

Leave the Rhino, and walk to Brine Street? **P19**

Stay on the Rhino

"I'll stay, thanks," you tell Captain Abdu.

He doesn't notice—he's too busy yelling at someone in a rowboat to get out of the *Rhino*'s way.

Eventually the *Rhino* starts moving again, its steam whistle tooting. The captain shouts so much that he soon sounds hoarse. The *Rhino*'s so slow that you're tempted to leave and walk after all, but the sidewalks are crammed too. Might as well stay on board.

You can't imagine pirates attacking with these crowds around, and you stop checking every single passing boat and bridge, and start daydreaming about what to have for dinner tonight after you've been paid. That's why you don't notice people abseiling down from a bridge onto the *Rhino*'s deck. Black and white striped bandanas cover their lower faces—it's the Piranha gang, the most fearsome slavers in the city. You try to yell a warning to the crew, but you're so scared that only a squeak comes out of your mouth.

One of the Piranhas twirls a baseball bat around her head and steps towards you. Do you:

Use your spear to defend yourself? **P9**

Or

Jump over the side of the boat? **P18**

Defend Yourself

You point your spear at the Piranha, but she just laughs and knocks it out of your hands with her baseball bat. She swings it again, this time at your head, and

Everything turns black P10

10

Boom-boom-boom-BOOM

An elephant's jumping up and down on your forehead—well, that's what it feels like. There must be a huge bruise, you can feel it throbbing in time with your pulse.

So, you're not dead after all. Phew. But your cap's gone. And your backpack and package. And your money.

Above you is a low ceiling of rust-streaked painted steel. You try to sit up, but now a dozen imaginary elephants start jumping up and down.

Captain Abdu looms over you. "Careful, kid, you've been out cold."

He's lost his red top hat. What's that around his wrists…handcuffs?

Oh no. You're wearing them too. So is the crew.

"Where are we?" you croak.

"The cargo hold of the *Rusty Rhino*. The good news is we're all alive, so far. The bad news is we're prisoners on my own boat. Damned Piranhas." He helps you up.

You've never been down here before. The cargo hold has rows of benches bolted to the wooden deck, with an aisle between. The benches are lined up with rows of small holes on each side of the hull. You've seen those holes before from the outside, but never knew what they were—too small to be windows. The holes are no longer empty—each now has a long pole poking through it.

The captain notices your puzzled expression. "We've been drafted as rowing slaves."

Your heart sinks. Looking out the nearest hole, you see that yes, the pole is an oar, its blade high in the air. "Why does a steamboat have oars?"

"I love my dear *Rhino*, but her engine's older than I am, and sometimes we have to row our way home or out of trouble."

"But…I can hear the engine, so why do the Piranhas need us to row?"

He sighs. "We've been wondering the same thing. This isn't the Piranhas' usual way of doing things. They weren't interested in our cargo—threw most of it overboard." A clang and a splash from outside interrupts him. "Hear that? They've been tearing off the *Rhino*'s stern armor plates and tossing them overboard too. Why go to the trouble of hijacking an ironclad, then remove some of its armor, and keep its crew as rowers?"

You try to think, despite your aching head. "They want to lighten the Rhino, but keep its front armor, and they want it as fast as possible, so…so it can ram something, really hard?"

He nods grimly. "That's what we think too. But not if I have any say in the matter. The *Rhino* may be old, but she has some cunning features the Piranhas don't know about. Okay, crew, let's see what we can do." He walks up to the front bench and pokes his fingers under it, and the whole bench hinges up, revealing a box of weapons and tools.

One sailor laughs, but is silenced by the captain's glare.

"We're still outnumbered, outgunned, and locked in," he says in a low voice. "One false move and the Piranhas will slaughter us." He rummages for a tiny silver tool and hands it to a sailor with a droopy moustache. "Grawlix, you're our best lock picker—get these handcuffs unlocked. But don't take them off—we need to pretend we're still cuffed." He turns to a short brown woman with a tattooed chin. "Crumb, you have the best ears of any of us. Sit yourself by the hatchway and listen for anyone coming. Be ready to raise the alarm with one of your famous sing songs."

She grins.

Grawlix soon has everyone's handcuffs unlocked.

Wondering where the *Rhino* is headed, you watch out the oar hole. Looks like the north end of Beach Road. What's worth ramming around here?

Captain Abdu distributes weapons around the crew. Not to you though. "Sorry, kid, but you're no warrior."

12

You remember how useless you were with the spear. "I know. When there's trouble, I'm only good at running away."

"That's often the best way to deal with trouble. And we may have need for a fast runner, depending on where the Piranhas are taking the *Rhino*."

"We're on Beach Road. The north end—King Volt's territory. Why, I don't know."

He chews his lip. "Me neither. Money is the only thing the Piranhas care about, and there'd be no profit in ramming one of Volt's power turbines."

The engine noise changes, and the *Rhino* starts to turn.

Crumb bursts into song, in a terrible squeaky voice. Everyone dashes back to their benches, and checks their weapons are out of sight and their handcuffs in place. The captain sits beside you, on a bench on the left side of the boat.

Two sets of footsteps clatter down the stern hatchway.

You glance out the oar hole again. The *Rhino* has stopped, facing south. Due south.

Of course. "They're going to ram Big Pig's Tollgate at the south end of Beach Road," you whisper to the captain.

He raises his eyebrows then nods. "Yes, that could be very profitable," he whispers back, barely audible over Crumb's singing.

A huge woman emerges from the hatchway, followed by a short man wearing spikey shoulder pads and spike-covered gloves, like he's some kind of pirate porcupine. Both have Piranha black and white striped bandanas around their necks.

"Shut up!" the woman yells at Crumb, marches to the front, turns and scowls at everyone. She has muscles on her muscles, and scars galore, and carries a buzzing stun-gun and a mysterious black box. Somehow even her hair—braided with pink teddy-bear ribbons—is scary.

The porcupine man blocks the hatchway steps, the only way out.

"We should have thrown you lot overboard and let the sharks chew on your flabby flesh!" Scary Hair yells. "And maybe we still will. Pick up those oars, or die."

"My crew will follow my orders," Captain Abdu says calmly. "We will row."

You're pretty sure that's his sneaky way of telling the crew to play along for the meantime.

Everyone grabs the oars—even you, although you've never rowed anything bigger than a raft.

"Not as stupid as you look," Scary Hair sneers. "Time to learn my favorite song." She presses a button on the mysterious black box, and a drum beat starts: boom-boom-boom-BOOM-boom-boom-boom-BOOM. For one crazy moment, you think she's going to start dancing or singing, but then realize the 'music' is a rowing beat.

"Pathetic!" she yells at the crew's first rowing stroke. She's right, the timing was terrible—yours especially, losing your grip and hitting your nose on the oar. "Synchronize or suffer!" She points her stun-gun at Grawlix.

The next stroke is better, everyone pushing their oars at nearly the same time, and the third even better. This crew have obviously had plenty of rowing experience together.

Over the drum beat, the *Rhino*'s steam engine chugs at full speed.

Out the oar hole, you see Beach Road whizzing past, faster and faster. The steam whistle blasts warnings every few seconds. There's a scream and a horrible crunch, as someone's boat doesn't get out of the way fast enough, and the Rhino doesn't even slow down. At this rate, you'll be at the Tollgate in minutes.

"Better," Scary Hair barks, marching up and down the aisle. "Perhaps some of you deserve to live a little longer."

"You know the Pimple?" the captain whispers to you, when she's not looking.

You nod. It's a huge broken concrete column near the Tollgate—people call it the Pimple because of the way it sticks out into Beach Road.

"Our only chance is to ram it," he continues. "Tell me when we're about twenty yards away."

"Less yapping, more rowing!" Scary Hair shouts.

Ram the Pimple? That sounds dangerous, and you have no idea how he'll do it, but you nod anyway.

Out the oar hole, Beach Road races past. Mermaid Street, Ocean View Road, and, wait for it… Armpit Bridge, which means the Pimple's close.

"Now," you shout.

"Hard to port!" Captain Abdu yells.

The whole crew stands. Everyone on the right pushes their oars extra hard. Everyone on the left jams their oars into the water and pulls backwards, you joining in.

The Rhino swerves left. Time seems to slow down. Scary Hair turns and snarls, raising her stun-gun towards the captain. The porcupine man waves his spiked fists in the air. The captain and crew drop their handcuffs and crouch down. Grabbing their weapons? No, grabbing the benches. You do the same, not knowing why.

Crunch! The *Rhino* jolts to a stop, so suddenly that both pirates are thrown to the deck. The *Rhino* crew pile over them. Moments later, Scary Hair stares nervously at her own stun-gun, now pointed at her by Grawlix, and the porcupine man is stuck to the wooden deck by his spiky clothing and two oars.

"No time to waste," the captain tells you. "Run to the Tollgate and raise the alarm."

He and most of the crew swarm up the hatchway. You're close on their heels.

The Piranhas up here on the main deck are still getting back to their feet, with no idea why the *Rhino* crashed into the Pimple. The last thing they expect is for their rowing slaves to burst out of the hatchway, waving weapons.

You dodge a pirate sword, hop over the crushed bow onto the Pimple's concrete, leap down, and race along the Beach Road sidewalk, heading for the Tollgate. "Piranhas!" you yell at the top of your lungs. "Pirate attack! They hijacked the *Rhino* and kidnapped her crew!"

That gets everyone's attention, especially at the Tollgate. Dozens of Big Pig's soldiers dash past you towards the *Rhino.*

The *Rhino*'s crew and the soldiers soon take the Piranhas prisoner, to the delight of the locals—the Piranha gang isn't popular around here.

Captain Abdu, who's somehow found his red top hat again, grins and claps you on the shoulder. "You can't fight and you can't row, kid, but you're quick on your feet. How'd you like to join my crew? Oh, and we found this in the hold." He hands you your backpack. The package is still inside, looking a bit squashed but intact.

It's time to make a decision. Do you:

Join the Rusty Rhino crew? **P16**

Or

Stay a Deadline Delivery courier? **P17**

16

Join the Rusty Rhino Crew

"Thanks, captain," you say. "I'd love to work on the *Rusty Rhino*."

Of course, it's not quite that simple—the *Rhino*'s still jammed onto the Pimple, with its bow crumpled and leaking.

But word quickly spreads through the under-city about how Captain Abdu's crew outsmarted the Piranha gang and saved Big Pig's territory from invasion. An hour later, Big Pig sends out his best mechanics and boat builders to rescue the *Rhino*. A few weeks later, the boat's been fully repaired. Its new bow is painted with an angry pig logo, signaling to everyone that the boat gets free passage through Big Pig's Tollgates. Forever.

"It's not entirely good news," Captain Abdu admits to you. "When Big Pig does anyone a big favor, he always expects a big favor in return too. But still, we've been attacked by pirates a dozen times before and this time ended better than most. Okay, kid, tomorrow we start our next voyage, transporting rat skins, dried plankton, and jellied eels across the city. Get ready to learn to fight, row, swim, and anything else I can think of."

"Yes, sir!"

Congratulations, this part of your story is over. You have survived a pirate attack and started an exciting new life on board the Rusty Rhino. But things could have gone even better—or even worse. You could have gone up to the over-city, or down to the mysterious domain of the froggies. And there are other pirates down here beside the Piranhas to worry about, like those Kannibal Krew. Or the mysterious Shadows.

It's time to make a decision. Do you:

Go to the list of choices and start reading from another part of the story? **P531**

Or

Go back to the beginning and try another path? **P1**

Stay a Courier

"No, thanks, captain," you say. "I'm not really sailor material. But, um, do you have a spare dollar? I'm broke, dead broke, and can't even pay my toll fee to get back home."

He laughs and gives you twenty dollars. Twenty! Then he hugs you. Half the crew hug you too, until you're blushing.

You wave goodbye, and run to Brine Street—your package delivery is late, and Miss Betty will probably yell at you.

After delivering it, you return to the Tollgate and hold out your dollar toll fee.

"You're that kid," says the guard.

"Um," you say.

"Helped save us from attack by the Piranhas," she says. "Thanks."

"No problem."

"No charge." She waves you through the gate.

Wow, that's never happened before.

Today's turned out pretty well. Twenty bucks in your pocket—enough for dinner and new shoes. Well, not brand-new, but new-ish, the right size and with no holes. Luxury.

You might only be a courier, but life's definitely improving.

Congratulations, this part of your story is over. Even though Miss Betty won't be impressed, helping to defeat a pirate attack was quite an adventure. Although if you'd made different decisions, today could have gone even better—or worse. What if you'd never gone through the Tollgate and caught a ride on the Rusty Rhino at all? Or if you'd left the boat after that building collapsed?

It's time to make a decision. Do you:

Go to the list of choices and start reading from another part of the story? **P531**

Or

Go back to the beginning and try another path? **P1**

18

Jump Overboard

You run for the side of the *Rhino*, getting ready to jump for your life. But before you can clamber up over the armored side, something hits you on the head, and

Everything turns black **P10**

Leave the Rhino and Walk to Brine Street

You wave goodbye to Captain Abdu and his crew. "Thanks for the ride."

"Good luck," he shouts, as the *Rusty Rhino* chugs away.

"You too."

Twelve blocks later, near a line of people queuing for who knows what, you find a dented steel door marked with 390 in peeling yellow paint. It doesn't look like much—in fact, you recheck your package's delivery address to be sure this is the address. Yep, 390.

Whatever this place is, they have a serious security system. Cameras watch you, and the door snaps open then shuts itself the moment you've walked through. Inside are white walls and long shelves, ceilings with humming tube lights, and a half-flower half-chemical smell that catches in the back of your throat.

Another smell too—dog, maybe?

A man in a white coat takes the package, scribbles an electronic signature on a data tablet, then walks away, arguing on his phone the whole time and barely looking at you.

Some customers are like that. You don't mind—the worst customers are the ones who blather about nothing for half an hour and make you late for your next job.

The security door lets you out then snaps shut behind you.

So, what now, walk back to Deadline Delivery and hope Miss Betty has another job for you? Unfortunately, that could mean waiting for hours in the dispatch office, watching her playing Bouncy Bunnies on her computer. But at least there's ten dollars waiting for you back there—that's better than some days.

As you start the long walk back to Nori Street, you have fun imagining the ways you're going to spend that money, starting with a delicious dinner tonight. Just thinking about it makes your stomach rumble happily. You're so busy daydreaming that you don't notice the shadows in an alley, not until they start moving. Too late, you realize they're not shadows but Shadows, the local pirate gang who dress in black from head to toe.

Before you can decide whether it's worth trying to run, something hits you from behind and everything goes dark.

You wake in the alley, with a throbbing headache. Surprised to be alive, surprised that you still have your clothes, even your cap. Your shoes are gone though. A few yards away is your backpack, slashed open—pointlessly, since it was empty anyway.

Oh. They found the coins in your pocket too, so now you're dead broke. Not even a dollar to get back through a Tollgate. What an awful day.

"Are you okay?" calls a voice.

You look around but can't see anyone.

"Up here."

From far above, an over-city boy looks down through a security fence.

"I called for an ambulance, but…they said they didn't service lower levels," he continues, sounding confused. "Security reasons, they said."

Stupid over-city kid. Ambulances never come down here, everyone knows that. "Go away," you tell him.

He doesn't. "And then I called the police," he continues. "But I don't think they believed me when I told them three ninjas attacked you."

Huh? "What are ninjas?"

He frowns. "Those guys in black."

"Those were pirates, from the Shadows gang."

He looks even more confused. "Pirates don't dress like that. Pirates wear eye patches and stripy t-shirts and old-timey captain hats. And they have cutlasses and flintlock pistols. And peg legs. And parrots on their shoulders. Well, not all at once, I suppose. And they say 'Arrrrrr!" and bury secret treasure and then find it again."

What on earth is he on about? "Go away," you repeat. "I have to walk across town to Nori Street in bare feet, and I'm tired of your stupid over-city babbling."

"Nori Street? That's near where I live. Why don't you catch a mag-lev train? It's only a five-minute ride."

"There aren't any trains down here, dummy. And even if there were, I don't have any money—the Shadows took everything."

"No, I meant the train up here. I'll pay for your ticket. Look here, there's a gap in the security fence where you could squeeze through."

You look up, ready to yell at him, but he's right—about the fence at least—he's flapping a loose section of steel mesh. Just maybe he's not completely crazy.

It's time to make a decision. Do you:

Go up to the over-city? **P22**

Or

No way, you're staying down here. **P29**

Up to the Over-City

"Okay, I'm coming up," you tell the over-city boy.

Easier said than done—you have to climb a slippery concrete wall, then shimmy along a creaking girder, in bare feet. The final part's the worst—clambering hand over hand across heavy steel mesh to where he is. One slip and the thirty-foot fall will probably kill you.

Just as you get there, he holds the mesh closed, blocking your way. "Are you a hooligan or a vagrant?" he asks.

"What?"

"My father says that under-city folk are hooligans and vagrants."

Stupid over-city dad, you want to say but don't, coz you're dangling over a thirty-foot drop, clutching rusty steel mesh that's already digging into your aching fingers. "See my cap? Deadline Delivery, that's the company I work for. I'm just a courier who got mugged by, um, nin joes, like you saw."

"Ninjas," he corrects, then holds the mesh open and lets you swing through. "Hi, I'm Albert."

"I'm, um…Rhino," you lie, trying to rub some feeling back into your sore fingers. No way is he getting your real name.

"Rhino? That's such a cool name, much better than 'Albert'." He points down through the mesh. "Rhino, are they hooligans and vagrants?"

Following his gaze, you see half a dozen people looking up. "Maybe some of them," you admit. Let's be honest, any route up to the over-city will attract some bad people before long.

Albert puts his thumb to his ear and talks into his little finger. "Hello, I'd like to report a broken security fence. Yes, sending a location-tagged photo now. Thank you." He puts his hand down and looks at you. "They're sending someone immediately."

"You have a phone inside your hand?"

He nods. "I got it for my birthday. I was always losing my phones or forgetting to charge them, this one's so much more convenient.

You should get one too, it'd be perfect for a courier."

You laugh. "Sure, after I find one of those pirate secret treasures you were talking about."

"C'mon, Rhino, the next train's in three minutes."

Rhino? Oh, right, he thinks that's your name. Stupid over-city kid.

Maybe it would be safer to leave him and travel alone. But looking around, you feel lost. Even though they're exactly the same streets and buildings, everything up here looks unfamiliar.

So you follow him, shading your eyes. It's so bright—for once there are no security fences between you and the sun. And everything's shiny and clean—buildings, people, everything. The under-city's an almost invisible shadow beneath security fences. No wonder that over-city people forget the under-city even exists.

A hover-van races past and stops where you came through the fence. Two people in overalls leap out, carrying tools.

Albert sighs. "Unbelievable. I report you being mugged down there and no one cares, but...I report a hole in the security fence and they turn up in three minutes flat. It's so unfair."

Maybe he's not so stupid after all. For an over-city boy.

He takes you down the street, past a building which has an entire wall showing a giant video ad for deodorant, to a line of seats which look like they're made of glass (although surely that's impossible). In front of the seats, a gleaming silvery rail continues in both directions down the street—the mag-lev track, and so this must be a train stop, you suppose, but are too embarrassed to ask.

A small train soon approaches. It's shiny and clean, of course, and looks like a spaceship. Albert somehow pays for tickets by wiggling his magic phone-hand again.

"What else can it do? Make coffee?" you ask.

Albert laughs.

From four rows away, two young women turn and glare at you, sniff, and then move further away. Do you stink or something? Yeah, okay, probably. Albert either doesn't notice or is too polite to mention it. He launches into a long story about pirates—his sort of pirates, not the real ones—which makes no sense. Something about walking on a plank and some guy named Jolly Roger.

"Nori Street," a computer voice announces five minutes later.

One block away is Ivory Tower, although you barely recognize it. This level of the building is covered in marble and chrome and glass, almost beautiful. For a moment, you think you're dreaming and this must be the wrong address. But when you peer down through the security fence, there are the grimy old under-city levels you know so well.

"What's wrong, Rhino?" Albert asks as you cross the street together, on a lacy golden bridge that plays tinkly notes with your every step. Musical bridges—is there anything they don't have up here?

"Just wondering how to get back to the under-city levels."

He frowns, confused again. "Why not use the elevators?"

"Ivory Tower has no elevators on our levels. And the stairwells are blocked, to stop us horrible hooligans and vagrants getting up here." Hmm, wait a minute. Surely the stairwells and elevators must have connected *all* the levels once, back when the building was built, before the city flooded. So…maybe some connections *weren't* blocked?

It's time to make a decision, and fast. Rolling towards you is a police robot, making a grumpy beep-boop-beep-boop noise. Do you:

Go into Ivory Tower? **P25**

Or

Run from the Grumpy Robot? **P27**

Ivory Tower

"I've just had an idea, Albert. It may not work, and it could get me in a lot of trouble, so…goodbye and thanks for all your help."

"Bye, Rhino. Hope I see you again one day." He bends down, takes off his shoes, and gives them to you. "Here, you'll need these, for running away from pirates."

"What?" They're great shoes, so great that you don't want to put them on your dirty feet. You feel a lump in your throat. "Thanks, Albert. They're the best present anyone's ever given me."

He shrugs. "They're just shoes. I've got dozens. Good luck, Rhino."

Clutching the shoes, you sprint up to Ivory Tower's front door before the police robot can catch you.

"Can I help you?" growls a doorman in a fancy uniform, glaring from your grimy bare feet to your dirty Deadline Delivery cap.

You smile at him. "Yes, please. I'm a poor under-city kid who needs to get back to the under-city levels as fast as possible. You want me out of here too, right? So—"

He grabs you by the collar and drags you inside. "How dare you smear your dirty feet over our nice clean floor," he shouts, then adds in a whisper, "Play along for the security cameras. I was born in the lower levels of this very building, and I remember Deadline Delivery. Is Miss Betty still there?" Before you can say a word, he drags you into an elevator and starts shouting again. "We don't want your sort up here, understand, kid?"

Why's he still yelling? Oh, the elevator has a security camera in the corner.

"You're a bunch of dirty, um…"

"Hooligans and vagrants?" you suggest.

"Precisely! Dirty vagrants and hooligans!"

The floor numbers blink down to "8", the doors open, and he pushes you out.

26

"And don't come back!" As the doors close, you see him wink.

The elevator doesn't even look like an elevator from out here—there are no control buttons, just two stainless steel panels that you know are really its doors. So, it's a one-way elevator—sneaky.

Yes, this really is Level 8—there's the tattoo parlor at the other end of the corridor, and next to it, Deadline Delivery.

Miss Betty scowls at you, as usual. But she pays you the ten-dollar delivery fee, as promised.

The steel door squeaks and starts to close, and you hurry out. Miss Betty doesn't say goodbye. She never does.

Congratulations, this part of your story is over. You've seen the over-city, and met Albert, who's pretty cool for a crazy over-city kid, and now you have a great new pair of shoes and ten dollars—this is the best day you've had in months. Would things have worked out so well if you'd made different choices?

It's time to make a decision. Do you:

Go to the list of choices and start reading from another part of the story? **P531**

Or

Go back to the beginning and try another path? **P1**

Run from the Police Robot

"Goodbye and thanks for your help, Albert. I'd better get out of here before that police robot catches me."

"Wait a moment." He bends down, takes off his shoes, and gives them to you. "Here, you'll run faster in these."

"Really?" They're great shoes, so great that you don't want to put them on your dirty feet. "Thanks, Albert. They're the best present anyone's ever given me." You feel a lump in your throat.

He shrugs. "They're just shoes. I have lots. Good luck, Rhino."

Clutching the shoes, you run down Nori Road. But the police robot accelerates. Halfway down the block, it catches up and clamps you around the neck with a metal hand. "You are unauthorized," it says, and grabs the shoes with two more hands—it has six hands, at least.

"They're mine, a gift—I didn't steal them," you protest.

"Correct," it says. A little TV screen on its body lights up, and there on screen is Albert giving you the shoes. "You are unauthorized," it repeats, and more pictures appear—you climbing through the security fence, you and Albert catching the train—you've been watched the whole time on security cameras. So much for sneaking around without being noticed.

The robot drags you down an alley, to a large cage labeled Trash.

"I'm not trash!"

"Correct. You are unauthorized," it says again. Robots aren't great conversationalists, that's for sure. It seals the shoes in a plastic bag, and hands them back to you. Huh? "Please hold your breath. Have a nice day." It pushes you into the cage, on top of piles of real trash, closes the door and pulls a lever.

The bottom of the cage swings open.

You fall, screaming.

Just as you hit the water, you remember to hold your breath, even though you can't swim.

But as you splash, you bounce on something. Somehow you're not drowning, you're in a huge rope net stretched over the water. Around you, people sift through all the trash that fell with you.

"Look, it's one of Miss Betty's Deadline Delivery kids," says a man with a dozen earrings.

"Dead?" asks a bald woman. "I know a guy who'll pay ten dollars for dead kids, so long as they're fresh."

"No, still breathing."

"What a shame. Never mind then."

Everyone laughs. You hope they're joking.

"Half a slice of pizza, and the cheese is still soft!" yells the bald woman, swallowing it with a huge smile.

"That's nothing, I found two apple cores!" the man shouts back

Lying beside you on the net is your Deadline Delivery cap. It's soaking wet, like the rest of your clothes (except for Albert's shoes, safe in their plastic bag), but you put it on anyway.

Back at Deadline Delivery, Miss Betty scowls at you, as usual. She pays you the ten-dollar delivery fee, as promised, but only after deducting two dollars as a Wet Uniform fee for your cap. So unfair. You scowl back at her silently.

The steel door squeaks and starts to close, and you hurry out. Miss Betty doesn't say goodbye. She never does.

Congratulations, this part of your story is over. You've seen the over-city, and met Albert, who's pretty cool for a crazy over-city kid.

Even that grumpy police robot was nice to you, in a way.

And now you have a great pair of shoes and eight dollars—this is the best day you've had in months. Would things have worked out so well if you'd stayed in the under-city?

It's time to make a decision. Do you:

Go to the list of choices and start reading from another part of the story? **P531**

Or

Go back to the beginning and try another path? **P1**

Stay in the Under-City

Did that over-city boy really expect you to trust him, a total stranger? Sure, a free train ride home would have been cool, but…he was probably only joking or trying to trick you or something, coz, well, over-city people are crazy. Everyone knows that.

You leave the alley. Where now—home? But how, with no shoes and no money?

Hmm, Beach Road is only a couple of blocks away, and has fairly good footpaths and a Tollgate at its south end. Yeah, heading that way makes sense. As for how to get through the Tollgate without a dollar toll fee…um, you'll think of something. Maybe try that secret tunnel you found on Krill Road last week, although that will mean a lot of climbing over rubble in bare feet.

Twenty minutes later, you've stubbed your toes three times, trodden in dog poop, come within an inch of stepping on a rusty nail, and been sniffed by a hungry-looking cat. Not too much further though—you can see the Beach Road Tollgate in the distance.

A steam engine chuffs behind you, and you turn and see the *Rusty Rhino* ironclad again. Maybe Captain Abdu will give you a ride, perhaps even loan you a dollar for the toll fee.

But…why is the *Rhino* going so fast, and using oars as well as its steam engine? And that's not Captain Abdu at the wheel, although he's wearing the captain's crumpled red top hat. Strange. The captain never ever lets anyone else wear that hat—it's his favorite. Just visible at the guy's neck is a black and white striped bandana—the uniform of the Piranha pirate gang. The *Rusty Rhino*'s been hijacked!

Where are Captain Abdu and his crew? Taken prisoner? Dead?

And where's the *Rhino* going in such a hurry?

You look further up Beach Road and see a line of speedboats are quietly following the *Rhino* at a distance.

You turn the other way and see the Tollgate in the distance. Why isn't the *Rhino* slowing down?

30

Oh. It isn't speeding *to* the Tollgate, it's going to ram its way *through* the Tollgate. The Piranhas are invading Big Pig's territory!

It's time to make a decision. Do you:

Run to the Tollgate and warn them? **P31**

Or

No, ignore the Rhino. The Tollgate can defend itself. **P34**

Run to the Tollgate

Is this really a good idea? Outrun a steamboat, in bare feet?

It's not impossible, you tell yourself. The *Rusty Rhino*'s just a slow old cargo boat, even when helped along by oars.

So you start jogging towards the Tollgate.

For the first block, you easily outpace the boat. But then you trip on a loose sidewalk plank and fall, stubbing your toe yet again and scraping your knee.

Ignoring the pain, you get up and carry on running. The *Rhino*'s close on your heels.

Faster.

The Tollgate's just three blocks away.

Two.

One block. The *Rhino*'s catching up.

"Pirate attack!" you yell at the top of your voice. "The Piranhas have hijacked the *Rusty Rhino*!"

Can the guards at the Tollgate hear you yet?

Maybe not, but the people on the street around you can. The locals hate pirates, and hate the slave-selling Piranhas most of all. Some people run off, and others start throwing things at the *Rhino*—stones, bricks, rotten food. Someone even fires an arrow. Not that any of that will do much against an ironclad boat.

The *Rhino*'s chugging alongside you now, and getting faster, or you're slowing down, or both. Onboard, a Piranha glares at you over an armor plate. "I hate loud-mouthed kids," he shouts, and levels a pistol at you. Before he can pull the trigger, a flying brick hits him and he falls, cursing.

Exhausted and out of breath, you stagger to a stop near Armpit Bridge, and shout "Piranha attack!" one last time at the top of your voice.

Just ahead is a huge concrete column, locally known as the Pimple because of the way it sticks out into Beach Road. To your amazement, the oars on the *Rhino*'s left side suddenly jam into the water, and the oars on its right side push extra hard. The boat swerves left, bouncing hard off the Pimple and snapping lots of oars.

How did that happen? It was no accident, you suspect.

The impact has damaged the *Rhino*, and slowed but not stopped it. Its engine's still going and it's speeding up again.

Somehow you find a second wind and dash the rest of the way to the Tollgate, passing the *Rhino* again and hoping no one else takes a pot shot at you. "Pirate attack!"

"Yeah, we heard you the first time, kid," mutters a guard from behind the heavy steel mesh. "Stand back and enjoy the show. Now!" He raises an assault rifle.

You duck into a nearby doorway, wincing at your bruised and bleeding feet, then turn to watch the approaching *Rhino*.

Something whirs and clanks, and five enormous spikes emerge from the water in front of the gate. People on the *Rhino* shout at each other, and the boat tries to turn away. Too late—with a shriek like a dying dinosaur, it collides with the spikes, gouging long holes in its side. Soldiers run out from the Tollgate, and there's more shouting from the *Rhino*.

Only a few shots are fired. Five minutes later, a line of unhappy pirates are sitting handcuffed on the sidewalk outside the Tollgate.

"Look what those damned Piranhas have done to my poor old boat," says a familiar voice.

It's Captain Abdu on the *Rhino*'s deck, looking down at her ripped and crumpled side. He's reclaimed his red top hat, and that's more ripped and crumpled than usual too.

"Are you and your crew okay, captain?" you ask.

He gives a sad smile. "Thought it was you I heard earlier, shouting pirate attack warnings—thanks for that. We were imprisoned in our own cargo hold, forced to be rowing slaves. A couple of broken bones and a stab wound, but we're all alive and grateful to be so. Could be worse, could be far worse. But I fear the *Rusty Rhino* has made her last voyage."

To everyone's surprise, the captain's wrong.

Big Pig takes the Piranhas' attack on his territory very personally, and has the *Rhino* recovered and repaired, at his own expense. He orders its bow painted with an angry pig logo, signaling to everyone that the boat gets free passage through the Tollgates.

Captain Abdu isn't completely happy about this. "Big Pig just wants to look good to the locals—he'll expect me to pay him back, one way or another. But at least I have my dear old *Rhino* shipshape again."

Somehow Big Pig hears about you too, and orders you to have an angry pig logo tattooed on your hand—that gives you free passage through the Tollgates too. You secretly hate the tattoo, but hey, no more Tollgate fees ever?—that sounds great. Life's definitely improving.

Congratulations, this part of your story is over. You're a hero to most people, except the local pirates. And Miss Betty, who doesn't care about anything except packages being delivered on time, but you don't care about that.

What might have happened if you hadn't raised the alarm about the pirate attack? Or what if you'd never gone up to the over-city at all?

It's time to make a decision. Do you:

Go to the list of choices and start reading from another part of the story? **P531**

Or

Go back to the beginning and try another path? **P1**

Ignore the Rhino

The *Rusty Rhino* steams (and rows) past you, followed by half a dozen speedboats, each crowded with people. No weapons are visible, but you spot several black and white striped Piranha bandanas beneath shirts and jackets. Definitely a surprise pirate attack.

Part of you feels guilty, wishing you could do something to warn the Tollgate. But still—outrun a steamboat in bare feet? No way!

Too late now anyway. The pirate fleet has already passed.

Limping, you carry on down Beach Road, watching where you're stepping with your sore bare feet.

There's a huge bang in the distance—either at the Tollgate or close to it—then lots of little bangs. Gunfire? A haze of smoke or dust hides whatever's happening. You keep walking.

Your left foot's bleeding and your right foot has a blister, but you soon forget that as you get closer to the Tollgate—the whole gate's been smashed open. There's no sign of the guards. A body lies face down in the water, and blood stains a sidewalk.

You sneak through the wreckage (not that there's anyone around to hide from) and walk back to Nori Road, detouring each time you hear screams, gunfire, and revving speedboats. There's no other sign of life, except occasional frightened faces peering out from barred windows.

Hearing a throbbing engine, you take cover behind a smashed crate. A cargo boat goes by, laden with weeping handcuffed people, guarded by grinning Piranhas.

An over-city fire control hovercraft whooshes past. It sprays water over a smoldering boat, then disappears, ignoring you and the slave boat. Typical. Over-city people only care about stopping fires spreading upwards—they couldn't care less what happens to anyone down here.

Getting back to Ivory Tower unseen takes half an hour. You hammer on the bulletproof glass doors. "Let me in!" You can see someone's shadow moving inside, but the doors don't open. "Let me in! I work here."

Someone grabs you around the neck.

"Not any more you don't, kid," a Piranha sneers, and handcuffs you.

I'm sorry, this part of your story is over. You're now a slave of the Piranhas, being herded with dozens of others into a long boat, on your way to…who knows where. If you'd made different choices, things might have worked out better. Or even worse…

It's time to make a decision. Do you:

Go to the list of choices and start reading from another part of the story? **P531**

Or

Go back to the beginning and try another path? **P1**

Secret Tunnel

You climb a creaking fire escape and clamber over the roof of a flooded car salesroom. Through holes in broken skylights, you can sometimes see car skeletons rusting under the water.

You cross a rickety rope suspension bridge, down an alley close to the Wall, and into a small building that everyone ignores because it's covered in bird poop and smells even worse. Then up a staircase with half of its steps missing, then under a broken door. You stop and wait, listening and watching through a hole in a wall, in case anyone's followed you. No point in having a secret tunnel if it doesn't stay secret. After five minutes, you decide you're alone. There are dog and rat footprints on the dusty floor, but no shoe prints except your own. No other people have been here in a long time. You only found this place last week, completely by accident, while looking for shelter during a rainstorm.

You carry on, through a room lined with shelves of rat-eaten books (and rat nests, judging by the rustling and squeaking) then past a concrete-walled room full of cables, pipes, vents, spider webs and a wall of giant fans. After swinging out the rightmost fan from its frame, you duck into the tunnel behind.

It's only an air duct, and so low you have to crawl on your hands and knees, your backpack scraping along the roof. With every move, the metal walls groan and creak and wobble like they're about to collapse. Don't think about that, keep going, it's worth it, because…

…when you get to the other end, and peer out through a jumble of torn girders, below you is Krill Road. You're through the Wall.

You wait again, watching, listening. Big Pig would be very unhappy if he knew this tunnel existed, and bad things happen to anyone who makes Big Pig unhappy.

Over there, under that floating tangle of blue plastic wrap—is that a pair of eyes looking back at you? No, don't be so paranoid.

Climbing down onto Krill Road, you're watched by a large three-legged ginger cat, but apparently no one and nothing else. The tunnel exit is invisible from here, just a shadow beneath an old upside-down sign advertising hot dogs. Why did people in the olden days always eat their dog sausages in bread rolls?

Everything's quiet. Maybe too quiet. That's always the problem with Krill Road. Long, wide and straight, with good sidewalks and three solid bridges. A great way to get across the city, for people or boats. And the reason pirate gangs like it too.

A line of ducks swims past. Must be safe, right? The ducks seem to think so, and barely glance up as you jog along the top of a crumbling concrete wall on Krill Road's left side.

Suddenly the ducks burst into panicked quacking and take off.

You turn to see a dozen wild dogs trailing you, led by a huge German Shepherd with a ripped left ear.

You know a dog that looks a lot like that. It knows you too, sometimes it even stops and says a doggy hello and you scratch behind its ears. But the dog you know doesn't have a ripped ear. Maybe this is the same dog and it's been in a fight recently, or maybe it isn't the same dog, and you're about to get your throat ripped out. Wild dogs eat almost anything, including kids.

Don't panic. Not yet. Avoiding any sudden movements, you look around, but don't see any ladders or other escape routes where a dog couldn't follow you. Around a corner chugs a wooden boat loaded high with cabbages. At the boat's center, sitting on a box behind a small steering wheel, is an old woman. There's a sawed-off double-barreled shotgun by her feet.

She smiles toothlessly and slows down. "Jump on, dearie," she says. "You don't look like a cabbage thief. If I see you being eaten alive by dogs, I'll lose my appetite for lunch."

The dogs are getting closer. It's time to make a decision. Do you:

Accept her offer of a ride? **P38**

Or

Decide not to trust her? **P50**

Cabbage Boat Ride

"Thank you." You climb down into the boat and sit behind the old woman, carefully avoiding cabbages, coiled ropes and an oar.

She revs the engine and the boat burbles off, to howls of disappointment from the dogs.

Something splashes nearby. No, not a dog, just a huge rat swimming past, perhaps escaping the dogs too. Another splash, a flicker of too many teeth, and the rat's gone, leaving only ripples. A shark? People claim there are crocodiles and giant octopuses prowling the flooded streets too. Or maybe it was froggies—the green-skinned mutant people who live underwater and snatch at anything and anyone on the surface. Not that you've ever seen a froggy, but everyone says it's true.

The dogs are soon out of earshot, but a few minutes later something else can be heard over the engine's burbling—a high-pitched roar, getting louder. Looking back, you see a blood-red speedboat approaching. On both sides of the road, people disappear behind doors and slam windows shut.

"Pirates!" yells the old woman, glancing back too. "Looks like the Kannibal Krew. So sorry, dearie." Everyone knows the Kannibal Krew really are cannibals.

"Not your fault." You grab the oar and start paddling. Every little bit helps, right?

She laughs sadly. "That's very sweet of you, dearie, but this old tub can't outrun a speedboat."

You scan both sides of the road, looking for somewhere safe to leap out.

The cabbage boat swerves around a corner, and the old woman cuts the engine.

"What are you doing? This is a dead end!"

She points her sawed-off shotgun at you. "Yes, I know, dearie. Drop the oar. Like I said, I'm so sorry, but the Kannibal Krew and I have an arrangement—I hand over any passengers to them, and in return they don't eat me."

"That's not fair!"

"Not for you, perhaps, but it's a pretty good deal for me. And you should know not to accept lifts from strangers."

"Look behind you. We're going to crash."

She sneers. "I'm not falling for that old trick—do you think I was born yesterday?"

The drifting boat really is about to collide with the side of the road. You have seconds to make a decision. Do you:

Jump out of the cabbage boat? **P40**

Or

Stay on the boat, jumping looks too dangerous? **P48**

Jump out of the Boat

With a bang, the cabbage boat hits a brick pillar on the side of the road, tipping the old woman onto the cabbages. Before she has time to recover, you leap off the boat and scramble onto the sidewalk, dodging from side to side to spoil her aim.

She yells some very rude words. Her shotgun blasts, and something stings your back.

It hurts, but you're still alive, so you keep running, and flee up a flight of worn steps that lead you don't know where. You randomly turn left and right half a dozen times, then fall in a heap behind a low wall, exhausted and gasping for breath and completely lost.

But safe. For the moment.

You check your stinging back. Just two shotgun pellet wounds and a little blood—you were lucky, very lucky. You can feel one pellet under your fingertips and dig it out, wincing in pain. The other's in too deep and hurts too much. Worry about it later.

Your backpack was hit too. What about the package inside? Pulling it out, you see three small holes and hear broken glass tinkling. Oh no. Miss Betty won't be pleased. Although…why isn't the package leaking more? A large broken bottle would be dripping everywhere, but this, there's just a little dampness and a weird sour smell. Not booze—that's a relief, you'd hate to have risked your life just so some rich person can get drunk.

You peer over the low wall. Carefully, in case any old women with shotguns are looking for you. Or pirates. Or anyone else.

Several blocks to the north is a tall green building you recognize—it's only a block from Brine Street, so you're closer than you'd expected. Maybe that old woman did you a favor after all.

Things are peaceful enough—people hanging washing from lines at windows, small children playing and arguing.

You make your way down to the street, ignoring two yapping skinny puppies. There's no sign of pirates or cabbage boats, so you jog north.

Two blocks later, you find a market you've never seen before, spread over the roof of a low building. Rows of stallholders are selling oily engine parts, electrical junk, toys, weapons, food, and all sorts of stuff. None of it's any good to you, not with only a dollar in your pocket. Ignoring the delicious smell of barbequed rat, you carry on.

Brine Street, at last. Most of the addresses aren't numbered, and it takes you a while to find the steel door marked 390 in peeling yellow paint. There's a long line of people queuing along the sidewalk, you don't know why—they're definitely not queuing for 390. Some of them pretty scary-looking. Nearly as scary as the three security guards, stomping around and keeping order with stun-guns.

You try to edge past the crowd, towards 390.

A man yells at you—maybe he thinks you're queue-jumping—and someone else joins in, and suddenly everyone's pushing and shoving and shouting. Then just as suddenly, everyone stops and backs away and pretends you're not there.

A security guard looms over you, his buzzing stun-gun in hand. "Where do you think you're going, kid? You steal that cap?"

"No, sir, I have a delivery for 390 Brine Street," you squeak, unzipping your backpack.

Without asking, he grabs the package and stares at it, then drags you over to the yellow door, hands you back the package, bangs on the door and walks away.

Huh?

A security cam swivels down at you. The door rolls open, then snaps shut the moment you're through.

What is this place? Lots of white walls and shelves, suspiciously clean, ceilings with quietly humming tube lights, and a half-flower half-chemical smell that catches in the back of your throat.

A huge grey dog shuffles towards you. He has no back legs, just two wheels held on with a frame of metal rods and leather straps. But even so, you're pretty sure he could eat you alive if he wanted to.

"Nice doggy," you stammer.

He sniffs at you suspiciously, and says, "Wuff."

A tired-looking woman in a white coat and a bulletproof vest marches through a doorway and snatches the package from you. She slices the plastic wrapping with a scalpel, revealing a Styrofoam box full of finger-sized bottles. "What happened?" she asks, holding up a broken bottle.

Oh no. Miss Betty deducts fees for any breakages, no matter whose fault they are.

"Shotgun blast. A couple of pellets hit me too."

"Show me," she orders.

None of her business, but she's still holding that scalpel and it looks really sharp, so you show her the two small bloody patches on your back.

She grunts, as if reluctantly believing you.

"What's in those tiny bottles?" you ask, even though it's none of your business—if she can ask nosey questions, then so can you, right?

"Drugs."

You choke. "I'm a drug smuggler?"

She laughs. "*Medical* drugs. To be precise, antibiotics, one week past their expiry date. They were donated to us by a wealthy over-city hospital across town—we need all the help we can get. I'm Doctor Hurst, and this is the Brine Street Community Medical Clinic. A shame that one bottle got broken, but there's enough left to treat half of the people queuing outside our main entrance next door. You want me to fix up those shotgun wounds?"

Is this really a medical clinic? The closest to a clinic you've ever seen is old Charlie on Level 6 of Ivory Tower—he charges a bottle of moonshine whiskey to stitch up any wounds, uses half of it to sterilize the wounds and drinks the other half while he's stitching. He's better than nothing, but not much.

"Um, okay," you say, deciding to trust Doctor Hurst. Well, she does look...doctory. And doesn't smell of whiskey.

It only takes her a few minutes to dig out the other shotgun pellet—which hurts, but not too badly. The dog sniffs you again, and licks your hand. Maybe it's being nice, or maybe it's tasting you.

The doctor dabs something purple on both wounds. "You were lucky, they're just flesh wounds. Keep them clean and dry and they'll heal fine." She walks over to a desk and types on a computer keyboard. The Deadline Delivery web site appears on screen, and she presses the green Delivery Received icon. "I won't mention the one broken bottle."

"Thank you. Thanks so much."

The doctor looks you up and down, and frowns. "How much do you make for a delivery like this?"

Another nosy question, but you answer anyway. "Ten dollars."

"No wonder you're so skinny. That's terrible—we pay the delivery companies far more than that, but you kids take the risks. Wait a minute, I've got an idea." She leaves through a door.

You can hear her arguing with someone, but not what they're saying.

"Wuff," says the dog, sniffing your trousers.

"Nice doggy," you repeat nervously.

He grins, showing lots of teeth and a long tongue, and says, "Wuff" again.

Oh, he can smell your leftover meatloaf from breakfast. You'd planned to keep it for lunch, but…never mind. You pull the plastic bag from your pocket, and share the meatloaf with him.

He swallows it in one bite, then licks your face. "Wuff, woof."

"You're welcome." You scratch behind his ears.

A few minutes later, Doctor Hurst returns. "How'd you like a permanent job as our clinic courier? It'll be hard work, and dangerous, but no more than what you do now, and you'll be better paid. And better fed."

No more working for Miss Betty? Hmm, that sounds good…but what do you really know about the Brine Street Community Medical

44

Clinic? It's time to make a decision. Do you:

Take the job? **P88**

Or

Think about it and decide later? **P45**

Decide Later

"Um," you say. "Can I think about it?"

"Sure, no rush," says Doctor Hurst. "Where are you going now?"

"Back to Deadline Delivery in Nori Road for my next delivery job."

"That's a rough neighborhood," she says.

"Yeah, but so is Brine Street."

She grins. "True. How'd you like an easy delivery job on your way back? 157 Nori Road. Twenty dollars, in advance."

"Okay," you say, before she can change her mind. Twenty dollars is heaps, and 157 is inside the Wall, only a block away from Ivory Tower. Easy money.

She hands you a small heavy box and the money.

You say goodbye to her and the two-legged dog, and leave.

Outside, the queue of clinic patients is even longer than before. Most of the people ignore you—you're just some boring courier coming out a boring yellow door—but a few stare, including a scary-looking woman with a Mohawk haircut and a necklace of teeth. A pirate, maybe? She's carrying a baby, and the baby stares at you too.

You pretend to ignore them, but the woman turns and whispers to an old man with his beard in dreadlocks and red beads.

Trouble?

That's the problem with wearing a Deadline Delivery cap—every few months, someone tries to rob you, even though the stuff you carry is hardly worth stealing. But Miss Betty insists all her couriers have to wear the stupid caps, and somehow she knows if anyone doesn't.

At the end of the block, you glance back ever so casually, and sure enough, the old man's following you, his red beaded beard glinting in the sun.

You're not worried. Not yet. You know this part of the under-city well. At the next alley, you turn left, still walking slowly. As soon as you're hidden by the building walls, you dash down the alley, turn left through an archway, and keep running. You dodge through the second-right doorway, down another alley, up a ladder, along the top of a wall, then jump down the other side and back onto the road, and stop, out of breath.

Hiding your cap in your backpack, you check in both directions. No sign of the old man.

Okay, back to Nori Road.

Easier said than done. Four blocks later, you turn left and find the whole road ahead blocked by a collapsed building. Must have just happened—there are still clouds of dust everywhere. Over-city police hovercraft and ambulances and news drones buzz around, a team of giant rescue robots lift girders and concrete beams, and of course a zillion people are watching. You'll never get through this way, not for hours, perhaps days.

So you turn right and detour around several blocks, hiding or changing direction whenever you spot suspicious people or boats.

Unfortunately, that all takes time, and hours pass before the Wall comes into view again. Your feet ache, and so do your shotgun wounds.

There's the hot dog sign up ahead. Not far now.

You stop. Something's different.

Oh. The sign—before, it was upside-down, but now it's more…sideways.

Has someone else found the secret tunnel?

Staying out of sight as much as possible, you get closer.

A hand clamps down on your shoulder. It's the old man with the dreadlocked beard. "You're a sneaky dodgy twisty-turny wee thing, that's for sure. Dragging me halfway across the city, when all I want is a nice wee chat. Young people today—so rude. Now, I can't help but notice your interest in this here wall of junk." He smiles, revealing shiny metal teeth. "That seems a remarkable coincidence, because I hear that just a few hours ago some of Big Pig's crew were also terribly interested in this very same wall. Spent two hours hammering and welding, they did, and then went away, without a word of explanation.

Quite a puzzle. Although by another remarkable coincidence, we're right by the Wall, aren't we? And what with you being a courier, and needing to get through the Wall so often…ah yes, I see by your eyes that I guessed right. Well now, losing that wee secret door is a shame for both of us, to be sure. We in the Kannibal Krew are also fond of having a few hush-hush ways of getting from here to there and there to here, yes, indeed." His smile widens, as though this is some huge joke.

A blood-red speedboat approaches, driven by the woman with the Mohawk. Next to her is a bald man with a skull tattoo covering his head. He's holding the same baby you saw outside the clinic. It stares right at you, same as before. Eying you up as lunch, perhaps.

"Let's go for a wee trip," the old man says, and nudges you towards the boat. For a moment, his grip on your shoulder weakens. This could be your only chance. Do you:

Try to run from the Kannibals? **P89**

Or

Follow the old man's orders? **P91**

Stay on the Boat

The collision rocks the cabbage boat to one side, and the old woman overbalances, her shotgun waving wildly.

You dive flat onto the hull—not that a pile of cabbages will protect you. The shotgun blasts over your head, so close that you're amazed to still be alive.

Looking up, you glare at her. "I told you we were going to crash."

She snorts and spits into the water. "Right little smarty-pants, aren't you, dearie? Fat lot of good it's done you—or will do, for what's left of the rest of your short life."

You sit up—slowly, because she's pointing the shotgun at you again. The side of your head hurts, and something's dripping down your face. Blood. You take off your *Deadline Delivery* cap and see two small bloody holes.

"Don't cry," she says with a sneer. "You won't bleed to death. Well, not from that."

Huh? Oh, of course, the pirates. The red speedboat swirls to a stop in front of the cabbage boat, blocking the road and your last hope of escape.

In the speedboat are two pirates—a bald man with a skull tattoo covering his head, and a woman with a Mohawk haircut. Both wear necklaces of human teeth. "Lunch!" they roar, grinning at you. They're not talking about the cabbages.

The man leaps onto the cabbage boat, giggling and waving a huge machete.

You scream. The last thing you ever see is that machete, glinting in the sun as it whooshes down towards you.

I'm sorry, this part of your story is over. You weren't careful enough in this dangerous city, so you died. Perhaps things would have gone better if you'd made some different decisions… and lucky you, you can try again.

It's time to make a decision. Do you:

Go to the list of choices and start reading from another part of the story? **P531**

Or

Go back to the beginning and try another path? **P1**

No Cabbage Boat Ride

“No, thank you,” you tell the old woman politely, keeping an eye on her hands. You know better than to trust a free ride from just anyone in the under-city.

Sure enough, she reaches down for her sawed-off shotgun.

You run, heading for the only nearby cover, a collapsed brick wall. Just as you duck around a doorway, the shotgun booms and the top of the doorframe disintegrates into splinters.

She yells some very rude words—well, some of them you haven't heard before, but they definitely sound rude. The shotgun booms again and you're showered in brick dust. She knows where you're hiding, and there are no easy ways out of here.

At least the gunshots have scared those wild dogs away.

You hear a speedboat approaching, then the woman arguing with someone. Sneaking a glance around the doorway, you see a blood-red speedboat with two pirates on it. Kannibal Krew, most likely—one is bald, with a skull tattoo over his whole head, and the other has a Mohawk haircut. Both wear strings of teeth around their necks.

“There!” the old woman yells, pointing straight at you.

Whoops. No time to lose, no time even to think. The only thing that matters is getting away, and fast. You run, ducking and dodging from side to side, not knowing where you're going.

Another shotgun blast, but nothing hits you. Hopefully you're out of range.

The pirates are a bigger worry than the old woman. No way can you outrun a pirate speedboat—your only hope is to go somewhere they can't follow.

You sprint towards an open door, but someone slams it shut and locks it before you get there. Can't blame them—everyone's scared of the Kannibal Krew.

Racing around a corner, you look for a half-remembered alleyway, but it's not there—oh, right, you’re thinking of a different road, three blocks away. No useful doorways, ladders, or stairways are in sight. The speedboat revs, getting closer. The pirates have spotted you.

You dash over a bridge and around another corner. The water's covered in floating trash here, and it's nearly low tide. Soon, some of these streets will be little more than deep sticky mud. Enough to clog a speedboat engine or strand the whole boat.

Apparently the pirates think the same—their speedboat slows, and the tattooed man clambers up to the bow and pokes a long pole into the floating trash, probably checking whether it's water or mud underneath. But the boat's still moving, still getting closer. From behind its wheel, the Mohawked woman waves at you and laughs like a hyena.

Through a broken wall, you spot a concrete stairwell leading upwards. No idea where it goes, but it's got to be safer than here. You run up the stairs—as quietly as possible, in case the Kannibals give chase.

At the top of two long flights of stairs is another level with broken walls. A pathway's been cleared through the rubble, to a narrow footbridge stretching over the street. Just what you need, except a group of people are blocking the way—they're crouched by a nearby wall, peering down at the street below. They're wearing black and white striped bandanas—the uniform of the Piranha pirate gang, the worst slavers in the city.

Heart pounding, you duck behind a pillar, hoping they haven't noticed you.

No, they're too busy watching the street and arguing.

"How about that boat there?" one grumbles, pointing down. "An adorable family with four little kids and no weapons. Easy pickings. Little kids sell for fifty bucks at the moment—more if they're cute."

"No, we don't want no adorable families, not today. The boss wants an ironclad boat," says another.

"Don't see why. Ironclads have heaps of armed guards. Risky target, very risky. What's he want an ironclad for?"

52

"How would I know? Sunday afternoon visits to his dear old mum, maybe. Some new special sneaky plan, that's all I've heard. I just do what I'm told, and so should you."

From the shadow of the pillar, you take a longer look. Six Piranhas, wearing harnesses, and with coils of rope at their feet—they must be planning on attacking a boat by abseiling down from the bridge.

The grumbly pirate has a good point—why go to the trouble of attacking an ironclad boat? The only ironclad you know is the *Rusty Rhino*, a cargo steamboat with a well-armed crew who'd have no trouble fighting off half a dozen Piranhas.

From behind you, clattering up the staircase, come two sets of footsteps—probably the Kannibal Krew searching for you.

Pirates in front, pirates behind. Big trouble. Then again, the Kannibal Krew and Piranhas hate each other—that could help you.

It's time to make a decision. Do you:

Make a run for the bridge? **P53**

Or

Stay where you are, and hope the pirates fight each other? **P67**

Make a Run for the Bridge

"Kannibal Krew! Help!" you yell, running towards the footbridge.

Not that you expect the Piranhas to help you on purpose. And they don't—exactly as you'd hoped, they charge at the surprised-looking Kannibals instead.

Perfect. You dash over the narrow bridge, feeling clever.

But as you reach the other side, a foot stretches out and sends you sprawling across a dusty floor.

A dozen more Piranhas surround you. Oh, of course, they were hiding on *both* sides of the bridge. And you've spoiled their ambush. No wonder they're angry.

One of them knocks your Deadline Delivery cap to the floor, and rips your backpack off. "A courier?" He grins nastily. "You're lost, kid. Dangerously lost. This is a bad part of town."

"Grinder's signaling us," says a scarred woman, looking over the bridge. "They got Kannibal Krew trouble."

Most of the Piranhas lose interest in you and dash over the bridge, yelling and waving weapons.

"Kill the kid. We don't want no witnesses," the scarred woman says to the man rummaging in your backpack, then sprints after the others.

The man pulls out the package and reads the label. His nasty grin turns...almost nice. "390 Brine Street? They've sewed me up often enough. It's your lucky day, kid—I won't kill you this time. Get out of here before I change my mind." He tosses you your backpack and package and disappears over the bridge, leaving you alone and confused. Who sewed him up? What's at 390 Brine Street?

Whatever. Those Piranhas could return at any moment, so you run out the door in the opposite wall.

This building's stairwells are mostly blocked or missing, so finding another way out is hard work. Eventually you decide to squeeze through a broken window, trying not to break any more of its jagged glass in case the noise attracts attention.

54

You make it through with just one long scratch, then notice a bloodstained green plastic card on a lanyard, lying amongst the broken glass on the floor. Looks familiar—where have you seen those cards before? Oh yeah, it's a security pass for day workers going up to the over-city.

On its other side is the name Ortopa Baskirl, whoever he or she is. Or was—that's probably Ortopa Baskirl's blood on it.

You're soon back down on the streets and on the way to Brine Street again, but you keep looking up at the over-city and fingering Ortopa Baskirl's security pass in your pocket. Could you use it yourself? You've always wanted to see the over-city with your own eyes, not just from through a security fence or on television.

Ten minutes later, you're at 390 Brine Street, and deliver the package to some grumpy guy who's in too much of a hurry (or too snooty) to say "hello" or "thank you". You hardly notice, still thinking about the over-city.

A couple of blocks away, you pass one of the long ladders which go up to the over-city. They're fenced off and guarded, of course—over-city people don't want under-city people sneaking up there and getting up to no good. A dozen day workers queue at the ladder's bottom, wearing green security passes just like the one in your pocket.

It's time to make a decision. Do you:

Pretend the security pass is yours, and join the queue of day workers? **P55**

Or

Try to return the security pass? **P64**

Pretend the Security Pass is Yours

You stuff your Deadline Delivery cap into your backpack, slip the security pass lanyard around your neck, and join the line of day workers. A couple of them glance at you, but don't say anything.

As each worker reaches a steel gate at the front of the queue, they swipe their pass past a glowing green light, and the gate says "hello" and the person's name in a cheerful computerized voice, and then lets that person through.

When it's your turn, you swipe your pass the same way, ready to run if alarm bells ring, but the gate just cheerfully says, "Hello, Ortopa Baskirl," and opens. More people are already queuing behind you, so you go through the gate, keeping your head down.

Stairs. Hundreds of stairs, all the way up to the over-city. And at the top, there's another queue at another security gate.

"You're not Ortopa Baskirl," says a voice behind you.

Uh-oh. You turn and see an olive-skinned man with no eyebrows.

"Ortopa's sick today, so I'm doing his job for him," you say. Not a very convincing lie, but it's the best you can think of.

Mister No-Eyebrows raises his non-existent eyebrows. "Really? Strange, coz Ortopa's a woman—we work together. I don't know or care who you are, kid, but you'd better be a hard worker, or else."

"I am a hard worker. Um, working at what?"

He doesn't answer.

The security gate lets you through, and you get your first proper view of the over-city. Everything's shiny and clean, and so bright it hurts your eyes, although maybe that's just because up here the sunlight doesn't have to filter down though security fences. All the over-city people look shiny and clean too, just like on television. They ignore you and the other day workers, as if you're invisible.

Mister No-Eyebrows leads you a few blocks away to a tall building, and you both enter through a narrow side door, after swiping your passes again. He pushes you down a carpeted corridor and through several more doors (swiping passes each time) then into a room full of mirrors and tiles. He hands you a pair of purple gloves and a bucket full of plastic bottles and clean rags. "Okay, show me how hard you can work."

Looking around, you realize this must be a bathroom, although nothing like any in the under-city—down there, you hold your breath and get out as fast as possible, hoping there aren't too many cockroaches and rats in there with you. If you can find a bathroom. This bathroom…well, those shiny things must be taps, but why are there five of them? And why does this place need cleaning anyway?—it's the cleanest room you've ever seen. But he's watching you, so you put on the gloves, then mop and scrub and wipe and polish everything in sight.

"Mmm," he says, unsmiling. "A bit slow, but not bad for a first try. Next."

Next what?

He leads you along a corridor to…another bathroom, like the first except this one is pale pink and has gold taps. Solid gold? Who knows—over-city people are crazy.

"Well, what are you waiting for?" he asks. "We've got eighty-three more to do today."

Eighty-three? Sighing, you pick up your sponge again.

This time he helps, showing you a faster way to mop the floor, and a trick for polishing taps.

Eighty-two to go. The next one is pale blue, with butterflies painted across the ceiling. Pretty, although not much fun to clean.

And so on, bathroom after bathroom after bathroom, with just one short lunch break, hours later—thankfully not in a bathroom.

Mister No-Eyebrows never tells you his name, and calls you "Fake Ortopa". The only things he ever talks about are cleaning-related—stain removal, the best way to polish mirrors, and unblocking clogged drains.

By the end of the day, your hands ache, your back hurts, and you've got a weird itchy rash on your left wrist. Today wasn't what you'd expected from your first visit to the over-city—you now know more than you ever wanted to about fancy bathrooms. All you saw of the rest of the over-city was a few glances out windows.

"Good work today, Fake Ortopa," Mister No-Eyebrows says, as you return to the over-city street level together. "You scrub toilets better than the real Ortopa, and that's what matters to me. Back tomorrow?" He swipes his card.

"Maybe." Is scrubbing toilets better than working as a courier? Depends—are you going to get paid for today, and how much? Or does he love cleaning so much that he does it for free, and expects you do the same?

You swipe your card, the door opens and you walk out, straight into the arms of a burly security guard. "Ortopa Baskirl?" she asks, grabbing your security pass lanyard and almost choking you with it.

"Um, yeah?" you squeak.

She grins like a shark. "Really? Ortopa Baskirl was found floating face-down in an under-city street this morning." She turns to Mister No-Eyebrows. "You. Scram!"

He does.

"I found Ortopa's pass by accident," you babble to the guard. "I don't know anything about her, or her death. It was probably the Piranha gang, but…"

"Shut up." She drags you over to a gleaming dark green luxury car hovering a few inches in the air.

From its open rear window, a well-dressed man smiles at you. "You're in a lot of trouble, kid. Trespassing, possession of stolen property, identity fraud, interfering with murder evidence," he says, counting each point on his fingers. Then he opens the car door. "Or this could be the best day of the rest of your life."

Who is this guy? No matter how much trouble you're in, you don't trust him one bit. No way do you want to get in this car—but the guard just picks you up, tosses you inside then slams the door.

58

The guard gets into the front seat and the car glides away so silently you wouldn't know it was moving if the street outside wasn't sliding past.

"Relax, kid, enjoy the ride," the man says, still smiling. "I'm Bradley Lime, recruitment specialist for the Avocado Corporation—I'm sure you've heard of us." You shake your head but he doesn't notice and keeps talking. "I've been watching you on security camera footage, deciding what to do with you. Naturally, under-city people try to sneak up here every day. Most of them want to steal something or smash something or hurt someone, or all three. Can't have that now, can we? No, the nice folks up here want peace and quiet, law and order, not a bunch of dirty under-city hooligans running around. But you, you sneaked up here and …spent the day cleaning bathrooms. Interesting."

Wasn't my idea, you feel like saying, but don't.

Bradley's still smiling like a toothpaste ad. "The Avocado Corporation thinks disadvantaged kids deserve a chance for a successful life here in the over-city, so we're offering you a job as trainee manager. All expenses paid, including food, accommodation, and uniform."

The car stops, next to a forest building—a skyscraper covered in plants and trees and flowers. You've seen them before, looking up from the under-city, but never up close like this.

"You'd be working here, at Avocado Corporation Urban Organic Farm number 29," he continues. "What do you say, kid?"

You don't understand half of what he's said. Some sort of job here in the over-city. That sounds good, but…what's an urban farm? And what does a trainee manager do, and what do they get paid?

It's time to make a decision. Do you:

Take the job, because it has to be better than being a courier? **P59**

Or

Say no, and get away from this crazy guy as soon as you can? **P62**

Avocado Corporation

"Okay," you say to Bradley Lime, and try to smile.

But you can't compete with his grin, which just got even wider. "Best of luck, kid."

The guard takes you into the "urban farm" building, through a door labeled *Management Only*, and slams the door shut, leaving you inside. You try the door, but it's locked.

It's a strange room, hot and humid. The walls are thousands of small panes of glass, and through them is nothing but green—endless rows of plants and trees. Oh, the whole building must be full of plants. Yeah, an urban farm, that makes sense now. Places like this must be where farmers grow food for over-city people.

"What do you want?" asks a voice behind you.

Turning, you see a sweaty young woman in a green Avocado Corporation t-shirt.

"Um, hi, I'm your new trainee manager," you say.

"No one tells me anything." She sighs and taps on a tablet computer. "Oh, right. Lucky you. Hi, I'm Marcie, junior assistant manager, welcome to your exciting new career at the Avocado Corporation." Marcie sure doesn't sound excited. "Follow me. I'll get you a t-shirt—they must be worn at all times. Corporate policy. And you'd better watch the New Employees video. Corporate policy."

Over the next few hours, you hear "corporate policy" about a million times from Marcie. Apparently the Avocado Corporation has rules for absolutely everything.

Then it's dinnertime in the Avocado Corporation staff cafeteria. There's plenty of food and it tastes okay, and you eat until you're stuffed. But you don't enjoy it much—sitting at the same table are eleven other trainee managers, and they're the glummest people ever. So far, the only happy Avocado Corporation employee you've met was Bradley Lime. Maybe he wasn't really smiling, maybe he was just showing his teeth. Or maybe it's against corporate policy for trainee managers to smile or laugh.

Marcie looks at her watch. "Evening shift starts in three minutes. Follow me," she tells you.

Maybe now you'll finally find out what a trainee manager does around here.

She takes you up and down stairs and along glass-walled corridors, stopping now and then to check numbers on computer screens—humidity, temperature and so on. Despite the zillion plants on the other side of the glass, you haven't touched one leaf yet. Who's doing the weeding and planting and harvesting? Robots?

Then you see movement through the glass—people trudging along, carrying trowels and baskets. They look even sadder than the trainee managers, and aren't wearing Avocado Corporation t-shirts. Hey, one of them is Mac, the owner of Mac's Greasy Spoon back at Ivory Tower! What's he doing here? Behind them swaggers a man wearing a Piranha black and white striped bandana and carrying a stun-gun in his meaty hand.

All of a sudden, everything makes horrible sense. "They're slave workers, aren't they? The Piranha gang supplies the Avocado Corporation with slaves to do the farm work."

Marcie rolls her eyes. "Duh! This farm has to supply nine thousand lettuces and three thousand cucumbers by 4 am tomorrow morning. Who do you think's going to do all that work? Better them than us. Behave yourself, or you'll end up as one of them—that's corporate policy."

I'm sorry, this part of your story is over. You've made it up to the over-city, discovered the Avocado Corporation's terrible secret and what happens to the Piranha gang's slaves. Working as a trainee manager is going to be awful, no matter how much they feed you and pay you—you don't want to have anything to do with slavery. Life was so much simpler back in the under-city—if only you hadn't taken that security pass…

61

It's time to make a decision. Do you:

Go to the list of choices and start reading from another part of the story? **P531**

Or

Go back to the beginning and try another path? **P1**

Get Away from Bradley Lime

"Thanks anyway, but I don't think I'd be a good trainee manager," you tell Bradley politely.

His smile disappears. "I guess you're not so smart after all."

The guard opens the car door, and she drags you over to the urban farm building. You struggle, but she's too strong. Without a word, she shoves you through a door labeled *Staff Only*, then slams it shut, leaving you inside.

You try the door, but it's locked.

What is this place? There are plants absolutely everywhere, in pots and on racks along the walls. Some are vegetables and fruits, but others you don't recognize. The air is hot and humid. Bright too—the walls are thousands of small panes of frosted glass. Above, instead of a ceiling, there's a layer of steel mesh, and above that, more plants. Hmm, maybe the whole building's nothing but plants on every level? Yeah, an urban farm, that makes sense now. Places like this must be where farmers grow food for over-city people.

But why did the guard put you here? Will you be forced to become a trainee manager after all?

From behind a tree walks Mac, the owner of Mac's Greasy Spoon back at Ivory Tower. You stare at each other in surprise.

"So they got you too, huh?" he asks. "At least you're alive—we lost some good people today."

"What are you talking about? What are you doing up here, Mac?"

"What are *you* talking about?"

"What?"

"Stop saying 'what'. How did you get here, kid? Weren't you caught in the raid with the rest of us?"

"What raid?"

"You really don't know?" He sighs. "The Piranhas hijacked an ironclad boat and rammed one of Big Pig's Tollgates. They grabbed a hundred or so people, killing anyone who resisted, then brought us back here."

Oh no. You overheard those Piranhas talking about hijacking an ironclad—they must have wanted it for the raid.

He frowns. "So how did you end up here?"

"Um, well, pirates were involved, but…it's a long story. Believe it or not, I've spent most of today cleaning over-city toilets."

"Back to work, lazy scum," yells a sour-faced woman holding a whip. She has a black and white striped bandana around her neck.

"What are Piranhas doing up here in the over-city?" you whisper to Mac as you follow him down a long tree-lined passage.

"The Piranhas supply slave labor to the Avocado Corporation, of course. You don't think over-city people dirty their own fingers weeding lettuces and picking tomatoes, do you?"

"Maybe we could smash a window and escape?"

He snorts. "Look at those little windows, surrounded by those solid steel window frames. This is a prison, and there's no escape. We're slaves, kid. For the rest of our lives."

I'm sorry, this part of your story is over. Trusting Bradley Lime was a big mistake—clearly, the over-city's just as dangerous as back in the under-city. What might have happened if you'd stayed down there? Or escaped the pirates earlier? Or not gone through the secret tunnel at all?

It's time to make a decision. Do you:

Go to the list of choices and start reading from another part of the story? **P531**

Or

Go back to the beginning and try another path? **P1**

Return the Security Pass

You walk up to the queuing people, holding up the green security pass. "Excuse me, does anyone know Ortopa Baskirl?"

Most of them ignore you, except an olive-skinned man with no eyebrows, who grabs the security pass. "Where'd you nick this from?"

What? "I didn't, I found it."

"Where's Ortopa?"

"How would I know?"

He turns to at the queue of people. "Anyone seen Ortopa today?"

While he's distracted, you run, ignoring his yelling and swearing, hoping he doesn't chase after you.

Luckily, he doesn't. He probably doesn't want to be late for work—workers at the front of the queue have started climbing the ladder up to the over-city.

Okay, that's far too much excitement for one day—time to head back to Deadline Delivery for your next delivery job.

A few blocks from the Tollgate, you realize someone's following you. Two someones, in fact. Big guys. Maybe pirates, maybe muggers.

You stop, take off your backpack, turn it upside down and shake it to show there's nothing inside, hoping they'll give up once they know you're not carrying anything worth stealing.

Doesn't work—they're still following you.

At the next corner, you clatter over a bridge of floating oil drums and run for a nearby alley.

They follow. As you emerge on the street at the other end of the alley, you can see the Tollgate in the distance. Safety. Except that between you and the Tollgate is a speedboat, which roars into life when the crew see you. Muggers, slavers, or cannibals, whoever they are—you're surrounded.

Your only hope is to cross the road, and get to that brick building on the other side of the water. It has a narrow hole in its side wall, too tight for most adults to get through—a great escape route. If you can get to it.

Unfortunately, there are no bridges on this block, and you can't swim, even your dog-paddling is terrible. The speedboat will be here in a minute, tops.

Just as you think things can't get worse, there's barking and growling behind you. It's those wild dogs again, only a few yards away, and leading them is the huge German Shepherd with a ripped left ear. The two guys in the alley see the dogs, stop and keep their distance.

And that's when you remember the wrapped slice of meatloaf in your pocket, left over from breakfast. You toss it to the German Shepherd, which gobbles it down then licks your face while you scratch behind its ears.

"Help me?" you beg. "Over the road? Please?"

It's a smart dog—it's already spotted the speedboat, and the men in the alley. But is it smart enough to understand you? And does it want to help you?

"Help!" you yell, leap into the water, and dog-paddle for your life. You swallow water and choke, expecting to drown. But suddenly there's wet fur under your hands, and the big dog is towing you through the water to the other side of the street.

"Thank you," you say, as you squeeze through the hole in the brick wall, with seconds to spare.

The dogs and the people on the boat growl at each other for a few seconds, then the boat roars away.

"Thank you," you repeat, reaching back through the hole and patting the German Shepherd. "Double, no, triple meatloaf for you tomorrow."

Congratulations, this part of your story is over. You're wet and tired and late getting back to Deadline delivery, but you've survived a dangerous day. What might have happened up in the over-city? Or if you'd done things differently around the Kannibal Krew and the Piranhas?

66

It's time to make a decision. Do you:

Go to the list of choices and start reading from another part of the story? **P531**

Or

Go back to the beginning and try another path? **P1**

Hope the Pirates Fight Each Other

The two Kannibal Krew reach the top of the stairs and run past the pillar you're hiding behind. Then they see the Piranhas, and stop so quickly that one crashes into the other. The Piranhas turn, equally surprised.

While both groups of pirates yell at each other, you sneak back down the way you came, unnoticed.

Brilliant.

But you soon hear running and raised voices behind you. Oh, of course, the outnumbered Kannibals are trying to escape down the same stairs you're on, and the Piranhas are chasing them.

Not so brilliant.

You leap down the stairs, two at a time, and slip, landing heavily at the bottom. Limping, you stagger past the Kannibals' red speedboat and hide behind an ancient fridge half-covered in broken bricks. Not much of a hiding place, but hopefully the pirates are more interested in each other than you. In the distance, the old woman's cabbage boat chugs away as fast as it can.

Seconds later, the two Kannibals dash out and leap onto their speedboat. The skull-faced man pushes the boat out into the water with a pole, while the Mohawked woman starts the engine. Or tries to—there's a whirring noise but nothing more. The man tries to start the engine too, but still nothing. They loudly blame each other. Hmm, you can see something they can't—wet handprints on the boat's stern, as if someone's been there in the last few minutes. Maybe they did something to the engine? But who?

Piranhas run out onto the sidewalk and screech to a halt—the boat is now several yards away from the sidewalk edge, probably too far to jump. One Piranha tries anyway, but instead lands in the muddy water with a huge splash. He coughs and curses, then dogpaddles through the floating trash towards the boat.

Abruptly, he vanishes under the surface. Didn't look like a dive, more like he was pulled down. By what? Froggies? The pirates stare at the water, as mystified as you are. Then they start yelling threats and throwing things at each other again.

Fine. So long as they're not yelling and throwing things at you.

Your left foot hurts, but you limp away.

Ahead is a rickety wooden sidewalk, its planks partially covered with flattened cardboard cartons. Or so you think, until you step straight through cardboard into thin air, and fall into the dirty water below. Weighed down by your backpack, shoes and clothes, you slowly sink.

An octopus swims through the murk and pulls off your backpack. No, impossible. Must be a hallucination—you remember reading somewhere that people see all sorts of impossible things when they're close to dying. The octopus somehow grows two brown arms and a body with green webbed feet. No, it's an octopus eating someone head first. No, that doesn't make sense either.

The creature drags you away, then pushes you up to the surface. You gasp for breath, coughing and spluttering and holding onto what feels like a rotting plank. Thick mud squishes between your knees, and there's nothing under your feet. The only light comes from one side. Where is this?

You cough again, and retch.

"Shut up," says the octopus. Oh, it's a girl, wearing a rubbery octopus mask over her head. She must be a froggy, yeah, that would explain the webbed feet too. Drowning would have been preferable, if half the stories about froggies are true. Worse than cannibals, people say.

She holds your plastic-wrapped package. With her other hand, she points a rusty harpoon at you. "Hate you." She points towards the light. "Hate them more."

You peer out, and realize you're under a sidewalk—the same sidewalk you were standing on before. On the other side of the street, the pirates are still shouting, but no longer at each other.

Grappling hooks and ropes have capsized the red speedboat. The Mohawked woman is shrieking and splashing somewhere in the water. There's no sign of the skull-faced man. Two Piranhas have ropes lassoed around their bodies and are being slowly pulled into the water, despite the other Piranhas trying to pull them back or cut the ropes. Some Piranhas are throwing bricks and rubble into the water, as if desperately hoping to hit someone or something.

As you watch, a nearby patch of floating trash rises a few inches above the surface and makes a kerchink noise. Something shoots out and hits a Piranha, who screams and falls to the sidewalk, next to the unmoving body of another pirate.

You hate pirates too, but not as much as these froggies do.

Out of the water next to you rises another pile of trash, with a man's mustachioed face underneath. (Unless it's a woman with a moustache—you're not going to ask.) He and the octopus girl peer at your delivery package and argue in loud whispers, glancing at you now and then. "Dry skins not for fungus deciding," he insists. "Verdigris afterwards delivery. Now fungus."

Or something like that—apparently froggies talk a special froggy language, and in a special froggy accent.

The mustachioed man disappears back under the water.

The octopus girl sighs, mutters to herself, and turns towards you. She's still holding that harpoon—and your package.

"That's not yours," you protest.

"Not yours either," she snarls, and shoves it back at you. Then she swims away, dragging you along by your shirt collar.

"I can't swim," you splutter, flopping around on your back, trying to breathe, trying to hold on to the package.

"True that." She takes you mostly under the shadow of sidewalks and buildings, and sometimes under piles of floating trash to cross streets. And once through a dark tunnel that seems to go right under a building from one street to the next. You try to keep track of the passing streets but are soon completely lost—the whole city looks different from down here.

At last she stops, by a steel ladder. The water's only waist-deep here, so you stand up. Above is a thick metal grate, with "390" scrawled next to it in orange spray-paint. Through the grate you can see part of a fluorescent light tube and a white ceiling.

"Hello, Chopper," she calls up.

A huge grey dog—presumably Chopper—looks down through the grate, and barks until a woman comes over and looks down too. She's wearing a white coat, a bulletproof vest, and a puzzled look.

"Delivery, 390 Brine," says the octopus girl.

This is Brine Street? You hold up the package, hoping the plastic wrapping hasn't leaked.

The woman frowns, looking at your cap. "Miss Betty's hiring froggies now?"

"I'm not a froggy," you protest.

"True that," agrees the girl.

The woman shrugs, unlocks the grate and swings it open. The girl pushes you up the ladder.

At the top is the whitest, cleanest room you've ever seen. What's that half-flower half-chemical smell?

Chopper stares at you, growling softly. He has no back legs, just two wheels held on with a frame of rods and straps. Even so, you're pretty sure he could still eat you alive if he wanted to, so you stay on the ladder, ready to drop back down if necessary.

The woman takes the package, slits it open and pulls out some finger-sized bottles. What would anyone put in bottles that small?

Chopper sniffs your trousers. Oh, your leftover meatloaf from breakfast. You pull the sodden bag from your pocket. What a yucky mess. "It's all yours, Chopper."

He swallows the lot in seconds, licks the bag, then licks your face.

"Okay, that's fine, thanks." The woman shows you a tablet screen displaying the Deadline Delivery web site, and presses the green Delivery Received icon. "Bye."

Just as you're wondering whether to try to escape up here, the octopus girl grabs your ankle and motions you back down with her harpoon.

"Um, bye." As you clamber down the ladder, the grate's closed and locked above you. "What is that place?" you ask the girl.

"Medical clinic. Obvious. No more nice—I save you only for package. Clinic good to froggies."

Huh? She saved you from drowning only because the package was for this clinic? If the package is that important, why not kill you and deliver it herself?

"Now verdigris," she says, grabs you by your shirt collar again and swims away again.

Verdigris? The mustachioed man said something about that too. Isn't verdigris the bluey-greeny stain you see on old copper and brass? What on earth is she talking about? Stupid froggies.

Perhaps ten minutes later, you arrive at a huge gloomy room with white tiled walls, balconies of seats on both sides and strange tall ladders at one end…oh, it's an indoor swimming pool, like you've seen in photos from the olden days. Why people back then needed a special room just for swimming, you don't know.

No-one's been swimming here since the city flooded. The tiles are lined with grimy horizontal tide marks—this whole room must flood every high tide. The pool is half-full of muddy water, and its far end has a large jagged hole, with daylight streaming in through it. More murky light filters in through dirty frosted glass windows along the room's walls.

Hundreds of froggies crowd the balconies above. To your surprise, none of them have claws, or fangs, or green skin, or webbed feet, like in the stories—they're just ordinary people. Except for their clothes, which are made from recycled…stuff, everything from plastic bags to metal bits to electrical cables. Lots of them wear hats or masks covered in trash—as disguises, presumably—and some wear goggles and web-toed flippers, also made from trash.

They all talk weird, like the octopus girl. But by listening hard, you realize some important stuff. Queen Verdigris is the name of their boss, a tall pale woman sitting on a deckchair on a tiny platform at the top of the tallest ladder, wearing a brass helmet from an old-fashioned diving suit. Fungus is the name of the girl in the octopus mask. “Dry-skins” is what they call anyone who isn’t a froggy—under-city people, pirates, over-city people, even you. Not that you’re dry at the moment.

Most importantly, the froggies are arguing about you. About whether to kill you.

“Dry-skin has seen too much froggy secrets,” says one, and lots of froggies nod.

“Dry-skin run from pirates, just like us, sympathy,” another says, and lots of froggies nod at that too.

“Dry-skin deliver for Brine Street clinic,” Fungus points out. Is she trying to help you?

After a while, Queen Verdigris bangs on her ladder. Everyone quietens down and looks up at her expectantly. “Crocodile Doom,” she announces in a gravelly voice.

A few people grumble, including Fungus, but most of them nod and shout, “Crocodile Doom!”

They’re going to feed you to crocodiles? Is this their idea of fun? Maybe they don’t have television down here.

Fungus shakes her head and mutters to herself, then pushes you into the pool.

The water’s less than waist-deep, and not too cold. Too muddy to see what’s below. As you stand, something crunches under your left foot and something else wriggles under your right foot.

Now what? Froggies with long spears are watching you from the pool edges, so clearly there’s no point in trying to climb out of the pool. Try to escape out the hole in the far end of the pool? Seems too easy. Maybe it’s a trap, and a hundred hungry crocodiles are hiding under the water, waiting. Or maybe this is all some stupid froggy joke, and someone wearing a crocodile mask will jump out and yell “Boo!”

and everyone will laugh. Probably not though.

"Doom!" chant the froggies. "Doom! Doom!" Over and over again.

Something moves under the water, creating a line of ripples heading in your direction.

The froggies see the ripples too, and cheer.

"Doom! Doom!" chant a line of little froggy kids at the front row of a balcony, stomping their feet.

You're scared, but staying here and waiting to die seems pointless. So you start wading across the pool, trying not to trip on the slimy debris under your feet, and trying not to splash too much. Doesn't work though—the ripples change direction to follow you. For just a moment, something long and scaly breaks the surface then submerges again.

Above, the shouting and stomping get louder and louder. Then something heavy screeches and snaps, someone screams, and the froggies start shouting and pointing. You look up and see a balcony's partly collapsed, probably from all that foot stomping. From a broken guard rail, a little froggy kid is dangling down over the pool.

It's time to make a decision, and fast. Do you:

Run for the hole in the far wall while everyone's distracted? **P93**

Or

Help the froggy kid? **P74**

Help the Froggy Kid

Trying to ignore the ripple from the approaching crocodile, you splash over to the broken balcony, and are just in time to catch the froggy kid as he screams and falls.

Ropes wrap around you both and you're dragged up into the air together. Just in time—moments later, a huge crocodile bursts out of the water, its long jaws snapping inches from your feet.

Hands pull you both up to a safer part of the balcony. Around you, dozens of voices yell and give advice and bicker all at the same time.

"Shut up!" Fungus shouts.

Everyone does. There's silence, except for the crocodile still snapping its jaws and thrashing around below, probably wondering where its lunch has gone, and the little froggy kid, crying in Fungus's arms.

"Why?" she demands, glaring at you. "Why help my bro Bucket?"

That's her little brother? What sort of name's Bucket? Although admittedly, it's no weirder than the name Fungus.

"I couldn't…do nothing and let a little kid get eaten alive," you say.

Bucket leans over and hugs you.

Queen Verdigris bangs on her ladder, and points at you. "Froggy friend," she announces.

Everyone cheers, and starts chanting, "Froggy friend," over and over. These froggies sure do like their chanting. There's no more foot stomping though, and everyone's keeping away from the balcony edges.

What "froggy friend" means, you're not sure, but it must be something good, coz everyone's smiling and no one's trying to feed you to crocodiles any more.

"Lunch," Queen Verdigris announces.

Everyone cheers again. For a horrible moment, you think maybe she means that you'll *be* their lunch, but they take you to a nearby room full of long tables and wonderful foody smells, and the queen insists you sit next to her. Fungus and Bucket sit on your other side, and Bucket gives you lots of shy smiles.

The food is…weird, like everything else down here, but it tastes as good as it smells, even if you can't tell what some of it is.

"Good, yes?" Queen Verdigris asks.

"It's the best meal I've had in months, your majesty," you say, and she looks pleased.

You gradually get used to their odd accent and language. They're talking about ordinary things—fishing, growing vegetables, recycling, playing sport, keeping safe, finding clean water and food. Sounds like life is even tougher for froggies than people like you, because absolutely everyone picks on froggies—not just pirates, but most under-city people too. You feel guilty, remembering the horrible gossip you'd heard and believed about froggies—almost none of it was true.

To be honest, now that the froggies have stopped trying to feed you to the crocodiles, they seem nicer than most under-city people you've known. They're like one huge family, all looking after each other. Not like most dry-skins.

"You froggy friend now," says Queen Verdigris. "We like you. So stay, be one of us, yes?"

Is she serious? "Become a froggy? Forever?" Part of their family?

She nods. Fungus and Bucket gaze at you, grinning.

It's time to make a decision. Do you:

Become a froggy? **P76**

Or

Stay a courier, and return to Deadline Delivery? **P86**

Become a Froggy

"Yes, I want to be a froggy." Your voice shakes a little. You won't be sorry to never see Deadline Delivery again (even though Miss Betty owes you ten dollars for the Brine Street clinic delivery), but giving up your old life is scary. What if this is a terrible mistake?

Froggies hug you and shake your hand.

"Fungus, find new froggy a job," Queen Verdigris orders.

Fungus nods. So does Bucket, even though no one asked him.

After lunch, they take you along dozens of gloomy tunnels and passageways, sometimes walking or wading, sometimes swimming and towing you. "Careful not get lost," Fungus says. "Tide rising now, some tunnels soon flood."

"I'm already lost, and I can't swim."

"We teach you," Bucket says, and Fungus nods.

Eventually they stop, in a huge hall that smells like a giant fart. There are tanks and pipes everywhere, and pulleys and pistons turning enormous wheels, and dozens of froggies busy on a long raised platform.

"Crabb Street sewage treatment plant," Fungus says proudly. "Filter sewer for city south suburbs."

"Mmm," you reply, trying to hold your breath.

"Stinky water down from over-city," Bucket explains, pointing to a row of pipes. "Clean water up to over-city." He points to another row of pipes.

They take you over to the long raised platform, where froggies are pushing giant sieves through a long tank of what Bucket calls "stinky water", and occasionally pulling out things like bottles and rags and rusty cans.

"Recycling," Fungus says. "Many things found, sometimes valuable—jewelry, phones, coins. We sell back to over-city."

You hope they wash the recycled stuff really, really well.

"And sell stinky sludge back to over-city for fertilizer," adds

Bucket, who seems to be an expert on stinky stuff.

Perhaps they can see you're not too impressed by sewage. They take you up and down more tunnels and corridors and streets for what seems like an hour. The farty smell is replaced by a fishy smell, getting stronger.

In the distance, at the end of a wide tunnel, you see bright light and water. Lots of water. More water than you've ever seen before. And the fishiest smell you've ever smelled before.

You reach the end of the tunnel, stop on a large platform and gaze out at the sea. Obviously, this is exactly the same sea which flows through the city streets. But you've never seen it like this before, with no buildings or security fences in the way, just endless waves, all the way to the horizon, under the biggest, emptiest sky ever.

To one side of the platform is a long boat full of glittering fish. On board is a golden-skinned woman with tiger stripe tattoos on her face. She frowns up at you.

"Move," snarls a voice beside you. Four froggies push trolleys with crates full of fish past you and down the tunnel. That looks like hard work.

Fungus turns to you and crosses her arms. Bucket copies her. "Which job? Sewage or fish?" she asks.

Not much of a choice. What about exciting jobs, like feeding the crocodiles, or ambushing pirates? Anyway, it's time to make a decision. Do you:

Work at the sewage treatment plant? **P78**

Or

Work at the fishery? **P81**

Sewage Treatment

"Sewage," you say glumly. You're not looking forward to working in that stinky sewage treatment plant, but you feel unsafe here by the sea—there's just…too much water.

After a few days working at the sewage treatment plant, you hardly notice the smell any more. Or maybe your nose has stopped working.

Anyway, the work's okay. One day you find seven one-dollar coins in your sludge sieve—it's amazing what over-city people lose down drains.

There's more to the job than just sieving sludge. You also learn how to clean tanks and pipes, to oil pistons and scrape filters, and to shovel dried sludge (which luckily smells better than wet sludge) into sacks labeled "All-Natural Organic Fertilizer".

At night, whenever the tide is right, you join groups of froggies outside, walking through the watery streets on long stilts, to collect recyclable bottles, cans and plastic. At first, you feel silly disguising yourself in a trash suit and hiding in the water whenever dry-skins walk by, but you soon start enjoying being a sneaky froggy. And it's fun helping the others scare away any dry-skins who get too close to the maze of froggy tunnels.

Fungus and Bucket teach you to swim. You're still terrible at it, but less terrible than before, and getting better every day—or so they claim.

Fog, the sewage treatment plant manager, says you're getting better at sieving sludge too.

Two weeks later, you spot something glinting in the sludge tank. Jewelry perhaps? Someone found a wedding ring down here last month. You grab at the glint with your sieve.

Wow. It's jewelry alright—a golden necklace, glittering with sparkly gemstones.

"Shiny," says everyone.

It sure is. But is it real gold and real gems?

Fog washes the necklace, examines it carefully, and then makes half a dozen phone calls. "Real," he tells you. "Worth fortune. Over-city owner offering return reward. Huge reward. Take now to Queen Verdigris."

You do.

"So pretty," the queen says with a sigh, holding the necklace up to the light. "Shame we can't keep."

"Yes, your majesty." You know the froggies never keep found valuables—that would be stealing, and would make froggies no better than pirates. But there's nothing wrong with claiming a reward. Even a huge reward.

"What to do with shiny reward? What you think?"

"Me, your majesty?"

"Yes, you find, so what you think, what to do? Maybe I agree, maybe not, but tell me even so."

"Well, um, I've only been a froggy for a few weeks, but, um, I was wondering…"

"Yes, yes?"

"Why don't we start a froggy courier business? We know a million routes around the city that dry-skins don't, and I reckon we could deliver stuff faster than anyone else. We'd make money, and…well, people might start treating froggies better if they knew we weren't monsters, just ordinary people making an honest living."

"Hmm," she says. "Hmm, hmm, hmm."

That afternoon, there's a meeting in the swimming pool room, and everyone else says "hmm" and argues and complains and disagrees. After an hour or so, they mostly agree that a froggy courier business is a good idea.

There's only one problem—other than you, no one's brave enough to be a courier.

But then Fungus stands up. "I be courier too." She turns to you. "If you teach me."

"And me," Bucket insists, sticking his bottom lip out.

80

He's far too young, you almost say. But then again, he's a far better swimmer than you, and can run faster than a hungry rat, so why not?

"Sure," you say. "Let's do it."

Congratulations, this part of your story is over. You've survived pirates and crocodiles and found a new life for yourself. And now, starting a courier business could change the lives of your new froggy family.

Things could have turned out very differently if you'd made different decisions. Maybe better, maybe worse.

It's time to make a decision. Do you:

Go to the list of choices and start reading from another part of the story? **P531**

Or

Go back to the beginning and try another path? **P1**

Fish

"Fish," you say glumly. All those fish smell really…fishy, but working here sounds (and smells) better than stinky sewage.

"New worker for you, Tiger Lily," Fungus tells the woman with tiger-stripe tattoos, then she and Bucket just walk off and leave you there.

From the fishing boat, Tiger Lily frowns at you again. "Can you swim, kid?" She has a strange accent.

"Not really, ma'am. Not yet."

"Call me captain, not ma'am. Can you catch fish?"

"No, captain. Well, I once found a small fish in my shirt after falling into the water—does that count?"

She rolls her eyes. "Can you push a trolley?"

"Not far, if it's full of crates of fish."

"Ever been to sea?"

"This is the first time I've even seen the open sea."

Some of the fishing boat's crew snigger.

Captain Tiger Lily rolls her eyes and gives a loud sigh. "Alright, get down here and help unload these fish."

"Captain, why don't you talk funny like the other froggies?"

More sniggering from the crew.

The captain glares at you. "What a nosy child. This is how everyone talked back in the over-city, where I was born."

"You left the over-city to become a froggy? Why?"

"Less talking and lift that fish crate, kid."

"Yes, captain."

After the crates have been unloaded and sent down the tunnel on trolleys, the crew do mysterious things with ropes and nets and sails, while you try to stay out of their way. Then the boat starts swaying and rocking and you realize it's moving, heading out to sea. Looking back, the city gets smaller and smaller. Will you ever see it again?

A wrinkled crewman claps you on the shoulder. "Feeling seasick yet, kid?" he asks cheerfully. "I still remember my first boat trip—I spent the whole time leaning over the railing, throwing up and groaning and wanting to die." He looks around at the other crew with a grin. "Two dollars says the kid will throw up in the next ten minutes!"

The crew laugh, and make complicated bets on how soon you'll throw up and how often.

The captain doesn't join in the laughter or the gambling, but she is watching you carefully.

This must be a test—if you fail, she'll probably send you to the sewage treatment plant. So you clutch a handrail, trying to ignore your lurching stomach, and wishing you hadn't eaten so much lunch. Closing your eyes doesn't help, and looking at the boat's deck makes it worse. Staring at the horizon helps you feel a little better.

Perhaps half an hour later, the sails are lowered, and the boat slows and stops in the middle of empty sea. To everyone's surprise, especially yours, you haven't thrown up even once.

"Well done, kid," says the wrinkled crewman, grinning even though he's lost his bet. "Perhaps we'll make a sailor out of you after all."

Lots of money changes hands. No one seems annoyed at you.

You spot fins approaching the boat. "Sharks!" you shout.

Everyone roars with laughter.

Even the captain smiles. "They're dolphins, our fishing partners."

Several dolphins stick their heads out of the water and they laugh at you too—well, not really, but that's what it looks and sounds like.

The captain whistles at the dolphins. They click and whistle back—they're talking!—then race away.

She shouts orders to the crew.

In the distance, the dolphins are returning.

"Wait," orders the captain, watching them through binoculars. "Wait…wait…ready…now!"

The crew launch a huge spring-powered net over the waves. It falls just in front of the dolphins, and the water fills with furious splashing from fish caught in the net.

As the captain shouts orders, everyone hauls the net in, even you. Dozens of ropes have to be pulled and tightened in just the right order. At just the wrong moment, you pull on the wrong rope and hundreds of fish spill from the net. The dolphins snap them up.

The captain bares her teeth and growls at you, looking more like a tiger than ever.

"Sorry," you mumble.

"The dolphins deserve their share," she snaps. "But not quite that much."

Desperate not to make any more mistakes, you watch and listen carefully, and do whatever anyone tells you. It's especially hard because the bits of the boat have such weird names, like the halyard—the line that raises and lowers the sail. And the boom—the horizontal pole at the bottom of the sail, that's nearly knocked you on the head twice already.

On the voyage back to the city, you don't make any more embarrassing mistakes or throw up. Sailing's cooler than you'd expected.

But during unloading back at the dock, you drop and nearly spill a crate of fish.

Captain Tiger Lily glares at you again. "See you tomorrow, 6AM," is all she says.

Tomorrow? So she wants you back, and you won't be sent to the sewage treatment plant? Yay!

Weeks go by. You go out fishing most days. Soon you can name all the boat's weird bits, know how to tie half a dozen different knots, can tack and jibe and trim as well as any of the crew, and duck under a swinging boom without even thinking about it. Sailing's hard work, even harder than being a courier, but the best fun ever.

Except for fish. Not the smell, you're used to that. But they're so slimy and slippery and wiggly and…fishy. You're always dropping them, or stepping on them, or tangling the fishing net, or doing something wrong. Every time, the captain rolls her eyes. Or sighs. Or both.

Most evenings, you're exhausted, but go for swimming lessons with Fungus and Bucket whenever they offer—a real sailor needs to be able to swim.

One morning at the dock, you see the captain talking with Queen Verdigris. They see you watching them, and turn away. If the queen's involved, this must be something serious. What if she decides you can't be a sailor anymore? Or worse, what if you can't even be a froggy?

They're walking over to you. Uh-oh.

"Would you like to hear a secret?" Tiger Lily asks you. "I hate fish. I hate catching them, hate their smell, don't even like eating them. Well, except for Swab's fish curry, but Swab can make anything taste good. So then why, you may ask, did I leave the over-city to come down here and captain a smelly old fishing boat?"

Good question, but you stay quiet, hoping she'll say more.

"Because I love sailboats," she continues. "I've loved them since I was a small child, staring out to the sea from the window in our thirty-ninth floor apartment." She points up to the over-city towers. "I gave up everything to sail. But even so, I wish there was more to froggy sailing than fishing. Don't you?"

You nod. "Sailing's like flying on the water."

She grins. "Yeah, you get it too. I could see that on your first day. Ever heard of Oasis?"

"The magical island where there's no over-city and no pirates, and froggies can live in peace and safety? That's Bucket's favorite bedtime story."

Queen Verdigris gives a mysterious smile. "More than bedtime story."

"What? Oasis is real?"

"Maybe," Tiger Lily says. "I've collected all the Oasis stories I've ever heard, and half of them contradict each other. But still, I reckon

Oasis is worth looking for. And if it doesn't exist, perhaps we'll find another island to turn into Oasis. So, I'm looking for brave sailors to join my crew."

"Me?"

Queen Verdigris laughs. "Yes, you. Why else we talking, huh?"

"It'll be dangerous," Tiger Lily warns you. "We may never return."

"Living here's dangerous too. I'm in."

It's not quite that simple. Queen Verdigris has bought Tiger Lily a boat—the Seahorse, named after an olden-days animal that could run underwater, or so Fungus say—but the Seahorse is old and leaks and needs lots of repairs. There are a dozen more crew to choose, and food and water and tools and weapons and a million other things to organize for the voyage.

But somehow everything gets done. A month later, you and Tiger Lily and the rest of the crew board the Seahorse, watched by nearly every froggy in the city. Bucket's crying because he wanted to come on the voyage too. You wave goodbye to everyone, knowing you'll miss them, wondering if you'll ever see them again. Or the city.

"Cast off. Make sail," orders Tiger Lily.

"Aye, captain." Blinking back tears, you turn to face the oncoming sea, and adventure.

Congratulations, this part of your story is over—who knows what the future will hold? And what might have happened if you'd made different decisions? Could you have ended up in the over-city? Or in the clutches of pirates?

It's time to make a decision. Do you:

Go to the list of choices and start reading from another part of the story? **P531**

Or

Go back to the beginning and try another path? **P1**

Return to Deadline Delivery

“Thanks, but I have to get back to my job,” you tell Queen Verdigris. Not that it’s much of a job. “But…I’d really like to visit again some time. If you’ll let me.”

She smiles. “You froggy friend forever.”

After lunch, Fungus and Bucket tow you back to Nori Road near Ivory Tower, using a special secret froggy route that goes right under Big Pig's Wall—no toll fee to pay, yay!

Bucket’s only half your age, but he can swim like…um, a frog.

“I wish I could swim,” you tell him. Working as a courier would be so much easier if you could use secret froggy routes.

“We teach you,” Bucket says, and Fungus nods.

You all say goodbye. A few minutes later, you’re back at Deadline Delivery.

Miss Betty scowls at you. “You’re late.”

Late? “I was attacked by Kannibal Krew, Piranhas, and a crocodile!” And by froggies too, sort of…but not really. You’re not going to say anything bad about the froggies.

“No excuses!” She counts out eight one-dollar coins.

“Eight? You said the job paid ten dollars.”

She gives a sour grin and points to your dripping cap. “Minus two dollars—Wet Uniform fee.”

So unfair. Maybe you should’ve become a froggy. Bet no one makes them wear stupid caps or pay stupid fees.

Miss Betty drops a long blue box on the counter. “Urgent delivery, Crabb Street. Pays nine bucks.”

You sigh, nod, and take the box.

The steel door squeaks and starts to close, and you hurry out. Miss Betty doesn’t say goodbye. She never does.

Congratulations, this part of your story is over. You have learned the truth about the froggies, and made new friends. Things could have happened very differently—you might have ended up in the over-city, or as a pirate slave, or rich, or broke, or with a different job. Or eaten by crocodiles.

It's time to make a decision. Do you:

Go to the list of choices and start reading from another part of the story? **P531**

Or

Go back to the beginning and try another path? **P1**

Become the Clinic Courier

Doctor Hurst was right—working as courier for the Brine Street Community Medical Clinic has been really hard work, and some days it's just as dangerous as your old job. But every day, you're thankful there's no more Deadline Delivery and no more Miss Betty. Never again.

The clinic feeds you, and pays you—pays you well. And they give you free treatment for gun wounds, rat bites, and plague mold.

On the downside, they also make you shower every single week, whether you need it or not.

You don't mind…too much.

Congratulations, this part of your story is over. You have a brand new life, and who knows where it might lead. What might have happened if you'd never taken that ride on the cabbage boat? Or not gone through the secret tunnel at all?

It's time to make a decision. Do you:

Go to the list of choices and start reading from another part of the story? **P531**

Or

Go back to the beginning and try another path? **P1**

Run from the Kannibals

You twist out of the old man's grasp and sprint past the slowing speedboat.

You'll be a goner as soon as that speedboat has time to change direction and follow you, but maybe you can get out of sight before that happens, and before the old man can chase you down.

Diving through the next doorway, you race down a short alley, then up a tall fire escape ladder.

Bad mistake. Every footstep clangs on the steel. Now he'll know exactly where you are.

Sure enough, you soon hear him at the bottom of the ladder, grunting and swearing.

At the top of the ladder is a mossy brick wall with a small window, its glass long gone.

No other exit, except a thirty-foot drop onto concrete. You're trapped. Unless you can squeeze through the window? Yeah, the pirates are bigger than you and won't be able to follow. Unless they send that scary baby in after you, ha ha.

You push your backpack through the window, then follow it. Your head and shoulders get through ok, just, but then your hips get stuck. The old man's footsteps on the ladder are getting louder—he must be close to the top. No way do you want to die halfway through a window, pirates eating you from the toes up.

Desperately, you wiggle your hips. Something rips and you're through. Back on your feet, you grab the backpack and run, run, run, ignoring the old man yelling that you're a "crazy kid".

You keep running, sometimes aiming for Tollgate and safety, but mostly at random, until your lungs shudder and legs shake and you fall to the floor of a moldy-walled walkway.

Lying there, gasping, you suddenly realize what ripped earlier—your trouser pocket with all your money. It's all gone. Every last coin.

How will you get through Tollgate now?

90

Once you get your breath back, you work out where you are—four blocks from Tollgate—and carefully make your way there, because maybe you're still being followed. But the sidewalks are more crowded with people around here, and there's safety in numbers—or at least a better chance of someone raising the alarm if pirates are spotted.

And then you wait. Hoping you'll see someone you know, someone who'll loan you a dollar.

You don't.

Hoping someone will feel sorry for your sad face, ripped clothes and bandaged shotgun wounds.

Fat chance.

Hoping a soft-hearted Gate guard is on duty.

No such thing.

The sun sets, and you're still stuck outside the Wall. Everyone's heard the stories about things which come out to hunt the streets at night. Things even worse than pirates and froggies. Just stories to frighten little kids, you tell yourself.

In what's left of the twilight, you find a hidey-hole between a collapsed wall and a sheet of rusty corrugated iron. Your dinner is the last crumbs from the meatloaf plastic bag in your pocket. You hug your knees to stay warm, and try to sleep, hoping something nasty won't find you in the middle of the night, hoping that tomorrow will be better.

This part of your story is over. Today was a disaster, but at least you're still alive. Would things have gone better if you'd taken that clinic courier job? Or stayed away from that old woman and her cabbage boat?

It's time to make a decision. Do you:

Go to the list of choices and start reading from another part of the story? **P531**

Or

Go back to the beginning and try another path? **P1**

Follow the Old Man's Orders

The Mohawk woman laughs at you, and the baby joins in. The bald man with the huge skull tattoo twists his mouth into either a smile or a snarl, it's hard to tell.

"What's so funny?" growls the old man.

"Your face," the woman tells him.

"Baa!" says the baby.

"Crazy kid," the old man tells you.

"What?" you say, completely confused. And surprised to still be alive.

"We know you're a courier, cap or no cap," he continues. "We saw you back at the clinic."

This is a robbery? They want Doctor Hurst's package, whatever it is?

"We do what we can to help the clinic, so we got you a present," the woman says. She tosses something to you.

You flinch, expecting something horrible.

The old man grabs it from mid-air and waves it in front of you. It's a necklace—alternating yellow and black plastic bottle tops and half a dozen human teeth on a long black string. Horrible, but not quite as horrible as you'd expected.

He places the necklace around your neck. "Any time you're in Kannibal Krew territory, just show this and no Kannibal will bother you."

"Um," you say, still confused.

The skull tattoo man frowns at you. "Well? Say thank you!"

"Thank you," you say. "I mean it. Thank you. Really."

The old man grunts. "You're welcome." He hops down into the boat and it roars off before you can say another word.

You hide the necklace under your shirt, put your Deadline Delivery cap back on, and walk the six blocks back to Tollgate, thinking hard. Safe passage through Kannibal Krew territory, forever? A necklace like this is worth its weight in gold, to any courier.

After paying your toll, you jog to Nori Road and deliver Doctor Hurst's package to 157, then return to Ivory Tower and Deadline Delivery.

Miss Betty scowls at you. As usual. But pays you the ten-dollar delivery fee, as promised. That's thirty-two dollars in your pocket—you're rich! Well, a lot richer than usual.

The steel door squeaks and starts to close, and you hurry out. Miss Betty doesn't say goodbye. She never does.

This part of your story is over. Today turned out pretty well, and who knows where tomorrow might lead. But things could have turned out differently—you might have ended up in the clutches of much nastier pirates, or gone to the over-city, or been captured by froggies, or eaten by crocodiles.

It's time to make a decision. Do you:

Go to the list of choices and start reading from another part of the story? **P531**

Or

Go back to the beginning and try another path? **P1**

Run for the Hole

You wade as fast as you can to the other end of the pool.

The mysterious ripple doesn't follow you. As far as you can tell. It's hard to be sure, what with the other ripples from you, and from bits falling from the balcony.

The froggies rescue the dangling kid before it can fall in the water. Good on them. But then they remember you, and all the "Doom" chanting starts up again, sounding even angrier than before. Someone throws something at you, and it lands in the water just a couple of yards away.

You run out through the jagged hole.

But it's not an exit after all, just a smallish room with one wall of glass bricks.

Two doorways.

One's blocked by a fallen concrete beam.

The other's on the far side of a raised platform occupied by a family of crocodiles. They stare at you. Two of them hiss then slip into the water.

You turn and look out the hole, only to see that ripple again, heading straight for you. At the front of the ripple, a crocodilian snout and eyes appear. The last thing you ever see is its jaw opening wide.

I'm sorry, this part of your story is over. You escaped pirates and the crazy old cabbage boat woman, but you were foolish to think you could escape the froggies and their Crocodile Doom.

It's time to make a decision. Do you:

Go to the list of choices and start reading from another part of the story? **P531**

Or

Go back to the beginning and try another path? **P1**

STRANDED STARSHIP

by Kevin Berry

Goodbye spaceport, hello space!

You stand at the observation window in your cramped, sparsely-furnished cabin, watching the Earth recede as *The Bejeweled Diva* leaves its berth at the orbiting spaceport and accelerates into space. You're keen to explore, but the view of your home planet is too spectacular to miss, a living, breathing ball of deep blues, browns and wispy white. Who knows when you'll be back?

A tight sensation grips your stomach. Your mouth feels dry, and you swallow. Nerves? Despite being the number one space cadet in your school, you've never been off-world until this trip.

No one ever told you space was this big.

And it's quiet. The soft thrum of the engine accompanies a slight vibration in the floor and walls, a bit like turbulence in an airplane. Except it's not turbulence because there's no atmosphere in space. So, it must be the spaceship shaking.

Better not think about that. The ship's not going to fall apart. It's an old, classic model, after all. Been flying for years. Or is it decades? Either way, ships of this type were built to last. Weren't they?

You shake your head to clear it of these disturbing thoughts. Instead, you wonder about the live animals the steward told you are in the cargo hold. What are they? Also, the other passengers looked an odd bunch, especially the two Proximeans, short, big-eyed, blue creatures.

After acing the school exams and cadet work, the school offered you a chance to exchange places with a student from the colony at Proxima B for a few weeks, live with a family there and learn more about operating starships. Your family readily agreed. You'll miss everyone, but this was too good an opportunity to pass up.

The little spaceport disappeared from view long ago. As you watch, the Earth shrinks to a bluish dot in the darkness of space. You turn away from the window. At some point, the starship must make the string jump to the Proxima B system.

The captain left you a message saying you could visit the Bridge or Engineering after the starship is underway. You grin. That's the best part of the whole journey, being able to see how a starship operates first-hand. Maybe you'll be allowed to take the controls sometime, too. That'd be awesome.

A jolt almost throws you off your feet. What happened? Did we hit something? It sure felt like it. And that gravel sound. How's that possible out here?

There's nothing but empty space outside the windows. No clues there, but you're not sure if you could see something that doesn't have its own illumination anyway. Face pressed to the viewport, you peer outside, straining to see. Is some of the view darker than the rest? A patch where there are no stars visible?

Maybe.

Something is different. What? You tilt your head, listening. The engine sound has changed. A louder, grinding, churning mechanical noise has replaced the soft thrum. The floor's wobbling more than before, too.

That can't be good. You bite your lip. Did some space debris damage the drive? What if we can't maneuver? There'll be no way for the starship to slow down. It'll hurtle through the solar system until we reach the asteroid belt and collide with an asteroid in a massive, fiery explosion.

You take a deep breath. Is this a good time to visit the Bridge? Or Engineering? See what's going on? Or should you save that for later and go make friends with some of the other passengers? It must be time for dinner, surely. But if you go to the passenger lounge, will you miss something exciting—or dangerous—happening on the Bridge or in Engineering?

It's time to make a decision. You have three choices. Do you:

Go to the Bridge and ask the captain about the grinding noise? **P98**

Or

Go to Engineering and ask about the grinding noise? **P103**

Or

Go and meet the other passengers over dinner? **P107**

Go to the Bridge and ask the captain about the grinding noise

You leave your cabin. The door slides closed behind you with a whoosh. You're standing in a corridor that curves in both directions, and you can't see far because of the bends. The walls glow with a soft light that flickers, which it's probably not supposed to do. The carpet is patchy in places.

The accommodation onboard is not the Ritz. It's more like the Pitz.

The ship's steward loaded a map of the starship onto your wristpad when you boarded, so you check that to find the way to the Bridge. It's a standard layout for a small cargo and passenger starship—the ship's drives, fuel tank and cargo hold are on the lower deck, and everything else is on the upper deck. The Bridge is at the front end of the ship.

You set off towards the Bridge. There are other doors along the corridor, some marked with cabin numbers. One on the left is labeled as a passenger lounge, but the door is closed, and you can't see inside.

The starship is about 50m in length, and your cabin is about halfway along the corridor on the starboard side, so your journey to the Bridge only takes a minute. The corridor curves around the port side of the ship, illuminated by the glowing walls. Perhaps, when you have two minutes to spare, you could explore that section.

You hold your wristpad up to the security patch for the Bridge, and the door whooshes open. You step inside without hesitation.

The Bridge is much smaller than you had imagined, only about twice the size of your tiny cabin. Windows wrap around the apex of the ship, providing a 180-degree view. Instrument consoles covered with metal levers, dials and display screens stand under them, with two cushioned bucket seats before those.

A woman with big frizzy hair—presumably the captain—sits at one, her back to you. She's wearing black leggings and a navy blue jacket, and talking into a communicator on her oversized shoulder pad. You catch the words "—what's going on?" before she slaps the communicator as if in anger.

Something's definitely gone wrong.

She spins to face you with narrowed eyes. "No passengers allowed on the Bridge. How did you get in here, anyway?" Her tone was sharp.

You hold up your wristpad. "With this."

Her expression softens. "Oh. You're the space cadet. Of course. Welcome to the ship."

"Thanks. May I come in?" It seems polite to ask, even though you're already a step through the doorway.

Just a slight hesitation before she agrees. "Sure. Take a seat there." She gestures at the other bucket seat.

It's stained and shows considerable signs of wear, but you sit down like it's a throne, beaming with delight, feet barely reaching the floor. You're sitting at the controls of a starship!

"So, what's your name, cadet?"

"Everyone calls me Ace. It's my nickname at school."

"Because you're good at cards, yes?"

You shake your head. "Top gun on the space combat simulator."

"Ah." She nods and smiles. Maybe she's warming to you now. "Call me Teena."

"Okay, Teena. Thanks for letting me onto the Bridge. I didn't know it would be so—"

"Compact? It's standard for this type of starship. We need a lot of fuel, and we have as much cargo space as possible. And, of course, we maximize passenger comfort," she added, apparently as an afterthought. "Are you happy with your spacious accommodation?"

No! "Yes," you say.

She nods and turns to the console, checking something.

"Is there no other crew on the Bridge?"

"No. Only me. I'm the captain, the navigator, the pilot. And I own this piece of j—this delightful ship. I've been flying it for twenty years, as did my family before that. And prior to that, I'm not sure. It's got history, this rust—trustworthy vessel, but it's sound and predictable, like an old movie."

"What was that crunching sound a few minutes ago? I felt a bump. And the engine noise has changed too."

The captain crosses her arms and sits back in her bucket seat. Nose wrinkling, she says, "You noticed that. Well … it's nothing for you to worry about."

You look away. That doesn't sound right.

"Hey, Ace," Teena says. "How would you like to maneuver the ship?"

Your eyes widen. "Really? You'll let me do that?"

"Sure. It's time to turn it around anyway."

Wow. You can hardly believe your luck. Hands-on experience! Your friends back at school will be so envious when you tell them.

"We've been accelerating at 2G for two hours, and we're about halfway to the string jump point," the captain explains. "Now we need to slow down, so we'll have slowed to a halt when we arrive. We—that is, you—have to perform a complete about-turn so we're facing backwards. Then the drive will decelerate us instead of continuing to speed us up. Are you up to it, Ace?"

You give her the thumbs-up. "I sure am. Point me to the controls."

Teena indicates a small backlit display on the console and an adjacent trackball. "The display shows the direction the ship is facing. It's like a compass that points to the Galactic center, which we'll call 'north'. We're currently pointing 25 degrees west of that. Now, you know your trigonometry, don't you, Ace?"

You gulp. Trigonometry, trigonometry …. That's math, right? Yeah, it must be. But what do you do with it, exactly?

The captain watches you closely as you struggle to find the right words. Or word. That would be 'No', but you don't want to say it.

"I never understood that stuff either," she says. "Look, this is how I do it. You get something with a straight edge, like"—she looks around for a moment and picks up something further along the console—"this chewing gum wrapper. Then you place it on the display, lining it up with the arrow showing our current bearing. Use the trackball until you've lined up the arrow with the other end of the gum wrapper. Okay?" She doesn't wait for an answer, but moves over to do something on a different console.

Wow, you're going to turn the starship around. What a responsibility. And with nothing but a gum wrapper to give you the right bearing.

You do as Teena instructed, moving the trackball. It's a skill you've mastered from bossing many computer games, so that part should be easy. But the arrow showing the ship's current bearing doesn't move. A quick look through the window confirms it. The ship isn't turning.

"It's not working," you say after half a minute of frustration.

The captain is busy on whatever she is doing and doesn't look up. "It can be a bit sticky. I got some gum in the trackball once, and I never managed to get it all out."

"It's not sticky. The trackball's working fine, but we're not changing direction."

Now Teena looks up. A frown creases her face. "That's not good," she says.

You knew it. You tried to tell her that something was wrong, but maybe she doesn't want to worry you. There's no denying it now, though.

"Why is the drive making that grinding sound, anyway? Do you think it's connected to the problem of the ship not turning?"

The captain sighs and nods. "You're a perceptive cadet, Ace. I agree, the drive shouldn't sound like that. And it does appear that it's not working properly. I need to call Karl in Engineering for an update. Thanks for your help."

"You're welcome."

She swivels her head as if trying to catch a sound more clearly. "Wait. Do you hear that?"

You listen hard. "I don't hear anything. Oh, that's it. The engine has stopped."

102

"Now I *really* have to call Engineering. I think it's about time for dinner in the passenger lounge. How about you head off there and leave this to me?"

Your stomach rumbles at the thought of dinner. Teena clearly wants you to leave, but you're curious about what the problem with the maneuver drive might be.

It's time to make a decision. Do you:

Stay with the captain and investigate the drive problem? **P131**

Or

Go and meet the other passengers over dinner? **P107**

Go to Engineering and ask the engineer about the grinding noise

You leave your cabin. The door slides closed behind you with a whoosh. You're standing in a corridor that curves in both directions, and you can't see far because of the bends. The walls glow with a soft light that flickers, which it's probably not supposed to do. The carpet is patchy in places.

The ship's steward loaded a map of the starship onto your wristpad when you boarded, so you access that to find the way to Engineering. It's a standard layout for a small cargo and passenger starship—the ship's drives, fuel tank and cargo hold are on the lower deck, and everything else is on the upper deck.

There's a stairway to the aft of the ship, and you make your way there. The stairs are metal and narrow. A handrail helps you keep your balance as you walk down to a plain door labeled:

ENGINEERING
KEEP OUT

You ignore that instruction and open the door with your wristpad, as it gives you access to the whole ship. You step inside.

You're in a large, double-height room. It smells of oil, grease and sweat. The lighting from the ceiling flickers intermittently. The grinding, mechanical noise is louder here. The drive shouldn't sound like that.

There's no one in sight. A metal railing to your right separates you from one of the drive housings. A corridor curves around it, so you follow that. The drive housing itself has small windows through which you catch glimpses of the drive as you go past. When you round the corner, you see the other bulky drive housing on your left. The corridor continues between them and leads to a space beyond about four meters square.

An office/workroom is on the other side of the space, and there's a rickety table and two chairs outside. A large red hammock is slung between the office and one of the drives' housing racks. Lying on it is a large man in his fifties reading a copy of *Deadline Delivery*. He turns his head as you approach and puts the book aside.

"Hey, yer must be the space cadet the steward told me about. Good to see yer, kid. It gets pretty lonely down here. What's yer name?"

"Everyone calls me Ace." You swivel your head from side to side, taking in the massive drives towering behind you on either side.

"I'm Karl, the ship's engineer. Yer want a tour of Engineering, Ace?"

You grin and give a thumbs-up. A tour sounds great.

Karl doesn't even get out of the hammock, but he jerks his thumb towards your left. "That's the string jump drive to yer left. A fine piece of machinery that no one understands completely, including me." That doesn't seem to bother him. He points to the drive on your right. "That's the maneuver drive. We're operating on that at the moment."

"It sounds odd. I felt a jolt a few minutes ago, and the sound of the drive changed. What happened? Is everything okay?" you ask.

"It's working, ain't it?" He slowly sits up on the hammock and dangles his legs over the side.

"Let me tell yer something, Ace. A piece of advice for yer. If yer become an engineer, don't tinker with anything that's working. Coz it might not work no more after you do that and a mountain o' blame will come yer way. Just try and fix things once they're broken. If yer succeed, then yer everyone's hero."

"Thanks for that," you say flatly. That advice sounds terrible. What about maintenance? Things may need replacing while they are wearing out before they fail completely.

A yellow light flashes in the office, and Karl gets down and slopes off into the small room. His pale gray overalls appear almost too large on his lanky body. You wait while he takes a short call. You can't hear anything of the conversation because of the gravelly sound of the maneuver drive.

Karl comes out of the office with a grave expression. "Yer were right, Ace. That was the captain. The ship's not turning around, so something's gone wrong with the drive. I have to investigate."

Wow. This could be exciting. You can see first-hand how a starship's engineer diagnoses and fixes a problem. Though you might not see much because Karl seems the lazy type. "Any idea what the problem might be?"

"It may be a disruption in the fuel lines, an electrical shortage, or a mechanical problem. Dunno which, yet. Electrical would be easiest to fix, mechanical's the hardest."

"Are you sure we didn't hit something?"

Karl hoists a bushy eyebrow. "Space is big and empty, kid. The chance of us hitting a rock or something is miniscule." He pinches his finger and thumb together and separates them barely to emphasize his point.

You nod reluctantly. You're sure you heard something before the grinding noise started …

"How about you give me a hand, Ace? I'll check out the electrical circuits. You check out the fuel lines." He jerked his thumb behind him. "Fuel lines are that way. Valves shut them off if any of 'em come loose." He heads into the small office.

From what you've learned at cadet school, you're doubtful that an electrical or fuel issue could cause the maneuver drive to sound like it's running on gravel. But you shrug and go to check it out anyway.

The fuel lines are behind the maneuver drive. All the valves are fine. You're about to make your way back when the drive makes a spluttering, crunching sound and winds to a halt. The silence seems deafening.

Karl shouts, "Klunderheads! The blasted thing's stopped."

When you get back to his office, he's on the communicator again. You listen in, even though it's impolite, because you want to find out what's going on.

He disconnects the call and turns to you, crossing his hairy arms.

106

"Seems as if it's a mechanical problem after all. But we might have another problem too. The captain says that there are animals in the cargo hold. Someone needs to check them, make sure they're not freaked out. Do you want to do that, Ace, or help me out with the maneuver drive?"

You think for a moment. It's important to fix the maneuver drive, but you are curious about the live animals in the cargo hold too.

It's time to make a decision. Do you:

Stay with Karl and help with the drive problem? **P156**

Or

Go and check the cargo hold? **P162**

Go and meet the other passengers over dinner

The passenger lounge is a vast space, the largest on the starship, designed to provide somewhere for the passengers to spend time and socialize rather than remain alone in their sparse cabins for the entire voyage. It hasn't been redecorated for a considerable time, if ever. The carpet is well-worn in places, and the wallpaper is tatty around the edges.

At one end of the room is a dining table that seats eight people. It looks a little worse for wear, as do the mismatching dining chairs. A large, flat entertainment screen is fixed to one wall, surrounded by comfortable seating. At the other end of the room are sofas, easy chairs, refreshments and a selection of books on coffee tables. A small display stand lists notices regarding entertainment and meal times. There's not a lot on it, but "Three Coarse Meal 5.30pm" is at the top. Looks like a spelling mistake.

The other seven passengers are sitting at the table, waiting. A couple of women are chatting together. They look similar, tall and slim with straight blond hair, so maybe they are twins. The steward approaches you. He's an overweight man in his late twenties with an expression that suggests he's been sucking on lemons. He grumpily escorted all the passengers on board before the journey, and it doesn't appear that his mood has improved at all.

"So you're here at last, then. Take a seat, kid."

"Ace. My name is Ace."

"Yeah, whatever. If you'd been five minutes later, you'd have missed the starter, and there'd be no point complaining to me about it. Now, take your damn seat!" He walks off and exits through a side door. You catch a whiff of something cooking in there. Cabbage.

You sit in the last empty seat, opposite the two Proximeans, short, stocky blue-skinned creatures with beaks instead of mouths. Are they a couple? Male or female? One of each? It's hard to tell. They're both wearing grey hats over pointy ears and black jackets.

"Hi," you say.

One of them smiles at you. You think it's a smile, anyway.

The side door opens and the steward returns, bearing a wooden tray of steaming bowls. Right behind him glides a robot about half your height carrying a similar tray. Metallic fingers curl around the front edge of the tray, holding it steady. It must be moving on wheels or tracks. Little green sensor eyes flicker around constantly, and its rounded top rotates a little way in each direction, checking for obstacles.

You're a little disappointed when the robot goes to the other side of the table to serve the guests there. Meanwhile, the steward plops a bowl of green soup down in front of you with a *thunk*. Some of it spills onto the ragged tablecloth. Lumpy green bits float in the bowl. They could be cabbage, or the steward might have sneezed in there. You can't tell.

"Best damn cabbage soup you can find," he declares. "If you've any complaints, I don't want to hear them. The next course is in ten minutes, so eat up."

Evidently, he made the soup himself. That makes sense. The starship has a small crew. He probably serves as the cook as well as steward. Maybe his duties also include being the ship's doctor. What would his bedside manner be like?

You look around the table. The two women look at their bowls, then at each other. A grizzled middle-aged guy scratches his head. The other two people sit back in their chairs, perhaps having decided they'll skip this course.

Opposite you, the robot reaches with a long arm to give each of the Proximeans a bowl of some kind of leafy mixture. They start eating the food with fat, hairy blue hands.

Perhaps they can't eat the human soup. You're not sure if you can eat it either. Spoon in hand, you look at the lumps rotating in it as if under their own power. But you'll give it a try.

"You will have good time Promina B?" the Proximean on the right asks you slowly. Its voice is high, and its English clear enough to understand.

You have a mouthful of the disgusting soup and don't really want to swallow it, so you give a thumbs-up in response.

The Proximean stares at you, brown eyes widening, beak falling open. Half-chewed leafy greens tumble out. The other one gasps and grabs its partner's arm. What's going on?

They gesticulate wildly to the steward, who hurries over. "That child! Rude hand sign!" they tell him.

He turns to you. "Are you upsetting the other guests?"

You swallow the awful soup, shake your head and give him the thumbs-up. "I did this because I had my mouth full."

The Proximeans shrink back in their chairs, quivering.

The steward leans in to you. "That's a death threat in their society, kid. Try to be nice." He claps you on the back. "I'll let you off with a warning because I see that you like the soup."

Oh no! Different customs. You apologize profusely to the Proximeans, who eventually understand and start to relax. Now you have to eat the whole bowl of soup to keep the steward happy, but the robot comes and takes your bowl away before you can.

"That was revolting." The grizzly man threw his napkin on the table.

"Are all the meals going to be like this?" the man sitting next to you asks.

"No complaints! This is top notch grub," the steward said. "If you don't like it, you're welcome to skip meals. No? Don't want to do that? Then don't complain. I won't have any damn passengers complaining about my damn food."

Ah. Coarse meals. Now you understand it wasn't a spelling mistake.

The steward and the robot go off and return with plates of meat and mushy vegetables. The meat is unidentifiable. So are the vegetables. The Proximeans have more leaves.

"So, let's introduce ourselves," the steward said. "Let's get friendly with each other. I'm Stewart, the steward. My robotic helper is Rocky. It doesn't talk. Now let's go around the table. It's your turn, now. Starting with you, kid."

You wish he wouldn't call you "kid" when he knows your name. "I'm Ace, a student on an exchange trip. First time in space." You smile.

The Proximeans introduce themselves, but you have no idea how to spell or even pronounce their weird names.

The grizzly-bearded man says in his gruff voice, "I'm Dan, a miner. I'm going to Proxima B to check out the potential for mining in the system."

The other man who spoke earlier says, "I'm Richard, a nurse. I'm going to a job out there in the new colony."

The two women at the end of the table explain they are Millie and Jillie, the animal handlers travelling with the animal cargo.

The remaining person, a smartly-dressed woman with long dark hair, speaks quietly. "I'm Teresa, a businesswoman." She doesn't elaborate.

Stewart claps his hands. "Great. Now get friendly. I'm going to rustle up the damn dessert."

You groan at the thought of another course and pick at the meat and vegetables. They're edible, though mysterious and tasteless.

Dessert isn't a lot better. The Proximeans have the same thing as the humans this time, a sloppy chocolate-flavored goop. Perhaps they like chocolate. After dessert, of which most of the passengers manage no more than half, Stewart encourages everyone to mingle. The robot brings out a tray of drinks. You grab an apple juice. Most of the others pick up a glass of wine, though by their expressions after they sip, it appears to be low-grade stuff. The Proximeans slurp brown frothy liquid from glasses with straws—possibly chocolate milkshakes.

It seems awkward. People shuffle around. Everyone starts off talking about the meal we've had. You approach the two animal handlers and ask them what they're going to do on Proxima B. They tell you they're going hiking in the rough hills around the colony once they've delivered their cargo.

"My Spacenet connector's gone!"

You turn. Richard, the nurse, was the speaker. Instinctively, you check your own Spacenet connector is in your pocket. It is, and you breathe a sigh of relief. Everyone has a connector to the Spacenet, the replacement for the Internet.

Stewart hurries over to Richard. "What do you mean, it's gone?"

"Stolen! It was in my pocket when I came to dinner."

"Mine too!" Dan says. "And it has my mining exploration license on it."

"Jewelry gone," one of the Proximeans says. "From pocket."

"And my necklace," Teresa adds, feeling under her collar.

Stewart looks around you all. "So five of you have lost something since you came to dinner?"

"Not lost. Stolen," Dan insists.

The steward scratches his head. You and the animal handlers look at each other. The three of you have been together since dinner ended and aren't missing anything.

Something doesn't add up. If there's a thief, it must be one of the five people who reported something stolen. But who?

"This is the last damn thing I need," Stewart says. "The robot and I will conduct an investigation. Everyone go back to your cabins for now. I'll make a search of the passenger lounge area and then come and talk to each of you in person."

Some of the passengers grumble, but everyone does as they're asked. You return to your cabin, but it's cramped and boring there. You don't want to stay. Maybe you can help with the investigation? Or start one of your own?

It's time to make a decision. Do you:

Go ask the steward if you can help with the investigation? **P112**

Or

Spy on the passengers to see who the thief might be? **P124**

Go and ask the steward if you can help him

You decide to go and find the steward. Waiting in your cabin with nothing much to do is boring. Instead, you can make yourself useful. What was that saying again? Two heads are better than one? Yeah, that's it. But what about too many cooks spoil the broth? Oh, never mind. Go offer to help anyway.

The cabin door whooshes closed behind you. The luminescent corridor walls provide a dull yellow illumination. You walk the short distance to the passenger lounge, which is on the left of the corridor. The steward rises from his knees as you enter. Evidently, he's been searching the floor under the dining table. The little robot circles the table slowly.

"Yes?"

"I want to help."

"I've got to treat everyone as a suspect, Ace, including you." Stewart glowers at you.

"But I was with the animal handlers the entire time after dinner. They and I can vouch for each other. We weren't even near the passengers who had their items stolen."

The robot beeps twice. Stewart glances at it. "Okay. Rocky confirms that. You and they aren't suspects any more. And I could use your help, so thanks for offering."

You grin. An investigation could be fun. "What would you like me to do?"

"We have to question everyone, ask if they saw anything suspicious. Draw a diagram to show where they were in the room, where they thought everyone else was and what their movements were. Then we'll check over everything for inconsistencies."

"Okay. I can do that."

"The main thing is not to annoy anyone. They're upset at having lost their things. We have to be delicate about this, damn it."

"I understand."

"Go talk to Dan the miner and Richard the nurse. Take Rocky with you. I'll interview the Proximeans because you upset them earlier. And I'll talk to Teresa. We'll meet back here." He tells you their cabin numbers.

"Got it." You are about to give him a thumbs-up but change your mind. It might remind him of how the Proximeans reacted.

With Rocky at your heels, you return to the corridor, find Richard's cabin, and knock. He answers almost immediately.

"I'm helping the steward," you explain.

Richard glances at the robot and at you, and then indicates for you to come inside. His cabin is identical to yours. He sits on the bed next to an overturned copy of *Once Upon an Island*. You sit in the only chair.

"What do you want to know? I've checked my room. My Spacenet communicator definitely isn't here. I'm sure I had it in my back pocket when I went to dinner."

"I want to record where everyone was. Who were you talking with? Anyone walk behind you?"

He wrinkles his nose and looks up, thinking. "I talked to Teresa and then Dan. The Proximeans were further away."

"So, only Teresa and Dan were near you the whole time?"

"Yeah. They both moved behind me, too, at different points, to get a top-up of their drinks."

"Okay, thanks." You scribble a note on a napkin you took from the dining table.

Richard doesn't appear to want to say any more, and you can't think of any more to ask, so you leave his cabin and move on to Dan's. You tell him the same thing about helping the steward, he lets you in, and you ask the same questions that you asked Richard.

He strokes his rough beard before answering. "The Proximeans were behind me. I didn't talk to them because they kept apart. I talked to Teresa or Richard the whole time. Richard went to get another drink at some stage, but he didn't move behind me. When Teresa went to get a top-up, she had to squeeze between me and the Proximeans to get past."

The robot beeps three times and hops. You don't know what that means. You write some notes, but you're almost out of napkin now.

"I miss my Spacenet communicator. If I could get my hands on the person who stole it …" Dan clenches his fists for a moment, and then lowers his head. "It's those funny cat videos people post. They make me laugh so much."

"I know what you mean, Dan. I couldn't do without mine either." You quickly check your pocket to make sure it's there. It is. "I read somewhere that a typical Spacenet communicator is more powerful than the computers that NASA used for the first manned mission to the moon. Amazing, isn't it?"

Dan grins. "Ace, even the smartphones people had way back in 2016 were more powerful than those NASA computers."

Wow. You didn't know that.

On the last small square of unoccupied napkin, you draw a picture of where people stood when the items went missing. "Is this correct?"

Dan pulls some glasses from a shirt pocket and peers at your small map. "Yep. That's it, all right. As I told you."

Rocky bounces twice and beeps some more. It wants your attention.

"Does your robot need to take a walk or something?"

"Maybe," you say. "Thanks, Dan."

You leave his cabin. Outside, in the corridor, Rocky extends a metallic arm. A titanium finger beckons.

What does it want? Oh. The map. Maybe it wants to look at the map.

You hold out the napkin. Rocky stabs at it with a finger. It goes right through, leaving a hole, obliterating the part of your drawing showing where Richard, Dan and Teresa stood together.

Never mind. You think you've worked it out anyway.

You return to the passenger lounge just as Stewart approaches from the other direction. You go inside, followed by Rocky.

"That didn't help much," Stewart says. "It's definitely not the Proximeans, though. They were pretty much by themselves most of the time and didn't see anything, damn it."

"What about Teresa?" you ask.

"She said both Dan and Richard seemed a bit shifty, moving around and looking sly. Darn it. I don't want to upset anyone, but I might have to make a search of everyone's cabins. Unless you found out something useful?"

"I think I did. And so does Rocky." You show Stewart your holey napkin. At least the notes are still readable.

He scratches his head. "This makes some sense to you, does it?"

"Yes. If you want to search the cabins, I think I know whose cabin you should start with."

It's time to make a decision. You have three choices. Do you:

Accuse Richard, the nurse? **P116**

Or

Accuse Dan, the miner? **P118**

Or

Accuse Teresa, the businesswoman? **P121**

Accuse Richard, the nurse

You lead the way to Richard's cabin and knock on the door with gusto. He opens it slowly, glances at you, looks over your shoulder at Stewart, and steps back into his room, leaving the door open.

"That's great you're here," he says. "I guess you've found the thief, and you've come to return my stolen Spacenet communicator."

"That's half correct," you say, winking at Stewart. "We've found the thief all right, and it's you, Richard."

"What? Don't be ridiculous."

In your peripheral vision, you see Rocky wobbling from side to side on his wheels. It must mean something, but you have no idea what.

Stewart leans in close. You feel his breath in your right ear as he whispers, "Are you damn sure about this, Ace?"

You nod. The steward waves his hand at Rocky, who zips around the room, a red light in its chest blinking on and off. The robot reminds you of a tracker dog, apart from the red light, of course.

"What's that robot doing?"

"It's conducting a search," Stewart says, "for the stolen items."

"This is absolutely crazy. You're both bonkers. Why do you think I'm the thief, anyway? Tell me that."

You point a finger at him. "You were standing right by Teresa and Dan. You had the opportunity to steal from them both."

Richard juts his chin forward and replies with a raised voice. "They had the opportunity too. And what about the Proximeans? I was nowhere near them."

Your mouth goes dry. You make a croaking sound. You'd forgotten that. Have you got this wrong?

"When I get to Proxima B, I'm going to lodge a complaint, you can be sure of that."

Rocky gives a long beep. Stewart clenches his teeth and glares at you. "Rocky found nothing. There's nothing here."

"Told you. Now get out and leave me in peace."

You stumble out into the corridor, followed by Rocky and Stewart.

The steward is red-faced. "You and your damn ideas. Now we're in trouble and the real thief might have had time to conceal the stolen items. I shouldn't have listened to you."

I'm sorry, this part of your story is over. You've met the passengers and got involved in an investigation to find a thief. However, your deductive reasoning wasn't up to par this time, and the real thief got away. Richard doesn't talk to you for the remainder of the voyage, and Stewart often leaves you out of the fun entertainment. Even the ship's robot seems to ignore you. However, you can change your last choice if you wish, because this book allows you to do that.

Alternatively, other pathways are waiting.

It's time to make a decision. You have three choices. Would you like to:

Go back to where you were helping the steward with the investigation? **P112**

Or

Go to the list of choices and start reading from another part of the story? **P532**

Or

Go back to the beginning of the story and try another path? **P95**

Accuse Dan, the miner

You hurry back to Dan's cabin with Stewart beside you and Rocky rolling behind. A sharp rap brings Dan to the door.

"What's going on?" he says, his eyebrows creasing into a monobrow as you all crowd into his cabin. He's squeezed back to the viewport.

"I think you know, Dan," you say, tapping him on the chest. "You couldn't wait to get to Proxima B to hunt for precious metals and gems. You had to pick some up on the journey, didn't you? Where is the stolen jewelry and the Spacenet communicators?"

Dan bends forward, poking you high in the chest, his bristly face almost nose-to-nose with you. "Are you for real, Ace? I was one of the victims. My Spacenet communicator was one of those stolen. I told you that already." He looks at Stewart, who stands with a blank expression, listening. "This is nonsense. Why do you think I'm the thief, anyway?"

You point a finger at him. "You were standing between everyone. You had the opportunity to steal from them all."

"And they were standing next to me, too. But I was in front of Teresa the whole time, except when she moved behind me. How could I have stolen from her?" He pokes a finger mere centimeters from your face. "Have you talked to her?"

You gulp. Have you got this wrong?

Stewart glances at you before turning his attention back to the miner. "We have to search your cabin, Dan. It's part of the investigation."

"Is that so? Are you searching everyone's cabin? No? Then it's harassment. I won't put up with that." His fists are clenched.

You bite your lip. Is Dan going to hit the steward? And you?

But Dan turns as Rocky whizzes across the room, beeping loudly, rounded top rotating. If the robot had a tail, you're sure it would be wagging right now. It bonks his top repeatedly against the small bedside cabinet.

"Aha!" you say, and march over.

"Wait," Dan says. "Don't look in there. There's nothing—"

"I bet there is. Let's see," you say, yanking the top drawer open. It falls to the floor, its contents spilling.

You all stare. No jewelry or stolen Spacenet communicators. Only chocolate. Dozens of chocolate bars, boxes of exotic European chocolates, thousands of M&Ms.

Rocky whirrs.

The steward strokes his chin. "That's much more than the personal duty-free allowance, Dan. You can't take all of that to Proxima B."

"I was going to eat most of it on the journey." Dan's voice falters.

You frown. Even you would be sick eating that much chocolate over such a short time.

"Even so, the quantity you left Earth's spaceport with is illegal."

"Okay, okay, I admit that I smuggled the chocolate. It's worth a fortune on Proxima B. I need some start-up capital when I get there."

Stewart folds his arms. You follow Rocky as it rolls around the remainder of the room, looking for the stolen items.

"I don't know anything about the other stuff. Honestly. Look for yourself."

Rocky rocks on his wheels from side to side. You look everywhere, but find nothing. Oops. Dan isn't the thief after all.

So who is? And how much trouble are you going to be in?

The steward sums it up. "All right, we were wrong to accuse you. Please accept our apologies. Right, Ace?"

You nod, head hanging, red-faced.

"The thing is," Stewart continued, "you're on board with too much chocolate, and that's smuggling."

Dan's craggy face is crestfallen. He gazes at his feet. "What are you going to do?"

Stewart taps the side of his nose. "How about you forget we accused you wrongly of theft and say no more about it, and we'll

120

ignore the fact that you smuggled so much chocolate out of the Earth spaceport?"

The miner lifts his head. "Deal." He spits on one hand and shakes first Stewart's hand, then yours. You wipe your moist hand on the back of your pants afterwards.

There's an opportunity here. "There's still the issue of you having too much chocolate to import to Proxima B. Way over the allowance, isn't it?" You don't even know what the allowance is, but you remember what Stewart said earlier.

"I—I'm going to eat some of it," Dan says.

You tilt your head and stare at him.

"I meant that I'll share it with you," Dan mutters. He doesn't look too happy about it though.

I'm sorry, this part of your story is over. You've met the passengers and got involved in an investigation to find a thief. However, your deductive reasoning wasn't up to par this time, and the real thief got away. On the other hand, you did end up with a lot of chocolate to eat during the remainder of the voyage, so it wasn't all bad. If you want to catch the real thief, you can retake your last choice (but that will mean giving up the chocolate).

Alternatively, other pathways are waiting.

It's time to make a decision. You have three choices. Would you like to:

Go back to where you were helping the steward with the investigation? **P112**

Or

Go to the list of choices and start reading from another part of the story? **P532**

Or

Go back to the beginning of the story and try another path? **P95**

Accuse Teresa, the businesswoman

You march to Teresa's cabin, confident that you'll reveal her as the jewelry and Spacenet communicator thief. Rocky rolls behind you, and Stewart strolls in the rear.

She doesn't respond immediately to your knock. You rap louder. Finally, the door whooshes open. Teresa stands there in the smart attire she wore at the dinner. Behind her, in her cabin, her suitcase lies open on her bed.

"Come in," she says. "Do you have some more questions? I'll be glad to do anything I can to help."

"Good," you say. "Then please hand over the stolen items. That would help a lot."

If looks could kill, you'd be obliterated right now, but her glare fades.

"You're joking, surely. I'm a respectable businesswoman. I was one of the victims."

"Saying you're a victim is a ruse to fool us."

"How ridiculous. Are you listening to this kid?" she implores the steward.

"Let's hear the kid out."

The little robot scoots around the room, whirring quietly, searching.

"We're looking for a pickpocket. Everyone else lost something from their pocket, but you said you had your necklace stolen. I didn't see your necklace at dinner." You remember seeing her feel under her collar when she reported it missing.

"It was under my collar." Teresa huffed, lifting her nose in the air.

"Then how would a thief have known it was there to steal it? Also, you stood near all the victims after dinner, and you passed behind all of them to top up your drink. That's the opportunity you had."

Stewart hasn't said a word, but he watches closely. Rocky scurries around the room and now rolls alongside the edge of the bed.

"Preposterous," Teresa protests. "It's scandalous for a person in my position to be treated like a … like a common thief."

"I'm going to have to search your room, ma'am," Stewart says, but he doesn't move an inch.

Teresa steps back and flings an arm wide flamboyantly. "Look, then. There's my luggage. Examine it if you must. Poke around among my skirts and panties. Oh, look in the bedside cabinet too. Anywhere else? No? This cabin is so tiny, isn't it?"

She sounds so assured. Have you made a mistake here? What trouble are you going to land in if you have?

Stewart takes a step towards the suitcase on the bed, but Rocky emits a high-pitched whistling that jars your ears. He's rolling around by the bed.

"Have a look," Stewart says.

You get to your knees, then lie on the floor. There isn't much space under the bed. You reach underneath. Rocky comes over and nudges your arm. It directs you a little further along. Reaching as far as you can, you touch a velvet bag that doesn't belong there. You yank it out, pull it open, then stand and tip the contents onto the bed.

"Look. Two Spaceport communicators and some jewelry. Proximean, I bet."

Teresa's fuming, but she's caught red-handed.

"Right, Teresa," the steward says, "it's the brig for you. I'll return these stolen items to their owners. Well done, Ace." He high-fives you. Rocky races over to join in.

Congratulations, this part of your story is over. You've met the passengers and got involved in an investigation to find a thief. Your observation skills and deductive reasoning solved the mystery. The pickpocket was put in the brig, and the other passengers think you're a hero. Dan gives you a heap of chocolate because you recovered his Spacenet communicator. The steward's grumpy demeanor has lifted, and he goes out of his way to make your journey comfortable and enjoyable, and even lets you hang out with Rocky most of the time.

Recovering their jewelry even helps you make amends with the Proximeans for offending them earlier.

But have you tried the other pathways in the book?

It's time to make a decision. Would you like to:

Go to the list of choices and start reading from another part of the story? **P532**

Or

Go back to the beginning of the story and try another path? **P95**

Spy on the passengers

You don't want to sit in your cabin doing nothing while there's a pickpocket to be found. This is an opportunity for you to help and make a lasting impression. They won't forget you if you find the thief.

You open your door but remain inside, listening. After a minute or two, another door whooshes open and closed. You can't see the door because of the curved corridor, so you step out cautiously until you glimpse the steward moving away from you. He knocks on a door further along. You strain your ears. The door opens and closes.

It's quiet now. He must have gone inside.

What is the point of this? You're about to go and wait for the steward when you hear footsteps in the corridor.

One of the other passengers has left their cabin. Whoever it is, they don't seem to be coming towards you. They're going the other way.

As quietly as you can, you follow, hurrying to catch a glimpse of the other person. You pass the passenger lounge on the left and all of the remaining cabins on the right. Then you have her in sight. It's the businesswoman, Teresa.

Staying back so she can't see you, you sneak around the curved corridor. She goes past the door to the Bridge and around into the port corridor. You don't even know what's down there.

You go past the airlock. She's walked almost halfway around the starship now. Is she going for a stroll? Maybe you're following her for nothing.

You hear a door whoosh open and edge forward, peering around the curvature. Teresa enters a room. She hasn't seen you. The door closes behind her.

It's the medic bay. Why is she here? Is she ill? Or is she the thief and she has gone in there to conceal the stolen items?

If she's ill, she might need help. But then why was she waiting in her doorway and didn't ask the steward when he left the passenger lounge?

No, it's suspicious behavior. And, if she's the thief, she's cunning, devious, possibly dangerous. Do you really want to mess with her?

You barely hear the whoosh of a door from around in the starboard corridor. That's probably the steward. You could race off and get him, or you could confront Teresa on your own.

It's time to make a decision. Do you:

Get the steward and tell him your suspicions? **P126**

Or

Confront the suspected thief on your own? **P128**

126

Get the steward and tell him your suspicions

Even if Teresa isn't dangerous, it'd be best to have a witness when you confront her, otherwise it's her word against yours. Also, if you're completely wrong about her being the thief and she's in the medic bay because she's sick from the dinner (possible!), getting the steward is a good idea anyway.

You backtrack a few steps quietly, then spin and race around the corridor to the starboard side, moving with the silence of a stalking panther. You're so quiet that you run almost up to the steward before he realizes you're there.

"Ace! Damn it, kid, you took me by surprise. Why aren't you in your cabin like I told you?"

"Quick, follow me. You have to come to the medic bay."

You turn and hurry off. He comes after you, but slower because he's overweight. Rocky the robot (who is not overweight) scurries up beside you, beeping softly, keeping pace with you until you reach the medic bay. You've been gone less than a minute. Teresa must still be inside.

Stewart arrives a few seconds later. "What's this about, Ace? I'm damned busy, you know."

The door whooshes open when you activate the sensor with your wristpad. Inside, you see Teresa putting something on a high shelf.

"I think that's our thief," you say.

Stewart slips past you into the room. "Can I help you with something, Teresa?"

"Um … no, I was only looking for a headache pill."

Light glints off cut diamonds in her hand. It's the stolen jewelry!

"Look!" you say, pointing. Rocky hops up and down on his wheels, lights flashing.

Stewart has seen it too. He reaches up and seizes Teresa's wrist. A pair of Proximean diamond rings tumble from her fingers.

He moves closer, reaching up to the shelf, and finds the Spacenet communicators there. "I suppose you planned to hide these here and pick them up just before we reach Proxima B."

Teresa doesn't answer. She's seething mad. But there's nothing she can do. She's been caught red-handed. She's not a businesswoman at all, but a pickpocket posing as one for cover.

"Right, Teresa," the steward says, "it's the brig for you. I'll return these stolen items to their owners. Well done, Ace." He high-fives you. Rocky races over to join in.

Congratulations, this part of your story is over. You've met the passengers and tracked down the pickpocket on your own. The thief was put in the brig, and the other passengers think you're a hero. Dan gives you heaps of chocolate because he's so happy to have his Spacenet communicator back. The steward's grumpy demeanor has lifted, and he goes out of his way to make your journey comfortable and enjoyable, and even lets you hang out with Rocky most of the time. Recovering their jewelry even helps you make amends with the Proximeans for offending them earlier.

But have you tried the other pathways in the book?

It's time to make a decision. Would you like to:

Go to the list of choices and start reading from another part of the story? **P532**

Or

Go back to the beginning of the story and try another path? **P95**

Confront the suspected thief on your own

Better not waste any time. The door whooshes open when you activate the sensor with your wristpad. Inside, Teresa stares at you in shock. She's emptying her pockets. In one hand is a Spacenet communicator. Another lies on the benchtop, along with a pair of diamond rings.

"Aha! Caught you. You're the thief. The pickpocket."

She scowls at you, then relaxes into a smile. "You're Ace, aren't you? Listen, Ace, we can make a deal here. I can cut you in for a share of the profits. Or you can simply take the Spacenet communicators for yourself and sell them on Proxima B. What do you say?"

You're not dishonest. "No. That's wrong. I'm certainly not doing that. I'm going to report you to the steward."

"You're making a big mistake, Ace. You'll regret this."

You shake your head, turn and step into the corridor, about to shout for the steward. Before you have a chance to call him, Teresa crashes into you from behind, and you both tumble to the metal floor in a noisy tangle of arms and legs.

The thumps of the steward's footsteps come closer. He skids to a halt by the medic bay door. "I heard a din. What in the blazes is going on here?"

You and Teresa sit up, then stand. You're not hurt, just a little winded.

The ship's little robot, Rocky, rolls up and leans back on its wheels as if it's looking at you.

"I caught her red-handed," you say. "Teresa. She's the thief. She was hiding the stolen items when I found her. I was about to call you when she knocked me down."

"That's nonsense," Teresa says. "Ace is the thief, as I suspected. After we all went to our cabins, I watched the corridor to see if your cadet would make a move. I followed Ace here, and the kid knocked me over trying to escape."

You stare at her, gob-smacked. That's completely the opposite of what happened!

Stewart looks from you to Teresa and back a couple of times. He seems uncertain what to do. Rocky whirrs.

"Where are the darned stolen items?"

"They're in the medic bay," you say, "on the benchtop."

Stewart turns towards the door, but Teresa reaches out and stops him. "Don't turn your back on the thief. Ace could run away with the stolen goods, or hide them while you're distracted."

He looks back at you, crossing his arms, jaw set.

Your throat feels tight. A pain begins in your stomach. Does he believe her?

Rocky rolls into your leg, nudging you. Stewart takes a step closer. What's going on?

"Where do you think the stolen items are?" Stewart asks Teresa.

"In those pockets," Teresa says, pointing at you.

"What? Of course they're not." Unless—

"Empty your pockets, Ace," the steward says, his eyes hard, his mouth straight-lined.

"This is ridiculous." Now it's your turn to feel indignant. You've caught the thief, and now you are being interrogated and searched! Why doesn't Stewart turn and look into the medic bay? He'll see the jewelry sitting on the benchtop in there.

You stuff your right hand in your pocket, ready to turn it inside-out like you've been asked, and gasp when your fingers strike something hard. Rings. And two Spacenet communicators.

Sheepishly, you pull them out. "I—I don't know how they got there," you mumble. But you do know. Teresa, the expert pickpocket, is as good at putting things into pockets as she is at taking them out. She's duped you. Landed you in it. You will get the blame for her failed pickpocketing spree.

Stewart shakes his head. "It's the brig for you, Ace. You surprised me. I thought you were a good kid. Guess I was wrong."

He escorts you to the brig, the last room on the starboard corridor to the aft of the starship. As you walk, you glance over your shoulder, distraught, hoping that Teresa will recant and confess. She doesn't. Instead, she gives you a little wave.

The brig is small, much smaller even than your cabin. There's a bed with a thin mattress, a wobbly chair and a book on a table. In the corner, not visible from the corridor, is a compact grubby shower cubicle and a toilet.

You're locked inside. A small window lets you look out into the corridor. The others walk off, but Rocky sits there for a few seconds longer, rocking back and forth on his wheels like a wagging finger telling you off.

I'm sorry, this part of your story is over. You've met the passengers and tracked down the pickpocket on your own. Unfortunately, not having any help or a witness when you confronted Teresa allowed her to turn the tables and put the blame on you. Teresa is acclaimed as a hero and you spend the rest of the journey in the brig with almost nothing to do. You're dismissed from space cadet school upon your arrival at Proxima B and have to take a number of dangerous and unpleasant jobs to earn enough money to pay for your passage back to Earth—but that's another story.

This may be the end of your space career, but it might turn out better if you try some of the other pathways in the book.

It's time to make a decision. You have three choices. Would you like to:

Change your last choice and get the steward before confronting Teresa? **P126**

Or

Go to the list of choices and start reading from another part of the story? **P532**

Or

Go back to the beginning of the story and try another path? **P95**

Stay with the captain and investigate

You can put off going to dinner for a while. Who knows when you'll get another chance to troubleshoot problems on the Bridge?

"I'd like to stay here," you say.

"Sure. I'll call Karl and see what he says about the drive."

Teena makes the call. You listen to her side of it. "Uh-huh … then unblock the drive! We can't maneuver … yes, I understand it'll take time to investigate … all right, call back when you have an update."

She disconnects. "Karl is the laziest engineer I've ever come across, but he does know his stuff. Hopefully, he understands how urgent this is."

"So … we're drifting?"

"Yes, if you can say that travelling at over five hundred thousand kilometers per hour is drifting. We've no way of slowing down until the drive is fixed."

"What about the string jump point?"

"We'll shoot past it. That doesn't matter much. I can recalculate a new jump point. But we can't jump at this speed, if that's what you're thinking. We might collide with something in the Proxima B system when we emerge."

"I see." A thought occurs to you. "What if … just saying … Karl can't fix the maneuver drive? How long until we're rescued?"

Teena laughs, but not in a happy way. "Rescue would depend on a faster ship catching us up. That'll be costly. And unlikely. I want to see if Karl can fix the drive first. If not, and a rescue ship isn't available, then we might be playing pinball in the asteroid belt."

You squirm a little. "How long until we get to the belt?"

The captain claps a hand on your shoulder in what you interpret as a reassuring manner. "Don't worry, Ace. It'll be two weeks before we get there at this speed. And whenever the maneuver drive has failed before, Karl has managed to fix it within a few hours."

You decide not to ask if it fails often.

132

There's a buzz, and a message appears on the main display screen in bold green letters.

Attn: The Bejeweled Diva. *This is a patrol ship. Please send over your flight documents. We believe there is a problem.*

Teena groans. "I don't need this right now."

You look out of the viewport. The big, dark shape you thought you saw from your cabin is still there, matching speed with *The Bejeweled Diva.* You can't pick out any details, but that's clearly where the message is coming from.

"I see it. The patrol ship. Out there."

The captain glances out. "It must have been following us for a while to have matched velocities with us."

"Is there a problem?"

"I may have forgotten to pay the port departure fee when we left."

"You may have?"

"I did."

You facepalm.

Another message comes through.

The Bejeweled Diva: *we await your documentation.*

Teena responds. "On its way." She attaches a copy of the flight documentation.

An idea occurs to you. "Can we ask them for help with the maneuver drive?"

"Yes, we can ask. Good idea, Ace."

Teena messages the patrol ship:

While you are here, we have a Mayday. Our maneuver drive is non-functioning. Can you please send an engineer to assist us in case my own engineer cannot fix the problem?

We await an answer, but nothing comes immediately.

"I wonder why they're not using audio?" Teena says. "That's standard protocol."

After a few minutes, a message comes back.

We can't help you. We are still checking your documentation. Stand by and await further instructions.

The captain turns to you. "You know, now I'm suspicious. Why haven't they picked up on the fact that I didn't pay the port departure fee? And why won't they help us?"

It doesn't sound right to you. "Can you check them with the scanner? What type of patrol ship is it?"

Teena sighs. "The scanner doesn't work. At the last annual maintenance review, the electronics engineers said it needed some new wiring, but I couldn't afford it at the time."

You have to ask. "When was the last annual maintenance review?"

"About six years ago," she admits.

You shake your head. This is crazy. Are you even going to get to Proxima B at this rate?

"Ask them their patrol ship id, please, Teena."

Puzzled, she messages across the request. A code comes back: 470.

"470? Means nothing to me," Teena says. "It's a 3-digit code, though, so I guess it's okay."

You work out something in your head. "No, it's not. All the patrol ship ids are 3 digits, yes, but they follow a particular formula. I learned about it in space cadet school. And 470 doesn't match the formula."

"Are you sure?"

"Absolutely. A valid patrol ship id is any three digit number that is a multiple of 17, plus 19. So if we deduct 19 from 470, we get 451. That's not evenly divisible by 17."

"I get it. So, they're not the authorities. They're probably 'unfriendlies', then. Though the authorities can be unfriendly too, of course."

"By 'unfriendlies', what do you mean? What do they want?"

"Let's find out."

Teena messages back.

Cut out the pretense. You're not a patrol ship. WHO ARE YOU?

No reply.

"This could be bad. I need to check the cargo bay. See if our cargo of cats is safe."

"Cats?"

"Pets for the colony at Proxima B." She hits the exit button, and the door to the corridor opens with a whoosh.

You follow, but when she gasps and stops suddenly, you bump into her back.

"Hide!" she whispers, nudging you with her foot. She stands in the doorway, blocking it.

The stomping sound of feet comes from the metal corridor, but dampened somehow. It sounds like two sets of footfalls, but they are light, as if they're padded.

You back away, so whoever it is can't see you from the corridor. Because of the curvature, you know they can be only meters away. But in this small Bridge space, what shall you do? They'll find you as soon as they enter, if they do.

Your gaze falls upon a door on the back wall on the starboard side. You don't know where it goes.

It's time to make a decision. Do you:

Stay in the Bridge and hope you're not found? **P135**

Or

Go through the door at the back of the Bridge? **P137**

Stay in the Bridge and hope you're not found

Whoever it is, they grab the captain and pull her into the corridor. She glances back at you, forehead wrinkled, realizing you didn't find a hiding place.

A creature steps into the Bridge and immediately sees you. It's a Space Pug! Mean creatures, known as Spugs, roam space looking for trouble. And they seem to have brought it to *The Bejeweled Diva.* And to you, specifically.

"Woof! I've found another one, Sluuffo." He grabs you with a clawed hand with such strength that it's hopeless to resist, and he drags you into the corridor with the captain.

"Quiet, now," Sluuffo says, putting a big smelly hand over your mouth. "Or else."

"Yeah. Gruff. We don't want any witnesses. This is supposed to be a quiet operation. Woof."

The captain tries to say something, but the other Spug clamps his furry clawed hand over her mouth.

"Let's go, Makkav," the one gripping you says. "We'll deal with these two first. Yap. Then you help our friends with the cargo, and I'll go collect the 'specials' from our collaborator. Woof."

They drag you along the port corridor. "Yap. Shame we have to do this, but we don't want witnesses. Woof."

You reach the airlock. They shove you both inside roughly and lock it behind you both.

"You can't do this to us!" shouts Teena. She bangs on the inner airlock door in vain.

On the other side of the airlock door, Sluuffo raises a hand to his flappy ear to indicate he can't hear. Makkav gives a brief wave goodbye, then flips the switch to open the outer airlock door.

You're both sucked into space.

I'm sorry, this part of your story is over. Not hiding from the boarders

136

when the captain warned you wasn't the best choice. It got you caught as well as her. If you'd hidden, maybe (just maybe) you might have found a way to help her. Perhaps you'd like to try that choice again?

Alternatively, other pathways are waiting.

It's time to make a decision. You have three choices. Would you like to:

Change your last choice and go through the door at the back of the Bridge? **P137**

Or

Go to the list of choices and start reading from another part of the story? **P532**

Or

Go back to the beginning of the story and try another path? **P95**

Go through the door at the back of the Bridge

Swiftly, you open the narrow door and slip through, pulling it closed behind you. Inside is a space not much larger than a wardrobe. There's a bucket seat and a timeworn instrument panel that you don't have time to investigate properly right now. You stand against the door, listening.

"What do you want?" That's the captain's voice coming from inside the Bridge space.

"Your cargo, what else? Yap. If you hadn't challenged us, we could have lifted your cargo without you even noticing while we … checked your documentation. Woof. But you didn't believe us, so we had to teleport over here. Now what are we going to do with you?"

Yap? Woof? The boarders are Space Pugs. Mean creatures that you've read about in your space cadet classes, a result of crazy genetic experiments between humans and dogs. Now they roam space. Spugs, for short.

"You don't have to do anything with me. I assume you're going to steal my cargo and leave the ship. Why do you need to do anything with me?" The captain's voice sounds shrill.

"Our clients insisted on no witnesses. You're a witness now. Gruff. We'll have to put you out the airlock. Sorry about that."

He didn't sound sorry. You cringe. If you hadn't told Teena the patrol ship id was invalid, she probably wouldn't have challenged them, and they wouldn't have had a reason to come over.

You shiver. Is the captain going to die because of that?

There's a scuffle. Maybe Teena's going to get away. You press yourself against the door, trying to work out what's happening.

"She's unconscious now, you dolt, Makkav."

"I didn't think I hit her that hard. Yap."

"You'll have to carry her. Let's get on with it."

You stifle a scream. You want to pound on the door, but it won't do any good. It'll only result in you going out the airlock with her.

"Shall I get rid of her right now, Sluuffo?"

"Woof. Nah. We might meet another one. She's not going to be any trouble now that you knocked her out. Go join our friends in the cargo hold, and I'll go and collect the 'specials' from Engineering."

Why Engineering? What are 'specials'? This sounds suspicious.

Their soft footfalls leave the Bridge and go into the corridor, so you slip out of the small room. Through the open door, you see the two Spugs strolling away. The one you think is Makkav carries Teena over his shoulder. Her frizzy hair and limp arms bounce on his back as he goes.

Quietly, you follow, keeping them barely in sight, so you can duck behind the curvature and remain hidden if one of them turns. You pass a door on the internal wall labeled "SHIP'S LOCKER: CREW ONLY". Makkav takes the stairway down to the cargo hold, and Sluuffo continues onward. You creep after them like a displaced shadow.

Someone, or something, lets Makkav into the cargo hold. More Spugs are down there! Further on, Sluuffo takes the steps down to Engineering. Trailing at a safe distance, you hear the door whoosh open as someone lets him in.

Who? Are there more Spugs down there too? Is Karl, the engineer, in danger? You try to recall Sluuffo and Makkav's conversation earlier.

It's not sensible to confront either of them. You made that decision when hiding in the anteroom to the Bridge. It would get you captured and possibly killed.

You need another option. Something more creative. Something to put the odds in your favor, so you can rescue the captain and prevent the Spugs from stealing the cargo.

But what?

Maybe there is something in the ship's locker that can help.

You hurry back to it, glancing down the stairs to the cargo hold as you pass. The door down there is closed. What's going on?

The ship's equipment cupboard will be locked, for sure. Have you been given access with your wristpad? Probably not.

You hold your wristpad up to the security sensor, and the door whooshes open. You grin. They must have trusted you to give you access to this.

Or maybe they simply forgot to withhold access.

Either way, you've opened the ship's locker. A dull yellow light from the corridor wall behind you illuminates a random ramshackle bunch of items inside. You want something like a laser rifle, Kevlar armor, perhaps a bunch of stun grenades.

Instead, you find a bowling ball, an extendable pole with a hook, and a spacesuit bearing a label from the second-hand store at the spaceport.

Not much use, you think. If you weren't trying to save the captain's life and prevent the cargo from being stolen, you might give the bowling ball a whirl around the curved corridor of the ship. Would it complete a whole circuit if you bowled it fast enough?

You shake your head. There's no time for that. There's not much time to think about anything.

Should you delve further into the cupboard? Scrounging around in there a little longer might waste time, or it might turn up something useful.

Sweat moistens your palms as you grip them tightly. You've got to do something.

Is the spacesuit any help? The captain probably bought it for herself. It'll be roomy, but at least you'll fit into it. But what can you do with it?

You could use it to get from *The Bejeweled Diva* to the Spug ship.

Scrunching your face and tilting your head to one side, you wonder if that's a good idea.

You can put the spacesuit on while you decide, so you tug the spacesuit from the cupboard. Two minutes later, you're inside it, fastening the helmet on. It seems to be in good condition, but there isn't time to check it thoroughly. It's a bit baggy on you. Now what?

140

It's time to make a decision. Do you:

Rummage through the ship's locker a bit more? **P142**

Or

Go to the airlock? **P141**

Go to the airlock

There's a chance the Spug ship is empty because they're all looting *The Bejeweled Diva.* You can't teleport there because starships of this type don't have a teleporter—and if *The Bejeweled Diva* had one, you wouldn't trust it to be working anyway. But you can get there with the spacesuit. If it's empty, you can take control of their ship and force the Spugs to surrender.

You grin, adrenalin pumping, and clunk down the corridor to the airlock, feet clicking on the metal floor because of the metal plates on the boots. After a quick check that nobody's around, you open the inner door and go inside, then seal it shut behind you.

The Spug ship isn't visible through the outer airlock door. Why is that? You try to facepalm, but the helmet visor gets in the way. The Spug ship is off the starboard side of *The Bejeweled Diva.* The airlock is on the port side. You'll have to go outside and then scramble over the hull of the starship before you can propel yourself across the gap.

You sway on your feet, tapping a gloved hand against the airlock door, mind racing through the options. They're basically all dangerous.

But what is the best choice?

It's time to make a decision. Do you:

Leave the ship, in the spacesuit? **P153**

Or

Change your mind about leaving the ship and return to the ship's locker? **P142**

Rummage through the ship's locker

Going to the Spug ship is an idea beyond crazy. You're not going to give that one any more thought. It shows how desperate you are to help the captain that you came up with it in the first place.

With the light from the corridor walls able to penetrate further into the cupboard, some shelves at the back are now visible. It's probably a good idea to check there. You peel off the spacesuit gloves and remove the helmet. You're not going to need them now that you've decided you're not leaving the starship. You breathe in the ship's air gratefully—the last person in that suit could have used more soap. You keep the rest of the suit on, as there's no time to lose.

You listen carefully in case Sluuffo or Makkav return, and investigate the shelves more closely.

Dust. There is a lot of dust, enough to make you sneeze. That could have been messy if you'd been wearing the helmet. But then you wouldn't have breathed in the dust, would you? You shake your head. Hurry! The captain needs you!

A few tattered books fall to the floor. You spread them out with a boot. Manuals on the string jump drive and the maneuver drive. They could be useful if you end up having to fix the drive problem yourself. There's also a guide to the Bridge controls. And, underneath, something interesting: a notepad with handwritten notes titled "'IN CASE OF 'UNFRIENDLIES'".

A quick flick through the brief notes reveals that electronic magnetic pulses (EMPs) disrupt Spug communications and teleporter signals. *The Bejeweled Diva* possesses an EMP shield. You hope it works.

A plan sprouts like an idea beanstalk in your mind, and you hurry to the Bridge with the guide to the controls. Once there, you locate the EMP shield, which you switch on, and for the ship's artificial gravity, which you turn off in the cargo hold only. That should cause some trouble for the Spugs.

The spacesuit boots have magnetic plates on the soles, and you'll need those to move in the cargo hold, so you keep the spacesuit on, but you won't activate the plates until you get there. You stride down the corridor to the stairs, stopping only to retrieve the extendable pole from the ship's locker. Then you go down the stairs, switch on the magnetic plates, open the door and step inside the cargo hold.

The cargo hold is a double-height area, large and airy. The walls give off a dim luminescence. A number of crates and boxes are stacked up, fastened together or bolted to the floor, but most of the holding area has been divided into cages, each containing ten or so cats. They are floating in their cages, literally bouncing off the walls.

What a racket. It sounds like every cat in the place is yowling for dear life. And it stinks. Perhaps you should have worn the helmet after all.

Several Spugs float around the cargo hold in the zero gravity, flailing their arms, somersaulting head over heels. A couple of them have managed to cling on to the crates or boxes around them. They're yelling, yapping and growling too.

Something grabs at your hair, and you duck. Above you, a snarling creature makes another attempt to reach you with a long clawed hand. Not a Spug. You gasp. It's a Space Pit Bull, or Spitbull, one of the wickedest beasts ever to be created in a laboratory.

You extend the sturdy pole from the ship's locker and poke it in the stomach up to the ceiling. It glares at you, dripping grey saliva from bared teeth.

The captain bounces along the ceiling some distance away, but she looks safe enough, although unconscious. You'll have to leave her a little longer, but keep watch in case the Spitbull tries to get to her.

With the magnetic-soled boots sticking you to the metal floor, you walk further into the cargo hold, keeping an eye on the Spugs around you and prodding any away who drift too close. You glimpse Makkav punching at his wristpad with a clawed finger, snarling. The Spugs' communications won't be working because of the EMP shield. How long will it take him to figure that out?

Now comes the tricky part. You unlock a cage and pull out two of the floating cats. Their fur stands on end, their ears pricked. There's no time to calm them. Quickly, you put them into a cage with some other cats, and then return for more. After a minute, you've emptied one cage and crowded all the cats in with those in another cage. It'll be cozy for them. Hopefully, they won't fight.

Then, using the hook on the extendable pole, you catch a Spug by the belt of his tight red pants as he floats past, pull him down, thrust him into the cage and lock it.

He glares at you, and you smile in return.

Ten minutes later, you've caught and imprisoned them all.

Makkav yells, banging on the cage bars, but he can't escape. "Woof. When we get out of here, we're going to find you, kid. Yap. There's nowhere in this galaxy you can hide. I'm dangerous, you know. I have the death penalty in twelve star systems!"

"I'll make sure I inform the authorities of that," you say and walk away.

Teena is awake now, holding her head in her hands. Somehow, she's managed to get down to floor level and is half crawling, half drifting towards the stairs. You hurry to help her, your magnetic plates clicking on the floor.

Back in the corridor, you feel the weight return, put down the pole and shrug off the spacesuit.

"Thanks, Ace." The captain claps you on the shoulder. "I don't know what I would have done without you. I'm making you First Officer for the rest of the voyage."

"Thanks!"

The door to Engineering closes. Heavy, padded footsteps come upstairs. Meowing and yowling too.

"Sluuffo!" you whisper. You'd forgotten about him.

"Quick! This way."

The captain takes your hand and jogs along the corridor the short distance to the ship's locker. "Get the bowling ball," she says.

You give her a quizzical look but do what she says.

"Get ready." She spins you to face the direction of Engineering.

A few seconds later, Sluuffo comes into view. He's carrying a large box in one hand. The "specials".

In his other hand, he has one of them, a beautiful golden exotic shorthair. The poor cat struggles as Sluuffo raises it above his open jaws.

Then he sees you. "Woof. What's going on?"

"Now!" Teena says.

You've never missed a target. That's why they call you Ace. Like a pro, you whip the bowling ball back, crouch and send it forward as speedily as you can. Straight for Sluuffo.

He drops the box and the exotic shorthair he was about to munch on and jumps in the air. The ball passes directly underneath him. He glares and growls at you, then turns. The bowling ball hits the outer wall of the curving corridor and continues on, racing around the edge of the corridor out of view.

Sluuffo drops to all fours and bounces after it.

You look up at Teena in surprise. She grins. "It's instinctive behavior. They can't help it."

"But what do we do when the ball stops?"

"It'll come all the way around first. Pass me that pole, will you?"

You give her the pole, and she motions you back to the inner wall of the corridor. A few seconds later, the bowling ball rolls past, though much slower now, with Sluuffo only meters behind. As he goes past, she clouts him with the pole, and he crumples flat onto the floor.

"That'll do. I'll put him in one of the cages. You've done well, Ace."

Teena puts on the spacesuit. You help her drag Sluuffo to the stairway, but once in the hold he doesn't weigh anything in the zero-G, and she can easily post him into the last empty cage.

You run your hand through your hair. The danger is not over yet. The Spug ship is still there, and *The Bejeweled Diva's* maneuver drive

146

doesn't work. And what happened in Engineering? Is Karl all right?

What shall you do? Every minute might count.

It's time to make a decision. Do you:

Go to Engineering and see if Karl is okay? **P147**

Or

Return to the Bridge and call for help? **P151**

Go to Engineering and see if Karl is okay

"I'm going to Engineering," you call out to Teena, and run around the corridor. You take the narrow, metal steps to Engineering two at a time, steadying yourself with the handrail. A quick flick of your wristpad at the door's security panel lets you in.

You're in a large, double-height room. It smells of oil, grease and sweat. The lighting from the ceiling flickers intermittently. It's eerily quiet. The maneuver drive still isn't working.

There's no one in sight. A metal railing to your right separates you from one of the drive housings. A corridor curves around it, so you follow that. The drive housing itself has small windows through which you catch glimpses of the drive as you go past. When you round the corner, you see the other bulky drive on your left. The corridor continues between them and leads to a space beyond.

An office/workroom is on the other side of the space, and there's a rickety table and two chairs outside. A large red hammock is slung between the office and one of the drives' housing racks. Lying on it is a large man in his fifties, presumably Karl, counting a bundle of money. He turns his head as you approach and jolts.

"Klunderheads! What are yer doing in here, kid?"

"I'm Ace, the student space cadet." This looks suspicious. What is all that money? Why isn't he fixing the maneuver drive?

"Scram. Yer didn't see anything here, or else."

You stay put. Something clicks in your mind, the dawn of understanding. "You sold a box of 'special' cats—exotic shorthairs—to that Spug."

Karl swings his feet over the side of the hammock and stands, stuffing the notes into his pocket. "I told yer to scram. It's none of yer business."

It all makes sense now. You stand, hands on hips. "You tipped off the Spugs that *The Bejeweled Diva* carried a cargo of cats. And I bet you thought you could make some extra money by smuggling those exotic shorthairs on board and selling them as extras."

Karl's lip rises, revealing yellowed teeth. His bushy eyebrows quiver.

"You must have disabled the maneuver drive yourself so they could teleport aboard. Didn't you?" There's no stopping you now with the accusations.

Karl takes a step toward you, fists clenched. "Yer too clever for yer own good, Ace. Now we has a situation here that I don't know how to fix. But it'll start with me getting my hands around yer neck."

You gulp and step backwards.

A reassuring hand on your shoulder steadies you. Teena steps past, raising a taser and pointing it at Karl. "Stop right there."

Karl stops, spreading his hands wide, palms open. "Surely, Captain, you don't believe what this kid says."

"I've had my suspicions. Now I know they're right." She gestures with the taser for Karl to walk past, and steps back to let him by. You step back with her. "Now, walk to the brig. I'll be right behind you."

Karl saunters past. He glares at you, eyes full of venom. You pull your head back in a shiver.

The brig turns out to be the room on the starboard corridor nearest the stairs to Engineering. You get a look at it when Karl goes inside. It's small, containing little more than a bed, a wobbly chair and a small table with a book on it called *Between The Stars*. No technology as far as you can see. Karl turns to say something, but the captain shuts the door on him, and it locks automatically. Karl shakes his fist at you through the small window as you turn away.

"Ace, you've done well again. Thank you. But we're not out of trouble yet. The Spug ship is still out there, and we can't maneuver because of whatever Karl did to the drive. I need to see if we can get it working, and I need to go to the Bridge and call for help, but I can't do both at the same time. Can you help?"

"Sure. I'll check out the drive."

She claps you on the shoulder encouragingly. "Great. Thanks, Ace.

Remember to switch off the drive before you do anything. The controls are in Karl's office."

Switch it off. Right. That's probably a good thing to remember.

You return to Engineering and locate an ancient control panel in Karl's office that has letters so faded you can barely make out the words, but you locate the maneuver drive switch and turn it off. There's a flashlight on the desk, and you pick it up.

Now, which is the maneuver drive? There are two drive housings, large, sound-buffered metallic structures surrounding the drives themselves to provide protection and reduce noise. You pick one at random and crawl inside, using the flashlight to guide your way, avoiding sharp corners and pipes. There's plenty of space in the central compartment, enough to stand up in once you've passed through the drive's outer shell.

It's the right one. One look at the drive core reveals the problem. Gravel and sand is spread through the drive core mechanism. Shredded sandbags are scattered among the enormous silver-colored drive blades. No wonder they stopped working.

That lot has to be cleared out before the drive can be restarted. You look around. The light is dim, but the flashlight reveals several tools on a shelf in a niche in the drive housing, fastened down in case the artificial gravity onboard fails. There's a hacksaw you can use to cut the sandbags away from the blades, and a supersized air blower to blow the grit out of the drive core.

Removing the pieces of the sandbags takes a few minutes. Then you turn on the supersized air blower. It makes a loud whining noise like a giant hairdryer, and a gale-force stream of air gushes forth. You hold the blower tightly, almost losing your balance with the recoil, as it blasts the sand and gravel bits out of the drive core mechanism.

When you're done, you put the tools back and inspect the drive blades again. It all looks fine. You can't tell if Karl did something else to sabotage the drive, but you guess not. He'll have wanted a quick way to undo his work.

150

You crawl out of the drive space and return to the office to switch the drive on. It starts up with a reassuring smooth sound. When you're sure it's working, you run upstairs and go to the Bridge.

"Well done again, Ace. Since you restarted the drive, I've turned the ship, so now we're decelerating. We got first move on the Spug ship, so they can't catch us."

"That's great, Captain."

"I called the spaceport for help. They'll send a patrol cruiser to relieve us of the 'unfriendlies'. And Karl, too."

"But what about your unpaid departure fees?"

The captain grins. "I think they're going to overlook that now. But unfortunately it'll delay our journey to Proxima B by at least a day while we return to the spaceport to refuel and find another engineer."

You don't mind. This has been the best adventure of your life.

Congratulations, this part of your story is over. You have met the captain, helped diagnose the maneuver drive failure, worked out that the ship alongside was not an official patrol cruiser, saved the captain and all of the cats from the Spugs by capturing them single-handedly, uncovered Karl's sabotage, cleared the debris out of the maneuver drive and got it working again in time for *The Bejeweled Diva* to get away from the Spug ship. And you've been made First Officer for the journey. Whew!

But it could have been a different story. Have you tried the other pathways in the book to see what happens when you make other choices?

It's time to make a decision. Would you like to:

Go to the list of choices and start reading from another part of the story? **P532**

Or

Go back to the beginning of the story and try another path? **P95**

Go to the Bridge and call for help

"I'm going to the Bridge to call for help," you shout to Teena, and run there. There are no new messages on the main display. If there are any Spugs remaining on their ship, they must surely be wondering by now what is going on. There may not be much time.

You scan the instrument panels, looking for a narrow-beam communicator that could penetrate the EMP shield you activated earlier. After a few seconds, you locate it on the far right-hand side. It's an old monochrome display screen and a worn keypad with half the letters indistinguishable. Luckily, you have keyboard skills.

There's a speed dial setting for the spaceport at Earth. Typing quickly, you send them a message:

Hello, Spaceport. This is The Bejeweled Diva. *My name is Ace. Our maneuver drive is out of action. We are travelling away from Earth. Also, we have captured some "unfriendlies". Can you help?*

After a minute, a response comes:

Hello, The Bejeweled Diva. *This is Spaceport Earth. We have a patrol cruiser already heading your way because we detected an "unfriendly" ship following your flight path. Hold tight. It will be with you as soon as possible. How many "unfriendlies" have you captured? Is your engineer able to fix your maneuver drive so you can decelerate?*

Teena comes into the Bridge. You offer the comms seat to her, but she indicates for you to carry on and takes the other seat. She scans the message screen and shakes her head. "We can't slow down until Karl has fixed the maneuver drive. I'll give him a call, see if he answers. If not, we'll have to go check on him." She gets on the radio to Engineering.

You type a new message.

I think there were eight or nine of them. Mostly Spugs. One Spitbull. I put

152

them all into cages.

Teena talks on the radio to Karl. You listen to their conversation while waiting for a reply from the spaceport. It sounds like Karl has figured out how to fix the maneuver drive.

Who are you, Ace? A bounty hunter?

You chuckle at that. Maybe you could be a bounty hunter in the future.

No, I'm a student on an exchange trip. I've been to space cadet school.

Well done to you for capturing those "unfriendlies". You might get a medal for that.

"Tell them we're going to have the maneuver drive fixed in ten minutes, and then we'll decelerate. They'll catch up to us a lot sooner, and they can take the Spugs off our ship."

"Okay. But what about your unpaid spaceport fees?"

"Oh, they might let me off that. We've done them a big favor by capturing these nuisances."

Congratulations, this part of your story is over. You have met the captain, helped diagnose the maneuver drive failure, worked out that the ship alongside was not an official patrol cruiser, saved the captain and all of the cats from the Spugs by capturing them single-handedly, and called the spaceport for help. To them, you're a hero.

But have you tried the other pathways in the book to see what would have happened if you'd made other choices?

It's time to make a decision. Would you like to:

Go to the list of choices and start reading from another part of the story? **P532**

Or

Go back to the beginning of the story and try another path? **P95**

Leave the ship, in the spacesuit

You may as well go for it.

If this works, you'll be the hero. Maybe you'll even get a medal for capturing the ship of the "unfriendlies".

You bang the depressurization button. The air leaves with a hiss. This will prevent you from being sucked out into space when you open the airlock.

Next, gripping a handrail for support, you hit the red button to open the outer door and swing onto the outside of the hull. The artificial gravity extends about two meters beyond the hull for most starships. It ought to be the same for *The Bejeweled Diva*, and you sense that it is.

You don't know how much time you have before the Spugs will complete their tasks. Time is of the essence.

You switch on the magnetic plates on the spacesuit's boots to help you walk around the outside of the starship.

It's dead quiet.

There's no sound from your movements because sound doesn't travel in the vacuum of space. It's eerie.

The murky Spug ship comes into view as you walk, rising over the horizon of *The Bejeweled Diva* like dark clouds gathering before a storm. You walk another quarter way around the hull until you judge you're at the nearest point.

Now for the hard part. You've got to push yourself off *The Bejeweled Diva* directly towards the Spug ship.

Crouching, you reverse the polarity of the magnetic plates and, as they repel from the hull, you propel yourself forward, arms outstretched, aiming for the center of the black blob that is the Spug ship.

This is fun! It's like flying, except there's no air … or gravity … or anything. Okay, maybe it's not much like flying.

You're on course. Other kids don't call you Ace for nothing! You never miss a target.

But how far away is it?

You bite your lip. You'd assumed it would be close alongside, like two schooners almost bumping sides.

It isn't that near, though.

You try to swallow, but you can't. And a headache is coming on fast. This was a bad, bad decision.

It's hard to know how far away objects are in space. The Spug ship is a long way off. A kilometer, at least. Maybe two. It's going to take ten minutes or more to get there, not seconds.

And, if it's that far away, it's a lot bigger than you thought. That means there are probably more Spugs on board.

The outline of their starship gradually grows in size and becomes clearer as you get closer, but it's now apparent to you that your movement vector isn't perfect. You're not heading for the center of their ship, but for the edge. Perhaps the ship has moved slightly, but it won't make a difference to the outcome. Sweating and hyperventilating now, you realize you might miss the Spug ship altogether.

Frantically, you grab at the edge of the hull as you pass over, but it's an arm's length out of reach. One arm's length out of a kilometer or more isn't much, but it's too much. This is the first target you've ever missed.

And it's going to be the last target you ever miss.

Tumbling from your frantic efforts to grasp some part of the hull, you see both ships rotating in and out of your vision as you steadily drift farther away into darkest space, wondering when your oxygen will run out.

I'm sorry, this part of your story is over. You were incredibly brave, but jumping off your ship in a secondhand spacesuit, untethered and with no way of getting back, was highly risky. And not sensible either. But don't worry, you can try again.

It's time to make a decision. You have three choices. Would you like to:

Change your last choice and go rummage through the ship's locker? **P142**

Or

Go to the list of choices and start reading from another part of the story? **P532**

Or

Go back to the beginning of the story and try another path? **P95**

Stay with Karl and help

You might not get another chance to help with a major engineering problem on a starship, so you decide to stay in Engineering.

"I'd like to help out if I can," you say.

"Okay, Ace, if that's what yer want to do, but it might be tedious work. Are yer sure yer don't want to go exploring?"

You shake your head. Why's he asking you again?

"All right, let's make yer Assistant Engineer for the trip. That suit yer?"

"Sure." You grin.

"Okay, listen up. Maneuver drive problems fall into two categories," Karl explains, "big and small. The small ones are easy to spot and simple to fix. There'll be a loose bit of wire or a connector that's slipped out or something like that. So yer stick it back in. Not too tight, mind—yer want it to come loose sometime so yer can fix it again and the captain remembers yer useful."

You open your mouth, about to say something about how that sounds dishonest, and then think better of it. Maybe Karl would have nothing to do without the occasional minor "mishap".

"The big problems are usually easy to spot too, especially if it's a burnt-out component. Then the solution is to take out the broken one and either fix or replace it. I have some second-hand replacement components in storage that might work. But I can't always do that."

"What then?"

"Let's not worry about that yet, Ace. Now, the captain's waiting, and she's not a patient lady. Let's get on with having a look at this drive." He gestures towards it.

"Okay. I'll crawl into the drive space," you say. That seems to be what Karl is suggesting.

"I've got a torch for yer." Karl snatches a flashlight from a holder attached to the drive housing and passes it to you.

You crawl inside carefully, using the flashlight to guide your way, avoiding sharp corners and pipes as you pass through a tunnel in the drive housing.

There's plenty of space in the central compartment, enough to stand in. The enormous silver-colored drive blades are motionless and quiet. The fuel lines come in from one direction.

One look at the drive core reveals the problem. You turn around. Karl crawls into the space and stands.

"Look, Karl. There's gravel and sand in the drive core."

"It must have come in through the heat vents." He shook his head vigorously. "That's a million-to-one shot. Unlucky."

Something else catches your eye. It's the color of sand, but it isn't sand. You take a closer look and gasp in surprise.

"Sandbags. There's sandbags caught in the drive core mechanism."

Karl looks, jaw hanging open. "Klunderheads! Yer right, Ace. This ain't no accident. Someone's fired bags of sand and gravel into the heat vents to sabotage our maneuver drive. We've gotta fix this pronto, Ace. Could be … 'unfriendlies'."

"'Unfriendlies'?"

"No time to explain. I've gotta tell the captain right away. Then we've gotta clear out the drive, get it working again as quick as we can. Until then, we can't maneuver. Yer with me?"

"Sure." You give him the thumbs-up.

"Great." He claps you on the shoulder so hard you wince. "Hang fire a minute while I call the captain." He turns and crawls out of the drive space.

Karl told you to wait, but he also said clearing the debris out of the drive is urgent. And who are the "unfriendlies"? Sounds like no one you want to meet in the depths of space.

You could start clearing out the drive. That'd save time. Even if it is only two or three minutes until Karl gets back, it might make all the difference. It looks like the sandbags are the main problem clogging the works.

Or should you wait like Karl told you?

158

It's time to make a decision. Do you:

Start clearing the debris by pulling out the sandbags? **P160**

Or

Wait for Karl to return before clearing out the debris with him? **P159**

Wait for Karl to return

You use the time waiting for Karl's return to examine the maneuver drive core and the drive blades, evaluating the situation. It looks like the sandbags stopped the blades rotating, and the drive cut out as a result. There's sand and gravel around the core and the blades, but that can be removed quickly with the supersized air blower you see tied down on the tools shelf.

But how did the sandbags get inside the starship? Karl said they'd come in through the heat vents, but you don't see any.

Something's not right. If heated air is vented out, it would be through a one-way airlock system, and there's no way anything could come in. Besides, why would the starship waste good energy venting it into space when it could be used elsewhere in the ship, like heating passenger areas?

A little lightbulb goes off at the back of your mind. In your studies at space cadet school, you learned about starship design.

Small cargo and passenger starships like this one don't have heat vents.

The hairs rise on the back of your neck. Karl told you a lie.

Maybe he sabotaged the drive himself.

It's time to make a decision. Do you:

Confront Karl about the heat vents? **P171**

Or

Get out of Engineering fast? **P174**

Start clearing the debris

Every second might count. Without pausing to think about what you're doing, you lean forward and tug at the first sandbag with all your strength. "Unfriendlies"—you don't want to meet them. You need to get the maneuver drive working again. Karl and the captain will think you're a hero.

Most of the sandbag comes away with a tearing noise. You fall backwards against the drive housing and hit your shoulder. Ouch. There'll be a bruise there tomorrow. Undeterred, you step back to the drive core and grab the end of another sandbag. But this one won't budge and doesn't tear.

Frustrated and wheezing with effort, you look around, using the flashlight. There may be tools somewhere in here. Yes—on a shelf in a niche in the drive housing, fastened down in case the artificial gravity onboard fails. You inspect what's available: hammer, chisel, screwdrivers, an oil can with oil, some rags, a supersized air blower, a hacksaw—that's what you need. You can cut through the clogged sandbag with a hacksaw. Then there'll be only the sand and gravel to get out.

The hacksaw must be diamond-tipped, because it rips through the tangle of sandbag like it is a cobweb. Suddenly, everything is free. The drive core heats up in a second. You leap back, feeling the heat like a bonfire. Now the drive blades begin to spin with a whirr that rapidly becomes a high-pitched whine. You turn and duck down, ready to crawl out, but it's too late. You're being sucked towards the giant blades. You scrabble on the metal floor, but your fingernails have nothing to grasp. You can't prevent yourself sliding backwards into the blades.

You fixed the drive so well that it's operating efficiently now. It makes mincemeat of you in moments, venting a thousand pieces out into space to float forever among the stars.

I'm sorry, this part of your story is over. It wasn't the best choice to start working on the maneuver drive when Karl asked you to wait. The good thing is that you got it operating again. Unfortunately, no one had switched it off first, and you got turned into space dust. But it's not too late to change your mind. You can change your previous choice and wait for Karl if you'd prefer.

Alternatively, other pathways are waiting.

It's time to make a decision. You have three choices. Would you like to:

Go back and wait for Karl to return before clearing the debris with him? **P159**

Or

Go to the list of choices and start reading from another part of the story? **P532**

Or

Go back to the beginning of the story and try another path? **P95**

Go and check the cargo hold

There's no direct access between Engineering and the cargo hold, even though they're both on the lower deck of the starship. You go up the stairs. The stairway to the cargo hold must be off the port corridor, because the starboard corridor has the passenger cabins and the passenger lounge coming off it.

As everywhere else, the walls are lit with an internal fuzzy luminescent light. About halfway down the corridor, you find a door labeled "CARGO HOLD". Your wristpad gives you access, and you descend the metal steps as quietly as you can.

Karl told you that he'd been told the animals should be checked. You don't know why, though. Hopefully, none of the cargo has escaped and is dangerous.

At the bottom of the steps, you grin. There's nothing dangerous here. Numerous cages contain domestic cats and kittens of various types, ten or twelve in each cage. You wander amongst them. They have plentiful food, water and playthings. Some of them purr when they see you. There is barely enough space between the cage bars to reach in with two fingers to stroke them, but they love it when you do. None of them seem distressed by the cessation of the sound of the maneuver drive.

The cats and kittens must be destined to be pets for the colonists on Proxima B. The colonists would love that. What a cool cargo. Better than transporting something boring like tax forms or stinky like fertilizer.

Crates and boxes are piled in the cargo hold too, but you can't see inside those. Maybe they contain food for the cats.

You wander around, checking everything carefully. Nothing appears to have come loose or fallen over. No animal needs help. Maybe the animal handlers have checked them recently. What was Karl talking about, then?

In the center of the cargo hold, the air blurs for a second or two, and a creature appears. You duck down behind a crate and peer around the corner. It looks around for a few moments, but doesn't see you, then it speaks into a wristpad. Several more of the creatures appear. You sniff. They smell of wet dog.

You study them closely. They're dressed in tight red pants and puffy blue jackets. They're not going to win any fashion contests. But when you look at their faces, you gasp.

They're Space Pugs, creatures that resulted from a genetic experiment of mixing human and pug DNA. Spugs, for short. The mad scientists behind that created all sorts of weird and disturbing beasts in some kind of modern-day Island of Dr. Moreau situation. Unfortunately, most of them escaped and left Earth. Your space cadet lessons covered this sad part of Earth's history.

There's one other creature amongst them, loitering by the stairway. It's bigger and meaner-looking, and it's scanning the cargo hold as if checking for threats. For a moment, it looks your way, but you're concealed by the shadows of the crates. You get a good look at it in that moment. It's not a Spug. It's a Space Pit Bull—a Spitbull. A real nasty piece of work, probably. You don't want it to find you.

So why are they here? They're not passengers. They must have teleported aboard from another starship.

"Woof. Let's get started," one of them says, directing the others. "We want to be gone before anyone knows we're here. Sluuffo's gone to get the 'specials', and we'll get these 'regulars'. Yap."

Specials?

One of the Spugs covers the video cameras in the cargo hold with tape. The others spread out, each moving to a cage. The cats go berserk at the sight and smell of them, yowling and clawing at the bars of the cages to get out.

They're going to steal all the cats!

You can't let this happen. But what can you do? They vastly outnumber you.

But they don't know you're there. You creep away behind the

crates, looking for anything useful. Yet what could be useful against a pack of these creatures?

On a small table you find some of the animal handlers' possessions. Maybe there'll be something here. You find a journal. A book of cat names. A small whistle labeled "FOR EMERGENCY USE ONLY". And a tiny electronic device with a switch labeled "CAGES OPEN / CLOSE".

You take the last two items and crawl back to where you can see what the Spugs are doing. They are busy attaching metal devices to the cages.

What are they for?

"Woof. Are we ready to start teleporting these tasty treats?" shouts a Spug. You think it was the one who spoke before.

There's a chorus of "Yes" and "Yap" in response.

You must do something, but what? You look at the two items you have with you. There's only a few seconds to decide. What will you do?

It's time to make a decision. Do you:

Open the cages? **P165**

Or

Blow the whistle? **P167**

Open the cages

You flip the switch on the electronic device. With a clang, the doors of all of the cages in the cargo hold simultaneously spring open. The moggies take the chance to jump out, yowling and screeching like a set of untuned violins played by demented minstrels.

They're too fast for the Spugs, who fall over themselves as they attempt to catch the darting cats and kittens. It would be hilarious if you weren't stuck in there with them, with a Spitbull guarding the only way out.

Within a minute or two, the cats and kittens have all found refuge on shelves and atop crates where the Spugs can't easily reach them. Down below, the Spugs jump in frustration, faces red from effort and rage.

"What idiot opened the cages?" shouts the Spug who appears to be in charge. "How are we going to catch these tidbits now? Gruff. As soon as we climb up after them, they'll jump somewhere else."

The other Spugs gaze at each other, frowning. They shrug. They show their empty hands, or paws, to the leader as if to say it wasn't their doing.

Uh oh. You have a bad feeling about this.

"Someone's in here," shouted the leader. "Find them!"

The Spugs spread out, overturning small boxes, looking behind things, searching anywhere that might conceal someone. Three of them come your way. It's not looking good for you.

It's time to make a decision. Do you:

Come out of your hiding place and surrender? **P166**

Or

Blow the whistle? **P167**

Come out of your hiding place and surrender

They're going to find you, you know it. Best get it over with. At least they won't be able to steal the cats now.

You stand and step out from behind the crates. The three Spugs coming your way see you. Their jaws quiver. Drool drips from their mouths. They're snarling.

This doesn't seem like a good idea now.

"Get him!" shouts the Spug leader over the sound of the caterwauling cats, then speaks into his wristpad.

The three Spugs grab you. They're not in the mood for a conversation. Behind them, you see the Spitbull rushing towards you, jaws wide open, closing in for the kill. Those teeth look sharp!

I'm sorry, this part of your story is over. What was that choice about? Surrendering to these nasty space-faring beasts when you've angered them by preventing them from stealing the cargo of cats? Not the best idea. At least the cats lived, though.

This needn't be the end (your end, that is). You can change it. Do you want to change it? Do you want to retake that last choice?

It's time to make a decision. You have three choices. Would you like to:

Change your last choice and blow the whistle instead? **P167**

Or

Go to the list of choices and start reading from another part of the story? **P532**

Or

Go back to the beginning of the story and try another path? **P95**

Blow the whistle

You blow the whistle with as much breath as you can muster. Sure, it'll reveal your presence to the Spugs, but it might be loud enough to summon help. And you need help to get out of this dangerous situation.

To your dismay, the whistle only makes a quiet hissing noise. Is it defective? You try again. The same quiet hissing comes forth. Perhaps you're not doing it right.

Only then do you look up. The Spugs have their clawed hands clamped over their ears. The Spitbull too. Two of them roll on the floor, whimpering. Another couple drop to their knees, groaning.

The cats, too, go wild. They screech. Their hair stands up on their backs. They jump about on the spot.

You stop blowing the whistle. Within moments, the Spugs and the Spitbull collectively gasp. A couple of the Spugs reach out to each other for support. Others look up, eyes closed, breathing heavily and looking unsteady.

The cats quieten down too.

Now you get it. It's a dog whistle that emits a sound at a frequency higher than the top range of human hearing, but within dog range, and it's as painful to them as a piercing shriek is to humans. Perhaps more so.

The Spugs gather together. The Spitbull stays by the stairway, blocking the only way out. You grimace. What should you do now?

The Spugs confer. Maybe they're making a plan. Maybe the plan involves finding you and doing something nasty to you.

You blow the whistle again, and keep blowing it.

The cats yowl, their fur and tails rising. The Spitbull collapses back against the stairwell, sniveling. Three of the Spugs flop face-first to the floor, groaning. All of them cover their ears against the sound that you can't hear, but seems to be torture to them.

Their leader, on his knees, speaks into his wristpad. The air around the Spugs and the Spitbull goes blurry. Seconds later, they disappear. They've teleported off the ship!

This is your chance. You slip the whistle into your pocket and run for the stairs, aware that most of the cats are glaring at you. You don't mind, you've saved them from the dinner tables of the Spugs. It's typical of cats to be ungrateful.

You take the stairs two at a time to the corridor, then race to the Bridge and use your wristpad to get inside. A frizzy-haired woman whirls to face you from a cushioned bucket seat in front of the control panels.

"I'm Ace," you gasp, catching your breath.

You look around. The Bridge is much smaller than you had imagined, only about twice the size of your tiny cabin. Windows wrap around the apex of the ship, providing a 180-degree view. Instrument consoles covered with metal levers, dials and display screens stand under them.

"I'm Teena, the captain. You're the space cadet student, are you, Ace?"

You nod.

"Welcome to the Bridge."

"I've come from the cargo hold. I was checking for damage after the jolt to the ship—"

"Thanks. I don't know what happened with that, but it knocked out the maneuver drive. We're drifting."

"I know. While I was down in the cargo hold, some creatures teleported aboard. Spugs. They were going to steal the cargo."

Teena gasps, her hand covering her mouth. "How did you get out?"

You explain about the whistle and what happened next.

Teena spins to face the controls. "There must be a starship nearby for them to teleport aboard. They'll be matching speed with us. I bet they disabled our drive."

Your gaze roams the control panels. "Doesn't their ship show up on the scanner?"

"The scanner's not working at the moment. When I got the last annual service done at a half-decent spaceport, they said it needed some maintenance or it wouldn't last much longer, but I couldn't afford it at the time."

"Oh."

"It costs a lot to run a starship like this. I barely make ends meet as it is."

You think of something. "When I was in my cabin, looking out the viewport, I thought I saw a black area in space. I mean, like something was there."

Teena grins at you. "That might be their ship. Show me."

You orientate yourself by looking at the stars for a few seconds, then point out the area that you noticed before. Now that you look more closely, it does look ship-shaped.

"That'll be it," Teena says. "But we can't get away from it because the maneuver drive isn't working. They might teleport back aboard anytime."

"I have an idea. Is there a way to send them a message they can't block?"

"Sure is. A one-way narrow-beam short-range communications spike will do the trick. What's your idea?"

You pull the whistle out of your pocket. Teena high-fives you and readies the communications spike. When she opens it, you blow the whistle and keep going, stopping only briefly to draw breath.

"They're leaving!" The captain points through the view screen. The black shape is getting smaller, moving further away. Soon you can't see it any more.

"Yay!" You give Teena the thumbs-up and then a high-five.

"Well done, Ace! You've saved the cargo! I'm going to make you First Officer for the remainder of the voyage."

Congratulations, this part of your story is over. You have raised the alarm about the maneuver drive, visited Engineering and the cargo

170

hold, and saved all of the cats from being stolen by the Spugs. And you've been made First Officer for the journey as a reward.

But have you tried the other pathways in the book?

It's time to make a decision. Would you like to:

Go to the list of choices and start reading from another part of the story? **P532**

Or

Go back to the beginning of the story and try another path? **P95**

Ask Karl about the heat vents

The supersized air blower might be useful to clear away the sand and gravel, so you unfasten it from its place on the shelf while you wait for Karl. You lift it up and find that it's surprisingly light for such a large tool, but it's cumbersome to use and requires both hands. A bulky switch is within reach of your left thumb.

After a few minutes, the engineer crawls back into the drive space and stands up. "I've turned off the drive. We can clear it out safely now."

He notices you frowning at him. "What's up, Ace?"

You gesture with the air blower as if it's a giant accusing finger. "Why did you tell me the sandbags came in through the heat vents, Karl? There *aren't* any heat vents on this type of starship."

Karl jerks his head back, sucks his cheeks in, and lets out a noisy breath. "Heat vents? Of course there aren't any heat vents on *The Bejeweled Diva.* A starship of this class don't have no heat vents." He guffaws. "Yer mistaken, kid. I told yer the sandbags came in through … through …"

"Yes?" You know you weren't mistaken. What's he going to say now?

He sighs. "Yer a smart kid, Ace, but yer poke yer nose where it don't belong. Yer don't leave me no other option now." He sticks his hand deep in his pocket and withdraws a laser pistol, which he aims directly at you. At the same time, though, you lower the mouth of the air blower to face him.

For half a minute, you stand facing each other, legs astride, an unlikely showdown out of some imaginary space Western mashup. A bead of sweat forms on Karl's forehead and runs down the left side of his face. A tic starts above his left eye, which winks rapidly. The hand holding the laser pistol trembles. Might he fire it accidentally? What will happen to you if he does?

"Put that thing down and come with me," Karl demands. "I'll tie

172

yer up and hide yer in the storage cupboard while I think about what to do with yer."

If you do as Karl says, you might have a chance to escape later. But you might not get a chance either.

Or you can fight back now.

It's time to make a decision. Do you:

Surrender and go with Karl? **P173**

Or

Switch on the supersized air blower? **P184**

Surrender and go with Karl

A supersized air blower is no match for a laser pistol. You gently lower it to the ground.

"Good kid. Sensible. Now, look behind yer. See them tools on the shelf there? There's a bunch of cable ties. Grab a handful."

Reluctantly, you do as he says. Now you're regretting your decision. Escaping from this situation won't be easy.

"Now, give 'em here."

You hold out the cable ties, and Karl snatches them with his free hand. He's sweating, and his left eye blinks rapidly from the tic that formed there.

"Crawl out of the drive space and wait for me. I'll be right behind yer with my laser pistol pointed at yer butt. Slowly, now. I gets nervous easy."

You go down to your knees and crawl into the low tunnel through the drive housing. Karl drops to his knees and comes after you.

Karl grumbles behind you. "Why did yer have to do this, Ace? Why'd yer have to ask so many questions? Yer a nice kid, why didn't yer just go to the cargo hold like I suggested? Then we wouldn't be in this situation, me and yer."

No kidding.

Karl is moving slower than you because he's so much older and he's holding the laser pistol and the cable ties. If you scoot through the tunnel fast, you'll have enough time to grab the small table by Karl's office and jam it in front of the tunnel entrance before Karl gets out. That could be your opportunity to escape. But what if he shoots you in the butt with the laser pistol when he sees you hurrying up to get out of the tunnel? How much would that hurt?

It's time to make a decision. Do you:

Crawl out fast and get out of Engineering? **P174**

Or

Ignore this opportunity to escape—wait for another chance? **P179**

Get out of Engineering fast

You crawl through the tunnel and out of the drive space as quickly as you can to escape Engineering. You take the steps to the upper level two at a time. At the top of the stairs, you skid to a halt, your sneakers squeaking on the metal floor, and glance backwards. Karl isn't behind you.

With a deep breath, you relax slightly. But only for a moment. You need to go and tell the captain what's been going on.

A movement down the port corridor catches your eye. Something's there. Small and quiet. But now it's gone out of view around the curve of the hall.

You have to know what it is. It doesn't matter which branch of the corridor you take, as they both lead to the Bridge at the bow of the ship.

Cautiously, you edge along the wall of the corridor, listening out for any sign of Karl coming up the stairs behind you. There's no sound of him, though.

"Meow."

You smile. A small cat sits at the edge of the hallway as if trying to hide, but the glowing walls all around mean there aren't any shadows for it to hide in. It peers up at you with sad, lonely eyes.

What an unusual kitten. You bend down to stroke the top of its head. Its face has a flat, squashed appearance, like a Persian cat, but it doesn't have the long, straggly hair that Persians do. It's an exotic shorthair, a female.

She purrs, loving your attention.

You can't hang around here. Karl might come after you. You have to get to the Bridge and tell the captain what's going on. The kitten looks so happy now you decide to take her with you. Maybe she's the ship's cat, and the captain can tell you her name.

At a jog, cradling the kitten in your arms, you follow the curving corridor towards the Bridge. You're on the side of the ship that doesn't have passenger cabins. There are a couple of doors, but you don't know what's behind them because they aren't labeled. Maybe they're cabins for the crew?

You glance behind you to make sure Karl isn't chasing you. He isn't. You turn around again and—wham! You crash into someone or something with your left shoulder and tumble, rolling so you don't land on your little feline friend. She meows in fear, but she's not hurt. You gather her close to your chest with one arm so she feels safe.

A gloved hand grabs the collar of your shirt and pulls you to your feet. You stare into a hideous dog-like face: bulging eyes, a big nose and protruding canine teeth. The creature growls at you menacingly.

"Gruff. Watch where you're going, you little—"

"Sorry." You gasp. It's hard to speak. The creature holds your collar so tight, your shirt is choking you.

Suddenly, you realize what it is. You've read about them in space cadet class. It's a Spug. A Space Pug. A nomadic race that wanders the stars, apparently looking for trouble. They must be the "unfriendlies" Karl mentioned earlier.

They're not passengers, so how did they get onto the ship? Probably by teleporting from another ship nearby. Maybe no one knows they're here. What do they want?

"Meow."

The Spug releases you. You drop to the floor, landing on your bottom. Another of the creatures comes into view from behind the first one. They're dressed identically with tight red pants and puffy blue jackets. Clearly, they have no fashion sense.

"Look what this kid has here," the newcomer says. "It's a little kitten. A 'special' one." It turns to the grumpy Spug you crashed into. "Woof. You like kittens, don't you, Makkav?"

"I sure do, Sluuffo," the one called Makkav says with a widening grin that reveals his unbrushed teeth in all their glory. "But I can't eat a whole one."

They guffaw.

"You can't have him." The little kitten will come to harm if these creatures get hold of it, and you don't want that on your conscience. You need to get away, but that won't be easy. The two Spugs have maneuvered to be either side of you in the corridor.

The one called Sluuffo takes a step closer, its arm outstretched, its hairy, clawed hand reaching out for the little exotic shorthair kitten.

You back into the wall of the corridor. There's a whoosh behind you. Your proximity to the sensor must have opened a door. With nowhere else to go, you step back into the room, spin and slam the button to close the door. You don't even see where you are.

The door slides with a whoosh, but at the last moment, when the door is barely a finger-width from closing, two claws poke through and prevent it from doing so. You groan.

"Yap, yap. I'll get this 'special' and collect the other 'specials' too," says Sluuffo. "You join our friends in the cargo hold and help them with the 'regulars'. Woof. We need to be out of here before anyone else notices we're here."

There are others? What are the "regulars" in the cargo hold?

You know the starship is transporting live animals. Cats! You facepalm. The cargo hold is full of cats, and the Spugs want them all! The exotic shorthair must be the 'special', and there are more of them somewhere, but not in the cargo hold.

There's smuggling of exotic kittens going on.

You turn your attention back to the door. Sluuffo is struggling with it, attempting to get the door to open wider while the door tries to close completely. At some point soon, it will retract. A shaft of light from the corridor comes into the room, but it's enough for you to see the light switch. You elbow that on, and bright light floods the room.

You're in a medic bay, about twice as large as your cabin. A couple of beds line two of the walls. The other has cupboards marked with a red cross and labeled with their contents. A chair, a small table and a benchtop are the only other furniture.

There's no other way out. You're trapped in here.

"Meow."

The little kitten senses your concern. You gently put her down on one of the beds. She snuggles under the cover, and you look around to see if there's anything that can help you in this situation.

The scraping of Sluuffo's claws on the edge of the door and the grunts of his efforts to prevent it from closing are unnerving.

You open the cupboards, even though their labels don't sound encouraging. How can you fend off a Spug with some bandaids or a gauze strip? It's not going to work.

An unlabeled drawer under the left-most cupboard is your last hope. You pull it open in desperation.

Inside is a plastic tray for injection pens. There's only one remaining. Bold lettering on the tray states, "SEDATIVES for DIFFICULT PASSENGERS".

Ah. This might be the thing you need. You grab the sedative pen as the door whooshes open and the Spug steps inside.

You position yourself in front of the bed in which the little kitten takes cover, and hide the injection pen behind your back.

"Come here, kitty, kitty," says Sluuffo in his gruff voice, his steely gaze roaming the room. "Where is it, kid?"

"I'm not telling you," you say. You'd cross your arms in defiance except you need one of them behind your back to conceal the injection pen.

The Spug laughs meanly. "The 'specials' are the most tasty. And their short hair isn't so ticklish in the throat. Gruff."

You gulp as Sluuffo moves towards you, bearing a cruel grin, readying yourself. You'll only get one opportunity with the sedative pen.

"Are you hiding the tasty morsel behind you? Let me see."

Sluuffo shoves you roughly to one side so hard you nearly lose your footing.

"Yap. There it is."

The bed cover is moving from the kitten's shivering movements.

Sluuffo reaches for it.

His attention distracted, you get up on one knee and bring your right hand around in a great arc to the Spug's butt, jamming the sedative pen into his bright red pants.

"Yowl!" Sluuffo turns towards you, raising a big, hairy, clawed fist. Then his eyes roll up into the back of his head and he collapses onto the floor, out cold.

Wow. That was a quick-working sedative.

Your heart's racing, and you breathe a big sigh of relief now this encounter is over. It was a close call.

But you know there's more Spugs in the cargo hold, stealing the cargo, which, you assume, is cats of some kind. Where are the other exotic shorthairs? And what is Karl up to?

The little cat pokes her head out from under the covers. She looks so cute with her flat, square face. You gather her up in your arms again, where she purrs softly.

You should do something, but what? The captain ought to know what's going on. Or you could go to the cargo hold, though it might be dangerous.

Your head spins with this decision. Perhaps you should go back to your cabin.

It's time to make a decision. You have three choices. Would you like to:

Go and tell the captain what you've discovered? **P188**

Or

Go to the cargo hold? **P193**

Or

Go to your cabin and hide? **P196**

Ignore this opportunity to escape and wait for another chance

You don't like the idea of a laser shot in the rear end, so you crawl out of the tunnel slowly like Karl said, letting him keep right behind you. Hopefully, there'll be a better chance to escape later.

Once you're both out into the main part of Engineering, Karl sticks the laser pistol in his pocket. Grim-faced, he says, "I don't wanna do this, Ace, but yer gave me no choice. Can't have yer running off and telling the captain. Put yer hands out."

Is this a chance to escape? No. Karl stands between you and the exit. Quickly, he wraps a cable tie around your wrists and tightens it. There's no getting out of that easily.

A fluttery sensation sweeps through your body, and you feel like throwing up. Nerves. What's Karl going to do with you? Should you call for help? Will anyone hear? Maybe. You could hear the maneuver drive from your cabin, so someone might hear you shouting for help.

Almost as if reading your mind, Karl fastens a long piece of tape over your mouth.

No problem. You can pull that off when he's gone even if your hands are bound together.

Karl pulls you around the corner of the office. There's several metal storage cupboards, each about the size of a medium wardrobe. He opens one of them. "In there."

Your eyes widen. Small spaces aren't your favorite. That's one reason you wanted to learn about space—it's so vast. The cupboard, on the other hand, is poky.

"In, I said." Karl pushes you inside. You stumble, but regain your footing. He tells you to sit, so you do. The floor is cold and hard. He fastens a cable tie around your ankles, and then secures your wrists to your ankles.

"Mmphf! Mmphf!" It's uncomfortable. The cable ties bite into your wrists. Your position is like one of those exercises where you have to touch your toes. You know it's going to get even worse as time passes.

And now you have no chance of pulling the tape off your mouth.

You wish you'd run when you had the chance. What's going to happen to you?

Karl shuts the door, leaving you in darkness. Your heart's racing. You're breathing fast and hard, not because your breathing is restricted, but out of fear. Sweat runs off your face into your shirt, and you feel rivulets running down the back of your neck.

Gradually, you bring your breathing under control. Karl seems to have gone. This is the time to make your escape, but you're no longer even able to move, let alone run. The situation has gone from bad to worse.

You try rubbing the cable ties together. With perseverance, one of them should break eventually, freeing either your feet or your hands.

Wait! Someone's coming!

You strain your ears. Definitely footsteps. Sounds like Karl's boots. But there's more than one person.

"Have yer got all my money?" Karl asks someone. It sounds like he's standing right outside the storage cupboard you're in.

"Yeah. Woof. You got the 'specials'? My team is in the cargo hold getting the 'regulars' right now. I want to see the 'special' ones for myself. Gruff. How many did you get?"

Your eyes prick up. You've never heard a voice like that before. It doesn't sound human at all. Low and gruff, slurring lots of the words together in a growl.

"I got ten 'specials', and they cost me two months' pay. I smuggled 'em in and hid them in here. You'd better have all my money."

"Relax, man. Woof. I already told you I had it all. Show me your 'specials'."

A storage cupboard door opens with the protesting screech of unoiled metal. It's not the one you're in, but it's nearby. You hear something being moved.

"I had to put the box in there, because one of 'em got out and ran off. The box tipped up when I jammed the drive, and the ship jarred a bit, see."

"There's only nine here."

"The other one hasn't come back yet. Maybe yer team found it."

"Woof. Maybe."

You hold your breath, listening hard. They've gone silent. After a few seconds, the growly voice continues.

"All right, man, here's all the money. Woof. Good doing business with you."

"Wait, Sluuffo. There's a problem." Karl sounded apprehensive.

"I told you, no problems!" The other voice had a definite growl to it that made the hairs on the back of your neck stand up. "This is a simple business deal. You stop the drive, we teleport in, we grab the cargo and your smuggled 'specials', and we leave. No problem."

"A kid worked out I jammed the drive. I can't let him tell the captain."

"That's your problem, not mine. You've got your money. I didn't pay you for problems. Yap."

Yap? Woof? What's going on?

"Get rid of him for me, will yer, Sluuffo? As a favor?"

You grit your teeth. This sounds bad. But there's nothing you can do, because you're bound up and gagged, completely helpless. Who is this Sluuffo? What kind of name is that, anyway?

"Where is this kid?"

The door to your metal prison is wrenched open. Artificial light bursts in, hurting your eyes and half-blinding you. Karl grabs your arm and pulls you out. You sprawl on the floor next to the box of 'specials'. Inside are several unusual kittens that look like short-haired Persians: exotic shorthairs.

A shadow crosses your face. Someone wearing tight red pants and a puffy blue jacket stands there. You look up into the face of a peering creature bending over you.

You gasp in horror. The creature is the size of a short human, but has the head of a dog. A pug, no less. Ugly and mean-looking eyes bore into you. A big purple tongue lolls out for a moment between a set of sharp canines.

A Space Pug. A Spug. You've read about these creatures in cadet class. They came about as the result of some disastrous genetic experiments, escaped Earth, and now they're nomadic space-faring creatures. Is this one of the "unfriendlies" Karl mentioned? And he's dealing with one of them?

Sluuffo straightens. "I'll take the kid."

"Yer won't eat the kid, will yer?" It almost sounds as if Karl cares.

"No. Woof. This one looks cute, just right for work as a pooper scooper in the puppy wards, cleaning up after the juveniles. Hey, like a pet for them, even. Gruff! It's not a problem at all."

The Spug slaps Karl on the shoulder in a friendly manner. He picks up the box containing the exotic cats in one hand. He pulls you to your feet and throws you over his shoulder with his other hand, holding you there by the feet so that you're upside down.

He's strong. You struggle, but you can barely move. "Mmphf! Mmphf!" is all you can muster.

Sluuffo talks into his wristpad. "I'm ready."

A few feet away, you see Karl counting a wad of money, his ill-gotten earnings from smuggling the exotic shorthair kittens. Everything becomes blurry for a few moments before you find yourself somewhere different. A teleporter! It's whisked you away from *The Bejeweled Diva*!

The Spug grasps you tightly. He lowers you to the floor, which is covered in dirt. Some of it gets on your face as you writhe around trying to see where you are. It looks like some kind of command center with lots of unfamiliar instruments and computer screens. The walls are green metal. Through a viewport you can see *The Bejeweled Diva* disappearing into the distance.

There are more Spugs here. You're on their ship!

Now you might never get home.

I'm sorry, this part of your story is over. Perhaps you should have taken the first opportunity to escape, because you never got another chance. Now you're going to spend the rest of your life scooping up puppy poop for the Spugs. Never mind though, you can try again and see what happens if you do take that escape opportunity.

Alternatively, other pathways are waiting.

It's time to make a decision. You have three choices. Would you like to:

Go back and try that opportunity to escape from Engineering? **P174**

Or

Go to the list of choices and start reading from another part of the story? **P532**

Or

Go back to the beginning of the story and try another path? **P95**

Switch on the supersized air blower

With a quick flick of your thumb, you turn on the supersized air blower. It makes a loud whining noise like a giant hairdryer as a gale-force stream of air gushes forth. You hold the blower tightly, almost losing your balance with the recoil.

The full force of the gust hits Karl squarely in the body. The laser pistol is whipped out of his hand, flies to the wall and bounces off, flying over your head and landing behind you. Karl is blown off his feet into the wall. He slumps to the floor with a groan and lies still.

Wow. That was fun.

You switch off the air blower and put it down. Karl looks unconscious, but he might wake at any time. He threatened to tie you up—does that mean there's rope or cable ties here? Yes, you see some cable ties amongst the tools.

It takes you only a minute to render Karl immobile by fastening cable ties around his ankles and wrists. You step back and admire your work. He won't get out of that anytime soon.

Next, you use the supersized air blower to clear out the sand and gravel from the drive, and a hacksaw to cut the sandbags loose. The drive is operational again. Should you find where to turn it on? Should you turn it on while Karl is in there?

Probably not.

You scratch your head. One thing you haven't worked out is *why* Karl sabotaged the maneuver drive. You recall him telling you he liked the ship to have little "mishaps" so the captain would remember he's useful. But this "mishap" seems too much, surely. And it wouldn't explain why he pointed a laser pistol at you.

You crawl out of the drive space. When you stand in the clearing by the hammock, you think for a minute. You should run and tell the captain what's been happening, but what about the maneuver drive? It's important to get that started again for the safety of the entire starship.

Can you drag Karl out of the drive space? He's lanky, but he's a big guy. You look around for inspiration or, preferably, something to help. Your gaze settles on a low wheeled platform—the sort that mechanics use to slide under vehicles they're working on. Perfect.

Lying on it, you scoot into the drive space. Then, with a bit of effort, you roll Karl over onto it. His head, shoulders and upper body fit on, but his legs will drag on the ground.

You give him a good shove. The wheels must be well-oiled, because even with all that weight, the platform shoots through the tunnel into the main part of Engineering. It slows a little before Karl's head bumps into the string jump drive housing opposite. Oops!

You crawl out. Karl told you he'd deactivated the drive, so somewhere there must be a switch to turn it on again. Where?

What was that noise? You whip your head around, but see nothing. It sounded like a cat meowing.

You listen intently, but you can't hear anything.

Maybe you imagined it. Anyway, there's no time to investigate. You have to start the maneuver drive.

A control panel in the office looks promising. Yes, it has various controls. The lettering has faded with age, but you can make out which of the switches is for the maneuver drive. You flip it on.

The drive starts with a whirring sound that quickly becomes a high-pitched whine. You listen carefully. There's no trace of the gritty, grinding, churning sound anymore. Success!

Now you need to speak to the captain. Where's the communication device that Karl used?

A light comes on, showing you where it is, and the captain's voice comes through a speaker.

"You've fixed the drive at last, Karl. And just in time, too."

"It's not Karl, Captain. It's Ace, the space cadet student. Karl's a little … tied up at the moment."

"Tied up? What do you mean?"

"He sabotaged the drive. I don't know why. But I got the better of him, cleared the mess out of the drive, and restarted it. We're good to go."

"Well done, Ace. I'll deal with that scoundrel later. Right now, there's a ship alongside us. I think it's 'unfriendlies', so I'm going to take evasive action."

You hang on tight to the desk in the office, expecting to be thrown to one side, but nothing happens. Then you realize the inertial dampeners have kept the maneuver smooth for everyone inside.

It's safe to move, then. You run up the stairs and along the port corridor towards the Bridge. About halfway along, you skid to a halt with a squeak of sneakers on the metal floor when you see a pair of beings in tight red pants and puffy blue jackets in front of you. The air around them is all blurry, and you don't get a good look at them. A moment later, they're gone.

You race to the Bridge and use your wristpad to get inside. A frizzy-haired woman whirls to face you from a cushioned bucket seat in front of the aged control panels.

"Ace, I presume? I'm Teena, the captain. Welcome to the Bridge."

You look around. The Bridge is much smaller than you had imagined, only about twice the size of your tiny cabin. Windows wrap around the apex of the ship, providing a 180-degree view. The instrument consoles covered with metal levers, dials and display screens stand under them.

"I just saw two people blink out of existence in the corridor!"

"'Unfriendlies'. I thought so. They must have teleported on board. But I took evasive action, and *The Bejeweled Diva* is moving away from their ship. We're getting further away each minute because I made the first move. The boarders had to teleport back before their ship got out of range."

You nod. That makes sense.

"Well done, Ace." Teena slaps you on the back. "I'm making you First Officer for the duration of the voyage. You may have saved us all."

Congratulations, this part of your story is over. You have uncovered Karl's sabotage, overcome him when he threatened you, cleared the debris out of the maneuver drive and got it working again in time for the captain to escape the "unfriendlies". And you've been made First Officer for the journey.

But have you tried the other pathways in the book?

It's time to make a decision. Would you like to:

Go to the list of choices and start reading from another part of the story? **P532**

Or

Go back to the beginning of the story and try another path? **P95**

Leave the medic bay and tell the captain what you've discovered

You grab the little exotic shorthair kitten from under the covers. One quick glance at Sluuffo lying on the floor suggests he isn't likely to wake up anytime soon. At least, you hope not. How effective are those sedatives on Spugs, anyway?

Maybe it's best to leave the kitten on the bed. You put her back. She purrs and rubs your hand. She seems to like you.

The corridor is empty. You scurry along it to the apex of the ship, where the Bridge is, and use your wristpad to get inside. A frizzy-haired woman whirls to face you from a cushioned bucket seat in front of the aged control panels.

You look around. The Bridge is much smaller than you had imagined, only about twice the size of your tiny cabin. Windows wrap around the apex of the ship, providing a 180-degree view. The instrument consoles covered with metal levers, dials and display screens stand under them.

"Hi, I'm Ace."

"Ace?" She looks at you with a blank expression.

"I'm the space cadet student."

"I realize that. I'm Teena, the captain. Welcome to the Bridge. Ace is a nickname?"

"Yes, from school. I'm top gun on the space combat simulator."

"Oh. Okay." She turns back to the instrument panels.

You sit in the bucket seat next to her. "I have to talk to you, Captain. It's important."

Teena holds up her index finger, signaling you to delay. "It'll have to wait. I'm a little busy right now. There's a starship alongside us. It's the authorities, I think. They demanded to check my flight documentation."

Now you're puzzled. That doesn't make sense. "But you're not sure it's the authorities? What does the scanner show?"

Teena points at a blank display screen on the instrument panel.

"The scanner hasn't worked for a while. It needs repairing. I can't see what kind of starship it is."

Now it makes sense. "It's not the authorities. It's Spugs."

"Spugs? Why do you say it's Spugs?"

"Some of them teleported aboard the ship. I think they're in the cargo hold now, stealing the cargo."

Teena leans in close to me. "This better not be a prank, Ace, or I'll revoke your special privileges."

Exasperated, you wave both hands in the air. "There's Spugs on board! Are there any cameras in the cargo hold?"

"Of course." The captain presses a button on a panel above a small screen currently showing the passenger lounge. The screen goes blank. She presses another one. "That's odd. Neither of the cameras is working."

"Can you view the medic bay? There's a Spug unconscious on the floor in there."

Teena gives me a sharp glance, then presses another button above the screen. This time, a picture appears. It clearly shows the Spug, Sluuffo, unmoving on the floor. The kitten sits on his chest, kneading him with its tiny paws.

The captain's eyes widen. She turns to you. "We have to act quickly. I don't know when Karl—he's the engineer—will get the maneuver drive working. So—"

"He sabotaged the drive with bags of sand and grit. They've jammed the drive blades."

Teena purses her lips. "Is that so? I'll deal with that scoundrel later. But he's left us unable to maneuver the ship. We can't get away from them, and we can't deal with the ones on board. They're too dangerous."

"Then what can we do?" you ask, scratching your head. Your stomach's churning. Is the situation hopeless?

"See that door there, Ace?" Teena points to the starboard edge of the back wall of the Bridge. There's a narrow door there you hadn't noticed before. "Open that, will you?"

You do as she asks. It opens into a space not much larger than a wardrobe. There's a bucket seat and a small instrument panel. Gunnery controls.

"That's the starboard laser cannon controls, Ace. In you go."

"Me?" You're open-mouthed.

"You said you were the top gun on the space combat simulator at cadet school. Get in there."

You scramble inside and have a look at the targeting controls. Most of them look familiar, if outdated. The space combat simulator at space cadet school is realistic. You can handle this.

Teena remains at the main Bridge controls. "We're only going to get one chance at this, so you'd better be on top form, Ace."

"Okay, Captain." Your fingertips stroke the controls and you aim the laser cannon at the Spug starship. The hull is dark, though. You can't see any details, only a rough outline and a large black splotch where it obscures the stars.

"We'll probably have less than thirty seconds after you switch on the targeting laser before they react, so be quick."

You flick it on. At low power, the laser cannon is harmless and operates merely for targeting. The display screen in front of you shows a magnified view of the target location. Currently, it's focused on part of the hull.

"What do you want me to target? Their maneuver drive?"

"No. We have to take out their weapons first. Look for a laser cannon or missile launcher."

With deft trackball skills, you spin the control rapidly, moving the focused laser beam around until you locate a laser cannon mounted on the Spug ship.

"Found it!"

"Full power and fire!"

You don't need to be told twice. With a deep breath, you slide the power level up to its maximum rating. A massive burst of energy issues forth from the laser cannon before it fizzles out. It'll need to recharge.

"Did you hit it?"

Without the targeting beam to illuminate the other ship, you can't see the damage, but you're sure you hit it. In space cadet training, you've never missed a target. The display screen is dark for a moment or two, and then blazes into color. The color of fire.

You give Teena the thumbs-up. "I did! Their laser cannon has exploded!"

Teena appears at the door of the cramped gunnery room. You high-five her and come out into the Bridge.

"Brilliant shooting, Ace. Now we have the advantage. They're going to message us any second. Wait and see."

The captain was right. A message comes through from the other ship onto the main display panel.

What the BLAZES are you doing firing upon an OFFICIAL patrol ship? I'll have your starship IMPOUNDED!

The captain types a quick response.

You're not the authorities. I KNOW you're Spugs. I've seen some of you on my ship. Now, get off my ship and pull away or we'll fire on you again! And don't think about taking any of the cargo with you. I'll be checking, and I'll blast your maneuver drive if you do.

No reply.

Teena turns to you. "I wondered why they didn't contact me on audio. Now I know. It would have been obvious they were Spugs."

"Yeah. They 'woof' and 'yap'." You chuckle.

"Look, they're leaving!" The captain points through the view screen. The black shape of the Spug starship with its burning laser cannon port becomes smaller, moving further away. Soon you can't see it any more.

192

"Yay!" You give Teena the thumbs-up and then a high-five.

"Well done, Ace! I'm going to make you First Officer for the remainder of the voyage. Now, I have to check that the cargo's safe, but I bet it will be. They wouldn't have dared steal it after your sharp shooting. Then I'll deal with Karl, get the maneuver drive fixed—maybe you can help with that, Ace—and then we'll be back on course."

Congratulations, this part of your story is over. You have raised the alarm about the maneuver drive, visited Engineering and discovered Karl's sabotage, encountered some Spugs and disabled one of them, met the captain, fired upon the enemy starship and saved all of the cats from being stolen. That's pretty good for your first day on board. And you've been made First Officer for the journey.

But have you tried the other pathways in the book?

It's time to make a decision. Would you like to:

Go to the list of choices and start reading from another part of the story? **P532**

Or

Go back to the beginning of the story and try another path? **P95**

Leave the medic bay and go to the cargo hold

Sluuffo isn't going to wake up anytime soon. You decide to leave the little kitten in the medic bay where it'll be safe for a while. You're feeling confident now. It doesn't matter how many of the Spugs are down there. You'll think of something.

You tie a strip of bandage around your head Rambo style and leave the medic bay. It's a short jog along the corridor to a door labeled:

CARGO HOLD

Your wristpad opens it for you. How did the Spugs get access? That's a mystery to be solved.

The stairs are metal. You clonk down them in a hurry, not even bothering to be quiet. Every moment might matter.

You rush into the cargo hold and pause by the entrance to look around. It's a big space separated from Engineering by a solid wall. The walls give off a dim luminescence. A number of crates and boxes are stacked up, but most of the holding area has been divided into cages, each containing ten or so cats. Most of them are moggies, but there's a batch of Siamese cats too. You don't see any exotic shorthairs, though.

What a racket. It sounds like every cat in the place is yowling for dear life.

A hand clamps down on your shoulder, and you jump.

"Yap. Look who's here. It's the kid from upstairs. What're you doing here, kid?"

You turn and stare into the snarling face of Makkav. "I'm going to stop you from stealing the cargo, you cat burglars." You have to shout to be heard over the cats' screeching. "So you can simply—"

Another clawed hand grabs you around the mouth from behind, truncating your defiant words. Its fur, up close, is much darker than that of Makkav, who lets go as the other creature takes a stronger grasp on you with both arms. You wriggle, but you're unable to struggle free. It turns so you can see the whole of the cargo hold again.

Several more Spugs have emerged from behind cages and crates. They're all wearing the same tight red pants and puffy blue jackets. It must be a uniform of some kind. You're so outnumbered that your bravery drains away. This wasn't a good idea. It was a really bad idea. You squirm, but it's hopeless. You can't get free.

You're forced to watch as, one by one, a Spug attaches a small device to a cage and puts his clawed hand on it. The air around the Spug and the cat cage goes blurry for a second or two, then both wink out of existence.

They're using a teleporter to get the cats off the ship. That's how they got on board.

Finally, all the cat cages and Spugs are gone, apart from Makkav and the creature gripping you. You sense the color draining from your face, and have a horrible feeling you might lose your lunch. What are they going to do with you?

Makkav speaks into his wristpad. "We're done here. Woof. Sluuffo isn't answering my calls. Teleport him out anyway, then teleport us. Gruff. It's time we left."

"What about this kid?" the creature growls, spinning you around and gripping you by both shoulders. "Can I eat this?"

You stare, horrified, into the terrifying dark-furred face of a Space Pit Bull, or Spitbull as they're known, one of the nastiest creatures to be found between the stars. He must be the muscle for the Spugs. Suddenly, the term "unfriendlies" seems a bit understated.

"I don't see why not," Makkav says. "We can't leave a witness here or we won't get to do this again."

"Yap. Take-out." The Spitbull grins widely. Its big tongue licks over long, sharp teeth. A gloop of saliva plops to the floor between you.

I'm sorry, this part of your story is over. You've managed to save one little exotic shorthair kitten from the Spugs, but they stole all of the cats in the cargo hold, which will end up on dinner tables throughout Spugworld. You end up as a take-out for the Spitbull. No one knows what became of you, only that you disappeared with the cargo, so you got the blame for the theft of all of the cats. Life isn't fair, sometimes.

It wasn't a good idea to go to the cargo hold and confront the Spugs when you didn't know how many there were and no one knew what you were doing. Luckily, this is a *You Say Which Way* adventure, and you can change your last choice to see what happens. Do you want to let the captain know what you discovered instead?

It's time to make a decision. You have three choices. Would you like to:

Change your last choice and tell the captain what you've discovered? **P188**

Or

Go to the list of choices and start reading from another part of the story? **P532**

Or

Go back to the beginning of the story and try another path? **P95**

Leave the medic bay and hide in your cabin

Venturing down to the cargo hold would be a crazy, dumb idea. Who knows how many Spugs are down there? And the captain probably knows what's going on. If not, it's not your business, right?

At the doorway, you look left and right. No one is in sight. You slink out quietly, hoping you don't encounter the Spugs or Karl on the way.

You can't see far because of the curved corridors. Which way should you go? Aft, past the stairway to Engineering, or forward, past the stairway to the cargo hold?

You choose to go past Engineering rather than risk another encounter with the Spugs. Luckily, you make it without any further incident.

There's barely enough room under your tiny cabin bed to hide, but you squeeze yourself in, cuddling the kitten close. Hopefully, no one will come in.

You stay there like that for several hours until the steward comes looking for you.

I'm sorry, this part of your story is over. You've managed to save one little exotic shorthair kitten from the Spugs, but they stole all of the cats in the cargo hold, and they will end up on dinner tables throughout Spugworld.

The captain is furious with you that you didn't tell her what you'd discovered. She revokes your status to access all parts of the starship, so the rest of your journey is boring. She also reports you to space cadet school, and they expel you for behavior unfitting a future officer. Finally, at Proxima B, after the authorities impound the captain's starship because she's arrived without her mandated cargo, she has you blacklisted as a passenger, so there's no way you'll ever get home again.

Fortunately, this is a *You Say Which Way* adventure, so you can choose again if you want to.

197

It's time to make a decision. You have three choices. Would you like to:

Change your last choice and tell the captain what you've discovered? **P188**

Or

Go to the list of choices and start reading from another part of the story? **P532**

Or

Go back to the beginning of the story and try another path? **P95**

The real Proxima B

Proxima B is a planet of a similar size to Earth in the Proxima Centauri system (constellation Centaurus), discovered in August 2016. Its discovery brought world-wide excitement because Proxima Centauri is the closest star to us besides our own sun, and the planet's orbit lies in the habitable zone—the 'Goldilocks' area in which, subject to other conditions, it could be neither too cold nor too hot to support life.

So … is it habitable? Could humans live there one day? Scientists want to know. Unfortunately, they don't have all the answers yet.

Here's what they do know:

Proxima Centauri is a red dwarf star 4.224 light years distant. That's 1.295 parsecs, or about 40 trillion kilometres.

Proxima B has a mass of about 1.3 Earths, so its gravity is similar. It's not known if it has an atmosphere, but a space telescope planned to be launched in 2018 will be able to determine that by sampling the star system's light.

It orbits only 7 million kilometres from the star, which is cooler than our sun, and has a 'year' of only 11.2 Earth days. Because it is so close, it is bombarded with X-rays and buffeted by stellar winds that may have blown away the atmosphere, if there was one.

So, sadly, it's probably not habitable, though scientists haven't yet ruled out the possibility.

Will we ever see it? Possibly. The Starshot project, funded by a wealthy Russian businessman, aims to create and send a mass of miniature unmanned spacecraft to the Proxima Centauri system. They'll be powered by lasers directed from Earth, giving them a push until they reach 20% of light speed. They'll take 20 years to get there. How they'll stop, I can't imagine.

Their pictures will take 4 years to get back to us.

I wonder what they'll reveal?

Mini Glossary

G = the acceleration due to the force of gravity (at the Earth's surface). That is about 9.8 m/s^2. *The Bejeweled Diva* accelerates at about 2G, or 19.6 m/s^2.

Inertial dampeners: these distribute the effects of the acceleration throughout the framework of the ship so passengers (and cargo) have a smooth ride. Remember the feeling of being pushed back in your seat when an airplane takes off? That's the effect of the acceleration.

Parsec: an astronomical measurement of distance equal to about 3.26 light years, or 30.86 trillion kilometres. Being a measurement of distance, and not time, Han Solo's declaration that the *Millenium Falcon* "made the Kessel run in less than twelve parsecs" doesn't make sense.

MYSTIC PORTAL

By Eileen Mueller

Enter Mystic Portal

Standing on a grassy knoll high above the sea, you pull on your biking gloves. Next to you, Sidney checks his full-face helmet. Your breath is a misty cloud in the crisp morning air. Tracey zips her jacket shut over her body armor—she's got all the latest mountain biking gear. [note: for mountain biking terms see **P360**]

Fastening her racing goggles, and tightening her helmet, Tracey calls, "My lid's good. Ready when you are."

Sidney glances at the trail leading down into the trees and bites his lip. Aside from your helmets and gloves, you and Sidney only have shin guards.

He's not the only one who's nervous. Breakfast is dancing in your stomach as if it knows you're about to enter Mystic Portal. The entrance to the track is a dark gaping hole in the pine forest. Toadstools stand guard on either side of a thin dirt trail heading downwards through the trees. At the bottom of the track is a sandy beach. Expert riders usually make it to the beach by lunchtime. It's not the entrance or the beach you're worried about, just all the tough obstacles in between.

You've all been training for months for this downhill ride. The three of you met at Tracey's house yesterday to tune your bikes. You all adjusted your shocks, bled your brakes, lubricated your chains and pumped your tires.

"I can hardly believe we're finally doing this," Tracey murmurs with a smile. "I'm glad we've already walked the trail a few times, so we know it."

"Me too." Sidney is nibbling his lip again.

Nudging him, you ask, "Still want to go?" Hopefully he'll back out, so you can keep him company.

Tracey rolls her eyes. "Not so fast, guys. You're not chicken, are you? We planned this. You can't go home now."

She's onto you. Just your luck.

Sidney's eyes flick back to the track. "Jase said weird things happen when you go down Mystic Portal."

"But it was fine when we walked it," says Tracey.

"Things that don't happen when you walk down," says Sidney, "only when you bike. You guys sure you want to go?"

"Jase says new jumps appear overnight." You fight to keep your voice steady.

"Yeah," says Sidney, "and other jumps vanish."

Tracey smiles at Sidney. "Okay, I'm nervous too, but if you want to take my bike, I'll go on your hard-tail."

Tracey has a top-of-the-range mountain bike, a downhill racing dualie, with the latest greatest shock absorbers on the front and rear suspension.

Sidney's hard-tail is a cheap mountain bike with no back suspension, so he hits the ground hard when he lands. Yours is a dirt jump bike without gears—even simpler than Sidney's. You've both had a turn on Tracey's new bike. It feels like you're landing on a giant marshmallow.

But neither of you can afford a bike like hers.

Sidney's eyes linger on Tracey's bike as he considers her offer. "Nah, I'm fine," he says, toughing it out.

"We can always use the chicken lines," you say. "We don't have to do every jump."

"Let's go," says Sidney, jutting out his jaw. He doesn't want to be the one to chicken out.

You know how he feels.

You get on your bikes.

Tracey zooms down the track, chewing up the dirt with her tires. Sidney's close behind, crunching over broken twigs and pine needles. Hard on his tail, you go over a tiny rise in the track and pull your handlebars upwards, lifting your bike off the ground.

"Hey you guys, I got some air." You yell, landing with a smack.

Sidney whoops.

"First jump is Camel Hump," Tracey yells as she goes past a makeshift sign with a badly painted camel on it.

Who built these cool jumps?" asks Sidney.

"No idea," she calls. "They say it's a mystery."

Tracy takes a corner tightly, stomping her foot on the ground. Sidney sticks to the middle of the trail, nice and safe, cruising around the corner. You rush at the corner, going high on the berm, then speed down the bank, back onto the track.

Ahead, the track splits in two.

"I'm taking Camel Hump," calls Tracey. "You coming or are you going to play chicken, Sidney?"

"I want to get to Ogre Jaws. The faster the better," calls Sidney. "That's the coolest jump ever."

You have to agree with him. Ogre Jaws is a great jump—it even has teeth. You can't wait to try it.

He crows like a rooster, then veers off to the left, bypassing the jump and going down the easier trail. He disappears into the trees, clucking like a chicken.

Tracey swoops up the steep reddish rise of Camel Hump. "Coming?" she calls. Her bike flies into the air, then disappears.

No, that can't be right. She can't have disappeared. She must've landed beyond your line of sight. Either that, or you've gone crazy.

204

Your spine prickles. Or has she really vanished? Weird things happen on this track.

You're nearing the fork in the trail. To your right is Camel Hump. To your left is the way out—the chicken line, which leads to Dino Drop and Ogre Jaws.

It's time to make a decision. Do you:

Hit Camel Hump? **P205**

Or

Bypass Camel Hump and go down the chicken line? **P234**

Hit Camel Hump

Your tires hum up the red compacted dirt of Camel Hump and hit the jump. The trees blur. Your bike is airborne. For a glorious moment you're flying—this is what you love.

The forest and Mystic Portal disappear.

You land with a whump. Your suspension is terrible, and you're swaying from side to side. Wait, this isn't your bike. What is it?

Rubbing your eyes, you squint against bright light and focus. You're on an animal, a camel, plodding down an enormous red sand dune. That's why you're swaying. You pitch forward, grabbing a handle on the camel's saddle to save yourself from doing an endo—wait would it still be called an endo if you go over the top of camel's head instead of over handlebars?

Another dune looms in front of you. The only things you can see are the deep-blue sky and endless red sand.

Where's Mystic Portal?

And where is Tracey? She went over Camel Hump before you and vanished in midair. She must be here somewhere.

"Tracey!" you yell. "Tracey, where are you?"

No answer. Only scorching heat beating down. A bead of sweat stings your eye. The air shimmers with heat waves. Dry air parches your throat. You're already thirsty and you've only just got here—wherever here is.

The camel plods on, making its way down the sand with even steps. It's a weird sensation, feeling as if you're going to tumble off the camel as it heads downwards. You soon find that leaning back helps you stay balanced in the saddle. At least there are cushions to pad your butt—you'd imagined camel humps to be soft, but there's nothing soft about the hump you're sitting on.

You pat the creature's back. "Hey, boy, thanks for giving me a ride. It sure beats walking in this sand."

The camel doesn't answer, but it does snort. You smile. Maybe it's not answering because it's a girl and you got it wrong. You laugh—the heat's affecting you already. Everyone knows camels don't understand people.

Soon the camel reaches the bottom of the dune, traipses across the sand and starts climbing the next dune. Maybe there'll be something interesting over the top. There has to be more to this place than dunes.

You were wrong. When you reach the top of the next rise, for miles in every direction, all you see is red.

You breathe through your nose, hoping it will cool the air so your throat isn't quite so parched, but it's so hot your nostrils feel like they're on fire.

"Not fair," you mumble. "How am I ever going to get out of here? I thought I was going for a bike ride."

It's then you notice the camel's leather harness is the same green and red as your bike. Astounded, you glance down at the saddle. It's red with silver edging, and so are the cushions—like your bike seat! Has your bike somehow transformed into a camel? Is that what Jase meant by strange things happening when you ride Mystic Portal? What on earth?

Or are you on earth at all?

With a sinking feeling, you realize it's no coincidence that jumping over Camel Hump has landed you on camelback.

A shriek sounds behind you. You whirl, grabbing hold of a brown bundle behind the saddle to save yourself from falling. Making its way toward you is a weird bird.

More than weird. Bizarre. Its wings are trailing stray feathers. Its body is way larger than a normal bird, and it flaps strangely. Usually birds flap evenly, but this thing moves haphazardly. Dangerously.

A giant desert vulture? Looking for a snack? You lean forward and pat the camel. "Come on, let's get going." As if the camel understands you, it plunges down the next dune. Soon you're hidden.

But not for long. The thing's shrieks grow closer. Something swoops overhead. Your hair ruffles. Oh, no, you're no longer wearing your bike helmet.

The bird shrieks again and swoops toward your head, narrowly missing you. "Hey," it cries, in a familiar voice, "why are you ignoring me?"

"Tracey?"

She swoops in front of you, hovering in the air beside the camel's head. It's not a bird after all! Tracey's on a tattered threadbare mat. A green and gold mat—the same colors as her bike.

"Steady," she snaps.

The flying carpet bucks and sways, nearly tipping her off.

You stifle a laugh. She had such a new shiny bike and now she's on the rattiest tattiest carpet you've ever seen. Your camel beats that old rag any day.

"What's so funny?" Tracey glowers as the carpet swerves, loose threads trailing behind it. She shoves her fist through a hole and grabs on to the edge with white knuckles. "I said *steady!*"

The carpet ignores her. Why wouldn't it? It's only a carpet—even if it is a flying one.

"Climb aboard and help me," she calls.

There's no way you're getting on that thing. It's way too dangerous. At least your camel is stable. As you shake your head, the carpet tries to buck her off again.

You can't help laughing out loud. "That thing's like a bucking bronco."

"Nah, more like a rollercoaster. You too chicken to ride it?"

"No way, I'm not chicken!"

"Yeah, I know you're braver than that." She raises an eyebrow. "You gonna help me?"

"Of course. I'll get on board!"

A deep voice comes out of nowhere, "You don't have to go with that tatty old thing. I'm a desert survival specialist and I can transport you to an oasis."

"What?" You gaze around. "Who was that?" You, Tracey, the

carpet and the camel are the only things you can see—apart from sky and endless sand.

"It's me, Jamina. Didn't you know camels talk?"

Wow, your camel understands you. Amazing. It may even be better than a bike!

"Come on," says Tracey. "I can't really fly this thing, but you'll probably be excellent. I need your help."

Travelling by flying carpet would be exciting.

Jamina turns her head around, snuffling at your hand. "Don't you want to see the oasis and meet all the people who live there?"

Being with a talking camel sounds exciting too.

It's time to make a decision. Do you:

Stay with Jamina the talking camel? **P209**

Or

Go with Tracey on the tatty flying carpet? **P219**

Stay with Jamina the talking camel

Tracey's carpet does a wild swerve and she slips, grabbing a fistful of tassels, her legs dangling off the side of the carpet. "Please," she says, "I really need your help."

"Sorry, Tracey," you say, "that thing looks too dangerous for me. Besides, Jamina is going to take me to an oasis. I'm looking forward to that."

"Don't blame you," she says. "Wish I had a camel." The carpet bucks, dumping Tracey onto its middle. Sprawled on the carpet, one of her feet hangs through a hole. "Hey, you." She punches the carpet. "What do you think you're doing? *Steady*, I said. *Steady*."

But the carpet seems to have a mind of its own. Zipping and bucking, it takes off across the desert—with Tracey yelling at it.

"Some tourists never learn," says Jamina. "The secret to training a flying carpet is speaking politely. Your friend is going to have a tough time."

"Why didn't you tell her?" you ask.

"People learn better when they figure things out themselves," says Jamina. "Are you thirsty?"

"Absolutely parched."

"Do you have any water with you?"

Of course. In your backpack. Feeling foolish, you reach for your forgotten water bottle to have a long drink.

Jamina interrupts you. "Not too much," she says. "It's better to take small sips often than to run out and go for hours without water."

You're so thirsty you could drink the whole thing in one go, but Jamina is the desert survival specialist so, after a few gulps, you stow your water bottle in your backpack. "I don't know much about camels, but I'm keen to learn. I thought all camels had two humps, but you only have one."

Jamina snorts loudly, fine-grained sand flying from her nostrils. "Asian camels have two humps. Camels in Arabia, like me, have one.

We're called dromedaries."

"So you're a dromedary?"

"I am," she replies. "How do you like the desert so far?"

You squint at the bright glare on the horizon and the miles of sand around you. "It's… um… hot."

Jamina stops, her large even feet creating depressions in the sand, and turns her head to gaze at you. "You're not wearing a hat. You could get sunstroke."

"I don't have a hat with me," you say. Fishing around in your backpack, you pull out a light sweatshirt and tie it over your head.

"That's better," Jamina says. "The first rule of desert survival is to drink water slowly, the second is to shade your head so your body doesn't have to work so hard to keep cool."

A refreshing breeze wafts across the sand, creating beautiful ripples on the surface. Jamina sniffs the air and continues walking, but faster. At first the wind feels good, cooling your skin, but soon it whips sand into your eyes, making them sting.

Jamina picks up speed, running down another dune, then stops. "A sand storm is coming. We'd better take shelter," she says.

There's nowhere to shelter. Nothing but sand. What is she talking about? She bends her front knees to kneel, nearly tipping you over her head, then bends her rear knees too. She's sitting down in the sand.

Panic grips you. Shouldn't she be running to get away from the storm? She said to take shelter, but how? You could hunker down next to her, hiding your face in her furry side. Or you could convince her to outrun the storm.

"Jamina, how fast can dromedaries run?"

"Forty miles per hour, but only in short bursts."

Really fast. Surely she could outrun that pesky wind. "Shouldn't we run?" you ask.

"We could try," she says. "Or we could pitch our tent and take shelter inside."

Our tent? You glance behind the saddle at the brown bundle you grabbed earlier to stop you from falling off. It's a tent.

The wind is getting stronger, flinging hard grains of sand at you, stinging your arms with fierce nips.

You don't have long to make a decision. Do you:

Pitch the tent to take shelter from the sand storm? **P212**

Or

Encourage Jamina to run from the sandstorm? **P218**

212

Pitch the tent to take shelter from the sand storm

Wind whistles between the dunes. A fine mist of sand swirls in the air, coating your teeth with grit. Climbing off her saddle, you untie the tent from Jamina's back and shake it out.

The tent's shaped like an igloo with a zipper in the door, an inner layer of mesh, and a floor sealed to the sides. You snap two long poles together and thread them through the fabric so the crossed poles curve over the roof and sides. You drive the unusually-long tent pegs deep into the sand.

Over the dunes, in the distance, a great red cloud of sand billows into the sky. The storm is approaching swiftly. You dive into the tent and pull the zipper shut.

Within moments, sand strikes your tent, pattering against the light fabric.

A voice asks, "Can you unzip the door a little so I can put my nose in? The sand is stinging my eyes."

It's Jamina. She's carried you all this way, now she's stuck out in the storm. You unzip the tent a fraction and she shoves her head inside at floor level. Pulling the zip down tight against her neck, you make sure the fabric is secure so no sand can sneak in.

Hundreds of tiny dark spots beat against the tent. Wind whistles around you, shaking the fabric. Soon the drumming of the sand is a dull roar.

"Jamina, why do you have your nostrils shut? I didn't know camels could do that."

"Keeps the sand out." She snorts, flaring her nostrils again. "Maybe it's time for some desert stories. I know a few. Would you like one?"

It looks like you're going to be stuck here a while. Opening your backpack, you pull out a sandwich. "A story sounds great. Would you like a bite?"

Jamina snorts at your sandwich. "No thanks. My hump is a great storage cupboard, allowing me to go for days without food or water.

Unless it's good food." Her eyes slide along your sandwich and her nose wrinkles, as if it's a rotting rat.

Her voice croons as she starts the story. "Once upon a time, there was a Bedouin with his camel, Jim, out in the desert when a sand storm struck. The Bedouin was clever—"

"Hang on," you say. "Why does the camel have a name, but the Bedouin doesn't?"

Jamina snorts. "Everyone knows that camels are the main character in desert jokes, not humans. Besides, Jim was my grandfather." She snorts again.

Her snorting's beginning to become a habit. Do all camels snort this much? "Oh, all right," you concede. "The Bedouin doesn't have to have a name then."

"The Bedouin was clever. He had a tent with him so, when the sand storm hit, he quickly pitched it and climbed inside. The storm was ferocious, making his tent buck. Soon Jim was braying outside. "Please let me put my nose just inside the door,' he cried. 'The sand is stinging my eyes terribly.' "

"Hey that's what you did!"

Jamina's lips pull back, showing her teeth—a comical-looking camel smile.

You grin back. "So, what happened?"

"The Bedouin let Jim the camel put his head inside the tent. The wind grew fiercer, whipping great gusts of sand at the tent, like a giant playing in a sand pit. 'Ow! The sand is stinging my shoulders,' Jim whimpered. 'Could I just put my shoulders in the tent to protect them?' What do you think the Bedouin did?"

"He let Jim bring his shoulders in," you reply.

"Do you know this story?" asks Jamina.

"No, I've never heard it before. I'm just good at guessing."

"Once Jim had his shoulders inside, the roar of the sandstorm grew even louder. 'Oh, my flanks ache. I'm sure my hide is raw. Could I please bring my hindquarters inside?' What do you think the Bedouin did?"

"Let Jim in?"

"Of course he did. He was a kind man, but a foolish one."

"Why was he foolish?"

"Just wait and see." Jamina snorts again.

"Jim heaved his back end inside, and the Bedouin zipped the tent shut, leaving only Jim's tail outside. Soon Jim was moaning again. 'My tail, my poor tail is being flayed to pieces by the vicious sand. What—"

"— do you think the Bedouin said," you finish the sentence for her. This story is getting rather predictable. "Of course the Bedouin let Jim bring his tail in." You're sure you're giving Jamina the right answer because she gives you one of her funny camel smiles again.

"That's right," says Jamina. "But by now there was no room for the foolish Bedouin, so Jim kicked him out into the sandstorm." She starts to bray. A weird guttural chuckling sound fills the tent.

She sounds so funny, you can't help laughing too, but a strange prickle travels down your spine. Is she warning you? Is she about to toss you out in the sand storm to die?

"Is this a joke?" you ask.

"No," she says, between chuckles.

"I hope your shoulders are alright," you say. "You don't need to bring them inside the tent, do you?" There's no way you'll let her, even if she asks.

Her chuckling bray grows louder.

You're about to block your ears when she stops.

"Of course not," she says. "I'm civilized and come from a long line of respected camels. I'd never do that to my riders."

"Respected camels? But Jim was your grandfather."

"Ah, yes. But Jim was also a rogue, the rebel camel in the family."

Rebel camel? Wow, maybe you're really going crazy. Rebel camels, flying carpets and endless sand were not what you expected when you headed through the forest down Mystic Portal. You touch your head. Maybe you fell off your bike and hit it—that would explain things. But your fingers land on soft hair, not hard biking helmet. Something really peculiar has happened today.

Jamina stops braying. "Did you hear that?" she asks.

It's all quiet, you can't hear a thing. "What are you talking about?"

"The storm has stopped."

Putting the rest of your lunch in your backpack, you throw it on your shoulders and leap to your feet to unzip the tent.

"No," cries Jamina, but it's too late.

Sand pours through the doorway covering your legs to the knees. The sand is heavy, weighing you down. You struggle, but manage to clamber out of the tent.

Jamina's body is half submerged in red sand. Stumbling to her feet, she raises her haunches with her rear legs, causing an avalanche of sand to cascade over her shoulders, burying you to the waist.

"Why did you do that?" you cry, spitting grit from your teeth. Grabbing a few sips of water, you rinse your mouth, then struggle to the top of the sand.

Chuckling, she raises her front legs to stand. "Camels always get up with their rear legs first. It's just the way we're made." She stamps on the spot, flinging more sand over you, until she's compacted the sand beneath her.

Oh well, you'd better get the tent, in case there's another storm.

As you reach towards it, Jamina says, "Please stand out of the way." She places her jaws over the top of the tent, lifting it where the crossed poles meet. She tips it forward so the doorway is face down, and the sand pours out.

"Wow, you're handy! An excellent dromedary and great desert survival specialist."

She winks.

Soon you're back in her saddle, the tent tied behind you, traipsing across the desert.

After an hour of listening to more of Jamina's stories about her rebellious Grandpa, Jim, you reach the rise of a dune, and gasp.

Below is an oasis. A deep blue lake winks in the sunlight, surrounded by palms, bushes and low buildings the same color as the sand. At one end of the oasis stand brightly-striped tents with camels tethered nearby. A wide swathe of trampled sand surrounds the settlement, as if camels have been dancing around it. Dancing camels? That'll be the day.

Snorting, Jamina picks up her pace and starts running. You're jostled from side to side, and hang on tight. She told you she could run forty miles per hour, but you had no idea it would feel like this. Your butt's being pummeled like a drum in a rock band, and your teeth clack like a row of tumbling dominoes. Sweat flies from your face as Jamina's hooves churn up sand behind you.

Stopping beside the tents, Jamina's sides heave. She folds her front knees to kneel, nearly tipping you off, but now wise to her ways, you grab the handle on the saddle, then dismount.

A bearded man wearing a white headscarf and loose red robes approaches. "Welcome home, Jamina." He pats her nose and she nuzzles his hand. "I see you've found a new rider who sits well in the saddle at high speed. Very well done. You're back just in time for the afternoon race."

Race? What race?

Oh! That wasn't a camel's dance floor surrounding the oasis. It was a race track.

The man extends his hand to you as a woman approaches. "I am Aamir, and this is my wife, Latifa. If you would like to stay and race Jamina in our camel race, you're welcome to stay with our family."

You gulp. That sprint on Jamina was crazy. It'll be a lot more dangerous racing with other camels.

"What will I do, if I don't race with Jamina?"

Aamir frowns, a thundercloud passing over his face. Latifah shakes her head, as if urging you not to provoke him.

"My camel has been on a long journey to find you. She has rescued you from the perilous desert. We have offered you a new career as a camel racer and shelter in our tent. To refuse would be the height of rudeness. We would have to banish you from the oasis."

Banish? That means you'd have to leave. Maybe you'd find Tracey out there in the desert or another way to get back to Mystic Portal and your bike. Or maybe you'd get hopelessly lost.

It's time to make a decision. Do you:

Race Jamina in the camel races? **P349**

Or

Leave the oasis? **P294**

218

Encourage Jamina to run from the sandstorm

Although the sand stings, the main cloud is far away.

"Let's make a run for it," you yell to Jamina, clambering back into the saddle.

She rises and takes off, racing up a dune and plowing down the other side. Sand billows around her hooves as she runs. You're jolted from side to side. Your bones shudder.

Behind, the sandstorm is racing toward you, high above the dunes.

"Are you sure you don't want to pitch the tent?" Jamina asks.

Will she be fast enough to outrun the storm?

It's time to make a decision. Do you:

Pitch the tent to take shelter from the sandstorm? **P212**

Or

Keep Jamina running from the sandstorm? **P297**

Go with Tracey on the tatty flying carpet

"I'm sorry Jamina," you say. "Thanks for offering, but maybe I'll come to the oasis another time. Tracey is my friend so I should really help her."

"That's okay," says Jamina. "Let me help you get onto that thing."

"Here, take my hand," says Tracey. She leans down over the edge of the carpet, stretching her arm out towards you.

Jamina stands still so you can balance on her back. This is crazy. You never thought a mountain bike ride would have you balancing on a camel like an acrobat while trying to climb up to a swaying flying carpet. Grasping Tracey's hand firmly, you push off Jamina's back with your feet and Tracey yanks you onto the magic carpet.

"Have a good flight," calls Jamina as she turns and wanders off into the desert. Soon she's a tiny brown spot in the vast tundra of red.

Being on the carpet is like sitting on a bouncy castle. Every time you move, your weight makes the mat undulate in the air. "Whoa," you cry, "no wonder it's so hard to stay on this thing."

"You can say that again," says Tracey. "Riding a bike is much easier." She tugs a tassel and yells again, "Straight ahead, but steady!" The carpet swerves, nearly tipping her off.

You grab a handful of tassels and slide to the middle to save yourself from falling.

"You try," says Tracey. "This thing must be deaf. I'm yelling as loud as I can and it's not responding. Let's see if it likes your voice better."

Whenever someone yells at you, you never feel like doing what they're asking. Maybe yelling at the carpet isn't the key. Maybe you could try something different, like telling the carpet a joke.

No, that wouldn't work, because it wouldn't know what to do. Your teacher's always saying good manners open doors, whatever that means. Maybe talking nicely would change things.

Wind streams into your eyes as the carpet zips up into the air. It

220

tilts, and you and Tracy start to slip off, your arms flailing. You both grab at stray threads. A loud ripping noise sends your heart thudding.

It's time to make a decision. Do you:

Yell at the magic carpet? **P221**

Or

Talk to the carpet politely? **P228**

Yell at the magic carpet

The hole in the carpet grows before your eyes. In a moment, you and Tracy will both be dumped on the sand, miles below. You'll break your arm, or your back, or something. Perhaps you'll both die.

"Stop!" You yell at the top your voice. "Stop or we'll die."

It works. The carpet screeches to a halt in midair. But the rip grows. With a tortured screech, the threads part and the carpet splits in two, Tracey holding one half, and you the other.

You both scream as you plummet through the air.

With twin whumps, you land on the side of a giant sand dune, letting go of the ragged pieces of mat as you land.

"Oof!"

"Ow!"

"Oh, no," moans Tracey, "there goes our transport!" She groans, shading her eyes as the carpet knits itself together and flies off. "Hey, come back!"

A faint laugh floats through the air.

Tracey turns to you. "There it is again. I could swear that thing was laughing at me the whole time it was trying to buck me off." She shakes her head and scrambles to her feet, brushing the sand off her bike shorts.

"It really did sound as if it was laughing," you say. "Perhaps I should've told a joke after all. Or tried speaking politely. Did you try either?"

"No, I was too busy panicking. That's why I kept yelling." Tracey blushes. "What now?"

Still sitting, you fish through your backpack and pull out some water. "Jamina said it was important to keep sipping water throughout the day, and to keep our heads shaded."

"Okay." Tracey takes a swig from her bottle and pulls a cap out of her backpack. "How will we ever get out of this desert?"

It doesn't look hopeful. Dunes surround you. That particular shade of red is beginning to get tiresome. And the sun is still doing overtime, working really hard to impress someone.

A loud snort startles you, making you jump. You whirl. It's Jamina, plodding over the crest of the dune, her broad feet stirring up puffs of sand as she walks.

"Here comes more transport," says Tracey. She points to Jamina, and yells, "Hey, you! Can you give us a ride?"

Elbowing Tracey aside, you mutter, "Stop yelling. Haven't you learned anything?" Your legs churn through the sand as you both make your way up to Jamina. "A sense of humor and some manners may come in handy. It's too late to try with the carpet, but there's no harm in trying with a talking camel."

You greet her. "Jamina, how wonderful to see you. It's great you came to check up on us. Would you please give us a ride to the oasis?"

"I'm sorry, the oasis is in the other direction. I had to change my course to make sure you two were all right." Jamina bats her double row of eyelashes at you. "But I'd be delighted to give you a ride to an Arab merchant, only an hour or two from here."

"Thank you very much," you answer. "Jamina, I hadn't realized you had two sets of eyelashes above each eye."

"Helps keep the sand out. Now climb up and let's get going."

You sit on the seat over Jamina's hump, and Tracey sits on a brown bundle of cloth behind you. "What's this?" She asks.

"A tent for sandstorms," replies Jamina.

"Let's hope we don't get stuck in one of those." You shiver. "I read about a terrible sand storm in an adventure book, once. It sounded awful."

After a while, Jamina's rhythmic swaying and plodding make your head droop. A gentle snore comes from behind. Tracey's asleep already.

"Have a snooze too," says Jamina. "I'll wake you before we get there."

Despite trying desperately to stay awake, your eyelids close and you soon doze off.

Loud snorting wakes you. Turning her head, Jamina says, "Wake up sleepy heads, we're nearly there."

Behind you, Tracey groans. "My neck has a crick and my bottom's sore," she moans.

"At least you're alive," you say. "Better than being stranded in the desert by that silly carpet."

"Guess you're right," says Tracey. "Hey, camel, where are we?" She points to a wide building made of pale concrete. In the middle of the building is a domed roof. It's surrounded by sand, not another building in sight.

Elbowing Tracey, you whisper, "Her name is Jamina. Remember to speak politely to the camel or she may dump you in the desert too."

"Sorry," Tracey mumbles.

Jamina snorts and turns her head to wink at you. "You're right," she says. "Manners go a long way in the desert. Especially with merchant Karim. This is his home."

"Home? It looks more like a fortress."

Jamina lopes closer. The building is surrounded by a tall concrete wall. Guards pace along the top, at the ready.

"What are they guarding, Jamina?" asks Tracey.

"Merchant Karim grew up in poverty. He became rich through hard work and shrewd trading," Jamina says as you approach the gates. "He helps finance schools in the city slums, giving poor kids a chance to change their lives. He's a fair man, but tough."

As you draw closer, the flash of sunlight on binoculars tells you that you're being watched.

"Desert bandits want a share of his riches. They're always breaking in to steal his gold and treasure, so merchant Karim hires guards to protect him." Jamina stops at the gate and a guard approaches.

"What is your business?" the guard asks Jamina.

"These two tourists have lost their way. I heard merchant Karim was hiring workers…"

What? Jamina's never said anything about you and Tracey working here. You shoot a worried glance at Tracey, but her eyes are glued to the guard's sharp sword.

"Ssh," she whispers.

She's probably right. It's best to stay quiet.

The guard looks over you and Tracey and says, "They look fit enough. Should be good workers. Follow me."

Jamina plods through the gate, following the guard. Once she's inside, she heads to the camel stables. After you dismount, the guard takes you through an arched doorway, down a wide corridor, to an enormous room.

A small man in yellow robes and blue headscarf greets you. "Aha, more workers?" He shakes hands with you and Tracey. "We have trouble with bandits attacking my home and preventing me from working with the poor," he says. "I need all the hands I can get. Are you willing to stay on as guards?"

"What would our duties be?" asks Tracey.

"Slingshots," answers the merchant. "We have long-range slingshots that shoot darts at the bandits' Land Rover tires, stopping them from attacking. We've found that young hands are much steadier at aiming slingshots than adults. What do you think?"

"We'll stay," says Tracey before you even have time to think, "if you can help us get home again."

"No problem. You've got a deal." Grinning, the merchant turns to his guards and they start a rapid conversation in Arabic.

You nudge Tracey, whispering, "Why did you agree to stay? You didn't even ask me."

"They have weapons," whispers Tracey. "We can always run away, if we want to."

Karim leads you out of the hallway and into the courtyard. "I'll take you to the training area so you can practice with slingshots," he says.

Before you get there, the massive gate to the compound slides open and a convoy of Land Rovers come inside. Drivers leap out of the vehicles and people rush from the building to help them unload their cargo.

"Ah, here are the supplies for my schools," says Karim. He disappears into the crowd to give a hand.

School supplies? No way. The boxes are labeled poison in large red letters, and skulls and crossbones are stamped on each one. "I don't trust him," you mutter to Tracey.

"Neither do I," she says. "It's now or never. Look, the gate is still open. Shall we make a run for it, or stay?"

It's time to make a decision. Do you:

Run away from the merchant and into the desert?**P226**

Or

Stay for slingshot training?**P340**

226

Run away from the merchant into the desert

"Let's go!" Grabbing Tracey's hand, you sneak towards the gate.

No one seems to notice you're leaving, not even the guards, who have come down from the wall to help unload the cargo. You both slip out the gate and run up the nearest dune.

"They'll see our tracks," says Tracey.

"Who cares? We just have to find a way back to Mystic Portal."

"How do we do that?" Tracey puffs as you head down the other side of the dune.

"Dunno, we'll think of something."

You race on into the desert, soon tiring. You share the last of the food and water from your backpacks, hiding behind a dune.

Tracey eyes the sun. "I've heard it's freezing in the desert at night," she says. "Do you have thermals with you?"

Tracey always thinks of good details when you plan a ride, so she'll have warm stuff with her. "Yeah, I usually bring extra gear when I go biking, but hopefully, we'll find a way home first."

"I'm tired," she says. "It's been a long day. Let's have a rest."

"Good idea. I'm bushed too." Using your backpacks as pillows, you both curl up on the sand and fall asleep.

A snort in your ear wakes you.

"Jamina? What are you doing here?"

"Merchant Karim sent me to save you. You'll die if you stay in the desert alone."

"But we want to get home to our families," says Tracey.

"He says if you come and help him, he'll help you get home. It's much better than dying here in the endless sand and heat."

You're parched and have no water left. Tracey nods. "Okay," you say. "We'll come and train to shoot slingshots, but after our first battle with the bandits we want to go home."

"Good," says Jamina. "Climb on my saddle and we'll get going."

Back at the compound, Karim welcomes you with open arms. "I

was terrified bandits would catch you in the desert," he says. "Help me defeat them and I will get you home."

You and Tracey agree, and he takes you both across the courtyard towards a training area.

The gates slide open, allowing more four-wheel-drive vehicles in. Once again, the guards rush down from the walls and people come into the courtyard to help unload the cargo. Again, the boxes are labeled poison, but the merchant pretends they're supplies for schools.

Tracey nudges you. "Do you trust him?" she asks. "The gates are open we could run away, or we could stay for slingshot training. What you want to do?"

It's time to make a decision. Do you:

Run away from the merchant into the desert? **P226**

Or

Stay for slingshot training? **P340**

Talk to the carpet politely

"Oh, wonderful carpet," you call. "We're so grateful to be your passengers."

Nothing happens. The carpet rips further. Your hands slip on the loose threads you're clutching. It's a huge drop to the desert sand below.

"Please!" you shout. "Please, let us back on board."

Before your eyes, the tear in the carpet knits together and the far end swings around and hits you and Tracey on your bottoms. Flying through the air, you land sprawled in the middle of a golden swirl on the carpet's green background.

Tracey thuds down beside you. She must be stunned, because she hardly says a word.

That was close, but thankfully, nice manners did the trick.

The carpet floats smoothly through the air, the desert's warm breeze caressing your face. You lie back and relax, staring at the brilliant blue sky.

Then Tracey moans, "Dumb carpet. Wouldn't listen to a word I did. Stupid thing."

Instantly, the carpet bucks beneath you.

"Told you that carpet's dumb," she screams. "I hate it!" The carpet tilts. She slides over the edge, her legs in mid air.

You grab hold of her hands. "Stop it! The carpet only listens when you're polite."

Her mouth hangs open and her eyebrows arch in astonishment. "W-what?"

She's getting heavier. Your arms ache from holding her. "You heard me. Oh great carpet, please forgive Tracey and let her back on board."

"Yes, please." Tracey's eyes light up. "I'm terribly sorry for my rudeness. I promise I won't do it again."

Tracey's side of the carpet lifts high into the air. She tumbles back on board, landing on top of you. She gasps, "Thank you, carpet. Thank you so much."

Was that faint tinkling sound the carpet laughing?

Grinning, you both lie back, gazing at the cloudless sky.

"This wasn't what I was expecting when we hit Camel Hump," Tracey says.

"Me neither. What a weird bike track. I had no idea Mystic Portal actually led to other worlds."

"Yeah, I guess each jump is some sort of portal," Tracey says. "Did you notice that the carpet is gold and green, just like my bike?"

"And the camel's saddle was the same colors as my bike."

"Intriguing."

After a while, faint noises float on the air. Sitting up, you spot some sand-red buildings and brightly-colored tents. "Look." You nudge Tracey.

"Some sort of settlement," she murmurs. "This should be interesting."

The carpet whisks you over the buildings, hovering above the tents. Below are striped awnings in all sorts of crazy color combinations. People sit on rugs with clay pots, food, crafts and trinkets spread out in front of them. Others are toasting peppers on metal skewers, the tantalizing aroma wafting through the air. Some are weaving. Children scamper between the stalls, laughing and calling to each other. Goats and camels are tethered on the far side of the marketplace. The bray of animals and the chatter of people bargaining rises above the busy market place.

"It's a bazaar," says Tracey.

"A what?"

"A Middle Eastern market. This is fantastic." She pats the carpet. "Thank you for bringing us here. Could we please get down?"

"Great that you asked politely," you say to her, "otherwise we'd be in for a bumpy landing."

The carpet drifts downwards and lands behind a tent. You and

230

Tracey get off. The mat rolls itself up and tucks itself under Tracey's arm, shrinking until it's only a foot long. It looks like a wall hanging now, not a carpet. Amazing.

"Absolutely awesome." Tracey pats the carpet. "Thank you very much."

"Are you Tracey?" You ask. "Or a polite alien in Tracey's body?"

Tracey mock punches your arm. "Thank you!"

You're making your way between the tents to the marketplace when a girl pops her head out of a tent flap. "Hello," she says in accented English, "is that a magic carpet?"

"Maybe," says Tracey, protectively tucking the carpet behind her back.

"Do you want to trade?" asks the girl. She ducks back into the tent and steps outside a moment later, holding a tarnished gold lamp. "This lamp is the home of a magic genie. If you polish it, the genie will grant you three wishes."

Wow, a genie! Three magic wishes! You could wish for anything you want, new bikes for all of you, a way to get home, and a custom-built mountain bike track in your own backyard.

Tracey's eyes are shining. No doubt she's imagining all the things she wants. "Do we each get three wishes?"

"Sure," says the girl.

"Hang on," barks Tracey. "If you can wish for anything you want, why don't you have a magic carpet already?"

"Um…" The girl's eyes slide away, and then she smiles, as if she's just come up with a good idea. "Because I've already used my wishes," she says, flashing her white teeth. "Now it's your turn. Do you want to trade the carpet for the lamp and genie?"

It's time to make a decision. Do you:

Trade the magic carpet for the lamp and genie? **P331**

Or

Keep the magic carpet and go to the bazaar? **P231**

Keep the magic carpet and go to the bazaar

You and Tracey glance at each other. There's something not quite right about what the girl said. "Um, no thanks," you say. "We need to go to the market."

"I can guide you around the bazaar and make sure no one rips you off," she says.

"Sure, that'll be great. I'm Tracey. What's your name?" asks Tracey.

"Daania."

"That's a pretty name," says Tracey, taking the girl's hand and heading towards the bazaar.

"It means beautiful." Daania says.

Even though Tracey's learned some manners on this trip, she's forgotten to introduce you. You trail behind them, your stomach rumbling as the scent of delicious food tickles your nostrils.

"Let's get something to eat," says Tracey.

"Just what I was thinking," you say. "What's good?"

Daania leads you to a stand. "This is my mother." A lady, wearing a brightly covered headscarf, smiles at you and thrusts some round bread towards you. "Her olive flatbread is the best in the bazaar. It's from my grandmother's secret recipe." Daania holds up flatbread smothered in olives and crumbly cheese. "I milk the goats and make the cheese myself."

"That's cool," you say.

"Cold?" asks Daania, obviously confused. "No, the milk is usually warm when it comes straight from the goat."

"Cool means good," you explain.

"Really? That's odd," she says.

"How much is the bread?" asks Tracey.

"As much bread as you can eat for a ride on your carpet," says Daania, eyeing the small mat still tucked under Tracey's arm.

Daania seems awfully keen on that carpet. Once she gets on it, who knows if she'll return.

Tracey must be thinking the same thing, because she says, "Let's all eat first, then go for a ride together once we've looked around.

"A good idea," says Daania, handing you the warm bread.

The goat's cheese is tangy and the flatbread is spicy, so Daania offers you both a drink of goat's milk, which tastes really strong.

Tracey wrinkles her nose as she drinks, but says, "Thank you."

You grin. This new polite Tracey is much better than the old Tracey, who was always fun, but often complained.

Munching on a handful of dates from Daania's mother, you and Tracey follow Daania around the bazaar, past rugs laden with nuts, seeds, dates, figs, olives and oranges. People wave and call out to you. A goat follows Tracey, butting her from behind.

"Stupid thing. Why is it butting me?"

"It likes you," says Daania. "If you ignore her, she'll keep butting your bottom. If you're nice to her, she'll stop."

Seems like there are a lot of lessons about being nice, here, in the desert. You try not to smile as Tracey bends down to pat the goat behind the ears. The animal bleats and licks Tracey's hand, then runs off between some tents.

"You've made a new friend," Daania says.

Tracey beams.

A man calls out, waving a beaded necklace and gesturing at bright strings of glass beads hanging under his yellow and red striped awning. "Nice for you," he calls to Tracey. "Nice necklet."

She smiles at his incorrect pronunciation and agrees. "Yes, very nice."

"You want to buy?"

"No thank you," she says politely.

Suddenly the roar of a motor fills the air. A Land Rover, with a red skull emblazoned on the bonnet, screeches through a gap in the tents. Churning up sand with its wheels, it races into the marketplace crushing produce and crafts and scattering people and animals. Men jump out of the vehicle, armed with long swords. One of them is splattered in pink paint.

Very odd.

"Bandits," says Daania urgently. "Quick, run!"

She tugs you and Tracey behind a tent and whirls to face Tracey. "The carpet. It's our only chance of escape."

Flinging the carpet onto the ground, Tracey says, "Please, carpet, help us get away."

The carpet unfurls, expanding to full size, and hovers just above the ground. The three of you leap on and take off past the tents. People are yelling, wailing and flinging pots and pans at the bandits. A chicken squawks, flapping past you.

Tracey ducks as a copper saucepan zips past her head. "Higher please, carpet, higher. We don't want them to hit you!"

Warm wind whistles past you as the carpet gains altitude, rising above the tents, zooming away from the hurly-burly of the bazaar and out over the desert.

"I fear for your safety if we return," says Daania. "These bandits create havoc and steal things, but they don't usually hurt us. I have heard that they sometimes kidnap foreigners to work in a factory. Up ahead is a way to get to your homeland, or we could return. What do you want to do?"

You glance at Tracey, but she just looks scared. "I dunno," she says in a small voice. "Up to you."

There's sand and blue sky ahead or bandits behind.

It's time to make a decision. Do you:

Fly the magic carpet straight ahead to get home? **P328**

Or

Return to the bazaar? **P307**

Bypass Camel Hump and go down the chicken line

"Not today, Tracey," you call, hoping she can hear you, even though she's out of sight. "I'm off to Ogre Jaws." Turning your handlebars, you go down the chicken line—the narrow trail leading around the jump that meets up with the main track further on

Even the chicken line is challenging, with gnarly roots and steep drops through tangled brush. Branches swipe at your face. You duck, just missing them. Twisting around a tree trunk and scraping under a branch, you spot the flash of Sidney's orange bike ahead of you.

He leaps a log, still making chicken noises, and lands with a thunk, zooming down the trail.

You crow like rooster, and jump the log too. If you're going to skip Camel Hump and be a chicken, you might as well be a funky chicken. You, Tracey and Sidney have always made a great game out of taking chicken lines. Not that Tracey takes them that often. With her new bike, she can conquer most jumps easily, and, you have to admit, she also has mean skills.

You shoot out onto the main track again. Sidney rounds the berm, disappearing around the corner. You follow. He rides over a small rise and gets air. You clear the jump by at least a yard.

"How much air did you get?" calls Sidney.

"About a half a yard," you yell, "but you easily got a whole yard."

"Yahoo!" he yells in triumph. "I'm taking the next jump."

After walking Mystic Portal, you know what's coming. You whizz around the corner, your back tire sliding in the dirt.

Sidney has stopped in the middle of the track.

You slam on your brakes and skid past him, churning up leaf litter and narrowly missing his bike. "Hey! Are you crazy? We nearly had a smash up." Your heart's pounding.

Sidney's staring at the track, shaking his head. "Something weird is going on."

"Yeah! You're trying to kill us!"

Frowning, Sidney points at the track. "Where's Dino Drop? It's disappeared."

He's right. When you walked down here recently, there was a giant redwood across the track, carved into a stegosaurus. To get to the drop, bikers had to go under the stegosaurus. But now it's gone.

"St-raaaange..." How could it have disappeared? "Perhaps someone took the stegosaurus away?" Even as you say it, you know that's not right, because the drop jump is no longer there.

"Do you think someone filled in the drop with dirt and covered it with dead leaves and pine needles?" Sidney sounds like he doesn't believe a word he's saying.

"Doubt it. Maybe we've just forgotten the track. It could be around the next corner." But all the times you've ridden with Sidney, he's always remembered every track—each jump, gap, corner, drop off and bridge. You shrug. "Nothing we can do, except keep riding."

"Yeah, I guess." He glances around again. "Where's Tracey? I haven't seen her since Camel Hump."

"Maybe she went down a different track."

"There wasn't a different track when we walked it," says Sidney, stubbornly. "How could there suddenly be one today?"

"Dunno," you reply. "This is really odd. Maybe she's ahead of us."

"Yeah, we'd better catch up." Sidney pushes off on his pedals and rides down the narrow trail.

Leaves flick into your face as the downhill track winds through a bushy area. The trail flattens, heading between groves of towering pines, then you face a short uphill climb. Legs pumping, you hammer the pedals, grunting as you mount the incline. You sigh in relief when you get to the crest. A whoosh of air escapes you as you zoom after Sidney down the hill.

Sidney breaks out of the trees and shoots over a pile of bark chips onto a grassy slope. The next huge jump is visible at the end of the clearing, just before the trail enters the forest again. A crudely painted sign sticks out of the grass: *Ogre Jaws*. It's a gap jump. The first dirt

236

ramp will spit you into the air above a pit of jagged chunks of old porcelain, shaped like monster's teeth. You have to clear the toothy gap and land your bike on the downward ramp on the other side. On either side of the downward ramp are huge mosaic eyes, like an ogre's. Whoever designed this jump has a wild imagination.

With a whoop, Sidney races up the ramp and is airborne, high above the jagged teeth. In a flash of red, he disappears, vanishing in midair like Tracey did.

Freaky.

Maybe you should follow him and see what happens. Maybe you'll have a great adventure, but it looks dangerous. Something could go wrong. Who knows where Sidney is. And Tracey. You haven't seen her since Camel Hump.

In a moment you'll be at the turn off to the chicken line.

It's time to make a decision. Do you:

Hit Ogre Jaws? **P237**

Or

Bypass Ogre Jaws and go down the chicken line? **P269**

Hit Ogre Jaws

Moments after deciding to take the jump, you're airborne, high above those menacing porcelain teeth. Wind rushes into your face, making you grin. It'll be no problem to clear the jump and land on the other side. You brace yourself for landing.

But that's not what happens.

Suddenly, the earth cracks open like an enormous mouth and a long red tongue whips out from between Ogre Jaws. The tongue wraps itself around the bike frame and your leg, and yanks you downwards.

The tongue releases you, leaving a slimy trail of goo over your leg. Gripping your handlebars, you plummet through darkness. With a soft whump, you land. That's odd, your bike seems to bend as it lands, as if it's made of rubber, not steel. Weird, because your suspension isn't that good and normally rattles your bones during landings.

Your bike keeps moving forwards through the dark, although the sound of its tires has changed. Something fluffy tickles your legs. You take a hand off the handlebars, and touch the frame. *It's fluffy*. Perhaps some mossy tree roots got stuck around the bike as you fell. You feel along the frame and up the stem towards the handlebars. Nope, not roots. Definitely fluffy.

Your bike goes over a lump in the ground and lurches. Green light beams out from your headlamp illuminating a dirt tunnel festooned with tree roots. Wait, your headlamp emits white light, not green. And it's in your backpack, not mounted on your bike.

Goosebumps break out on your arms and a cold trickle of sweat runs down your neck. Something creepy is going on. Where's Sidney?

"Sidney!" you holler.

The bike trills beneath you. "What is Sidney?"

What? The bike's talking to you? "H-he's m-my friend," you stutter.

"Aha, the other human!" a chirpy voice replies. "I think Bog the ogre got him."

"Bog the ogre?" Your voice shakes as you answer. Your bike is talking to you. Are you going mad?

The green light swivels from side to side, as if it's searching for something. Light catches on the handlebars which aren't handlebars at all. You're holding horns protruding from an orange furry head.

You're riding a one-eyed monster that beams green light from its eye.

Swallowing hard, you try to speak, but only a squeak comes out. "Eep."

"Bog likes human-toast for breakfast," sings the monster, still racing along the dark tunnel with its bright-green eye beam flickering over the walls. "He plunges a fork through the middle of the human and toasts it over fire. Says it's his favorite snack. Can't say I've ever tried human, but, then again, I'm vegetarian."

"G-glad to hear you're v-vegetarian," you reply. "P-please, wh-who are you?"

"I am Sharmeena, a track-keeper," the furry creature replies. "Track-keepers look after Mystic Portal."

"Wh-where are we g-going?"

"Why, to rescue your friend," says the track-keeper. "What was his name? Sidney?"

"Um, yeah, Sidney." You try to swallow the lump in your throat again, but it won't budge.

"You do want to save your friend, don't you?" she chirps.

Of course you do, but you'll have to face an ogre that toasts kids for breakfast! "Um… sure."

"You don't sound that sure," says the track-keeper. "If you want, I can save him myself, and leave you here, but if you choose that, I can't guarantee your safety."

It's time to make a decision. Do you:

Go with Sharmeena to save Sidney from Bog the ogre?**P239**

Or

Stay in the tunnel on your own? **P241**

Go with Sharmeena to save Sidney from Bog the ogre

"Of course I'll save Sidney," you reply. "He's a good friend. I'd never let him down."

"Hold on tight," calls Sharmeena.

She races down the tunnel, leaping over tree roots and flying through the air. This track-keeper is as good as a mountain bike—except she has four legs and you have no control over where you're going.

"Bog's lair is in a cave along here," Sharmeena says. "Keep your eyes peeled, in case we miss the entrance."

Wrapping your arms around her neck, you lean low with your chin on the track-keeper's head, peering out over the orange fur between her horns. The eerie green light from Sharmeena's eye flashes over the walls. Her hooves thud along the ground.

"There's an opening ahead," you call in a hoarse whisper, pointing at a yellow glow coming from a fissure in the tunnel wall.

Sharmeena slows and creeps along the passage, hugging the walls. Rumbling drifts down the tunnel, getting louder as you approach the cave entrance. The light from the track-keeper's eye dims, until you're plunged into darkness, except for that unusual yellow light ahead.

Your heart thuds. Sharmeena cranes her neck around the wall and you peer into the mouth of the cave. In the yellow glow of a lantern, an enormous ogre with a red Mohawk lies stretched on the floor his snores rumbling through the cave—Bog.

Behind Bog, in a flimsy-looking cage, is Sidney.

Sidney's eyes light up when he sees you, but he holds a finger to his lips, cautioning you to be quiet, and points at Bog with his other hand.

Still riding Sharmeena, you creep into Bog's lair, around the sleeping ogre. A stench wafts from Bog's feet, making you pinch your nose. Foot odor deluxe. No way you want to breathe that in.

When you're out of the stink-zone, near Sidney's cage, you hop off your new orange-furred friend.

"Boy, am I glad to see you," Sidney whispers. "Can you get me out of here?"

"This is my friend Sharmeena, a track-keeper. We've come to rescue you," you whisper. "These bars don't look very strong. We should be able to bend them in no time."

The track-keeper turns her single luminous-green eye towards you. Her pupil is a swirling spiral, which focuses on you, as she leans over and whispers, "Be careful. The bars are trickier than they look."

"Bog told me the bars were dangerous," says Sidney. "He used a key on one of these." He points at a row of locks on the door of the cage.

"Fat lot of good a key will do us, if Bog has it," you say, reaching for the bars. "I don't want to wake him up."

"No. Listen!" Sidney says. "That gold thing glinting under his head is the key. All you have to do is move his head while he's sleeping and slide the key out. Then I'm free. No risk, that way, see? Not like the bars."

"No risk?" you hiss. "What about my hand while I'm trying to move his head? Or my arm? I quite like having hands, thanks. I'll take my chances with the bars."

Sharmeena flicks her orange tail back and forth like a wary cat. "The bars are dangerous," she says. "Be careful."

"Why? What happens when you try to bend them?"

"Whenever humans touch the bars, they're never the same again," the track-keeper says. The spiral in the middle of her eye swirls faster, as if she's panicking.

It's time to make a decision. Do you:

Try to use Bog's key? **P242**

Or

Bend the bars to free Sidney? **P261**

Stay in the tunnel on your own

The tunnel is creepy, but being pierced with a fork and toasted has got to be worse.

Yawning loudly, you stretch. "Um, I'm quite tired. Perhaps I should rest here, while you save Sidney."

That should sort things out nicely. Sidney will be saved by Sharmeena and you won't risk your life facing Bog.

The track-keeper stops suddenly, throwing you headfirst over her horns into a heap on the tunnel floor.

You slam into a mass of tree roots. "Ow! What did you do that for?"

Sharmeena turns her gaze on you in a flood of green light. Her eye is luminous green with a swirling spiral at the centre. "Are you sure you want to me to save him and leave you here?" There's a touch of scorn in her voice.

It's time to make a decision. Do you:

Go with Sharmeena to save Sidney from Bog the ogre? **P239**

Or

Stay in the tunnel? **P241**

Try to use Bog's key

"If I get hurt touching the bars then we're both stuck, so I'm going to try the key."

"Good idea." Sidney sighs in relief. "If you touched them, I was worried something awful would happen."

Sharmeena nods. "You would've have transformed into a creature. Most humans react badly when it happens."

"Thanks for warning me." You grin. "I'm quite happy as a human."

Bog gives a loud splutter in his sleep, then his rumbling snores continue to echo around the cave. The golden key glints under his left ear.

"The key's right under Bog's head. If I touch him, he'll wake up and eat us." You scratch your head. "There's got to be another way. Can you think of anything, Sidney?"

"You could tickle him so he moves," suggests Sidney, "then snatch the key."

"And get snapped up in those giant jaws when he wakes up?" You shake your head. "No way. But you're right, we need him to move so I can grab it."

Bog farts. A creeping purple haze spreads from beneath his bottom out along the floor. A rotten-egg stench threatens to overwhelm you.

"Whatever you do, do it quick." Sharmeena coughs. "Those farts are toxic. I can't stand them much longer."

The ogre's belly grumbles in his sleep. He's hungry. You have to move fast before he wakes up for toasted Sidney.

Bog's stomach growls again, like a prowling tiger.

That's it! You can use his hunger! You snatch a cookie out of your backpack and approach Bog's head.

"That'll never work," says Sidney. "He's way too hungry to only eat a cookie. If you wake him, he'll just snap down the cookie, and then have us for main course."

Sharmeena pipes up, "And me for desert."

You place your finger on your lips to hush your friends. Leaning over Bog's head, you hold the chocolate chip cookie above his nose.

"Snaarrck." Bog gives an enormous snore.

You twitch, dropping the cookie in surprise.

With fingers like lightning, you snatch it before it hits Bog's face—luckily, your reflexes are fast.

The scent of chocolate chip wafts towards you. Bog's nostrils flare, quivering as he takes in the aroma. Gradually, you move the cookie towards his right ear. Bog turns his head, his nose following the delicious scent.

The stem of the giant key is poking out from under Bog's head. You grasp the stem with your left hand, but it won't budge. You'll have to move the cookie further so Bog will move his head and free the key. Leaning over Bog's face, you stretch your arm as far as you can.

Oh, no, your sleeve brushes his nose!

Bog snorts and rolls his head, trapping your left hand. Oily green wax dribbles out of Bog's ear, running onto your hand and the floor. Blech! It stinks. Odd brown blobs fleck the greasy wax. Ooh, gross, they're dead insects. You wrinkle your nose.

Gently, you try to remove your hand. Bog snarls in his sleep. There's no way you can pull your hand out, or you'll wake him.

In his cage, Sidney grimaces and his eyes grow wide. The track-keeper steps towards the cave wall and seems to melt against the rock until she disappears. Cool magic, but how are you and Sidney going to escape this mess?

You could yell and startle Bog so he moves, and then dash out of the cave—but that would leave Sidney with an angry ogre. Or you could try with the cookie again.

Leaning over Bog's head again, you dangle the cookie in front of his nose. As soon as his nostrils twitch, you move the cookie away. His nose and head follow. In moments, you've pulled your sticky hand out from under his head. The golden key is safe in your grip.

You yank the cookie away, but Bog lets out a vicious snarl and his eyelids flutter. Beads of sweat break out on your forehead. In a desperate move, you toss the cookie into his mouth and dash over to Sidney's cage. Munching in his sleep, Bog finishes the cookie in seconds, then starts snoring again.

"Phew, that was close," whispers Sidney. "Which lock?"

The track-keeper's orange fur gradually emerges from the rock. "How did you do that?" Sidney asks her. "You disappeared."

"It's just camouflage," she replies.

"Just?" says Sidney. "Imagine the tricks we could play on Tracey, using camouflage like that on our bike tracks."

"Stop fooling around." You wave the key. "Which lock does this key work on?"

"Dunno," says Sidney.

Your heart is still pounding. You've just risked your life. "Not helpful," you snap.

The track-keeper interrupts before the two of you start a full-on argument. "The keys works on all the locks, but only one will open the cage. The rest are enchanted."

That news makes you want to scream, but you don't dare—you might wake Bog.

"Look this one has a lightning show going on." Sidney points at a silver lock with traces of blue light flickering across its surface.

Sharmeena backs away from it. "That's a powerful enchantment." Her eye swirls.

"This one's got camels on it," you point at a brass lock with tiny engraved camels around the base.

"And that one has dolphins," says Sharmeena, nodding at a lock encrusted with green, as if it's been pulled out of a sunken ship.

"What about this rusty old lock?" you ask. "Did he use this one when he locked you up?

"Sorry," Sidney says. "I don't know. He threw me into the cage and locked it up before I had a chance to see."

It's time to make a decision. Which of the four locks will you try with the key?

Try the silver lock with blue flashes running across it? **P246**

Try the brass lock engraved with camels? **P247**

Try the green-encrusted lock with dolphins on it? **P250**

Or

Try the plain rusty lock? **P253**

246

Try the silver lock with blue flashes running across it

"This one looks the most exciting." You grab the lock. A buzz shoots through your fingers. You drop it, shaking your hand.

"What?" says Sidney. "Did it hurt you."

"Not really. It just gave me a fright."

Sharmeena nudges your elbow with her nose, her eye whirling rapidly. "Careful."

You grip the lock again. A buzz runs through your hand, making your arm will tingle all the way to your elbow. There's no way you're letting magic get the better of you. You have to free Sidney. It takes a moment to get used to the weird sensation running up your arm.

"You okay?" Sidney's eyes are doing that wide thing again. He looks like he has a couple of saucers in his head instead of eyeballs.

"Yeah, I'm fine." Well, almost.

You raise the key towards the lock, but before you insert it, blue light zaps between the lock and the key, crackling, and making your other hand buzz and your ears tingle. You gasp, but hold the lock and key firm.

"Watch out!" calls Sidney. "You have blue sparks in your hair."

It's time to make a decision. Do you:

Go ahead despite the sparks? **P289**

Or

Choose a different lock? **P260**

Try the brass lock engraved with camels

"This one looks interesting." You finger the heavy brass lock.

"I like camels," says Sidney. "We should try it."

Behind you, the ogre groans in his sleep and turns over.

If only Bog had rolled over before—you could have snatched the key without getting your hand covered in greasy earwax.

"Be quick," says Sharmeena.

As you bring the key towards the lock, your skin grows warm. Sweat beads upon your forehead, as if you're sunbathing on a baking summer's day. Something snorts.

You whirl. But only Bog and the track-keeper are behind you. "What was that?"

"Sounded like a camel," said Sidney. "I heard one at the zoo last week and it was just the same."

Turning the lock over, you examine it. You could swear the position of the camels has changed. Surely they were walking in a straight line around the bottom of the lock before? Now they're heading upwards, towards the keyhole. "Look. Has this changed?"

Sidney peers at the lock. "Maybe. Nah, that's not possible." He blows out his breath in frustration. "Dunno. Are you going to get me out of here?"

"Hurry, Bog will be awake soon." Sharmeena's eye whirls. She's worried.

It's time to make a decision. Do you:

Turn the key in the camel lock? **P248**

Or

Choose a different lock? **P260**

Turn the key in the camel lock

The warm sunny sensation that this lock radiates sure beats waiting in an underground tunnel with an ogre who wants to eat you.

"Let's go for it." You shrug. "We've got nothing to lose."

"Famous last words," says Sidney as you turn the key in the lock.

In a flash of blinding white light, you and Sidney are suddenly back on Mystic Portal on your bikes.

"Thanks," calls Sidney, "I couldn't have got away from Bog without you."

"All good," you call.

Tracey is further down the track in front of you. Sidney races behind her on his hard tail. Sharmeena is galloping along next to you as you ride.

"It's been great meeting you." She grins. "Well done saving Sidney from Bog. But now I have to go. Track maintenance is calling."

"Bye," you call.

Her orange fur flashes between the trees, and then she's gone.

Track maintenance? What did she mean? Surely she's not the mysterious Mystic Portal track builder? How could a four-legged creature hold a spade, carve trees or sculpt rock? You pedal hard to catch up with the others.

Tracy takes a corner and Sidney follows. You zip around the corner, then speed down the track.

Ahead, the trail splits in two. It looks familiar. Deja vu! There's that makeshift sign with the badly painted camel that you saw at the beginning of the track.

"I'm taking Camel Hump," calls Tracey.

"I'm taking the chicken line!" Sidney clucks like a chicken, then turns left to bypass the jump. He disappears into the trees.

Tracey swings to the right. "Woohoo! Camel Hump, here I come." Her bike crunches through gravel on way down the hill to the jump. "Coming?" she calls. She wooshes up the steep reddish rise of Camel

Hump. Her bike flies into the air. She disappears.

No, that can't be right. You must be mistaken. She must've landed beyond your line of vision.

You're nearly at the fork in the trail. To your right is Camel Hump. To your left is the way out—the chicken line.

It's time to make a decision. You have 3 choices. Do you:

Go back and choose another lock? **P260**

Hit Camel Hump? **P205**

Or

Bypass Camel Hump and go down the chicken line? **P234**

250

Try the green-encrusted lock with dolphins on it

"Try that one," suggests Sidney. "It looks interesting."

"I think so too." You reach out and cradle the chunky lock in your hand. It's heavy. Bits of green debris break off, revealing engravings of seahorses, turtles and more dolphins.

"Very beautiful." Sharmeena peers over your shoulder. "A good choice."

"It's like an underwater world," you murmur.

You insert the key in the lock. Cold washes over you. Your ears are filled with the whoosh of the sea.

"What's that?" Sidney's eyes are huge again.

"Could you hear it too?"

"I did as well," says the track-keeper.

Behind you, Bog yawns and stretches in his sleep.

"Quick, he's waking up. Get me out of here. Please," Sidney begs.

It's time to make a decision. Do you:

Turn the key in the dolphin lock? **P251**

Or

Choose a different lock? **P260**

Turn the key in the dolphin lock

Bog stirs, rolling over and muttering.

"Quick," whispers Sharmeena. "Now."

You turn the key in the dolphin lock. The whooshing grows, vibrating in your ears. Your vision goes blue. The cage door flies open and all three of you are propelled through the air.

Bog leaps to his feet, roaring, "No! My toast is running away!"

In a flash of blue light, Bog and the tunnels disappear.

You and Sidney are on your bikes going down Mystic Portal, with Sharmeena running beside you.

"Congratulations on choosing a good lock," she calls, veering off the track. "Now that you're safe from Bog, I have to go. Track maintenance is calling."

"Bye," you call, as her orange fur disappears into the trees.

"Track maintenance? Is that what track-keepers do?" asks Sidney.

"Hey, there's Tracey. Let's catch up with her."

You race down the track behind Tracey and Sidney and come to a loop heading across a stream. You pass a sign: *Dolphin Slide.*

"Great to see you guys," yells Tracey. "Let's jump!" She zips up a rock shaped like a dolphin, and leaps off the top, over the stream. Tracey and her bike disappear.

"Here we go again," calls Sidney. His bike sploshes through a puddle, up the rock. He jumps and vanishes.

Your tires hiss against the wet rock as you shoot up over Dolphin Slide.

In a flash of blue light, the trail and trees are gone. You're riding on a dolphin through the ocean. Sidney and Tracey are riding dolphins too. The sun slants through the watery blue. An orange octopus floats past, waving its tentacles, then disappears into a mass of green seaweed nestled in a bank of colorful coral. Light wink among the coral, casting a yellow glow. What are they? Underwater glow worms?

"Wow," says Tracey. "Can you believe this? It's incredible."

252

"Hey, we can talk underwater." Bubbles rise from Sidney's mouth as he speaks. "And breathe."

"Amazing. What's next?" you ask.

"I thought you'd never ask," says the dolphin you're riding on.

"Squee," replies Tracey's dolphin, "let's tell them."

Talking dolphins? Wow.

"Welcome to the underwater portion of Mystic Portal," your dolphin says. "My name is Squee, leader of this pod. We're your hosts, today, but you won't just be riding us. In order to get back to Mystic Portal, you need to compete in a race or take a tour. You can choose to ride seahorses in the Round the Coral Peninsula Extravaganza race, or go by turtleback on a Terrific Turtle Tour and see all the underwater sights."

"Cool." Bubbles tickle your nose as you speak. "What do you guys want to do?"

Sidney's eyes are shining. "I'm all for racing. The Round the Coral Peninsula Extravaganza by seahorse is for me."

Tracey's grinning. "I've always wanted to dive, so I'm going on a Terrific Turtle Tour to see all the underwater sights."

"Sounds good," says Squee, swimming under a coral bridge. "What will it be for you?"

It's time to make a decision. Do you:

Ride a seahorse in the Round the Coral Peninsula Extravaganza? **P272**

Or

Ride a turtle on a Terrific Turtle Tour? **P281**

Try the plain rusty lock

The dolphin lock, camel lock and the lock that's flashing electric blue all look like they're enchanted. Maybe it's safer to go with a normal-looking rusty lock. But it wouldn't harm to inspect them all again before you try.

You raise your key, hovering over the electric blue lock. A tingle goes up your arm. Is that a good sign? Hard to tell.

As you touch the dolphin lock, your body goes cold and roaring fills your ears. Odd.

Your fingers graze the camel lock, and you instantly feel warm.

When you handle the rusty lock, nothing happens.

"I think I'll go for this one," you tell Sidney, putting your key into the rusty keyhole. Flakes of orange rust fall to the floor, the same shade as the track-keeper's fur.

Bog groans in his sleep.

"Quick," Sharmeena says, "I think he's waking up."

Sidney shakes his head. "The rusty one is the plainest of all. Surely Bog wouldn't have chosen normal lock to keep me in here. He must've used one of the enchanted ones."

Bog's murmuring. You must be quick.

It's time to make a decision. Do you:

Turn the key in the rusty lock? **P254**

Or

Choose a different lock? **P260**

Turn the key in the rusty lock

Bog snarls in his sleep. His eyes are still closed, but at this rate, they won't be for long.

With a flick of your wrist, you turn the key in the lock, but it's stuck and won't turn the whole way.

"It's jammed," you whisper. "I can't turn it."

"It can't be the right lock then," Sidney says. "Hurry up, choose another one."

Bog stomach rumbles. "Hungry, hungry," he mutters in his sleep. "Make toast."

You twist the key again, but it won't budge. "It's too stiff. If I only I had some oil..."

Bog thrashes on the floor, then stretches and burps.

Maybe, just maybe, the ogre's grossness could be useful.

In a shower of rusty flakes, you yank the key out of the lock and race over to Bog. Bending, you dip the key in the patch of his greasy earwax. As you run back to the cage, the gold key shines in the lantern light, slick with oil.

"This should do the trick." You jam the key into the lock and turn it. Stuck. Again.

"Try again." Sharmeena urges.

Sidney's breath is rasping. His eyes are fixed on Bog, who lets out a giant fart that makes Sharmeena cough.

"Wassat?" Bog mutters in his sleep.

You jiggle the key in the lock, trying to turn it. It clanks against the bars.

"My toast!" Bog's bellow makes you jump.

"He's awake." Sidney's pale and trembling. "Run. Save yourselves," he hisses.

Frantically, you give the key one last twist. The lock springs open. Sidney's cage door swings ajar. He scrambles out of the cage, knocking you over.

"Hop on," cries Sharmeena.

Sidney leaps upon her back and reaches down, pulling you up to sit in front of him.

"No! Mine!" Bog roars, "I want toast!" He shoots a jet of flame from his jaws towards you.

Sharmeena springs through the air above the flame, with you and Sidney clinging to the fur on her back.

But Bog dashes to the entrance, blocking it with his enormous body. His loincloth swings as he stamps his foot. "Not fair! I'm hungry!" His bellows make the cave shake. A rock falls from the ceiling, narrowly missing you, showering you with dirt. "My food." He waves an angry arm at Sidney and opens his mouth, about to blast you with flame.

You have to think fast. "Stop, Bog."

He stares at you, startled.

There must be something you can do to stop him from making toast out of you all.

"I'm scared," Sidney whispers. He's squeezing your waist so tight, he's making something in your backpack crinkle.

That's it! Your backpack.

"Bog, you're hungry, right?"

"Yes, eat toast." A tendril of smoke curls from his lips. He smiles. "Eat toast. Two human toasts. Now." He opens his mouth wide, showing a great set of teeth.

"Bog, have you ever tried potato chips?" you ask. "They're much tastier than human toast." You click your fingers and hold them up above your shoulder. Sidney unzips your backpack and passes you a packet of potato chips.

You open them and hold them out to Bog.

Warily he approaches, sniffing the air. He snatches the pack and tosses the chips into his open mouth, wrapper and all.

"Yucky," he snarls, spitting out bits of wrapper. "Human tricked me."

"Peanut butter and jelly?"

Sidney shoves your sandwich into your hands. Unwrapping it first, you smile and hold it on your extended palm.

This time Bog approaches, snarling and gnashing his teeth. "If this no good, I blast you all." Bog stomps back to the entrance with the sandwich, sniffing it with narrowed eyes.

Holding your breath, you watch Bog nibble your sandwich.

Behind you, Sidney's rummaging in his backpack. He taps your shoulder and passes you his own peanut butter and jelly sandwich.

"Hold on tight," whispers Sharmeena. "We'll make a run for it. Keep your faces down so he doesn't burn them."

Bog swallows your sandwich. His eyes light up. He beams at you. "Much better than human toast," he says. "You give me more, I let you go." His eyes land on Sidney's sandwich in your hand. He licks his lips.

"Not so fast, Bog," you say.

"Why not?" hisses Sidney in your ear. "Let's get out of here."

Bog eyes up Sidney's sandwich. "Want it, NOW." He's about to have an ogre-sized tantrum. He could cause a cave in. You could all be buried alive.

"If I give you this sandwich and teach the track-keepers how to make you more peanut butter and jelly, do you promise not to hurt them anymore?"

"Never wanted hurt them," says Bog. "Just hungry. Very grumpy when hungry.

"Really? Is that all?" Sharmeena says. "We track-keepers never realized. We'd be happy to feed you peanut butter and jelly when you're hungry. But please, let us know before you're starving and grumpy."

"No problem." Bog toasts the last piece of Sidney's sandwich with a puff of flame. He pops it in his mouth, then burps. "Thanks for feeding me," he says. "See you soon."

He waves as Sharmeena leaps through the cave entrance back into the tunnel with you and Sidney on her back.

Away from Bog's lantern, the tunnel is pitch black. Sharmeena lights the way with the green beam from her eye. Soon she's racing along the tunnel, leaping up the sides and bounding back down to the floor again.

"This beats any mountain bike ride," calls Sidney, still clutching your waist.

"It's awesome," you reply. "Mystic Portal's my new favorite trail."

You race along the tunnel for a few minutes, your adrenaline pumping and the breeze rushing into your face. Sharmeena skids to a halt. There's a fork in the tunnel.

"Thank you for helping us with Bog," she says. "Hopefully he won't trouble us again, except when he needs peanut butter and jelly. I'd like to thank you by throwing a party in your honor. But maybe you're tired. If you want, you can have a rest in our library and read some adventure books, then join us later at the party when you're ready."

"What do you want, Sidney?"

"I'm fine either way," he says. "It's up you."

It's time to make a decision. Do you:

Go to the library and read before you go to the party? **P258**

Or

Go to the track-keeper party now?**P334**

Go to the library and read

"Some quiet time would be great." You climb off Sharmeena's back. "I'd love to read for a while, then come to the party after."

A soft glow shines from the left passage.

"It's only short way to the library," says Sharmeena. "When you're done, I'll bring you to the party."

"Thanks, I'd love that. What about you, Sidney?"

"I'll stick with you."

"I'll gather everyone for your party. See you soon." Sharmeena bounds down the tunnel.

A few moments later, you and Sidney enter the library. It's rather small, with a single shelf of books that all look similar.

Sidney settles onto a large cushion and falls asleep. He must be worn out after his ordeal with Bog.

A track-keeper gestures to the shelf. "Read as long as you like, and call me if you need anything."

Wandering over to the shelf, you investigate the contents. All the books are You Say Which Way adventures. There are many different titles to choose from. You see one about starships, another about dolphins, there's a dangerous delivery service, and even a magician's house.

It is time to make a decision. You do:

Read *Deadline Delivery*? **P1**

Read *Stranded Starship*? **P95**

Read *Danger on Dolphin Island*? **P365**

Read *In the Magician's House*? **P465**

Or do you:

Change your mind and go to the track keepers' party? **P334**

Change your mind and go to the track-keeper's party

It's time to find out how the track-keeper's are going. You shake Sidney.

Sidney stretches and yawns. "Is it time to go to the party?"

"Yeah."

He stands up. "Sounds good to me."

Sharmeena prances through the door. "Ready?"

You nod. "Good timing."

"Great, hop on."

Go to the party **P334**

260

Choose a different lock

It's time to make a decision. Which of the four locks do you want to try this time?

Try the silver lock with blue flashes running across it? **P246**

Try the brass lock engraved with camels? **P247**

Try the green-encrusted lock with dolphins on it? **P250**

Or

Try the plain rusty lock? **P253**

Bend the bars to free Sidney

Bog is still snoring, his warty lips parting to show big teeth when he inhales. As he breathes out, his lips flap like a grandmother's knickers on a washing line. You stifle a snort, until you glimpse another flash of his fangs.

You shudder. "No thanks, I'm not disturbing Bog for the key. He looks way too nasty to tangle with."

You grab the bars of Sidney's cage. A strange tingle goes through your fingers. Weird. You shake your hands and re-grip the bars. There's that tingling sensation again. Ignoring it, you strain with all your might, gritting your teeth and using all your force. The bars start to bend as you force them apart. A soft grunt escapes you.

"Ssh," says Sidney, glancing at Bog, who is stirring in his sleep.

Shaking your hands, you gasp for breath. "Just a little more."

The track-keeper shuffles from hoof to hoof, as if she'd rather be elsewhere.

This time when you grip the bars, your hands start to itch, but you've no time to worry about that, because Bog moans in his sleep and tosses and turns.

"Quick," whispers Sidney.

An enormous fart ruptures from Bog's bottom, and a cloud of purple smelly fog fills the cave. The stench makes your nose itch and eyes water. You stifle a cough and get back to work. Bog could wake up at any moment.

The itching on your hands intensifies, but you ignore it and strain to pull the bars apart until there's a gap wide enough for Sidney to escape.

The moment your drop your hands from the bars, orange fur sprouts from the back of them and spreads along your fingers. Your arms start itching and soon they're furry too. The itch travels over your body, up your neck and face, and down your legs, until you're covered in orange fur. A green beam of light shoots from the middle of your face, shining on Sidney as he clambers out of the cage.

"Wow," he says. "What a great disguise. You look just like our furry track-keeper, here." He gestures at Sharmeena, who is grinning.

Great disguise? Sidney must be joking. This is terrible. You're covered in orange fur, have four legs and only have one eye.

"I told you the bars are enchanted," says Sharmeena. "The only other human that touched them turned into a track-keeper too."

"Not fair. I want to be a track-keeper too," announces Sidney. "Just in case Bog wakes up. There's no way I want to end up as human toast." He rubs his hands up and down the bars until fur starts growing up his arms. It quickly spreads to the rest of the body. Then his head morphs and one giant eye appears in the middle of his face with a grinning mouth underneath. "So cool," he yells.

"No! You'll wake—"

Too late!

With a roar, Bog leaps to his feet. "Where's my toast?" He bellows in a voice that makes the walls of the cave shake.

"Run," calls the Sharmeena, and takes off out the cave door.

With a giant leap, you bound after her with Sidney at your heels.

Your powerful track-keeper legs propel you through the air, yards at a time, like a mountain bike taking a gap jump. This is incredible. Your eye paints the dark tunnel in a green glow, as you chase Sharmeena.

"Amazing," calls Sidney. Then he yelps in pain.

The stench of singed fur fills your nostrils. Behind Sidney, Bog belches fire.

"Come on, Sidney," you yell. "Let's hoof it!"

Sidney gallops up beside you. Together you take off, speeding along the winding tunnel. You belt around a corner and nearly crash into Sharmeena, who is standing staring at the wall. The green beam from her eye is focused, unwavering, on one spot.

"Hurry up," you urge her. "Bog's got flambéed track-keeper on his mind. I don't want to be next on his menu."

Bog's roars make the air pulsate around you.

Sharmeena stands motionless, staring at the wall, as if she's hypnotized. As if she can't hear you. Or Bog.

Sidney tugs at her fur with his mouth, trying to pull her along the tunnel, but she's frozen to the spot.

"Come on," you yell. You can't leave her here for Bog to eat. Not after she helped you.

The glow of Bog's flickering flames dances in the shadows around the corner. He's coming.

"Sidney! What shall we do?" Panic stricken, you turn towards Sidney, but now he's focusing his eye beam on exactly the same spot as Sharmeena. They're both standing still, ignoring the danger.

"Are you two crazy?"

You shoot one last terrified glance backwards. A jet of flame shoots around the corner. Any moment, Bog will be here.

You can't leave Sidney and Sharmeena behind, but you're terrified. Your legs tense to run as one of Bog's giant feet stomps around the corner, making the tunnel floor shake.

"Sidney! Sharmeena!"

Then you notice what they're doing. The beams of green light from Sidney and Sharmeena's eyes are cutting through the rock at the side of the tunnel, like lasers. Maybe they are lasers. Concentrating, you focus your green light on their hole in the rock.

Bog's roars fill your ears. You cringe as a surge of heat blasts along the tunnel, but you stand fast, staring at the rock, your combined laser beams melting a narrow passage through the hard stone.

Bog's flames are getting closer. The heat is nearly unbearable. A spark of pain shoots through your tail. "Ow!" The stink of singed fur hangs in the air.

Gritting your teeth, you send a surge of energy through your eye. Your laser beam blasts through the hole, shattering the last piece of rock standing between you and freedom. Daylight pours through the hole.

"Run!" yells Sharmeena. She shoves you through the hole and leaps in after you.

A moment later, the tunnel behind you is engulfed in flame.

"Quick. To the surface," she yells. "Or he'll burn us alive in this passage."

Your track-keeper legs frantically scramble through the passage. Sidney's breath rasps in your ears. He pushes you forward. Bursting out above ground, you collapse in an exhausted heap, your tail still throbbing where Bog burned it.

Sidney scuttles out behind you and slumps to the ground. Sharmeena climbs out of the tunnel, a lick of flame chasing her. But instead of sprawling on the ground next to you, she kicks dirt down the narrow passage.

Leaping back to your feet, you call to Sidney, "Come on, let's help."

With your strong hind legs, you and Sidney join the track-keeper, kicking dirt until your escape hatch is blocked.

Sharmeena grins. "That should stop Bog for now."

Sidney's pupil whirls with excitement. "Awesome. We filled the hole so fast, it's almost like our hooves are purpose made for digging."

Sharmeena laughs. "They are. We dig all the time. It's part of our job."

Her job? What's she talking about?

"Come on," she says, "I have something to show you. But first, let's get have a drink. That was thirsty work."

You and Sidney reach for your backpacks to grab your bottles, but you don't have arms and you're no longer wearing your backpacks because you're track-keepers. Glancing at each other, you burst out laughing.

"Jase was right, Mystic Portal is a really strange experience," says Sidney.

Grinning at him, you follow the track-keeper through the forest to a stream.

Once you've all slurped up some water, you sit in the stream until your tail is nice and cool again. You climb out onto the bank and shake yourself like a dog.

"Now," says Sharmeena, "you can either become human again and keep riding Mystic Portal on your bikes, or you can stay a while longer and help me build some new jumps."

"So you're the mysterious trail builder?" asks Sidney.

"Yes, it's not just me though. There are many other track-keepers that help."

You smile. "That's generous of you to build trails for us."

"We build them for ourselves. We love doing the jumps and racing each other downhill." Sharmeena laughs. "Of course, we don't mind mountain bikers using them too. Do you want to build a jump or go back to riding?"

Both options sound good. You and Sidney glance at each other.

It's time to make a decision. Do you:

Return to ride Mystic Portal? **P322**

Or

Stay with the track-keeper to build new jumps? **P266**

Stay with the track-keeper to build new jumps

"I don't know about you, Sidney, but I'd love to stay and build some jumps. Digging with these hooves is much easier than with a spade."

"And that's only half of it," says Sharmeena. "Watch this." She taps the back of her heel against the ground. A flat bone-like blade slides out from the front of her leg, just above her hoof. She leaps into the air and kicks out. The blade slices a chunk out of a log, bark chips spraying into the air. Time and time again, she leaps, lashing out with her hooves at the log.

Soon, the log is curved along the sides and she's formed a diamond pattern on top.

"It's a diamondback snake!" calls Sidney. "That's impressive."

"Wow." The mystery of the track builders has been solved. "So you're the sculptor who has been creating all these cool jumps!"

"Not just me. There's a whole team of us. But this snake is going to take a lot of work to finish. We'll need to build a downhill gap jump over there, and then secure the snake across the top, like a bridge, so bikers can ride along it."

"So you're building a skinny?" you ask.

She nods.

Sidney frowns. "How will the bikes get traction so they don't slip off?"

Sharmeena grins. "The diamond pattern should help the wheels grip. And we can fill the gap with a bed of pine needles in case someone falls."

"Just no pine cones," says Sidney. "I'd rather face Bog than land on a pile of cones." He rubs his bottom, grinning.

She laughs. "Use your bone-blades as spades. They work well for digging too."

You and Sidney tap your heels against the ground. With a strange crunching sensation, blades slide out above your hooves.

"I'll summon more help." Sharmeena lets out a piercing whistle.

Sidney rolls his eyes. "As if that's going to bring an army running."

The ridged bark on a tree trunk in front of you swells and morphs into orange fur, then a track-keeper steps away from the tree. The green leaves of a bush part, and another track-keeper steps out. Another emerges from a pile of dirt. A rock moves, then a green eye appears and orange fur ripples over it. A track-keeper drops down from a branch. All around you, track-keepers are appearing.

"Usually we camouflage ourselves," says Sharmeena. "Humans can't see us, because we look like dirt, trees or rocks."

"Awesome." Sidney's eyes nearly fall out of his head.

"If you hear a biker coming," says Sharmeena, "hold your breath and you'll instantly be camouflaged. Whatever you're standing next to is what you'll look like."

"Great," you reply, "we'd hate to blow your secret."

Sharmeena grins. "That's the idea. Now let's build that jump."

The track-keepers purr, sounding like a swarm of bees. Some of them fly at the snake, helping to shape it with their blades while others etch diamonds onto its back.

More track-keepers head downhill to start work on the takeoff ramp for the skinny bridge.

You nudge Sidney, who's motionless, staring at them. "Let's get to work." You head down the hill to join the jump builders.

Soon dirt is flying as you, Sidney and the track-keepers churn up earth. Placing a stump on the slope, you sculpt dirt over it. With their teeth, track-keepers drag branches onto the pile until you've built a huge mound, taller than Sidney. Together, you cover it in dirt. Then you and the track-keepers trample all over it, packing it down until it's hard.

When you're finished, you go down the track a few yards to start work on the bridge's off-ramp. In the middle of building, the crunch of approaching tires sounds further up the track. Instantly, the track-keepers take deep breaths and start merging with the trees, dirt and rocks as their camouflage kicks into action.

268

"Hold your breath," you hiss to Sidney, and gulp in a mouthful of air. An instant later, Sidney is indistinguishable from the dirt he's standing next to, and you look like a rock.

Tracey yells your name. She skids around a corner, and zooms down the track a few yards from where you're building.

"Sidney," she calls. "Where are you both hiding?"

If only she knew you were in orange fur, camouflaged as a rock!

Her bike zooms past the half-finished jumps, spraying you with loose dirt from your digging. She's frowning, looking really anxious.

A twinge of guilt nags at you. You and Sidney are having the time of your lives, but she looks really worried.

Tracey follows the track around a corner, soon gone from sight.

Around you, track-keepers reappear, emerging from their camouflage.

"Was that your friend?" Sharmeena asks.

"Yeah," answers Sidney. "Maybe we should get back to her, so she doesn't get too stressed out."

It's time to make a decision. Do you:

Leave the track-keepers and join Tracey? **P309**

Or

Finish building the snake bridge? **P324**

Bypass Ogre Jaws and go down the chicken line

With your spine prickling, you head down the chicken line. It's spooky the way Sidney disappeared in midair. Where has he gone? And what happened to Tracey when she went over Camel Hump? Are you the only one left on the track? Your tires crunch over loose stones and you shoot around a bend, joining up with the main Mystic Portal trail.

Stopping, you place your feet on the ground and take a swig from your water bottle. You glance up and down the trail. No sign of Tracey. Or Sidney. Are they really missing? Or is this just part of the Mystic Portal adventure?

The track in front of you drops away in a steep slope through more forest, thick with undergrowth on each side of the trail. With everyone disappearing, will you ever make it to the beachside exit at the bottom of Mystic Portal?

Tucking your water bottle away, you hop on your pedals and push off.

Thunk! Sidney lands on the trail a few yards in front of you, his tires puffing up a cloud of dust. "Yahoo! Ogre Jaws was awesome!"

"Whoa! Where did you come from?" you yell. It's great that he's here again. Now you don't have to worry. "Seen Tracey?"

"Nah," he calls. "But I bet she's having a *wild* time." Sidney pedals hard, shooting down the track, zigzagging between the trees.

You race after him.

Smack! Tracey's bike drops out of nowhere, onto the track, between you and Sidney.

Freaky.

"Wow, this trail is amazing," she calls, passing Sidney on a straight. "Let's do the next jump."

You zoom down the track behind Tracey and Sidney, cornering to take a narrow bridge across a stream. A few minutes later a switchback heads towards the stream again and you pass a sign: *Dolphin Slide.*

"Yay, last jump," yells Tracey. "No chicken line!" She shoots up a huge rock shaped like a dolphin and leaps off the top, over the stream. In midair, she disappears.

"See you at the beach," calls Sidney as his bike splishes through a puddle, then zooms up the rock. He jumps and vanishes.

You gulp. That's right. There's no way out, no chicken line. The track goes straight ahead and the trees and bushes are too dense to break through. You head down the steep slope, through the puddle, your tires hissing against the rock as you whizz up over Dolphin Slide.

In a flash of blue light, the trail and trees are gone.

You're underwater, riding a dolphin through the ocean. Sidney and Tracey are riding dolphins too. The sun slants through the watery blue. A school of purple fish swim past. Below you, a stingray is hiding in the sand. Green seaweed waves in the current, like huge bushy underwater shrubs. A vast bank of colorful coral rises above you like a brightly-colored mosaic. Among the coral, tiny yellow lights wink, casting an eerie glow. What are they? Underwater glow worms?

"Wow," says Tracey. "Can you believe this? It's incredible."

"Hey, we can talk underwater." Bubbles rise from Sidney's mouth as he speaks. "And breathe."

"Amazing. What's next?" you ask. "And how do we get back to Mystic Portal again?"

"I thought you'd never ask," says the dolphin you're riding on.

"Squee," replies Tracey's dolphin, "let's tell them."

Talking dolphins? Wow.

"Welcome to the underwater portion of Mystic Portal," your dolphin says. "My name is Squee, head of this dolphin pod. We're your hosts, today, but you won't just be riding us. In order to get back to Mystic Portal, you need to compete in a race or take a tour. You can choose to ride seahorses in the Round the Coral Peninsula Extravaganza race, or go by turtleback on a Terrific Turtle Tour and see all the underwater sights."

"Cool." Bubbles tickle your nose as you speak. "What do you guys want to do?"

Sidney's eyes are shining. "I'm all for racing. The Round the Coral Peninsula Extravaganza by seahorse is for me."

Tracey's grinning. "I've always wanted to dive, so I'm going on a Terrific Turtle Tour to see all the underwater sights."

"Sounds good," says Squee, swimming under a coral bridge. "What will it be for you?"

It's time to make a decision. Do you:

Ride a seahorse in the Round the Coral Peninsula Extravaganza? **P272**

Or

Ride a turtle on a Terrific Turtle Tour? **P281**

272

Ride a seahorse in the Round the Coral Peninsula Extravaganza

You love riding bikes and enjoy racing Sidney whenever you get a chance, but obviously you've never raced on seahorses. It's time to try something new. "Racing seahorses sounds fun."

Sidney's glance slides to you. "I reckon I could beat you," he challenges.

"Oh yeah?" You grin. "Let's see."

You wave as Tracey's dolphin veers towards a group of turtles swimming in and out of some seaweed.

"Turtles look like fun too," Sidney mutters, releasing a trail of bubbles in front of his face. "Maybe we can try those later." His hair floats around his head, like seaweed waving in the current.

Without warning, Squee rolls, tipping you off near a cluster of seahorses. They're huge, big enough for you to sit on, and are all wearing cowboy hats.

"What a laugh." You tap Sidney, who's floating nearby. "Look at their hats."

A blue seahorse wearing a shiny silver sheriff badge swims over to you. He has a belt with holsters holding tiny guns carved of coral. "I beg your pardon?" says the seahorse with a Texan drawl. It has an enormous belly. Could it be pregnant? "I'm Sheriff Kingpin. Did you just laugh at my hat?"

"No, sir, um… ma'am? I was admiring it."

The seahorse stares at you for a few seconds. "Sir to you. Didn't you know that male seahorses carry the mature eggs?" He preens his fins with pride. "I'm the leader of this seahorse ranch. You two will be riding Hippo and Kampos."

A red seahorse sidles over to you, curling his lip as he speaks, "Hippo is my name. Saddle up and climb aboard. It's a shame there are only two of you. Some of our foals and fillies also wanted to race today."

You shoot a nervous glance at Sidney. Hippo seems tough.

"I'm Kampos," a yellow seahorse says to Sidney. "Sheriff Kingpin's carrying my eggs, so I'm racing."

"Um, Hippo," you ask, "why are you named after an enormous mud-wallowing mammal?"

Hippo's lip curls again. "Hippocampus means seahorse."

"And Kampos is ancient Greek for sea monster, so watch it." Kampos laughs, making Hippo smile. Maybe he's not so tough after all.

You ask another question. "You asked me to saddle up, Hippo, but there's no saddle…"

With another of his infamous lip curls, Hippo says brusquely, "Of course there aren't any saddles. We're underwater creatures, not land horses. It was just a saying. Climb aboard and stop mucking around. We want to get this race underway. I've won this race every month and my father and grandfather before me. We have to keep up family tradition." He gives a sly wink and leans towards you, whispering, "Be my rider and we'll win. I know a shortcut. Family secret."

You'll get to take a secret shortcut and beat Sidney. Sounds great.

You and Sidney clamber on the back of Hippo and Kampos.

Sheriff Kingpin addresses you all. "The first event in today's Round the Coral Peninsula Extravaganza is electric eel hurdles. Under no circumstances should you touch a hurdle. If you do…" His face pales.

"What will happen if we touch the eel hurdles?" Sidney pipes up. "Will we get a shock?"

Sheriff Kingpin ignores him, but it can't be good because his face never regains the blue tinge he had when he first swam over.

"Then you'll swim through the treacherous waters of the snapping clams," Kingpin avoids looking at you and Sidney. "Make sure you get through alive. We all know what happened to—"

"Ahem." Hippo clears his throat noisily, then coughs, so you miss most of what Sheriff Kingpin is saying.

"… starting in a few seconds."

Did you miss you something important? Could you die in this race?

You nudge Sidney. "What did he say?"

Sidney shrugs. "Don't care, I'm in. This sounds like fun." At least both of you missed it, so he won't have an advantage in the race.

Two young brown seahorses hold a long piece of seaweed tight in front of you. "Three, two, one, go!" they shout in shrill voices.

Hippo takes off, breaking through the seaweed. You fling your arms around his neck to stop yourself from falling off.

In a flash of yellow, Kampos is swimming alongside Hippo. Sidney whoops. "We're going to beat you," he sings. They race ahead.

"Just try, Sidney," you cry.

"Don't worry. We'll take the shortcut," Hippo whispers.

He surges towards a narrow gap between jagged rocks. Seaweed waves across the entrance, like some bizarre guardian warning you not to pass.

"Are you sure about this?" you ask Hippo.

Clammy seaweed fingers brush across your face and arms as Hippo dives through the rock tunnel with you on his back.

"You'll see," Hippo pants. "This is the fastest route."

The tunnel is so narrow your arms skim jagged outcrops. And so dark, you can only feel and hear Hippo, not see him. You keep your limbs wrapped tight around him. The dark passageway seems to take forever. And this is a shortcut! Hopefully Sidney's route is way longer.

Hippo's panting rasps through the water. He's sounding tired, which doesn't make sense because he told you he always wins. What's wrong?

Ahead, it's growing lighter. A glimpse of blue expands as you near it. You shoot out into the blue ocean, gasping with relief.

"Thankfully we made it," puffs Hippo. "My claustrophobia was kicking in. Sorry about the panting. It always happens when I'm in a tight space."

You laugh in relief. "And I thought you were tired."

"I never get tired." Hippo puffs himself up with pride. "We're nearly there. Remember, whatever you do, don't touch the hurdles."

You round a rocky outcrop. Below you in the pale sand are blue hurdles that flicker with luminous yellow lightning. They're eels with their tails and heads in the sand, and their bodies arched. The hurdle closest to you is a small eel, so it's low, but each gets higher. The last hurdle is a giant eel that towers above the others. How will you ever get over that?

"See, there's Squee." Hippo flicks his tail toward the sleek grey dolphin swimming alongside the hurdles, Sheriff Kingpin beside her. "She's the race marshal."

"Why do we need a marshal when you already have a sheriff?"

"The sheriff protects us against outlaws and leads our ranch. The race marshal makes sure the Extravaganza rules are kept. There are two hurdle rules. First, we must touch the sand between each hurdle. Secondly, we must never—"

"I know. Never touch the hurdles. Will they zap us? Or is their lightning just for show?"

A cry bubbles through the water. It's Sidney, arriving on Kampos.

Ignoring your question, Hippo surges forward, bouncing his tail on the ocean floor. A puff of sand rises around you as he leaps the first hurdle.

Your head-start is tiny, but hopefully it will last.

With another bounce in the sand, Hippo flies over the second hurdle. This is fun. The third hurdle is a little higher. You feel Hippo strain, but he easily clears it.

As Hippo bounces up towards a fourth hurdle, Kampos lands below you, stirring up the sand on the ocean floor.

They're gaining! "Come on, Hippo," you cry.

Sidney and Kampos clear the next hurdle and touch down beside you on the ocean floor. Kampos and Hippo are neck and neck as they jump over the next hurdle. Everything becomes a blur of sand and hurdles as you and Hippo grunt, straining to keep up with Sidney and Kampos.

Landing on the sand, the final hurdle looms above you. In a blurry

276

yellow streak, Sidney and Kampos zoom over it and race off.

"I can't do it," pants Hippo. "I've been too lazy, not training because I always win, but Kampos has been practicing every day. I might not clear the final hurdle. We could end up touching it."

"And what will happen then?" You ask.

"You don't want to know. But it's horrible." His red face pales to pink.

"So we're giving up?"

"It's your choice," Hippo says. "We could still catch up on the snapping clams. There's always a chance that they'll run into problems, so we could still win and honor my forefathers."

"I have an idea!" you exclaim. "I can help you over this hurdle by kicking as we leap upwards. That should help us clear it."

"We can try if you want," says Hippo. "I still think it's too risky, but it's your race, so it's your choice."

Sheriff Kingpin is floating nearby. He stares at the hurdle, shaking his head, his expression grim.

"Be careful what you choose," warns Squee.

It's time to make a decision. Do you:

Kick to help Hippo over the last hurdle? **P277**

Or

Go to the snapping clams? **P278**

Kick to help Hippo over the last hurdle

What could be so dangerous about touching a hurdle? Maybe these seahorses are really chickens, too scared to try. Or perhaps they're superstitious. Besides, you're not planning on touching the hurdle. Your legs are strong from mountain biking. Their added strength should make a difference and help Hippo clear the flickering hurdle towering above you.

"Come on, Hippo." You pat his back. "Let's leap this hurdle and catch up to Sidney and Kampos."

Hippo starts trembling. "S-sure," he stutters.

He seems really scared. Have you made the right choice?

It's time to make a decision. Do you:

Abandon the highest hurdle and go to the snapping clams? **P279**

Or

Leap the final hurdle? **P290**

278

Abandon the highest hurdle and go to the snapping clams

You hate to see Hippo so frightened. "Sorry, Hippo I didn't mean to scare you." You pat his trembling body. "Let's just go to the snapping clams and try to catch up to Sidney and Kampos."

Hippo stops trembling. "I'm so glad," he says, swimming away from the hurdles.

Sheriff Kingpin cheers. "Great choice."

Go to the snapping clams. **P278**

Go to the snapping clams

"Snapping clams sound dangerous too," you say, "but I'm going to take your advice. You know these waters better than me."

"Good idea," calls Sheriff Kingpin.

Squee nods her head in agreement.

With a flip of his tail, Hippo zooms under the hurdle, and out over the sand. "I'm glad we didn't touch that hurdle or we really would've suffered."

"How?"

"Brrr. I don't want to discuss it. It's too awful."

"Come on. What?"

"Can't tell, but let me say, you're in the ocean," says Hippo, "not on some tame mountain biking trail."

Mystic Portal is far from tame, but you don't argue. You're just glad you didn't crash into one of the squid's hurdles. What's ahead of you, now? Snapping clams don't sound very tame either.

Skirting a large bank of seaweed, you come to a series of rocks with giant clams perched on top of them. The clams are opening and shutting their shells.

As Hippo approaches the clams, Sidney and Kampos swim out from the third clam, racing towards the fourth.

"Eight snapping clams in all," says Hippo.

"What are the rules?"

Hippo rolls his eyes. "Pretty obvious. Don't get snapped." With that, he zooms forward, his body nearly parallel with the ocean floor.

The first giant clam looms in front of you, its shell wide open, exposing its fleshy interior. That's strange, you thought clam meat was white or creamy, but this clam has bluish-yellow flesh. Perhaps it's the underwater light that makes it look that way.

Before you have more time to think, you're out the other side, shooting towards the second clam. This one has its wide jaws half open. It stretches them further as you pass through. In the middle of

280

its flesh, something shiny winks at you. "Is that a pearl?"

"Of course." Hippo shoots out of the clam leaving the pearl behind.

It's the size of a baseball. With a pearl like that, you could buy a new mountain bike. Maybe even one for Sidney too. "Is there any chance of me grabbing a pearl?"

"Don't even think about it," snaps Hippo. "It's way too dangerous."

When Hippo enters the next clam, a giant pearl is lying on the flesh. If you jump off Hippo's back, just for a second, you could grab it.

It's time to make a decision. Do you:

Leap off Hippo's back and grab the pearl? **P301**

Or

Stay on Hippo's back and go to the next clam? **P303**

Ride a turtle on a Terrific Turtle Tour

Cruising by turtleback sounds much more relaxing than racing on a seahorse.

"I'm coming too, Tracey." You grin. "I'd love a tour on turtleback."

"I wonder what we're going to see." Tracey's eyes are alight with excitement.

Squee and Tracey's dolphin swim over to a group of turtles playing leapfrog in some seaweed. Golden flowers glint among the seaweed. It's hard to tell how many turtles there are, because the brown and green seaweed camouflages their shells so well.

Squee whistles.

Three giant turtles break away from the group and swim towards you. One of them has a piece of seaweed wrapped around its leg.

"I'm Tuck," says the largest in a deep voice.

"And I'm Nip," says one with a ragged edge on its shell.

The turtle with seaweed around its leg bobs up and down in the water. "And I'm tagging along to learn how to be a tour guide. I've never done this before and I'm really excited. I'm especially looking forward to—"

"Ssh!" Nip whispers. "That's enough, just tell them your name, Junior."

"I'm Junior." The turtle pipes up, beaming.

Junior doesn't look any smaller than the others, but his voice is squeaky, like a child's.

"Pleased to meet you," you reply. "Do you mind telling me what that seaweed is for?" You point to the seaweed around his leg.

"Sure, that's my leash." Junior puffs up his chest. "When I'm a proper tour guide, I won't have to use it."

"Thanks for offering to take us on a Terrific Turtle Tour," says Tracey in her best polite voice, the one she uses with adults. "What would you like to show us?"

"A Terrific Turtle Tour?" says Junior before the others can get a word in. "Here's a tour of a terrific turtle. Well, here's my shell. These are my forelegs and these are my hind legs. He spins in the water. "And this is my tail." He lifts it and a stream of bubbles drifts out from the back end of his shell. His face goes bright red. "Um, sorry," he mutters.

"Junior!" Nip reprimands, tugging his leash.

"Um, time to swim over here," says Tuck, but not before an unpleasant odor drifts on the current towards you.

Tracey splutters and leaps off her dolphin to swim after Tuck. She clambers aboard his shell.

Squee whistles goodbye and you swim after them, leaving the smelly water behind.

Nip nods her head. "Climb aboard."

You glance at Junior.

"Sorry," he says, "I had too many kelp cakes for breakfast. By the way, I can't carry you because I'm too inexperienced to carry passengers. Soon I'll be qualified with my passenger license then I'll—"

"Ssh!" Tuck tugs his leash. "That's enough. Get on with the tour introductions."

"Oh, yes." Junior nibbles his lip.

He reminds you of Tracey when she's trying to come up with a quick excuse for not doing her homework or Sidney when he's trying to explain to his mom why his pants are ripped—again.

Junior speaks slowly, concentrating. "Today you can choose between the Sunken Ship Tour and the Underwater City Tour."

"Go on," says Nip. "Say the rest."

"But you're always telling me to say less," says Junior.

"Junior!" snaps Tuck.

Junior winks, without his parents seeing. You get the feeling he's used to stringing them along like this. "Our sunken ship tour—"

"Junior," interrupts Nip. "Sunken Ship Tour has capitals."

Junior rolls his eyes and puts on a voice like a TV news anchor.

"Our Sunken Ship Tour has a variety of interesting aspects. The *Pyromania*, an ancient pirate galleon, has been on our ocean floor for years, giving the ocean's flora and fauna a chance to flourish in new habitats within this man-made structure. Of particular interest is the shark hatchery." Junior's voice changes and he sounds like himself again. "Oh, the ship's fun, and really, really exciting. You should see it."

"What about the underwater city?" asks Tracey. "That sounds interesting too."

Junior puts on his TV voice again. "The underwater city of Hydropolis was flooded approximately twenty years ago when sea levels rose. Fortunately, the people of Hydropolis fled and survived. The city, however, was not so fortunate, and was flooded overnight. The waterlogged landmass slowly subsided into the sea over two years, creating a fantastic tourist attraction for Terrific Turtle Tours. Should you choose the Hydropolis Underwater City Tour, you're guaranteed a thrilling adventure of adrenaline rushes." Junior grins, then continues, "Of course the *Pyromania* Sunken Ship Tour is also a veritable wonderland of undersea treasures—a murky pirate world full of intrigue and mystery."

Tuck clears his throat. "So, which will it be? The Hydropolis Underwater City Tour? Or the *Pyromania* Sunken Ship Tour?

Straddled across Tuck's shell, Tracey shrugs. "Both sound exciting. It's up to you."

It's time to make a decision. Which Terrific Turtle Tour would you like to go on?

The Hydropolis Underwater City Tour? **P316**

Or

The Pyromania Sunken Ship Tour? **P284**

The *Pyromania* Sunken Ship Tour

"I've always wanted to see a pirate ship. Could we go on the *Pyromania* tour?"

"What does *Pyromania* mean?" asks Tracey.

"Not sure," says Junior. "Maybe it means you're mad about being a pirate. You know, Pyro for pirate and mania…"

"Ahem," coughs Tuck. "*Pyromania* means crazy pirates. Everyone knows that."

You smother a chuckle. Your teacher taught you that a pyromaniac is someone who likes lighting fires. What a weird name for a pirate ship.

"Let's get going," says Nip, "before the next tourists get here for a tour."

You cling to her shell as she swims into deeper water.

Fish cruise the ocean searching for tasty treats—blue fish with yellow fins, red ones, and others with purple and orange stripes. A shoal of tiny silver fish flit past. Starfish laze around on rocks, like sunbathers. A stingray moves along the ocean floor, churning up clouds of sand.

A dark shape looms on the ocean floor. As you get closer, the shipwreck comes into view. The *Pyromania* is leaning to one side. Colorful seaweed adorns the mast. The wood of the hull is nearly black, aged from years under the sea.

"Is there any pirate treasure?" asks Tracey.

"Treasure?" says Junior. "No. Dad thought treasure hunters would've been bad for Terrific Turtle Tours' business, so he got rid of the treasure long ago."

Tracey rolls her eyes and leans over towards you, so the turtles can't hear. "I bet they threw it away," she whispers. "What a waste."

You feel the same. You could have bought new bikes for everyone with a single gold doubloon. Turtles probably have no idea how valuable treasure is.

Nip and Tuck settle on the railing of the ship. "Junior, we're a little tired, so we'll rest here. You've done this tour often enough, so today you can guide our adventurers. Be careful and remember everything we've taught you."

Junior guides you and Tracey through the hatchway. Below deck, loose planks are strewn around the floor.

"Treasure seekers did that." Junior shakes his head. "Imagine ripping planks off a perfectly good wreck. It's such terrible vandalism!"

Vandalism? You never would have thought that hunting for treasure could be vandalism. But it obviously is in the eyes of these sea creatures.

You come to a door. "What's behind that?"

"My parents tell me never to let people open that door." Junior winks. "But they're not around, so maybe we can have a look."

"Why?" you ask. "What's in there?"

"It's a shark hatchery," says Junior. "But they're only tiny, so they'll be harmless."

"Wow, I've always wanted to swim with baby sharks," says Tracey. "Go on, please open it."

You glance at Tracey. She shrugs, and tugs the rusty metal handle. "It's stiff. I'm going to need your help."

You grab the handle and heave. The door flies open and a swarm of silver baby sharks shoot past you.

"They're cute," Tracey croons. "No one would ever believe they could grow up to be killers."

You peer inside the hatchery, but it's too gloomy to see much. "I can't see any more babies. Is it a problem that we let them out?"

Before anyone can answer, a sleek white and grey form fills the doorway and opens its massive jaws. A wall of jagged teeth fills your vision.

"No," screams Junior, diving between you and the shark.

The shark's mouth snaps shut. Junior squirms and writhes, but his shell is caught between the shark's teeth. "Swim!" He cries. "Swim

286

away, fast!” Then his eyes close and he goes limp in the shark’s jaws.

It’s time to make a decision. Do you:

Flee from the shark with Tracey? **P300**

Or

Save Junior from the shark? **P311**

Stay in the tunnel

Sidney's a good friend, but you have no idea how to fight an ogre and you're not keen to learn. "I'm not going with you," you state firmly, staring into Sharmeena's eye. "Besides, I don't know how to fight ogres so I'd probably get in your way."

"You're too scared." She pokes out her tongue. "Anyone who abandons their friend to Bog is no friend of mine."

With a flash of fur, bathed in the eerie light from her eye, the track-keeper leaps over you, and disappears around a corner.

You gulp. It's darker here than inside a trouser pocket.

No point in staying here. If you follow Sharmeena, at least you'll be able to see something. Feeling your way along the tunnel walls, you round the corner. Wow, that track-keeper moves fast. The glow of her eye is a pinprick, miles down the tunnel.

You can hardly see a thing. Hands out, you run your fingers along the tunnel wall, over roots and crumbling dirt, and inch your way forward. Soon the track-keeper's green light is gone.

But what's that?

Something yellow and glowing is coming towards you. It's a naked flame. It could be someone carrying an old-fashioned torch.

"Hey," you call. "Over here."

An ominous roar ripples down the tunnel towards you, making the ground tremble.

Uh-oh. That doesn't sound like good news. Spinning, you race back the way you came, stumbling over tree roots and skinning your knees. Scrambling to your feet, a blast of heat radiates down the tunnel towards you.

You whirl.

And face an ogre belching fire, its teeth glinting among the flames.

No wonder he can toast kids, Bog the ogre breathes fire. Your knees shake so hard, you can't move.

Bog approaches. The stench of swamp wafts towards you. That

288

must be how he got his name.

"My toast ran away," Bog roars. "Need another toast. Don't worry, I gobble you fast. Too fast for pain."

Although you struggle to move your feet, you're paralyzed, too scared to move.

Bog roars, belching flame. "Caught you!"

Sorry, this part of your story is over. You've taken a great jump, met a cool creature and had a wild adventure, but abandoning Sidney to Bog was not the best choice you could've made. There are still many other adventures. You could ride a camel, fight desert bandits, meet dolphins or build a new bike jump with Sidney and the mysterious track builders of Mystic Portal.

It's time to make a decision. You have 3 choices. Do you:

Go back and help Sharmeena save Sidney from Bog? **P239**

Go to the list of choices and start reading from another part of the story? **P534**

Or

Go back to the beginning a try another path? **P201**

Go ahead despite the sparks

You were warned about playing with electricity when you were child, but you're desperate. You have to save Sidney.

"I'm fine. I've got this."

"I wouldn't, if I were you," Sharmeena cautions.

You jam the key into the lock. A jolt flies down your arms and your whole body shudders. Your heart spasms painfully, then everything goes black.

Sorry, this part of your story is over. The lock gave you an electrical shock, killing you instantly. Taking a chance on a lock charged with an electrical force field was not the best choice, so you didn't save Sidney from Bog. But you can choose again. You could become a camel racer, have an underwater adventure on a sea turtle, or tame Bog the ogre.

It's time to make a decision. You have 3 choices. Do you:

Choose a different lock? **P260**

Go to the list of choices and start reading from another part of the story? **P534**

Or

Go back to the beginning a try another path? **P201**

Leap the final hurdle

"Come on, Hippo," you say, "have courage."

"Alright." Some of his earlier bravado sneaks back into his voice. "Let's do this. On the count of three. One, two, three."

He jumps up from the sand, then lands again and bounces, swimming up towards the hurdle. "Kick, now."

Releasing your grip around his stomach, you fling your feet backwards and kick like crazy. It's working. You're rising upwards towards the top of the hurdle. The eel's skin flickers with luminous yellow electricity. You keep kicking, churning up bubbles as you rise through the water.

The hurdle is nearly in reach, when Hippo starts to falter. "I c-can't do it,'" he pants.

"Yes we can," you yell. "Don't give up."

Within a huge kick, you both surge above the hurdle. "We're over!" you yell, bubbles flying around your face. "We've done it."

"No we haven't," shrieks Hippo. "My tail's stuck."

He's right. The curly end of his tail is hooked under the top of the hurdle. Yellow sparks flit around his trapped tail.

"No problem. I'll just swim down and free it."

"No," shrieks Hippo. "Swim away while you can. Hurry."

The lightning from the electric eels must be dangerous, but it's your fault Hippo's stuck. You leap off his back and open your backpack. "Hold on I'll get my bike's spare inner tube. Rubber is a great insulator, so this won't hurt either of us." Fishing out a tire tube, you hook it around Hippo and yank him off the hurdle. The yellow lightning running across the eels bodies dims.

"Are you okay?" you ask.

He nods. "Sure, I'm fine." But his tail has lost its cute curl and hangs limp in the sea. "Brace yourself."

"For what?"

The electric eels' lightning goes out. The lights on all those underwater glow worms die. The sea is darker than inside a sunken treasure chest.

"Blistering barnacles and crusty coral, now we've done it!" Hippo curses.

"What? Where are you, Hippo? I can't see a thing. And where are Kampos and Sidney?"

"We've deactivated the grid," answers Hippo.

"What grid?"

Before he can answer, beams of light shoot through the dark and a school of anglerfish surround you. The lights hanging off their heads illuminate the area.

"Fins up, you're under arrest for deactivating the power grid."

You don't have fins, so you raise your hands.

Hippo's fins poke straight up.

"As members of the Municipal Eel Charmers, we hereby arrest you and recruit you to eel charming, until all the eels that power this area have been persuaded to resume their duties in the power grid."

That's when you realize the electric eels are nowhere to be seen.

The angler fish pass you flutes made of coral. "Using the eel's power grid as hurdles is fine, as long as you don't tamper with the power. But now, as a result of your clumsiness, you must patrol the Coral Peninsula and charm the eels out of their hideouts, so Seahorse Ranch has light again. You will be assigned two guards who will report back to us when the eels are in place."

Two angler fish with gaping sharp-toothed smiles flank you as you ride off with Hippo. But when you play the pipe, an awful screech comes out, making you wince.

"Agh! I hate that noise," Hippos snaps. "But the electric eels love it."

An eel pokes its head out of the coral and follows you.

"This is like snake charming," you mutter, as the eel weaves through the seaweed towards you.

"What's that?" asks Hippo.

"Um, don't worry." You play another squeaky tune. It's horrible, off key and discordant. The music grates against your teeth.

By late afternoon, you've summoned all the eels from their nooks and crannies with your bad melodies. Your ears ache. You never want to play another coral pipe in your life.

It takes another hour of Hippo's smooth talking to convince the electric eels to take their positions back in the grid. When they're all lined up in their hurdle spots again, tiny lights among the coral flicker on again. The area is bathed in light.

"Don't touch the hurdles again," warn the anglerfish before they leave.

You nudge Hippo. "Those aren't undersea glow worms. They're lights."

Hippo winks at you. "Want to jump the eel hurdles again?"

"No thanks, I don't fancy playing more tunes on that pipe. My ears are still ringing from the last lot."

"Mine too."

His lip curls as Sidney and Kampos appear. "Where have you two been? You missed all the action."

"It was so dark," says Sidney. "We couldn't see a thing until a minute ago, so we had to sit tight."

"You tripped the grid, didn't you?" asks Kampos.

You and Hippo grin. "Yeah, we've been charming eels," you reply.

"Rather you than us," Kampos says.

Sheriff Kingpin appears, rubbing his huge belly. "Power outage, huh? Glad to see you fixed it, but it's time for you to go home now. The race is over."

Kampos and Hippo swim under a coral arch.

"Farewell," they call.

"Bye."

Moments later, you and Sidney are riding along Mystic Portal on your bikes. "I'm changing to my granny gear," calls Sidney as you head up a hill.

He's forgotten you don't have gears. You groan, but as you ride up the slope, your pedals crackle and small bolts of lightning fly from them. Humming, your bike zooms up the hill.

"Hey," calls Sidney, "our bikes are powered with electricity. How did that happen?"

Tracey is parked at the top of the hill. "You guys are motoring," she calls. "Tell me your secret."

"Haven't got one," yells Sidney.

That's when you spy the engraving of an electric eel on your handlebars.

Congratulations, this part of your adventure is over, even if your ears are still ringing from those awful tunes. You rode a seahorse, sorted out the eel's power grid and had fun on your mountain bike. You could go back and see what happens if you choose not to jump the final hurdle, but there are also many other adventures on Mystic Portal. You could tame an ogre, ride a magic carpet, learn how to survive in the desert, or help build a mountain bike jump.

It's time to make a decision. You have 3 choices. Do you:

Go to the snapping clams? **P278**

Go to the list of choices and start reading from another part of the story? **P534**

Or

Go back to the beginning a try another path? **P201**

Leave the oasis

"Excuse me, Aamir, I don't mean any offence, but I have a family too, and need to return to them."

"Very well." He nods, but doesn't look happy at all. "The law of the desert states that every visitor to our oasis is welcome to water from the lake and fruit from the trees. I cannot spare a camel to transport you. The nearest town is a day's walk in that direction." He points beyond the lake. "Straight ahead. Good luck."

Next to him, Latifah looks worried.

You gaze out over the burning red sand and gulp. A whole day's walk? "Um, maybe I will race your camel."

Aamir scowls. "I'm sorry. Racing a camel is a great honor. You turned me down." As Aamir turns his back on you, Latifah passes you a water skin, and a small pouch containing oranges and dates.

Jamina nuzzles your hand. "Good luck," she says. "Remember the desert survival lessons I taught you."

There's nothing for it, you have to face the desert alone. Squaring your shoulders, you nod farewell to Jamina and Latifah, and start walking over the hot sand. Heading over an enormous dune, your feet flounder but you reach the top. Soon the oasis is out of sight.

You can do this, you know you can. As long as you head in the right direction, you should reach the city. Determined to make good time, you race down the dune, keeping an eye on the sun to make sure you're heading in the right direction.

The sun beats down mercilessly, hour after hour. You drink deeply from your bottle until it's empty, munching on oranges and figs to keep your strength up. Your feet drag in the sand. Your eyes are dry and gritty. It's important to stay hydrated, so you open the water skin and have a drink from that too.

Sweat beads your face, running into your eyes, stinging them. As you stumble up yet another dune an ominous buzz sounds on the other side.

Dropping to your belly, you crawl commando style to the top to take a look. Flies are buzzing around an animal's carcass as vultures tear strips off it. You wrinkle your nose—even from here it stinks. Oh well, the city lies on the other side of that carcass so, as exhausted as you are, and as much as it smells, you'll have to pass it.

You take another deep swig from the water skin, only to realize it's now empty. Alarm bells ring in your head. How silly could you be? Jamina taught you to only take small sips of water, but in your desperation to get to the city, you've finished all your water in a few hours. And you only have one orange left.

Sliding down the dune towards the carcass, you hope there'll be another oasis on the way so you can refill the water skin. Not wanting to disturb the vultures, you make a wide berth around the carcass. But as you pass, a cloud of flies rise into the air and zoom towards you. You scramble across sand.

The flies are faster. They swarm onto your face.

Hands thrashing, you try to swat them away, but the minute you succeed, more land on your forehead, cheeks and neck. It's a losing battle. They're drinking your sweat—here in the desert every drop of fluid is precious. Perhaps that was one of the reasons Jamina said to sip water—to prevent sweat. You continue walking, flies crawling over your face.

If only you had a wide-brimmed Australian hat with corks dangling around it. That would keep the flies off. Hey, you don't have a hat, but you do have a sweatshirt. Pulling it out of your backpack, you tie it around your head, covering most of your face so the flies can't land.

Hours later, you come over a dune and see footprints in the sand. Parched and dizzy from lack of water, you follow them, hoping to catch up with someone who can give you a drink. Soon you're shuffling through the sand, exhausted, when you notice there are two sets of footprints. Two people? You press ahead, ignoring your throbbing skull and dry throat.

Now there are three sets of footprints.

296

With horror, you realize you've been walking in circles, following yourself. You stare at the sun, trying to orient yourself, but no longer know which way the city lies. Or the oasis.

Striking out into the hot red sand, you press forward. Soon you're crawling up a huge dune that seems to go on forever. Your hands and knees sink into the soft sand, but you drag yourself upwards until you crest the hill. Below is a tiny oasis. At the foot of a lone palm is a pool of sparkling cool water.

"Yahoo." Your voice only comes out as a croak. Giving into exhaustion, you roll down the dune, and then crawl across the sand to the oasis. Scooping up cool water with your hands, you bring it to your mouth, drinking greedily.

And end up with a mouthful of sand.

"Gah!"

It was a mirage—a hallucination from being dehydrated and exhausted. There was no oasis. It was all your imagination. You're never going to get to the city. Exhausted, you sink to the sand. If only you'd stayed for the camel races.

Sorry, this part of your adventure is over. You die in the desert. Turning down camel racing was not the best idea, especially when Aamir warned you to accept. You and Tracey never re-appear from Mystic Portal. For the rest of their lives, Sidney and your families wonder what happened. But don't worry, there are lots of other adventures in Mystic Portal, so you can choose again. Maybe you'd like to race Jamina, meet an ogre, explore the underwater city of Hydropolis or build a mountain bike jump.

It's time to make a decision. You have 3 choices. Do you:

Go back and race Jamina in the Camel races? **P349**

Go to the list of choices and start reading from another part of the story? **P534**

Or

Go back to the beginning a try another path? **P201**

Keep Jamina running from the sandstorm

"We can make it, I'm sure we can. Keep running."

Jamina increases speed, jolting you even more. Hanging onto the saddle with one hand, you tug your sweatshirt tighter around your face to keep the stinging grains away from your skin.

Red dust thickens the air, making you choke and cough. Squeezing your eyes shut against blasts of sand, you hang on to Jamina. She dashes forward, lurching and stumbling, nearly pitching you from the saddle.

Clutching the reins tightly, you catch your balance, but the camel's lurching gait nearly knocks you off again. For ages, you hang on, eyes shut tight, as she bucks like a bronco trying to make headway against the vicious storm.

"Mwoooaaaah!" Jamina shrieks.

You're jolted from the saddle, flying through the cloud of red. "Oof." Sand is harder than you thought, but luckily none of your bones are broken. You attempt to scramble to your feet, but the wind knocks you down.

Through the surging red sand, you hear Jamina bellow. You crawl towards her. Despite the raging sandstorm, you soon butt against something warm and solid.

"Jamina. Are you okay?"

"I was worried I'd lost you."

"I'll try to pitch the tent." You feel your way along her saddle, the sand pelting your fumbling fingers. But as you loosen the tent, the wind catches it and hurls it out of your grasp. You squint through the red haze, but it's already lost from view.

"Burrow into my side," says Jamina.

The wind dies down.

"Welcome to Sands of Time Industries," someone says.

You raise your head. The sandstorm is gone. You're in a warehouse—no wait, it's the biggest tent you could ever imagine. At one end, there's something that looks like a pizza oven, where people are working with long thin pipes.

As you watch, a female factory worker blows into the pipes and a bubble starts forming. That's right, glass is made from sand. That woman is glassblowing. The object on the end of the pipe is forming a familiar shape, like a three-dimensional figure of eight.

It's an hour glass.

"You'll start here," says a woman beside you, tugging your shirt. She's pointing to a table where three other kids, also dressed in mountain bike gear, are putting sand into hour glasses.

"Went down Camel Hump, did you?" asks one of the workers at the table.

"Didn't pitch the tent?" asks another.

You nod, stunned. One second you were drowning in sand and now...

"Well, you only have to work for one hour before you get to go home," says the first worker. He's looks like Jase, a fellow-mountain biker, but older. Perhaps he's Jase's big brother.

"Do you know Jase?" you ask.

He frowns at you, puzzled. "What do you mean, 'Do I know Jase?' I am Jase!" He grins. "Welcome to Sands of Time. Just fill this hour glass and you can go home. The good news is, like I said, it'll only take an hour." He passes you an hour glass.

"Th-thanks." You gulp. Jase has aged. He looks years older—but you and Sidney only went riding with him a week ago.

You pick up a few grains of sand and drop them into the open end of the hour glass. One grain trickles slowly into the neck of the glass. The others float out the top, back onto the pile.

"Just a grain at a time, no more is allowed," a girl next to you says.

Crazy. This'll take forever.

"Hey, I used to know you. A shame you didn't pitch the tent. You could've been home by now." She looks like an older version of Tracey.

Grinning, Jase says, "It's only an hour, but there's bad news too. Time goes a lot more slowly here, but our aging process doesn't slow, so we become wrinkled and old in no time at all."

Your spine prickles as you pick up your next grain of sand.

Sorry, this part of your adventure is over. Running away from sandstorms is usually fatal, so you were lucky to be saved by Sands of Time Industries. Pitching a tent against the storm would've been a much better strategy, because you, Tracey, Jase and the other workers spend the rest of your lives each trying to fill an hour glass. Sidney waited for ages at the bottom of Mystic Portal, but never saw you or Tracey again. The only thing he could tell your families was that you both disappeared in midair. There are lots of other adventures in Mystic Portal, because you can choose again. Maybe you'll ride the magic carpet with Tracey, tame an ogre or turn into a furry creature. You may even get to visit a sunken pirate ship.

It's time to make a decision. You have 3 choices. Do you:

Go back and pitch the tent? **P212**

Go to the list of choices and start reading from another part of the story? **P534**

Or

Go back to the beginning a try another path? **P201**

300

Flee from the shark with Tracey

"We have to save him," Tracey screams.

"It's too late. He's dead. We have to save ourselves." Grabbing Tracey's arm, you tug her away from the shark, which is now shaking Junior from side to side in its jaws.

You and Tracey swim towards a porthole and scramble through. The shark will never fit through, so you should be safe.

Tracey's voice shakes. "Wow, am I glad we escaped that—" Then her mouth opens in an underwater scream.

You spin to face two great white sharks, twice as large as the one you just fled from. Their jaws open and they lunge at you. There's no escape. You're fish food. This is your fin-ale.

Sorry, this part of your story is over. Abandoning Junior in his time of need (when he tried to save you) was not the best decision. But don't worry, you can choose again. Maybe you'd like to go back and save Junior, explore the underwater city of Hydropolis, or ride a seahorse in the Round the Coral Peninsula Extravaganza. Or perhaps you'd like to do another jump on Mystic Portal.

It's time to make a decision. You have 3 choices. Do you:

Go back and save Junior? **P311**

Go to the list of choices and start reading from another part of the story? **P534**

Or

Go back to the beginning a try another path? **P201**

Leap off Hippo's back and grab the pearl

Without thinking, you dive off Hippo's back, landing in the clam's soft flesh. The clam quivers as you walk towards the pearl.

Hippo charges out of the clam, then spins to face you. "No. Don't touch that pearl. It's not yours to take." His voice is panicky. "Get out of there, quick."

The pearl glints at you, full of promise. This pearl could give you new mountain bike—a bike with full suspension, just like Tracey's. It'll be like landing on a feather duvet every time you make a jump.

"I'm fine," you yell, stepping towards the pearl. The clam's flesh quivers again, more violently. It grows darker. Swiveling, you realize the jaws of the clam are closing.

You lunge, diving across the clam. Gripping the enormous pearl with both hands, you tug it.

It holds fast.

You can't let go. This pearl represents your dreams, your new bike. You yank hard, and the pearl comes free in your hands.

The clam snaps shut and you're enveloped in darkness. You sit down, the pearl in your arms, and wait for the clam to open.

You wait.

And wait.

Your chest grows tight. There's less and less oxygen in the water inside the clam.

Outside, someone knocks on the shell. Voices yell. They're trying to get you out.

But it's too late. Your breathing becomes shallow. Suddenly, like a flat tire, you're out of air.

Sorry, this part of your adventure is over. Your guide, Hippo, told you that the pearl was not yours to take. Ignoring his advice was not the wisest decision. Never mind, you can go back and make another choice. There are plenty of other adventures on Mystic Portal, so do choose again.

It's time to make a decision. You have 3 choices. Do you:

Stay on Hippo's back and go to the next clam? **P303**

Go to the list of choices and start reading from another part of the story? **P534**

Or

Go back to the beginning a try another path? **P201**

Stay on Hippo's back and go to the next clam

Although you could buy a new bike with this pearl, Hippo said it would be dangerous to take it. He also mentioned that it wasn't yours to take. With one last backward glance, you cling tightly to his back as he churns through the water, out the other side of the clam.

The clam shell snaps shut behind you. You shudder. If you'd delayed to get the pearl, you may have had a limb snapped off in that shell, or even worse, been trapped inside.

You zoom through two more clams, glad you're not trapped.

"Am I imagining it, or are these clams shutting their shells faster than the others?"

Hippo laughs. "That's part of the fun. These ones are much faster. That's why they're called snapping clams."

He picks up speed, rocketing towards a closed shell. Just when you think you're going to hit the hard grey exterior of the clam, it opens. Hippo zooms through the middle. The clam clicks shut behind him.

"Close call." A voice drifts on the current.

Startled, you glance around. It doesn't sound like Sidney.

There, to your left, swimming above the wreckage of an old ship, are a two turtles with kids riding on their backs.

"Just ignore those turtle tours," says Hippo, snorting. "Those tourists have nothing better to do than stare."

He's right. They're just hanging around in the water watching you race. You grin, glad you're having fun, and zip through the next clam.

Only two more clams to go.

When you clear the next clam, you give the tourists the thumbs up sign.

They're looking worried, but they've nothing to be afraid of. It's you who's taking the risks, not them.

The last clam is right in front of you.

"Hold on tight, and stay flat against my back," urges Hippo as you whizz through the clam.

Leaning low, you keep your head down. Ahead, the clam shell is shutting—there are only seconds to get out.

Now, it's only open a crack.

Hippo makes the gap. You sit up, waving your arms in victory.

The next moment, you're yanked off Hippo's back. You pull and tug, but you can't move. Glancing over your shoulder, you realize the end of your backpack straps are trapped in the clam shell.

Hippo speeds away, without you.

"Hippo!"

He doesn't seem to hear you.

You try to struggle out of your backpack, but as you tug, the straps only get tighter, held fast by the clam. Your shoulders ache from yanking against the clam's grip. You're stuck.

Something touches your arm, making you flinch. Is it the clam? You turn your head. "Oh, hi."

"Need a hand?" On turtle back, a kid is holding up a knife. "I can cut the ends of your straps off, and get you out."

"That'd be great."

The kid balances on the edge of the turtle's back, leaning with one arm on the clam's shell, and saws at your backpack straps.

You tumble through the water, landing on the sand. The ends of your straps are hanging from the clam's shell.

"Thank you." You grin, flexing your shoulders. "You saved my life, and my straps were too long anyway."

"No problem, I'll see you around Mystic Portal." The turtle swims away and the kid rejoins the tour.

A familiar voice sounds behind you. "An excellent solution, even if it was from a turtle rider."

You whirl. "Hippo! I thought you'd gone."

"By the time I realized I'd lost you, that turtle rider was already helping. Climb aboard, we have to get to the finish line."

"But we've lost the race already."

"No we haven't." Hippo's lip curls. "There are no losers in this race, except those that don't finish. Although the first home is the winner."

You hold on tight as Hippo races over coral bridges, through gardens of purple and yellow anemones, and waving forests of green seaweed. He swims past a wall of coral, twisted in beautiful multi-colored formations.

"When I was a young seahorse, I played a game with my brothers and sisters, imagining what these coral sculptures were."

"I see what you mean. That one looks like a goblin." You point at a green formation with appendages like arms and legs and a gaping hole that could be a mouth.

"This one looks like a seahorse's belly, full of eggs," says Hippo, nodding his head towards a smooth round formation.

"Um, yeah, I guess."

Moments later, you're over the finish line.

Sidney swims toward you, looking relieved. "I was beginning to get worried. Did something happen?"

You show him your backpack. "The clam got my backpack, but a turtle rider helped me escape. See, it's hardly damaged. The straps are just a bit shorter."

Sidney's eyes gleam in admiration. "Wow, sounds like you had a bigger adventure than me."

Squee swims up to you, giving you a big dolphin smile. "Open your backpack," she says. "I have a surprise."

From beneath her flipper, she produces a large pearl. "Everyone who completes the Round the Coral Peninsula Extravaganza gets a prize."

"That's amazing. Thank you."

"I got one too," says Sidney. "Imagine the new bikes we can get now."

"Yeah." You nod. "But first we have to get back to Mystic Portal."

"We can arrange that for you," Squee says.

"Goodbye," calls Sheriff Kingpin, entwining his blue tail around

306

Kampos' yellow one.

"Good luck with your little seahorses," you call.

Hippo butts you with his nose. "Come back soon, right?"

In a flash of blue light, you're on the beach, with Sidney and Tracey, standing next to your bikes.

"Hey." Tracey waves. "I explored a sunken ship with the turtles. It was really dangerous, but we got out okay. How was your race?"

"We jumped squid hurdles and raced through snapping clams." Sidney grins. "And we each got these." He pulls his pearl out of his backpack.

Tracey's eyes boggle. "Wow, that's bigger than a tennis ball. You could buy hundreds of top quality bikes with that."

"That's the first thing I'm going to get." You grin. "But for now, let's take these bikes for another spin down Mystic Portal."

Congratulations, you've travelled down Mystic Portal, been for a ride on a dolphin and a seahorse, and escaped a squid and the snapping clams. But have you survived a sandstorm? Met a track-keeper? Found the You Say Which Way library? Been on a magic carpet? Or been transformed into a furry creature?

It's time to make a decision. You have 3 choices. Do you:

Go back and take a Terrific Turtle Tour? **P281**

Go to the list of choices and start reading from another part of the story? **P534**

Or

Go back to the beginning a try another path? **P201**

Return to the bazaar

"There's nothing out there." You wave towards the empty desert.

"I agree," says Tracey. "We came here to get away from the desert, we don't want to go back out there and die in that heat."

"Going back is dangerous," says Daania. "There's a magic gateway out in the desert that can get you home, but if we go back, the bandits will probably kill you."

"I don't care," says Tracey. "I'm tired and we've been in the hot sun all day. Can't we go back and have a rest in the tent? Surely there's somewhere we can hide from those horrible bandits."

"There may be one place we can hide…" Daania scratches her head. "But you'll have to be really quiet."

Daania tells the carpet to go back towards the bazaar. It bucks and sways as if it's reluctant to follow her orders, but she finally soothes it. Soon, you're near the market place. The carpet sneaks across the sand, barely above ground level so it's not visible behind the tents.

It's quite handy, not walking, because the carpet is much quieter than your feet would have been.

Behind the plain brown tent, Daania gets off the carpet, putting a finger to her lips to remind you both to stay silent. She lifts a small flap at the rear of the tent and crawls inside. You and Tracey follow.

In the dim light, you see sleeping mats on the floor and a bed along one side of the tent. Daania's grandmother is in the bed, coughing, under mounds of stripy cotton blankets. Daania gestures that you and Tracey should hide under the bed. Tugging some blankets so they hang over the side of the bed, Daania crawls in after you.

Not a moment too soon. Boots stomp up to the tent. The fabric walls shake as the flimsy fabric door is flung open. A male voice yells. Objects crash to the floor as they search the tent.

Tracey grips your arm. Heart pounding, you freeze, barely breathing. If they hear you…

The boots get closer to the bed. Someone barks at Daania's

grandmother. She coughs as she replies. Will they search under the bed?

At last the boots start to tromp towards the door. On your arm, Tracey's grip tightens. Why is she freaking out, now? The bandits are about to leave.

Suddenly, Tracey sneezes.

A cry comes from the tent entrance. Boots pound towards the bed. The blankets are flung back.

A man looks under the bed, brandishing his sword. "Got you! Hey boss, I've got another slave to work at Sands of Time Industries."

Sorry, this part of your story is over. Going back to the bazaar led you into the hands of the bandits. They kidnap you and take you to work in a factory making magical hour glasses that slow time to a snail's pace. Unfortunately, your aging process doesn't slow, so you become wrinkled and old in no time at all. But, never mind, you can have another adventure on Mystic Portal. There are other exciting jumps that take you to strange worlds. You could transform into a furry orange creature, ride a giant turtle or meet an ogre.

It's time to make a decision. You have 3 choices. Do you:

Go back and fly the magic carpet straight ahead to get home? **P328**

Go to the list of choices and start reading from another part of the story? **P534**

Or

Go back to the beginning a try another path? **P201**

Leave the track-keepers and join Tracey

"You're right, Sidney." You frown. "It's not fair to let Tracey get upset. We'd better go back and join her."

Sidney waves his arm towards the snake bridge. "When will the skinny be ready?"

Sharmeena shrugs. "Jumps need to weather in the sun and rain before they're ready. One day when you come back, this snake will be ready and then you can try it out. In the meantime, go and enjoy our other jumps."

"Thanks," you both say.

In a flash of orange light, your body changes back into your own. Your orange fur has disappeared.

Instead, you're wearing mountain biking gear, sitting astride your bike.

The snake jump is nowhere to be seen and neither are the track-keepers.

Sidney's standing by the side of the track, holding his bike.

"Hey," he calls, "you look much better with two eyes than one!"

"So do you. That was crazy. Do you think we've gone nuts? Or is there really a snake jump being built somewhere around here?"

Sidney shrugs. "If there is, it's invisible now. But I'm so glad I can't see any ogres. Come on, let's catch up to Tracey."

Congratulations, you've taken a crazy mountain bike jump, stumbled into an alternate reality, escaped an ogre and made friends with the track-keepers, the secret sculptors of Mystic Portal. When you and Sidney catch up to Tracey, she insists she's had wild adventures too. You all vow to come back to Mystic Portal another day and try out more jumps.

Maybe you'd like to go on an underwater trip with Terrific Turtle Tours, fight desert bandits, ride a magic carpet or skip through snapping clams on the back of a seahorse.

310

It's time to make a decision. You have 3 choices. Do you:

Go back and finish building the snake bridge? **P324**

Go to the list of choices and start reading from another part of the story? **P534**

Or

Go back to the beginning a try another path? **P201**

Save Junior from the shark

Junior was trying to save you. You can't let the shark eat him.

"Hey, shark!" You wave your arms, trying to distract the shark, so it'll drop Junior.

It doesn't work.

"There." Tracey points to the loose planks. "Grab one. I'll tug the shark's fin to distract it."

Diving through the water, you grab a plank and swim back to the shark.

It's still shaking Junior from side to side, like a dog worrying a bone. Tracey is straddling the shark's back, yanking its dorsal fin.

You bring the plank down on the shark's head as hard as you can. But you're pushing through water. It's not the same as air. Your aim goes off.

Instead of hitting the shark's head, the plank smacks its nose.

The shark's jaws fly open and Junior tumbles out.

"Aagh, my nose," bellows the shark. "My sensitive nose."

You and Tracey swim to a porthole, dragging Junior through the water by his leash. You push Junior out the porthole. "Go Tracey, help him get to the surface."

She slips out the porthole.

Out of the corner of your eye, there's a flash of white. The shark! You push your head and shoulders through the porthole, and shove off with your arms, propelling yourself outside, just as the shark's teeth graze your leg.

Pain lances though your calf and your blood floats through the water. Your leg has been bitten. You'd better get to shore before more predators smell your blood and come looking for lunch.

Heart pounding and leg throbbing, you make for the surface.

Above you, Tracey is swimming upwards, towing Junior by his seaweed leash. He's so large. How is she managing?

Something nudges you from below.

No. Another shark. You kick harder, determined to get away.

"Hold still," snaps a familiar voice. "How can I get you on my shell if you keep kicking me in the head?"

Tuck! You relax and let the turtle lift you to the surface.

Tracey is astride Nip, gripping Junior's leash. Junior floats beside her, his eyes shut. He's so peaceful, so quiet, so unlike Junior.

"He's such a sweet turtle," says his mother, Nip. "How we'll miss him."

"He was valiant," you say. "A shark attacked and he gave his life to save mine. I'm sorry."

What's that? Did Junior just move his head?

His head moves again.

He's not dead, although his eyes are still shut. No one else seems to have noticed that he's still alive. They're too busy talking and swimming.

He opens an eye and winks at you.

Ah, he's playing a trick on his parents. You decide to go along with it.

"Let's get you tourists safely to shore," says Tuck, "before that shark comes after us. Nip, have you got any healing weed?"

Nip pulls her head into her shell, then pokes it out again, holding a piece of yellow seaweed in her mouth.

"Wrap that around your injured leg," says Tuck.

Taking the weed from Nip's mouth, you bind your leg with it. Your shark bite stops bleeding. The throbbing in your leg dies down.

"Take the weed off now," says Tuck, "then rinse it, and give it back to Nip."

"But I've only had it on for a moment."

"That's all you need."

He's right. When you remove the binding, there's only a faint pink scar on your calf.

Tuck coughs. "You know, Junior's quite a good boy. Not sure if I ever told him that. I wanted him to take over the family business when we retired. Terrific Turtle Tours would have been his."

Junior's dad is tough. Maybe it would be good if Junior heard a few good things about himself. "What was Junior really good at?"

Nip pipes up. "He told such wild tales. He was a great storyteller and very kind."

Tuck sighs. "A strong swimmer too. And he had the gift of the gab, why he could talk a father seahorse out of its eggs."

"Really Dad?" Junior squeals. "You love the way I talk? Oh, wow, have I got a story for you."

His parents are so pleased he's recovered, that they let him chatter as much as he likes.

"The shark was so vicious. I knew our friend here was a goner, Dad, so I leaped right in there, diving into its jaws. You see, with its jaws full, there was no way it could eat our tourist."

"But it nearly ate you," says Tuck, his voice choked up.

"No, I was saved by these brave tourists. We really ought to reward them you know."

"Good idea," says Tuck thoughtfully. "But you saved them too, Junior. You've proven you can keep our tourists safe, so you've qualified for your passenger license."

"That's great!" you exclaim. "Could I ride home on Junior?"

"Of course." Tuck swims alongside Junior so you can hop off his shell onto his son's.

"Wow, wow, wow. My first real live passenger." Junior is so excited that his voice is higher and squeakier than usual. "I can't believe it. I really can't. This is so cool. I really truly honestly have my passenger license. Wow, I'm qualified. It's amazing. This is absolutely fantastic. It's the best day of my life ever. And it's all because of you!"

You can't help smiling as he swims over some giant snapping clams. Tracey points out seahorses with kids on their backs, zipping in and out of the clam shells.

"Is that the Round the Coral Peninsula Extravaganza?" you ask.

"Sure is," says Junior.

The seahorses are fast, popping out of the clam shells seconds before they shut.

"Oh no, look!" A kid's backpack straps are stuck in a clam shell. The kid struggles, but the straps only pull tighter. "Come on, Junior, let's help that kid."

Junior plunges downward. You extract a pocketknife from your backpack and cut the kid's straps free.

"Thank you." The kid grins. "You saved my life."

"No problem," you say. "I'll see you around Mystic Portal."

Junior swims back to Nip and Tuck and you all head back to the Terrific Turtle Tours' hangout, by the seaweed. Tuck disappears into the seaweed, through a patch of sunlight that makes the golden flowers glint among the seaweed.

Strange. Even though Tuck's sometimes a little grumpy, you'd expected him to say goodbye.

You pat Junior's shell. "Thanks for the tour, Junior, and thank you for saving my life."

"Will you come back and play again?" says Junior. "That was fun. Scary, but fun."

"It's been great," says Tracey to Nip and Junior. "You've taken good care of us."

Tuck swims out of the seaweed, holding strands of weed with golden flowers in his mouth.

"How sweet, Tuck." Tracey smiles. "You brought us some flowers."

You take the stems from Tuck's mouth. The blossoms are strange, perfectly round and flat, tied onto the seaweed. "What? These aren't flowers. They're gold coins."

"I know." Tuck grins. "The seaweed is a great hiding place for the pirate treasure, isn't it?"

You and Tracey laugh.

"You saved our son's life," says Nip. "Even though he is fully grown, he's the only child we have. Please accept our small gift in return."

Congratulations, you and Tracey use your gold coins to buy new bikes for you and Sidney—and more bikes for the school mountain biking club, so other kids can go riding too. You often return to Mystic Portal to have more adventures. Maybe you'd like to join the Round the Coral Peninsula Extravaganza, see what happens if you don't save Junior, ride a magic carpet or meet an ogre. Or you may prefer to build mountain bike jumps, or try your luck on Camel Hump or Ogre Jaws.

It's time to make a decision. You have 3 choices. Do you:

Go back and flee from the shark with Tracey? **P300**

Go to the list of choices and start reading from another part of the story? **P534**

Or

Go back to the beginning a try another path? **P201**

The Hydropolis Underwater City Tour

"It's a hard choice," you say, "but I like the sound of the thrills in the underwater city, so let's go there."

"Great, great, Hydropolis is my favorite!" Junior spins around in a circle, trying to nip his tail, churning up bubbles in the water and creating a mini whirlpool.

"Settle down, Junior!" snaps Tuck, "or we'll have to leave you behind."

"Please don't, sir," you interject. Junior will be much more fun than his parents. "We'd love to have him along. It's important that he completes his training so he can get his passenger license."

"Good point," says Nip.

Still spinning in his whirlpool, Junior winks at you.

"Oh, all right," Tuck concedes. "He can come along, but he'll have to behave himself."

Flipping out of his swirling water, Junior straightens up, as if he's standing at attention in an army inspection. "Yes, sir. I won't disappoint you."

"That's to be seen," says Tuck. He turns and swims off with Tracey on his back.

"Um, this way." Junior follows him, waving you forward with one of his forelegs.

Nip chuckles as she swims behind them. Vibrations run through her shell, tickling your legs, but you're glad she's laughing. You don't want her to be grumpy with Junior. He's more fun than Tuck.

You eye the uneven edge of Nip's shell where a chunk is missing. "How did you chip your shell?"

"Shark bite, but I swam off, so it only got a mouthful of shell."

Sharks? You look around, but can't see any—unless they're hiding in the seaweed. "How far to Hydropolis?"

"Not far. Just a few more yards."

What's she talking about? There's only blue ocean and fish ahead.

Oh, and Tuck, Tracey and Junior.

Without warning, Tuck and Junior dive downwards, disappearing from sight with Tracey.

"It's the drop off, my favorite part." Nip plunges over the edge of a coral-encrusted cliff.

Below, a vast city of skyscrapers and industrial-like buildings is sprawled on the seabed. Enormous rusty bridges span gaps between rooftops. Spires are festooned with colorful weed that waves as you approach. Crumbling office blocks look like mouths with more holes than teeth, as fish swim in and out of open windows where there must've once been glass. A lobster pokes its head out of a gaping window as you pass. The tentacles of an octopus are hanging from the orifices of a building.

Creepy. Weird. Amazing.

Landing on the roof of a skyscraper, Tuck, Tracey and Junior wait for you.

"Isn't this place awesome?" Tracey asks as you land.

"Just wait, it gets even better," squeaks Junior. "Dad, can I show them? Can I show them, please?"

Tuck nods. "Yes, son, you can."

"Follow me. Whee!" shrieks Junior, sliding down a plastic tube along the outside of the building and into a window.

Shrugging, Tracey follows. You jump after her. The chute curls and twists down the side of the building. "Hey, it's a waterslide," you call to Tracey.

She laughs.

You both erupt from the chute in a tangled mess and float above the concrete floor among darting fish.

"Look!" Junior points towards a rack of bicycles. Lobsters hold the bikes in place, each with one enormous pincher grasped around the frame and another around the bike rack. "This is best part of the Hydropolis tour." Junior beams. "Choose one and hop on."

Tracey pats a lobster on the head. "Thank you for taking care of this bike. I'd like to ride it now please." She's using her polite voice—good call. Those lobsters' pincers look pretty sharp.

You choose a bike at the other end of the rack, thank a lobster, and get on. "Hey, this is unusual. I've never been on a floating bike before." No matter how hard you grip the handlebars, your butt floats off the bike seat, and your feet don't want to stay on the pedals.

"Fasten your seatbelt," laughs Junior. "And put your feet in the pedal clips." He picks up a long flat object in his mouth and swims over to you.

"What's that?"

"Mff, mff ivvnning mrrfff."

You can't understand him, because of the thing in his mouth.

"A diving belt," says Tracey. "It has lead in it to stop you floating to the surface."

Once you and Tracey secure your belts, seatbelts and pedal clips, Junior swims out a window and you follow. Pedaling the bike turns a propeller on the back, which moves you through the water. "Hey, this is cool."

A purple fish swims past your face, turning its bulbous yellow eyes towards you. It darts away to join a school of other purple fish, moving in unison like they all know the same dance.

Junior leads you to the rooftop of another building. "Visitors from Mystic Portal often enjoy biking," he says. "They tell us these bridges are the best feature of the city, and often want to bike over them. Follow me." He takes off across the rooftop, then swims just above the surface of a bridge.

"Let's go," calls Tracey, biking off after him, her propeller leaving a trail of bubbles that stream past as you follow her.

This is great. The propeller provides extra power, shooting you across the roof of the building and up over the high arc of the bridge. The ironwork on the bridge's rails is rusty and hung with streamers of seaweed. At the highest point of the bridge, you fly high into the water, then float down, landing next to Tracey and Junior.

"This is incredible. We should try some directional jumps too."

Tracey nods. "Brilliant idea. With the combination of a propeller and water, directional jumps should work well."

"Let's do a team jump," you say. "I'll go left, you go right."

You and Tracey race side-by-side up an arched bridge. At the peak, you twist your handlebars and lean to the left. Your bike follows, floating effortlessly through the water.

Tracey has veered to the right. You land on buildings at the opposite ends of a narrow flat bridge. Hunkering down on your bike, you tighten your seatbelt and pedal like crazy. Tracey's doing the same. There's no room to pass each other. It's a classic game of chicken. Which one of you will give way first?

You keep your eyes ahead. Tracey's getting closer. And closer. Too close. You're about to crash. Yanking your handlebars vertically, you lean back, pedaling hard. Your bike speeds up towards the surface. Tracey does the same.

Her laughter drifts on the current. You push your bike back into a horizontal position and circle round to meet each other. You experiment with your water bikes, dodging in and out of buildings, somersaulting over obstacles and pedaling around abandoned factories. Junior makes sure you don't go near the octopus' lair, just in case it attacks.

Soon Nip and Tuck arrive to guide you back.

"This has been awesome," says Tracey "I've learned so many new skills, so much about balance. You can't always test that stuff on land, because you'd hurt yourself."

"Yeah." You can't help grinning. "It would have been too risky to try these stunts on Mystic Portal."

"Can we come back again?" Tracey's eyes are pleading. "Please?"

"Of course you can," says Junior. "Oh, I mean, can they, Mom? Dad?"

"Sure," says Tuck. "You've given Junior some good practice at tour guiding today."

"But how will we find you?" Tracey asks.

"That's easy," you answer. "We'll go down Mystic Portal and over Dolphin Slide again."

"Can you come again tomorrow?" asks Junior, wagging his tail.

"We'll come again as soon as we can," you assure him. "We love it here, don't we, Tracey?"

The turtles swim to the edge of the shore.

"Thank you," you and Tracey call as you climb out of the sea onto the soft white sand.

"Hey, look." Tracey points at your bikes, leaning against a tree at the edge of the sand.

"Hey, how were the turtles?" Sidney calls, emerging from the water. "I had a blast on the seahorses."

"Hydropolis is an incredible underwater city," calls Tracey. "You'll have to come with us next time."

"Sure will," says Sidney, wringing out the dripping hem of his shirt. "Let's come back tomorrow. There are so many cool things to do on this trail."

"I can't wait." You grin as Tracey, you and Sidney high-five each other.

Congratulations, you and Tracey often return to Hydropolis underwater city, bringing Sidney with you.

You all become so good at jumping and bike tricks that you become the best bike acrobatics team in your area. Sponsors clamor to provide you with the latest fanciest mountain bikes and biking gear. You keep your old bike, just for fun.

Often, you take a quick trip down Mystic Portal with Tracey and Sidney to try out the new jumps that mysteriously appear on the trail. There are many more adventures on Mystic Portal. You could visit the sunken ship, ride a seahorse in the Round the Coral Peninsula Extravaganza, ride a magic carpet, face bandits, or tame an ogre. The choice is yours.

It's time to make a decision. You have 3 choices. Do you:

Go back and ride a seahorse in the Round the Coral Peninsula Extravaganza? **P272**

Go to the list of choices and start reading from another part of the story? **P534**

Or

Go back to the beginning a try another path? **P201**

Return to ride Mystic Portal

The ground trembles beneath your feet. Usually you'd think it was an earthquake, but now you know it's Bog. Your fur stinks of smoke and the bright daylight up here makes your eye squint.

Sidney leans in and whispers, "I don't fancy getting caught by Bog again. What say we go for another bike ride?"

"Good idea," you mutter as the ground quivers again. "The sooner we get back on our bikes, the better." You turn to Sharmeena. "Thanks so much for saving us from Bog. It would be fun to build trails, but we're pretty tired right now, so maybe we could come another day."

She nods and blinks her large eye at you. "I'll be here, building more jumps. Feel free to join me anytime you want." She vanishes in a flash of orange light.

Suddenly you're standing on the side of the track, holding your bike. Sidney's next to you, taking a swig of water from his drink bottle. His bike's leaning against the trunk of a nearby pine.

What just happened? Did you imagine everything? Are you going crazy? Or are there really strange creatures running around beneath the track? You clear your throat awkwardly.

Sidney's eyes dart around as if he's expecting Bog to charge out of the trees.

"Um…" You clear your throat again.

You're just downhill from Ogre Jaws. There doesn't appear to be anything odd lurking in the trees, but something strange is hanging off the back of Sidney's bike.

Walking over, you reach out and touch the orange fluffy tail dangling from his seat post. "I guess we didn't just imagine everything."

"Look, you've got one too," says Sidney, pointing at another orange tail on the back of your bike. He looks relieved. "I thought I was going nuts, but now I know I'm fine."

"Fine?" You laugh. "We're back on the bike trail, alive, with cool tails. That's better than fine. It's great."

"Beats being stuck in a cage with a fire-breathing ogre waiting to eat you," says Sidney, shuddering.

"Sure does." You get back on your bike. "Let's do some more jumps. I'm dying to see what happens next."

With a thrum of tires, Tracey bursts out of the trees. She's just come down the chicken line around Ogre Jaws.

"Hey, am I glad to see you two!" Her bike skids to a stop. "I had the craziest adventure. When I went over Camel Hump, my bike turned into a magic carpet. I've been battling desert bandits and I even met a genie from a magic lamp."

There are long gold and green threads wound around Tracey's handlebars. Could they be from the magic carpet?

"Sounds like fun," says Sidney, "but we've been fighting an ogre!"

"Fighting an ogre? Stop teasing me," groans Tracey. "I'm serious."

"So are we," says Sidney.

You nod. "He's telling the truth."

"Yeah, right," Tracey rolls her eyes then stares at the orange tails on your bikes. "Wow!" She raises an eyebrow. "Let's go. I want to see what happens on our next jump."

Congratulations, you saved Sidney from an ogre, became a track-keeper and cut your way through rock with a laser beam. Every chance you have, you come back to Mystic Portal. The track is never the same twice and each jump takes you to a new adventure. You may like to build a new jump with the track-keepers, go on Tracey's magic carpet, meet a talking camel or visit the underwater city of Hydropolis.

It's time to make a decision. You have 3 choices. Do you:

Go back and stay with the track-keeper to build new jumps? **P266**

Go to the list of choices and read another part of the story? **P534**

Or

Go back to the beginning a try another path? **P201**

Finish building the snake bridge

"Tracey's used to us disappearing and hiding from her," you say.

"That's true," says Sidney. "Maybe we can stay a few more minutes and finish off this bridge."

"Team," calls Sharmeena, "finish the landing ramp and snake bridge while I take our friends to get some water."

"But we're not thirsty." The last thing you want is to miss is jump building. It usually takes months to make a jump. These cool track-keepers are doing this jump in an hour or two.

"This time, the water is not to drink. Well, it is in a way." Sharmeena laughs. "Come on, I'll show you what I mean."

You go back to the river and Sharmeena bends down and starts drinking. And drinking. And drinking! At her throat, the fur swells, creating a huge bulge.

"Wow," says Sidney, "you're just like a pelican, with a pouch that swells up when it's full of fish. Only yours is for water."

Sharmeena motions with her foreleg for you to do the same. You and Sidney bend down to drink. It's amazing how much water your pouch can hold. A huge bulge swells out under your fur so you can hardly see your hooves.

You both follow Sharmeena back to the new launch ramp. She spits water all over the jump.

"Come on," she says. "Every jump needs to be weathered with the rain and sun to make it hard enough for bikes to go over it. This speeds up the process."

You and Sidney spit your water over the ramp too. Once you're finished, track-keepers stomp all over the ramp to compact it. Racing back to the river, the three of you gather more water for the off-ramp, then join in, stomping down the damp earth.

"Can't wait to jump this," says Sidney, "but it won't be ready for months. What a shame we don't have a giant hairdryer to dry it all out and make it hard."

"Yeah," you answer, "or a whole month of scorching hot days."

"We have something better," says Sharmeena. "Hide over here, and watch."

A group of track-keepers carry a bundle of silver ropes in their teeth. They stand on the track just down from the off-ramp and spread out, tugging the ropes. It's a silver net. How is that going to harden the jumps and make them more stable? Maybe it's for bikers who fall off? No, the net is placed *after* the bridge, not under it.

Sidney elbows you. "What are they doing?" He frowns.

A thunderous roar echoes through the trees.

"Quick," says Sharmeena. "Deep breath. Use your camouflage."

Together, you and Sidney take enormous breaths and are instantly camouflaged.

A moment later, Bog crashes out of the trees, chasing a tiny track-keeper. The wee creature runs, flat out, its orange fur ruffling in the wind. Bog stomps along behind it, bellowing.

"Can't catch me," calls the tiny one, racing up the on-ramp.

Roaring, Bog blasts the little track-keeper with an enormous jet of flame.

But the little one leaps high in the air, clearing the huge gap where the snake bridge will go, and scampering down the off-ramp.

With another ear-splitting roar that makes your knees tremble, Bog leaps over the gap and blasts fire at the off-ramp. He charges after the tiny track-keeper, who nimbly ducks in and out of the silver net. The other track-keepers discard their camouflage and they pull the ropes tight around Bog.

"No, not net. I hate nets," Bog cries as the ropes ensnare him. His writhes in the net, trapped.

Sharmeena steps forward. "We won't use the net on you again, Bog, if you promise to harden our jumps with your fire and to stop chasing us."

"But I so hungry," says Bog. "You so tasty. Takes lot of food to feed big guy like me. You let my human toast go." He starts to cry.

Poor Bog, its sounds like he's having a rough time.

Beside you, Sidney mutters, "Can't fool me. He'd try to eat me again if he had a chance."

"That's no excuse, Bog," says Sharmeena. "If you help us build these tracks for humans to play on, we can bring you plenty of vegetables to eat, but you have to promise to stop hunting people and track-keepers."

Bog's Mohawk is crushed, and his skin is red and inflamed from the net.

"I bet that net's enchanted," you whisper to Sidney.

"Looks like it," he says.

Bog stops crying. "Yes. Anything to stop the net."

"We'll let you lose, now," says Sharmeena. "But you have to prove your loyalty by lifting that snake bridge onto this jump and making sure it's secure."

Bog wipes his nose, leaving globs of snot on his arm, then nods.

Moments later, the bridge is in place. The ogre stomps on the ends, pressing them deep into the ramps so the bridge doesn't wobble. He shoots jets of flame over the surface of the dirt to harden it.

The track-keepers cheer, and praise him.

Bog stands back to admire his work. A tear glints in his eye. "I never… um… never made anything before," he says. "I only destroyed things." He pats the tiny track-keeper on the head. "Never had friends before."

Bog comes over to Sidney and grins. "Sorry about toast. We be friends too?"

"Sure." Sidney gulps. "Um, no problem, I think." Only a few hours ago, he was going to be Bog's human toast. You don't blame him for freaking. "Um, I like your hair." He points at Bog's red Mohawk.

"Thank you." Bog's stomach growls.

The track-keepers laugh. "Let's get you some vegetables now, shall we?" says Sharmeena. "Before you get too hungry..."

Great idea. Neither you nor Sidney want him to eat you or your new friends.

"Yummy," Bog says. "I roast them?"

"Sidney," Tracey's voice yells through the trees. "Where are you two?"

"We'd better get back to Tracey." You wave to Bog, Sharmeena and the other track-keepers. "We'll see you again soon."

In a flash of orange light, you're suddenly both human, on your bikes again, riding along the track behind Tracey.

"Hey, Tracey," you call out. "Where have you been? We've been looking for you for hours."

"I went down Camel Hump." Tracey stops at the side of the track. "Wait until you hear where Camel Hump took me." She grins. "What have you two been up to?"

You and Sidney exchange a glance. Whatever happened to her, she's never going to believe your story.

Congratulations, you escaped Bog and made friends with him, met the secret track-keepers, and helped build a new feature on Mystic Portal. You could ride a magic carpet, fight desert bandits or ride a seahorse. You could also find the track-keepers' secret library, visit a sunken ship or win some gold.

It's time to make a decision. You have 3 choices. Do you:

Go back and try to use Bog's key to free Sidney? **P242**

Go to the list of choices and start reading from another part of the story? **P534**

Or

Go back to the beginning a try another path? **P201**

Fly the magic carpet straight ahead to get home

Even though you can only see sky and sand ahead, and can't see any way of getting home, you'd rather trust Daania than those bandits. "We'll go home," you tell her. "Show us the way."

Flying over the desert, you marvel at the ripples and patterns in the sand far below.

"Beautiful, isn't it?" asks Daania. "Those patterns are caused by the wind."

"Incredible," says Tracey. "Not a camel's hoof print in sight."

The desert seems to stretch on forever, endless dunes merging with the sky on the horizon.

"What are those blobs over there?" Tracey leans forward, shading her eyes with her hand.

"Those are rocks," answers Daania. The carpet zooms closer. "See that big one with the arch?"

"You mean the one that looks like an elephant?" you ask.

"Exactly," says Daania "it's called elephant rock. That's where we're heading."

The enormous reddish-brown rock rises out of the desert plateau. Other large rocks are scattered nearby. Its resemblance to an elephant is so uncanny you almost imagine its ear twitching. One end of the rock is similar to an elephant's head, with a hollow where its eye would be. A thick trunk runs from its head down into the ground.

Daania points to the space between the trunk and the body. "We're going through there," she says. "If the carpet flies under the elephant's trunk, anyone on it will instantly go home. Well, that's what local legends say."

"Legends?" questions Tracey, her voice trembling. "We're relying on an old legend?"

You place your hand on her shoulder. "Just like legends of magic carpets," you say, "and talking camels. Now we know they're true too."

Tracey grins. "Yeah, we're the stuff of legends, now!" She taps Daania on the shoulder. "If this works, I'm happy to leave the carpet with you. Take good care of it, and remember: always speak to it nicely."

Daania's eyes shine with tears. "Thank you," she says. "My grandmother needs an operation in hospital, but she's too old to go by camel. Now I can take her on the carpet." She kisses Tracey's cheek. "I promise to take care of it, until you both return."

"Thanks Daania."

Elephant rock looms in front of you. "Look," you cry, pointing at the shimmering air under the trunk. "That looks really weird."

"It's your gateway home." Daania smiles. "Have a nice trip."

You and Tracey barely have time to call, "Thank you," before the carpet zips under the elephant's trunk.

With a whump, you're both back on your bikes, riding down the lower part of Mystic Portal. Sidney's shirt flashes on the trail ahead of you.

"Hey, Sidney," you call. "Wait up."

He stops his bike. "Man, I thought I'd lost you both," he says when you catch up. "What's that on your wheels?"

You and Tracey look down. "Wow," murmurs Tracey, winking at you. Twisted around your spokes are gold and green threads from the magic carpet.

Sidney would never believe your adventure. "Oh, that's um…," you say, trying to improvise like crazy.

Tracey saves the day. "Dunno. Must've come from that sandy patch we rode through."

You laugh aloud. She's right. You *did* ride a camel and a magic carpet through a *sandy* patch—an enormous patch of the Sahara desert!

Sidney looks puzzled. "I didn't see any sand," he says.

"That's because you went down the chicken line," you answer.

"By the way," says Tracey, "did you see any chickens? After all, we saw a camel on Camel Hump."

330

"Ha, ha. Come on, let's get riding." Sidney jumps on his bike and you and Tracey follow him down the hill, grinning.

The next jump is tiny, hardly worth mentioning, except when you're in the air, the tinkling laughter of the magic carpet floats up from your wheels. As if your bike has a mind of its own, it starts sweeping and loop-the-loop-ing, high above the trees.

Tracey's bike has gone wild too, somersaulting her through the air. "Yay," she cries. "Now we can be bike acrobats."

With carpet in your spokes, you'll never need a new bike. This one will always fly.

Congratulations, you survived the desert, met a talking camel, made friends with a magic carpet and Daania, and now have a new bike that flies. You could also find seahorses or an ogre, confront a sand storm, race a camel, or work for an Arab merchant.

It's time to make a decision. You have 3 choices. Do you:

See what happens if you return to the bandits at the bazaar? **P307**

Go to the list of choices and start another part of the story? **P534**

Or

Go back to the beginning a try another path? **P201**

Trade the magic carpet for the lamp and genie

"Magic wishes sound awesome," you say to Tracey. "We should trade."

"I agree." Tracey hands the carpet to the girl.

The girl passes the lamp to Tracey, unrolls the carpet and climbs on, speaking to it gently in her own language. The carpet whooshes into the air. "Be careful how you use your wishes," she calls out, before she speeds off into the desert.

Tracey bites her nails, and hands the lamp to you. "You go first."

You can't believe *she's* nervous. She's always calling you and Sidney chickens. "Surely you aren't afraid of a little lamp?" you ask.

"No, I'm fine," she says, stepping away from the lamp, as if it will bite her. "Come on, rub it and see what happens."

The lamp is old-fashioned. A long spout extends from its belly with a wick set in the end of it. The top surface is carved and has a small lid for refilling the oil. The handle is warm in your hands. "Oh well, here goes," you say, polishing the tarnished gold with your fingertips.

Purple smoke wafts from the spout. The pungent smell of lavender fills the air.

"Whaddaya want?" says a grumpy voice. "Can't you see you've woken me?"

The smoke thins and a little man is standing in front of you. His ears and nose are decorated with gold rings. His purple and gold waistcoat and golden billowing trousers sparkle in the bright desert sun. Frowning, he stamps a foot, making tiny bells tinkle on the end of his pointy crimson shoes. "I said, why did you wake me?" He twirls the ends of his droopy moustache.

Tracey replies, "Daania said you'd grant us each three wishes."

"What? Daania gave me away?" The genie folds his arms. "Well, I'm having a bad hair day. I don't feel like granting any wishes."

"But you don't have any hair!" exclaims Tracey, staring at his bald brown head.

"So what! I don't have to work just because you rub my lamp and ask me to." He folds his arms and turns his back on you. "I'm striking. I'm feeling off-color."

There's nothing off-color about his bronzed skin.

"Please?" asks Tracey. "Just for us."

This is amazing. She's nearly begging. You've never seen her plead for anything before.

The genie ignores her.

Tracey's voice grows soft as she cajoles the genie. "We're terribly sorry for waking you. We don't want much," she says. "Just new bikes and to get back home. Please."

Tracey is using the P-word again. Incredible.

"Nope, I said I'm on strike." He stomps his foot again.

This is a losing battle. You have to do something. Maybe flattery will work. "All we want is to get home. Surely you can help us? After all, you're so strong and powerful."

"Sneaky tourists with their nasty tricks, flattering camels and carpets and pretending to have manners," he roars, whirling to face you. "I've had enough of you. Be gone!" The genie flings his hands outwards.

In a blinding flash of purple light and smoke, the tents disappear.

You're standing next to your bikes near the bottom of Mystic Portal. Just below you, Sidney takes a small jump and lands on the pale dunes above the beach.

He turns and waves. "Hey, where have you two been? I've been waiting for you for ages. Come on."

"Wow, that was amazing," murmurs Tracey, "but I'm glad it's over."

"Yeah, it was incredible, but what a shame that genie didn't grant us any wishes."

"Well, at least we survived." Tracey gestures at the track. "After you."

Tracey's letting you go first? Unheard of. Perhaps she learned some manners in the desert, after all.

"Thanks." You get on your bike, wondering if you dreamed everything.

A high tingling laugh rings through the forest. The carpet? No, you can't see a flying mat anywhere. Until you glance at your handlebars and notice tattered threads of gold and green carpet twirled around them.

You take the small jump at the bottom of the track. Maybe, just maybe, the genie did grant one of your wishes. "Take me home please," you say.

Instead of landing, your bike the veers to the left and heads through the sky towards home.

Laughing, Tracey instructs her bike to do the same.

Upon the white dunes far below, Sidney stares at you both, his mouth hanging open. "Hey," he calls, "wait for me."

Tracey laughs again. "Dear carpet," she says, "Could you help Sidney?" She takes a strand of carpet off her handlebars and throws it down to Sidney. "Wrap this around your bike."

Sidney catches the thread and winds it around his frame. Moments later, he's in the air beside you. "Hey," he calls, "Mystic Portal is the best!"

Congratulations, you survived the desert, taught Tracey to be more pleasant, met a talking camel and flew on a magic carpet. Although the genie didn't directly grant your wish, he did send you and Tracey home, and gave your bikes new powers—mountain biking will never be the same again. Maybe you'd like to take some of the other exciting jumps on Mystic Portal. Who knows what new worlds are down the track waiting to be explored?

It's time to make a decision. You have 3 choices. Do you:

Go back to the bazaar and keep the magic carpet? **P231**

Go to the list of choices and read another part of the story? **P534**

Or

Go back to the beginning a try another path? **P201**

Go to the track-keeper party

"Let's party!" you and Sidney cry.

"Great!" Sharmeena bounds down the right-hand tunnel, jostling you and Sidney on her back. Her green light beam bounces off the walls.

At the back of your mind is a nagging worry. Bog is happy now with his belly full, but what will happen when he gets hungry again? You and Sidney don't have any more peanut butter and jelly. Although you promised Bog you'd teach the track-keepers how to make it, what if they don't have the ingredients?

After a few minutes, the passage leads to an enormous cavern. Green lights around the walls illuminate a large crowd of track-keepers, chatting, playing leapfrog and doing gymnastics.

"Wow, there are so many of you," Sidney exclaims. "I thought there might be a few track-keepers, but not hundreds."

He's right. There are way more than you'd imagined.

Sharmeena leaps onto a small stage in the front of the cabin and lets out a shrill whistle. The hubbub ceases. All the track-keepers turn to face you. Still on Sharmeena's back behind you, Sidney grips your waist even tighter.

Sharmeena raises her voice so it carries throughout the cavern. "These two adventurers have tamed Bog. They discovered he was only fierce because he was hungry, and they found food that satisfies him."

Cheers and whistles ring through the cavern. Track-keepers stomp their hooves. Others do somersaults in midair, the green beams of their eyes ricocheting around the room. You can't help grinning. Sidney's grip on your waist relaxes and he lets out a whoop.

"Party! Party!" The track-keepers chant.

But then it hits you again—Bog could attack at any moment.

Dismounting, you stride to the front of the stage and hold your hand high. Soon the mayhem stops and the track-keepers are silent, watching you. Except for one small track-keeper, who keeps whistling and bouncing around.

"We may have tamed Bog for now," you say, "but I'm afraid we haven't solved your problem." An undercurrent of murmurs runs through the cavern. Clearing your throat, you continue. "Bog will need more peanut butter and jelly. I doubt you have any and I don't know how we're going to make it."

To your surprise, the little wriggly track-keeper laughs. "No problem," it squeals, turning another somersault.

"But—"

Low chuckles break out, then giggles and loud raucous laughter. Some of the creatures roll around the floor. Sharmeena is cracking up too.

Sidney nudges you. "What's so funny?"

"I don't know." You shrug. "Maybe they're delirious with fear, but Bog will eat them if we can't make peanut butter and jelly."

The laughing crowd parts to let a group of track-keepers through. They're dragging something fastened to two long ropes. As they get closer, you see that it's a huge earthenware pot, mounted on wheels.

Sharmeena whistles to quiet the crowd, then turns to you. "This is why we're laughing."

An ominous roar floats down the tunnel.

Bog! He could be here any minute. "You think a piece of pottery is going to stop an ogre?" you cry. "It's not even big enough to block the cavern door. And even if it was, he'd shatter it in moments. How is this going to help?"

Sharmeena smiles. "Take the lid off."

Lifting the lid, you peer inside. "It's empty." How disappointing. Bog roars again. "I wish it was full of peanut butter," you say, shooting a nervous glance towards the corridor. "That would solve our problem."

Around you, track-keepers start laughing again, pounding the floor with their hooves. You're about to snap something rude at Sharmeena when you smell the delicious aroma of peanut butter and raspberry jelly. Your nostrils flare. Your nose twitches.

Sidney is sniffing the air, too. "Is that what I'd think it is?" He points at the pot.

It's full to overflowing with peanut butter, shot through with beautiful thick swirls of raspberry jelly.

"Impossible," you murmur.

"No it's not." Sharmeena laughs. "The pot of plenty makes sure we have whatever food we wish for. If we'd only known that Bog was hungry, we could have fed him."

"Yum." Sidney scoops a fistful of peanut butter and jelly out of the pot, and licks it off his hand.

"Ew, yuck, Sidney." You wrinkle your nose. "No one will want to eat out of the pot now that your hand's been in it."

"Except me!" booms a voice from the door of the cavern.

You gulp. It's Bog, looking meaner than ever in the eerie green glow of the cavern. His red Mohawk bristles and his nostrils flare.

Then he grins and races towards the pot, sticking his face inside to suck out the peanut butter and jelly. Moments later, the pot is empty. Bog's face is covered in smears of peanut butter and blobs of jelly. He burps happily. "Someone say party here?" he asks.

"Lights," calls Sharmeena.

The green lights around the edge of the cavern pulse. Only they're not lights at all—they're track-keepers, using their eyes as lights, blinking in rhythm with one another.

Sidney raises his eyebrows. "Wow, these creatures are handy."

"Drums." Sharmeena claps her hands.

A ring of track-keepers stomp their hooves, creating a drumbeat.

"Music," she calls.

Track-keepers start to sing bizarre yodeling songs with a catchy beat. You can't stop your feet from tapping in time to the music.

"Dancers," Sharmeena yells over the music.

Track-keepers somersault through the air, and land in formation. They twirl and jump to the music.

Sharmeena nods at you. "Get on."

You climb upon her back and hang on for dear life as she leaps among the dancers. Your adrenaline surges. Exhilaration flows through you. This party is in your honor. You saved Sidney and the track-keepers from Bog.

Bog surges into the crowd, heading your way. He scoops you off Sharmeena's back and flings you into the air. With a whump, you land in his arms and he hoists you onto his shoulders.

"My hero," he sings at the top of his rich bass voice. "You brought peanut butter and jelly, oh so lovely and smelly, so I can fill my belly."

Amazing. Whoever thought that ogres could sing?

You dance for hours, and then you and Sidney flop onto some large cushions in a corner.

"Let's try out the pot of plenty," says Sidney, eyes gleaming. Before you can stop him, he says, "I wish for chocolate brownies."

The aroma of warm chocolaty brownies wafts from the pot. Grabbing a handful, you both munch them down.

"I wish for curry," says Sidney.

The brownies disappear and a spicy scent fills the air, making your belly grumble—although you've just eaten.

"That wasn't very clever." You roll your eyes at Sidney. "We don't have any cutlery."

"That's okay." He reaches for the pot. "We'll just drink the curry down."

No he won't. "I wish for candy."

The jar is immediately filled with all sorts of sweets in brightly-colored wrappers.

You only have a chance to take one, before Sidney calls, "I wish for kumara fries."

"What's kumara?" You peer inside the pot.

Small wedges of orange and yellow vegetable, coated with seasoning, fill the pot. "These smell incredible," you say. "What are they?"

"Kumara," says Sidney smugly. "Sweet potato from New Zealand. It's famous all over the Internet. I've always wanted to try one."

You bite into a kumara fry. "This is the best food I've ever tasted."

"Great, isn't it?" Sidney grins. "It's a shame Tracey isn't here to enjoy these. She'd love them."

Tracey! What's happened to her while you've been underground? You'd better get back to Mystic Portal.

As if she can read your mind, Sharmeena appears beside you. "The party's winding down, so you'll need to go home," she says, "but because you've helped us, we'd like to give you both a gift before you leave."

Sharmeena leads you to a small tunnel at the back of the party cavern. Her eye lights up the passage. You round a corner and come to an enormous pile of bikes.

"Careless riders abandon these on Mystic Portal. We bring them here to tidy up the litter, but we can't use them. Would you both like one?"

Litter? These bikes are top quality!

"Would we ever!" Sidney selects a bike that's the same model as Tracey's new one.

You choose a top-of-the-range mountain bike with the latest front and back suspension, high-tensile forks and mag wheels. "This is awesome. Thank you, Sharmeena."

She grins. "Follow me." Sharmeena takes you up a steep spiraling tunnel. It's so tight, your bikes just squeeze around the corners. The tunnel ends in a rocky wall. There's no way out.

"What now?"

The beam from Sharmeena's eye shoots out and hits a small red button embedded in the rock.

"Didn't notice that button," says Sidney.

The rock slides away. Outside is Mystic Portal. You and Sidney wheel your bikes out onto the trail. You both turn to Sharmeena.

"Thanks so much for the new bikes." You wave.

"Yeah, they're great." Sidney waves too.

"You deserve them for taming Bog," says Sharmeena. "See you around." The rocky door on the side of the cliff slides shut.

Tracey rounds a corner and skids to a halt in front of you. "Hey what are you two doing here? And where did you get those bikes?"

"You're never going to believe this!" says Sidney excitedly.

You shake your head. "Yeah, he's right. We've had an adventure, but it's been unbelievable!"

"Why don't you try me? I've just had a really strange ride," says Tracey. "After what happened to me, I'd believe anything!"

Congratulations, you freed Sidney and tamed Bog the ogre, keeping the track-keepers safe so they can build more jumps on Mystic Portal. You've also had a great party and have a fantastic new bike. There are plenty of other adventures on Mystic Portal. Maybe you'd like to fly on a magic carpet like Tracey, see giant pearls inside snapping clams or confront a shark. Or you could go back and see what happens if you bend the bars to free Sidney.

It's time to make a decision. You have 3 choices. Do you:

Go back and bend the bars to free Sidney? **P261**

Go to the list of choices and start reading from another part of the story? **P534**

Or

Go back to the beginning a try another path? **P201**

Stay for slingshot training

"I think we'd better stay," you say. "We'll never survive in the desert, and we don't know how to get home."

"Yeah," says Tracey. "I don't fancy being the main course for vultures."

"Or their desert dessert," you reply.

Tracey smiles. "Let's help them unload."

Although poison seems like odd cargo for schools, you have nothing better to do, so you agree to help.

As one of the guards passes Tracey a box, she stumbles, dropping it. The top flies open and plastic bottles of brightly-colored stuff spill out.

Poison must come in all shades of the rainbow. You bend down to help her pick up the bottles. "Hey!" You hold up a bottle, pointing at the label. "This isn't poison. It's poster paint!"

The guard laughs, and calls, "Hey, these kids thought we were shipping poison to school children."

Other guards join in laughing. One of them calls, "Why would we do that? My son goes to the school that these supplies are being shipped to."

"And my daughter," calls another.

Karim comes over. "I'm sorry, that must have given you a fright. I should have explained earlier. I made my fortune importing rat poison, years ago. We're just re-using these old boxes." He opens some other boxes. "See?"

The cartons hold rubber bands, balloons, crayons, colored pencils, paper, books and other school supplies. You and Tracey grin foolishly.

"We're glad you're helping children. That's awesome." Both of you pick up boxes and follow the guards to the storage room.

After the school supplies are unloaded, a guard shows you the slingshot training area—a wide hall with tires mounted on targets at one end. An odd metal track runs along the side of the room. Children are a few yards in front of you, shooting metal darts from modern-looking slingshots. They hardly ever miss the tires.

"How are we going to get that good?" whispers Tracey.

"Dunno."

A man with a braided beard, a thick gold ring through his nose and a chest wider than a camel's, strides towards you. "New trainees?" He shakes your hands. "I'm Achmed. We'll have you shooting as well as these youngsters in no time." He nods to dismiss the guard and takes you both to a stand in a corner of the room.

Upon the stand is an ornate full-face helmet. Its polished black surface reflects your face, like a glassy lake. Crouched upon the front of the helmet is a sleek golden panther, its legs coiled with power as if it's about to leap out and devour you.

"That panther's real gold, isn't it?" asks Tracey.

Achmed nods. "24 carat."

"Wow," you breathe. The helmet's beautiful. You can't help yourself, you reach out to touch the panther.

"STOP!" shouts Achmed.

Just in time. Red laser beams spring to life, criss-crossing the area around the helmet.

Instinctively, you yank your hand back.

"You were lucky," Achmed says. "You only activated the warning system. Any further, and you would've lost your fingers. The bandits have been trying to steal this helmet for years, so we had to set up this system."

Rubbing your fingers with your other hand you stutter, "Th-thanks."

"Close call," mutters Tracey. "Are you okay?"

Achmed twists one of the braids from his beard around his finger. "This helmet will be awarded after our next battle—to the youngster who prevents the most bandits from reaching our compound."

You want that helmet. You'll do whatever it takes to get it. "How effective are the slingshots and darts?" you ask. "And how many bandits has the best kid stopped so far?"

"The slingshots are good," Achmed says, "but the bandits know we have them, and they're always coming up with ideas to outwit us. So far, we've managed to keep the bandits away from our compound by disabling their vehicles, so no one has been hurt. The best youngster has stopped four vehicles of bandits, so far this month." He points to a girl. "Bahar is our best shot," he says proudly. "She's my daughter, and will probably win the helmet."

Not if you can help it. You'd love that helmet.

"Here." He passes you and Tracey each a newfangled slingshot.

Weird. These slingshots are nothing like you've ever seen before.

Achmed shows you how to hold it by the sturdy plastic handle. It's strange, the handle goes sideways, not straight up and down like you'd imagined. It attaches to a rectangular metal frame. Yellow tubes hang off the back of the frame. A small barrel, like a gun barrel, is attached to the top of the rectangular frame, with clear plastic beneath, marked with a red cross.

You pull at the tube, saying, "We pull this to fire the darts, don't we?"

Achmed nods.

"That means the dart flies through the middle of the frame," says Tracey. "But what's this barrel on top?"

"The plastic's probably for sighting, but I don't know what the barrel does," you answer, turning to Achmed.

"That's a laser to help you sight your target accurately."

Tracey looks impressed. "Laser? That's hi-tech."

Achmed nods. "A microcomputer calculates how far the laser is from the target, and shows you where to aim." He waves at his daughter. "Bahar, come over and demonstrate. You other youngsters, stand by the wall, so you don't get hit."

Tracey and the others move aside.

Bahar is tall, about your age, with a long dark plait. Holding the slingshot up, she pulls a dart from a pouch at her side, fits it in the yellow tubing, and pulls it back. "Just press this button on the handle," she says. At the far end of the room, her green laser lights up a spot on a tire. "Then line up your laser spot with the red cross on the plastic sight, and release the tubing." She looks through the clear plastic and lets go of the tubing. Her dart hits the tire.

Achmed nods at you. "Your turn."

You miss your first few shots, but that's not so bad because Tracey does too. After ten minutes, you're both hitting the targets every time.

Tracey's eyes shine with pleasure. "This is so much fun."

With a groan, the metal track along the side of the room starts to move. A hatch opens and a cutout wooden panel of a Land Rover moves along the rail. It has real tires mounted where the wheels should be, and is followed by several others.

The kids line up and shoot their darts at the moving targets, hitting the tires. You and Tracey join the queue. You both keep firing until your battery packs are flat and need recharging.

"Come on," says Achmed, "it's getting late and you must be famished."

After a fine feast of meat, salads, dips and flatbread smothered with herbs and goat cheese, you fall into a huge bed, exhausted. In no time, you're asleep.

In the morning, you're woken by loud rapping on the door. Tracey calls, "Quick! Get up! Bandits are coming."

You scramble out of your room and meet her in the hallway. "Here," she says, giving you your slingshot. "The batteries are fully charged."

When you're further down the hallway, Achmed calls you. "In here, come and get your armor."

Armor sounds serious. The room is crowded with guards and the slingshot crew, preparing for battle. Achmed thrusts bullet-proof vests and trousers at you and passes out sturdy grey helmets and binoculars. Bullets? No way! But, like soldiers in a war zone, you're ready in no time.

Achmed points to a burly guard. "Stick with Duba, he'll look after you."

You dash behind Duba up narrow stairs to the top of the compound wall, Tracey's feet thudding behind you. The distant whine of motors echoes across the desert. Clouds of dust billow on the horizon. Your heart pounds. The bandits will be here soon.

Tracey gives you a tight nervous smile and raises her binoculars to her eyes. "I had no idea there'd be so many. Take a look."

The drone of four-wheel drives makes your neck prickle with anticipation. You stare through the binoculars. There must be at least ten vehicles out there, all filled with bandits. The first has a red skull with silver teeth painted across the hood. The rest are behind it, hidden in the dust churned up by its wheels. As they get closer, their motors roar.

Suddenly, your slingshot seems flimsy, your bulletproof vest too thin.

The Land Rovers stop. The dust dies down.

"Slingshots ready," calls Duba. "Aim and—"

"Duba!" Bahar cries from along the wall. "Their tires are hidden."

Shocked, you realize she's right. Metal sheets are attached to the bandits' vehicles, shielding their tires from your darts.

"No," cries Duba. "We have to stop them from getting closer, or they'll attack us. Youngsters, get down from the wall to safety. Bahar, take everyone to the training hall."

There must be some way to stop those vehicles. Something you can do.

"This way. Fast." Bahar hustles you all down from the wall, across a courtyard, past the storage room for the school supplies. The door is ajar.

"That's it!" You cry. "Follow me."

Dashing into the storage room, you rip open boxes of balloons and paint. "Quick, pour the paint into balloons and tie a knot in the top. We'll paint bomb their windscreens so they can't drive any closer."

"Great idea," calls Tracey. "Come, Bahar and you others, help!"

With so many kids helping, you soon have a box of paint bombs. You, Tracey and Bahar race back to the top of the wall.

"Get back down," yells Duba. "I told you youngsters to stay away. It's getting too dangerous. I said—"

The roar of Land Rovers drowns out his voice. The bandits have nearly reached the compound.

Bahar ignores Duba. Crouching behind the raised outer edge of the wall, she tips the paint bombs onto the floor so you and Tracey can reach them.

You fire a paint bomb at the nearest Land Rover. It splatters over the windscreen, fluorescent pink paint dribbling down over the red skull on its hood. Yellow follows. Then green. Blinded by paint, the bandits grind to a halt.

"Good thinking," calls Duba.

Beside you, Tracey has covered another Land Rover in blue, gold and silver. Bahar has covered hers with green and brown, the colors merging so the windscreen looks like it's splattered with poo.

Turning, you aim more bombs at nearby vehicles. You're just about out of paint, when the bandits lunge out of the Land Rovers, holding wicked knives.

"Hide," Duba yells. "We've got this. Agh—"

His cry is cut off as a knife flashes past you, hitting him in the arm.

"Grab him Bahar!" You load. Fire at a bandit just outside the wall. Paint splatters over the bandit's face. Reloading, you fire another paint bomb.

The bandit screams, rubbing his eyes and flees back towards the vehicles. Another bandit races towards the wall, his knife raised. Reaching for a paint bomb, you fumble. There are none. They're all gone.

Out of the corner of your eye, you glimpse the blue paint-splattered Land Rover that Bahar hit, and have an idea.

Down in the courtyard, a woman is tending Duba's wound. Bahar is heading up the stairs to the wall with another box of paint bombs.

"Bahar," you call, "Tracey will grab those. Go and get sacks of camel dung as fast as you can."

Grabbing some youngsters to help her, Bahar dashes off.

Tracey plonks the carton of paint bombs down next to you. You both reload, fire, and spray more bandits with paint.

Soon, Bahar is passing large bags of camel dung along the wall to the guards and slingshot crew.

You pick up a ball of dung. It's smelly and warm. Even though the outside is firm, you can tell the inside isn't.

"Gross," says Tracey, going for paint bombs instead. "That stinks."

"That's the point."

A grappling hook flies up over the wall past the guards. The rope on the end pulls taut. You glance over the edge. A bandit with a huge scar on his cheek is making his way up the wall. You load your camel poop in the yellow tubing and line your laser up on Scar Cheek's face.

Scar Cheek bellows to his friends to join him. You fire. The dung hits him in the face, some of it entering his open mouth. Yowling, he spits, letting go of the rope, and falls to the desert below.

The rest of the slingshot crew leap to action, firing dung balls at more bandits. The old hard dung makes them yelp with pain. The fresher dung makes them bellow and curse.

Paintballs fly. Every bandit is covered in paint, poo or both. Some are chased by swarms of flies.

Scar Cheek shouts, signaling his men to retreat. You were so busy firing, you hadn't realized all the bandits had cleaned their Land Rovers' windscreens. Within a few minutes, only empty balloons, scattered camel poo, and abandoned ropes and weapons remain—and a cloud of red dust marking the bandits' retreat.

"Phew," says Tracey, wiping her paint-splattered hands on her even-more-paint-splattered armored vest.

Your own hands are covered in dung and you smell like a camel's rear end. "Oh well," you say, "someone had to get their hands dirty."

"I'm just glad it wasn't me," says Tracey. "Paint is bad enough. The dung was a great idea though."

"Yeah, it worked."

"It certainly did," says a deep voice.

You spin.

Duba's behind you, holding his bandaged arm against his body. "Excellent job. Everyone helped, but due to your great ideas, we got rid of those bandits. As soon as you've cleaned yourself up, Karim wants to see you." He wrinkles his nose. "Make sure you use lots of soap."

Everyone laughs.

Duba addresses the whole slingshot crew. "Well done, youngsters. Merchant Karim wants to reward you all for your hard work."

Reward? Could that mean…?

Tracey nudges you. "Come on, stinky, I'm dying for a shower."

It turns out, Karim doesn't have showers, only baths. You soak in a huge warm tub of bubbles, but not for long. You're keen to see what that reward is.

Once you're dried and dressed in clean clothes, you're dismayed at the dirty multi-colored ring you've left around the bath.

A maid bustles in. "Don't you worry about that. You're a hero today, so no cleaning for you. Go and see merchant Karim immediately."

Grinning, you race to the training area.

Tracey smiles. "You smell much better," she says, digging her elbow into your ribs.

Entering the hall, Karim shakes your hand vigorously and greets the slingshot crew and guards. "You have all shown great resourcefulness and resilience today. Those bandits are terrifying, but you faced them with bravery." He strides to the cabinet in the corner and presses an alarm pad on the wall, turning off the lasers. Lifting the beautiful helmet from the stand, he brings it over and faces you. "Everyone was brave today, but you were brilliant, coming up with paint bombs and dung balls. Wear this helmet with pride when you return home."

"Thank you." You grin. "Um, did you say *return home*?"

"Yes, I'm sending you home." He places the helmet on your head.

Wow, you can hardly believe you won the helmet. It fits perfectly and makes you feel amazing. With a helmet like this, you don't need a new bike.

The merchant calls to a guard, "Saddle up Jamina. They're ready to go home."

"How?" asks Tracey.

"Easy," he replies. "When Jamina jumps off the compound wall, a portal to your world will open."

"J-Jumps off the c-compound wall?" stutters Tracey.

"I'm sure that'll be simple for two adventurers like you." He laughs, winking at you.

Everyone cheers as you and Tracey climb up on Jamina. How she negotiates the narrow stone stairs up the compound wall is a mystery, but soon you're at the top.

"Ready?" she asks. Without waiting for an answer, she leaps.

In a brilliant flash of light, you're back on the trail at Mystic Portal.

Congratulations, you've ridden a camel and a magic carpet, defeated the desert bandits with your brilliant ideas and become a hero. On every trail you bike, people admire your amazing helmet. You often return to Mystic Portal to have many more adventures. You could ride a sea turtle, explore an underwater city, or go to a party with hundreds of furry orange creatures. Or you could continue your desert adventure by finding out what happens if you speak politely to the magic carpet.

It's time to make a decision. You have 3 choices. Do you:

Go back and talk to the magic carpet politely? **P228**

Go to the list of choices and start reading from another part of the story? **P534**

Or

Go back to the beginning a try another path? **P201**

Race Jamina in the Camel Races

"I'd love to race Jamina, you say, shaking Aamir's hand and smiling at Latifah, even though you're not looking forward to another bone rattling ride. "And thank you for your generous offer of accommodation. The desert is a harsh place so I'd be happy to stay with you."

You'd also be happy to go home, but you don't mention that. It'll probably upset him again.

In no time at all, you're in Aamir's tent, eating a delicious salad of couscous, juicy figs and oranges, and drinking cool fresh lake water from a water skin.

When you're finished, Aamir whisks you into another part of the tent and pulls a large red headscarf from a bag.

"Here, this will protect you from sand and dust," he says, wrapping the scarf around your head and over your nose, and securing it. "Red is my family's color. You honor us by wearing it."

Taking you outside, he checks Jamina's saddle is secure, and helps you up.

Holding Jamina's halter, Aamir leads you past a hubbub of people among the tents, and through date palms and orange trees—which account for today's lunch. Soon you're out on the track that surrounds the oasis. Camels and their riders are milling behind a rope held by two young children—an improvised start line. There are ten camels in all, and a betting stand with a queue of people placing bets. The sidelines are crowded with spectators. The whole oasis must be here.

Flashing his teeth, Amir smiles up at you. "If you win today, I'll split the prize with you."

Prize? "That's generous of you, Amir. What's the prize?"

"Half a pound of gold. Good luck." He strolls off to the sidelines.

Half a pound of gold? Your mouth hangs open like an empty saddlebag as you think of all the things you could do with gold. You could even buy new bikes for you and Sidney, just as good as

Tracey's—if you ever get home again. Now the race seems like a much better idea.

"Are you ready?" asks Jamina, striding over to stand behind the starting rope.

"Sure, any time."

An official strolls along the row of camels, inspecting them and prodding the jockeys. He finds a leather pouch under one jockey's saddle and opens it, sprinkling a pinch of yellow powder on the ground. In a guttural voice, he sends the jockey and camel off the racecourse.

"Why aren't they racing?" you ask Jamina.

"That's a saffron bomb. It makes camels sneeze and their eyes water. Saffron bombs are banned, so that rider's disqualified."

The official prods a young rider's ribs and sends his camel away too.

"Some families starve their jockeys to make them lighter so they can win the race," says Jamina. "They're also disqualified."

At the far end of the line, the official yells and two camels are dispatched from the racecourse.

"What was that about?"

Through her solid body, Jamina's camel chuckle makes her sides thrum and tickles your legs. "Those two have hidden small rockets under their saddles. They get out in front, and explode the rockets, making their camels run faster and the ones behind run away in fear." Jamina snorts. "Some camels are sillier than others. I'm not spooked by a stupid rocket."

With four camels disqualified, there are only six left—Jamina and five others. "Do you think we have a chance of winning?" you ask.

"More chance than those cheats," replies Jamina, snorting again.

You really must talk to her about snorting so much.

The crowd quiets. Aamir gives you the thumbs up and winks.

A man in gleaming white raises his arm, and then drops it. The children let go of the rope.

With thundering hooves, camels race off, dust rising around you. You wish you had your sunglasses on, rather than in your backpack in Aamir's tent. Your body lurches wildly from side to side. You try to move in time with as Jamina speeds up.

The rider on the camel to your left whips his camel. It cuts in front of you, blocking off Jamina's path. With one of her infamous snorts, Jamina nips the other camel's flank. It veers off the race course. You and Jamina spurt forward through the gap.

All the other riders have whips. They beat their camels, and surge forward, leaving you and Jamina to eat their dust.

Even if you had a whip, you wouldn't want to use it on Jamina. She's been your friend and saved your life. You mentally kiss the gold goodbye. It was a nice dream, but there's no way you're going to catch up with those other camels now. You can't even see them, the cloud of dust is so thick. Glad for the headscarf over your mouth, you hunker down on Jamina's back. The dust seems thicker. The camels' hooves, louder.

Through the haze, camels appear. You're gaining on them. You pass one and pat Jamina's side. "Well done, girl."

The dust starts to clear. Palms on the side of the track peek above the dust cloud. There are only three camels in front of you. Wow, you may have a chance of winning after all. But as you pass the camel on your right, the rider flings something. A billowing cloud of yellow fills the air—a saffron bomb. The official must have missed one. Water streams from your stinging eyes as Jamina runs straight through the yellow haze, snorting and bellowing. Ahead, an inhuman shriek of pain fills the air. One of the camels has stumbled. It lies on the ground, its hind legs splayed right in your path. Jamina will never be able to stop in time. You're going to crash. Your race will be over.

Jamina charges. Leaps. And clears the camel's legs.

"Yahoo! Go girl," you shriek at the top of your voice.

Another snort. Jamina's hooves thunder along the compacted sand, chasing the lone camel. Not far now. Nearly there.

352

The leading rider glances back, shooting you a panicked look. She reaches under her saddle and pulls out a roll of something. A blanket? How is that going to help her? She flings the blanket in front of her and it unfurls hovering just above the race track.

Not a blanket! A flying carpet. The camel jumps on board, rider and all. They take off, zooming along the track, just above the sand.

There are no spectators here. Palm trees and bushes around the oasis shield this pair of cheaters from being spotted.

"Not fair," you yell, although it's no use. You'll never win now. Oh, well, at least the thought of gold was nice for a while.

You're tossed from side to side as Jamina bolts along the track.

"Slow down, girl. We're never going to win."

Ignoring you, she charges ahead, kicking up dust behind you.

Yeah, she's right. If you're going to race, you may as well finish. Palm trees blur as Jamina races past them. Something flashes among the palms, but you've no time to look, because the carpet in front is slowing.

"Come on, Jamina. Let's race!" You slap your hand against your thigh.

Jamina spurts ahead. She wasn't joking when she said camels could run 40 miles an hour. Her speed is brutal, but your butt will never be the same again.

Through the palms, you catch a glimpse of the lake, and beyond it, colorful tents. "Come on, girl, we're nearly at the finish line."

Giving one last spurt of speed, Jamina shoots ahead, narrowing the gap between you and the cheaters on the magic carpet.

Abruptly, the carpet stops. The camel steps off.

Jamina races forward. She's nearly caught up to them.

The cheater's camel lashes out with its hind legs. A thud ricochets through Jamina's body.

"Mwoooaaaah!" Her shriek of pain knifes through you. She lurches. Staggers. Nearly throws you off.

"Jamina, are you okay?"

Her breathing is labored, heavy, but she keeps going, staggering forward at a half run, around the corner.

In the distance, the cheaters cross the finish line. Spectators roar.

Behind you, around the bend, telltale dust rises in the air. The other camels are closing the gap, catching up. Still, Jamina staggers forward, running unevenly.

Patting her flank, you encourage her. "You doing well, girl. We're nearly there."

You glance behind to check your competitors. What are those dark splotches in the red sand? Deep-crimson splotches. Jamina's blood!

She's been so faithful, run so well, and saved your life in the desert. It's so unfair. "Jamina, you're hurt." Tears well in your eyes. "You don't have to finish. You've run well."

No answer. How you wish she'd snort, chuckle, or say something. The only sounds are her harsh breathing, the uneven thuds of her hooves, and the drumming hoofbeats behind you, getting ever closer.

The finish line looms. The crowd becomes distinct faces. Worried and anxious, you ignore the spectators, rubbing Jamina's neck as she slows, plodding across the finish line.

A moment later, the other camels catch up and race past you, leaving you and Jamina standing in the middle of the track, eating their dust.

The crowd cheers.

Don't they realize your camel's hurt?

She bends her front legs, kneeling. You're off her back before her rear haunches sink to the ground. Racing around to her head, you inspect her for damage.

A gash in her chest is bleeding. You rip your headscarf off and use it to staunch the blood.

Aamir rushes to your side. "How did she hurt herself?"

"She didn't. The rider in front of us cheated, and then that camel hurt her."

"Looks like a gash from a hoof," Amir announces. Before you can explain any further, he signals some men to take care of Jamina, and a loud horn blows.

The rest of the racing camels gather back near the finish line.

"They're announcing the results," Aamir says.

The official strides over to the cheater whose camel gashed Jamina and holds the rider's hand high in the air. They both beam as the official calls out something in Arabic.

You're about to protest, when the crowd parts and man strides forward, a camera with an enormous telescopic lens hanging around his neck. Yelling at the official, he grabs the camera and points to the screen.

The official steps over to take a look. Sidling closer, you peer over the man's shoulder. The photo clearly shows the cheater and camel using a flying carpet to win the race. That flash in the palms as you were racing, must have been from his camera.

Shouting, the official waves his arms in the air like an agitated windmill. Two men run over and drag the rider away.

Aamir approaches you. "They're disqualified. That means we won the race." His white teeth gleam against his dark beard in an enormous grin. "Well done."

Within moments, you're hoisted on people's shoulders. The crowd cheers. People stomp and whistle. Somewhere, a loud horn is blown.

You look for Jamina, but she's gone.

"It's alright," says Aamir, when he sees you searching. "My best healers are taking care of her. Soon she'll be well enough to do the victory lap with you."

Victory lap? There's no way she can run, but you nod, too tired to argue. When will you ever get home again? And where are Tracey and Sidney?

In the evening, as you're nestled in the sand next to Jamina, leaning against her side, Aamir approaches. "You raced well today," he says. "You must have a lot of racing experience."

Thinking of all the bike tracks you've been on with Tracey and

Sidney, you smile. "I have done some racing, but not on camelback. The credit really goes to Jamina."

Jamina raises her head and snorts. A good sign, she must be feeling better.

Aamir peels back the bandage on her chest. Taking a small clay pot from his robe, he smears smelly salve over Jamina's wound. Grinning, he replaces the bandage. "This salve will do wonders," he says. "You should both be able to do your victory lap by tomorrow."

No way, she'll need longer to heal, but you don't say it out loud.

Aamir gives you a blanket. "I'm guessing you'd rather sleep out here, under the stars by Jamina."

"You're right." Your eyes grow heavy and you fall asleep to the sound of his footsteps traipsing away through the sand.

Someone shakes you awake. You squint in the bright morning sun.

Aamir is bending over you. "Let's check Jamina's wound."

When he rips off the bandage, you're astounded. "How's that possible? Her wound's gone!" You rub Jamina's smooth fur, amazed that the gash has healed.

Aamir hands you your backpack, an orange and some figs. "I've put some wonder salve in your backpack," he says, "just in case you need it one day. You looked tired, so I let you sleep late, but now you must eat. The victory lap is in a few minutes."

The orange is juicy and the figs are sweet—a breakfast for royalty. Aamir saddles up Jamina while you're eating and soon you're astride her, heading for the race course.

"Wow, I didn't expect this. There are nearly as many folk as yesterday." They start cheering as you approach.

Jamina snorts. "Of course there are," she says. "We're important, we won the race."

"So now we race again?" you ask.

Another snort tells you you're wrong. "Of course not," Jamina replies, stepping on to the track.

An official stands before you with two bulging leather pouches. He passes one to Aamir and the other to you. The gold. Wow. Hastily, you stuff yours in your backpack as Jamina walks along the track. The crowd's clapping and cheering nearly deafens you. People throw handfuls of leaves and flower petals towards you, like confetti swirling through the air. As Jamina walks, she turns her head to gaze at the crowd. Her eyelashes flutter, and her lips are pulled off her teeth in a weird camel smile. She looks like a queen greeting her subjects.

You smother a chuckle.

A short distance along the track, two children hold a rope.

"We only go that far?" you ask Jamina.

She nods. "Thank you for being such a loyal rider. I have a special gift for you."

"There's no need for a gift," you say. "You saved my life in the desert and I've had a wonderful time with you. That's enough."

Instead of snorting, Jamina turns her long neck towards you. Did she just wink?

The crowd is still cheering from the sidelines as you cross the finish line.

With a flash, Jamina and the desert disappear. You're back on your bike, trees zipping past you, as you burst out of the forest into the sand dunes at the bottom of Mystic Portal. Crashing breakers on the beach below tell you that you're at the end of the bike trail.

Bracing yourself for the shock of your tires sliding on sand, you gasp when your bike whizzes through the sand smoothly. How is it possible? You glance down. The rims of your wheels are wider and you have enormous fat tires, especially made for traversing sand. Laughing, you realize the fat sand tires are Jamina's gift. They remind you of her wide feet tromping through the desert. At the top of the dune, you launch your bike into the air and as you land, small puffs of sand rise around your tires. You could swear you heard a camel snort.

A whoop sounds behind you and Tracey and Sidney break out of the tree line, heading over the dunes towards you. Thinking of the gold in your backpack, and all the great biking gear you can buy for you and your friends, you grin and call out, "Hey, have I got something to tell you two!"

Congratulations, you've had a successful adventure on Mystic Portal. With all the gold you've earned racing camels, you buy new bikes for Tracey, Sidney and yourself and set up a mountain biking charity to help kids who can't afford bikes. Every now and then, you jump over Camel Hump to visit Jamina for old times' sake. There are many more adventures on Mystic Portal. Maybe you'd like to tour the underwater city of Hydropolis, tame an ogre, discover the mysterious track builders or ride a seahorse.

It's time to make a decision. Do you:

Go back and ride with Tracey on the tatty flying carpet? **P219**

Go to the list of choices and start reading from another part of the story? **P534**

Or

Go back to the beginning a try another path? **P201**

General Glossary

Asian Camels — Asian camels are known as Bactrian camels, and have two humps. These camels have high tolerance to cold, drought and high altitudes. In 2002 the population was estimated at only 800 camels, so now they are listed as a critically endangered species. A small number of these camels are found in Australia, although most Australian camels are dromedaries. (See dromedary below).

Camel eyelashes, eyebrows and nostrils — Camels have a double row of eyelashes to prevent sand entering their eyes. They also have prominent bony ridges above their eyes, which also helps shield their eyes from sand. Their large bushy eyebrows stop glare from the sun, and their nostrils can shut against sand. (See closed nostrils in picture below).

Camel Feet — Camel feet are large and wide, which helps them walk on sand more easily. Camels have two toes on each foot. These are joined by webbing underneath the foot which allows the toes to spread as they walk on sand. The pads of their feet are covered with thick protective soles, and near the heel, camels have a ball of fat which cushions them as they walk.

Camel's Gait — A camel's gait, or the way it walks, is unusual. Camels and giraffes have long legs, short bodies, and large feet, so they walk in a similar manner. Camels and giraffes move both legs on the same side of their body at the same time. Most four-legged animals move a foreleg (front leg) then the back leg (hind leg) on the opposite side of their body.

Camel Hump is a Storage Cupboard — A camel's hump stores up to 80 pounds (36 kilograms) of fat. The camel breaks this down into water and energy when food and water are not available. These humps mean camels can travel up to 100 desert miles (161 kilometers) without water. A camel can go a week or more without water, and several months without food. They can drink up to 32 gallons (46 liters) of water at one drinking session! Camel's humps are quite firm to touch.

Unlike most mammals, a healthy camel's body temperature changes throughout the day from 93°F-107°F (34°C to 41.7°C). This allows the camel to conserve water by not sweating as the air temperature rises.

Camel Races — Camel races are often held in Arab countries and large amounts of money can be won when betting on camels. Recently, laws were made to outlaw child-jockeys (riders) in camel racing, because people were starving child-jockeys to make them lighter so their camels could win. No one starves their jockeys in Mystic Portal and all riders treat their camels with the love and care they deserve.

Dromedaries — The dromedary is a species of camel found in Arabia. Dromedaries have one hump. Fully-grown males weigh 880—1,320 lb (300—600kg), while females weigh 660—1,190 lb (300—540 kg). Camels have a long curved neck, a narrow chest and are covered in long, usually brown, hair. Camels are well-known for their tolerance to heat and for carrying burdens and riders across the desert. Camels are herbivores—they eat desert vegetation, such as grasses, herbs, and leaves.

Hippocampus — Seahorse is the name given to 54 species of small marine fish, also known as Hippocampus. "Hippocampus" comes from the Ancient Greek word *hippos* meaning "horse" and *kampos* meaning "sea monster."

Male seahorses carry their eggs — Male seahorses carry their young after the female inserts mature eggs into a pouch on the male's belly.

Turtle Group — A group of turtles is known as a bale, nest, turn or a dole of turtles.

Mountain Biking Glossary

You don't need to know these terms to enjoy the story but we thought you'd enjoy learning mountain biking slang.

Mountain Biking (MTB) — Mountain bikes are bicycles that are used off roads, over rugged terrain. Mountain bike and mountain biking are often abbreviated as MTB in mountain biking communities. There are various styles of mountain bike riding. Specialized bikes are often used for each style. Some common biking categories are: cross country, Enduro, downhill, slalom, freeride, dirt jump, trials, street, marathon and trail riding. Definitions of these styles and some other mountain biking terms are below.

Air—Air describes how high you get off the ground when you take a jump. "Hey, I just got nine feet of air." "Did you get any air?" "How much air did you get?"
Air time—How long a bike is in the air after a jump. "I just had two seconds air time."
Berm—A built-up wall of dirt at the corner of a trail, or an embankment on a trail, or banked corner.
Boulder Garden/ Rock Garden—A section of the trail which is covered with big boulders that the rider needs to jump or bike over.
Chicken Line—A chicken line is a part of the trail that gives a rider the chance to go around a jump or an obstacle, instead of doing the jump, i.e.: an alternate less-risky route.
Cross Country (XC)—Riding from a start point to a destination (or in a loop) over various types of terrain. Cross country riding usually includes climbs and descents.
Directional Jump—In a directional jump, the rider has to change direction in midair before landing.
Dirt Jumping (DJ)/Dirt Jump Bike—Dirt jumpers ride bikes over shaped mounds of dirt (take-off ramps) to become airborne. They land

on the landing ramp—usually another mound of dirt, some distance away. Some dirt jumps are designed to propel the biker high in the air. Others are designed to see how far the rider can get. Dirt jump bikes are simpler, with less moving parts (no gears etc), so they break less easily upon landing (or crashing).

Downhill / Downhill Trail / Downhill Ride (DH)—Mountain biking downhill on steep, rough terrain with obstacles such as jumps, drops or rock gardens. The fastest rider to the bottom wins. Downhill riding is often done on ski slopes or other steep areas, where riders get back to the top by ski tow, cable car or bus. Downhill riders have a reputation for speed and, sometimes, recklessness.

Downhill Jump—A bike jump designed so the take off point is higher than (or uphill from) the landing point.

Downhill Gap Jump—The take-off point is uphill from the landing point and there is a huge gap between both. See Gap Jump below.

Drop Jump / Drop / Drop Off—A ledge you can ride over. The rider drops off the ledge onto the trail below.

Dropping In—Dropping in is entering a steep track when other riders are around.

Dualie—A bike that has both front and rear suspension, i.e.: dual suspension. Suspension is a mechanical system that cushions the rider from hard landings and jolts, so a dualie is most comfortable to ride.

Endo—A crash when you fly over your handlebars, i.e.: over the end of your bike.

Enduro / All Mountain—A riding style similar to the type of racing in the Enduro World Series. This includes uphill climbs and downhill racing over technically challenging terrain. Enduro rides can take a whole day to complete.

Freeride / Big Hit / Hucking—Freeride is a do-anything style of riding that includes downhill racing, enormous jumps and skinny elevated bridges. It also includes stunts that require skill and aggression. Many of the most popular mountain bike videos online are freeriding.

Four Cross / Slalom (4X)—Riders compete on separate tracks, or on a short slalom track, with dirt jumps, berms and gap jumps.

Gap Jump—A gap jump has a take off ramp and a landing ramp, which are separated by a huge space in between. The most common example is a jump made of two dirt mounds with a pit or flat area between them. The aim of a gap jump is to be able to clear the distance easily. Failing to clear the gap often means smashing into reinforced timber at the front of the landing ramp.

Granny Gear—The lowest gear available on a bike, which only a grandmother would need to use. Designed for steep uphill climbing, but extremely easy to pedal in on flat ground.

Gravity Check—A fall.

Grinder—A long uphill climb.

Gutter Bunny—Someone who only bikes on the road—to school or work.

Hard-tail—A mountain bike that has no rear suspension—less comfortable to ride than a bike with full suspension. Suspension is a mechanical system that cushions the rider from hard landings and jolts.

Lid—Helmet.

Marathon/Touring—Long distance riding on dirt roads or a long single track. This includes mixed-terrain touring, which is riding over many types of surfaces on a single track with a bike suited for all types of surface.

Nose Wheelie—A reverse wheelie riding technique. The rider elevates the rear wheel while still rolling on the front tire.

Shred—Riding trails with speed and skill so other riders are impressed.

Skinny—A narrow bridge, sometimes high above the ground, which bikers ride along.

Step Up—A jump, with a gap, that takes you to a higher level. You jump your bike up over a step to the next level up a slope. Many bikers say step ups are the ultimate thrill, so these are often placed at the end of a trail, so the ride ends with a great jump.

Street Riding / Urban—Riders perform tricks by riding on (or over) man-made objects.

Switchback—A sharp corner on a trail, like the corners in a zigzag. Usually switchbacks help you climb hills that are too steep to pedal straight up.

Tabletop Jumps—This kind of jump has a flat platform connecting the on-ramp and off-ramp. Less experienced riders can land on the tabletop (platform), but more experienced riders will clear the entire jump and land on the off-ramp. Some people believe that table-tops are less risky than gaps because there is no gap to clear. But all jumps are dangerous. Table-tops look easier than gap jumps, so less-skilled riders may be tempted to try table-tops that are beyond their ability.

Trackstand—A riding technique: when the rider stops without putting a foot down.

Trail riding—Riding trails, such as unpaved tracks, forest paths, and signposted routes in recreational reserves. Trails can be a single track or a group of trails that form a trail center. (Don't confuse this with Trials riding).

Trials—Trial riders hop and jump bikes over obstacles, without touching their feet on the ground. Trials riding can be off-road or in town. Street-trials riders use man-made structures in a city or town. (Don't confuse this with Trail riding).

Wipeout—Crash. An old surfing term, used by bikers.

Wheelie—Lifting the front wheel off the ground, usually done by pulling on the handlebars, pedaling harder, and balancing well.

Wheelie Drop—A combination of a wheelie and a jump. Riders use wheelie drops to jump off a ledge at low speed when they only have a short run-up.

Whoop-De-Dos—A series of up-and-down bumps, suitable for jumping.

DANGER ON DOLPHIN ISLAND

By Blair Polly

Lagoon Landing

From the float plane's window, you can see how Dolphin Island got its name.

The island's shape looks like a dolphin leaping out of the water. A sparkling lagoon forms the curve of the dolphin's belly, two headlands to the east form its tail, and to the west another headland forms the dolphin's nose. As the plane banks around, losing altitude in preparation for its lagoon landing, the island's volcanic cone resembles a dorsal fin on the dolphin's back.

Soon every camera and cell phone is trained on the fiery mountain.

"Wow, look at that volcano," shouts a kid in the seat in front of you. "There's steam coming from the crater."

The plane's pontoons kick up a rooster-tail of spray as they touch down on the lagoon's clear water. As the plane slows, the pilot revs the engine and motors towards a small wooden wharf where a group of smiling locals await your arrival.

"Welcome to Dolphin Island," they say as they secure the plane, unload your bags, and assist you across the narrow gap to the safety of the wharf.

Coconut palms fringe the lagoon's white-sand beach. Palm-thatched huts poke out of the surrounding jungle. The resort's main building is just beyond the beach opposite the wharf.

Between the wharf's rustic planks, you can see brightly colored fish dart back and forth amongst the coral. You stop and gaze down at the world beneath your feet.

You hear a soft squeak behind you and step aside as a young man in cut-off shorts trundles past, pushing a trolley with luggage on it. He whistles a song as he passes, heading towards the main resort building. You and your family follow.

"Welcome to Dolphin Island Resort," a young woman with a bright smile and a pink flower tucked behind her ear says from behind the counter as you enter the lobby. "Here is the key to your quarters. Enjoy your stay."

Once your family is settled into their beachfront bungalow, you're eager to explore the island. You pack a flashlight, compass, water bottle, pocket knife, matches, mask, snorkel and flippers as well as energy bars and binoculars in your daypack and head out the door.

Once you hit the sand, you sit down and open the guidebook you bought before coming on vacation. Which way should you go first? You're still a little tired from the early morning flight, but you're also keen to get exploring.

As you study the map, you hear a couple of kids coming towards you down the beach.

"Hi, I'm Adam," a blond-haired boy says as he draws near.

"And I'm Jane."

The boy and girl are about your age and dressed in swimming shorts and brightly colored t-shirts, red for him and yellow for her. They look like twins. The only difference is that the girl's hair is tied in a long ponytail while the boy's hair is cropped short. Both are tanned brown and have peeling noses. You suspect they've been at the resort a few days already.

"What are you reading?" Adam asks.

"It's a guide book. It tells all about the wildlife and the volcano. It also says there might be pirate treasure hidden here somewhere. I'm just trying to figure out where to look first."

Jane clasps her hands in front of her chest and does a little hop. "Pirate treasure, really?"

Adam looks a little more skeptical, his brow creases as he squints down at you. "You sure they just don't say that to get the tourists to come here?"

"No, I've read up on it. They reckon a pirate ship named the *Port-au-Prince* went down around here in the early 1800s. I thought I might go exploring and see what I can find."

"Oh, can we help?" Jane says. "There aren't many kids our age staying here at the moment, and lying by the pool all day gets a bit boring."

"Yeah," Adam agrees. "I'm sure we could be of some help if you tell us what to do. I could do some filming with my new phone."

There is safety in numbers when exploring, and three sets of eyes are better than one. But if you do find treasure, do you want to share it with two other people?

It is time to make your first decision. Do you:

Agree to take Adam and Jane along? **P368**

Or

Say no and go hunting for treasure on your own? **P371**

Agreed to take Adam and Jane along

You have a good feeling about the friendly twins. "Sure, why not," you say. "It will be nice to have some company."

"Arrr me hearties," Jane cries out, getting into the spirit. "So where do we go first to find these pieces of eight?"

Adam glances at his sister and shakes his head. "Don't mind her. She does amateur dramatics at school. She always acts like this."

Jane frowns at her brother, closes one eye and growls out of the side of her mouth. "You'd better watch it, you lily-livered land lubber, or I'll shave yer belly with a rusty razor then make you walk the plank!"

You can't help chuckling at Jane's pirate imitation. Even Adam cracks a smile.

Pleased to have made friends so quickly, you point to the map of the island in the guide book. "I've read that cyclones—that's what they call hurricanes in this part of the South Pacific—usually sweep down from the north. So I'm thinking we should start on the northern part of the island. I reckon that's the most likely place for a ship to hit."

Adam nods. "As good a theory as any."

"North is on the rocky side of the island," Jane says. "I know because I was talking about stars to one of the staff the other night. They showed me how to tell which way is south by using the Southern Cross." Jane points to the sky out over the reef that protects the lagoon from the ocean swells. "South is that way, so north is the opposite."

You pull out your compass. "Yep, you're dead right. I guess it's time for us to trek to the other side of the island."

"Better get some gear then," Adam says. "We'll meet you by the pool in five minutes."

While Adam and Jane go to get their stuff, you wander through reception and to the paved courtyard where your family and other tourists are sprawled on loungers around the pool.

"I'm off to the far side of the island with some friends," you tell your family. "I've packed myself some things for lunch so don't worry about me."

Your family waves you off. Their noses dive back into their books before you've taken a step.

When Jane and Adam arrive, the three of you follow a sandy path between the buildings, past more bungalows tucked in amongst the lush garden, and head inland.

Before long, the path narrows as it weaves its way between broad-leafed shrubs, ferns and palms. Many plants are covered in beautiful flowers of red, blue and yellow.

When you hear a loud squawk, you stop and look up into the canopy. Adam and Jane look up too.

"There it is," says the sharp-eyed Jane. "See, on that branch near the top. It's got a green body, yellow wings and red head."

The parrot squawks again before swooping down and sitting on a branch not far away.

"Wow, so pretty," Jane says.

Adam pulls out his cell phone and takes a few shots of the bird.

You look at Adam's phone. "Nice. I bet it's got GPS. That could come in handy if we find treasure."

"Unfortunately there's no signal on the island," Adam says, zipping the phone back into his pocket.

"That's a shame," you say. "Just as well I've got my compass then."

For about half an hour, the three of you follow the main path. The ground slowly rises and the soft ferns give way to taller trees as you work your way inland around the lower slopes of the volcano.

Jane hums softly behind you.

When you come to a fork in the path, you're not sure which way to go. Then Adam spots an old sign covered in vines. He pulls the greenery aside and reads the faded writing. "It says there's a waterfall ten minutes' walk to the right and a place called Smuggler's Cove straight ahead."

370

You pull out your guide book. "Smuggler's Cove is a small bay on the far side of the island. It's here on the map. Might be some good treasure hunting there."

"Let's go and check out the waterfall first," Jane says. "I feel like a swim."

Adam shakes his head, "I think we should go on to Smuggler's Cove and start looking for treasure."

The twins look at you. You have the deciding vote. What should you do? It's only 10am, but it's already hot and a swim would be nice. But then treasure is the main reason you've come to this side of the island.

What should you do? Do you:

Go to the waterfall and have a swim? **P376**

Or

Go on to Smuggler's Cove? **P380**

Say no and hunt for treasure on your own

Adam and Jane look friendly enough, but you've always preferred doing things on your own.

"Thanks," you say, "but I'm a bit of a loner. I think I'll check a few things out on my own first. Maybe another time, okay?"

When their smiles disappear, you feel a little sorry for them, but you've been planning this expedition for ages and you don't want to be distracted.

"Okay," Jane says, looking down at her feet and kicking the ground. "If you change your mind, let us know."

Adam shrugs and wanders a short distance down the beach where he sits in the sand and starts digging a hole with his toes. Jane joins him.

Trying to forget the look of disappointment on the twin's faces, you study your guidebook. There are a couple of options you can take. The first is to head across the island to Smuggler's Cove, a sheltered inlet and only safe anchorage on the rocky, northern side of the island. The northern side, without a protective reef, is pounded constantly by ocean waves, which makes it a treacherous place for ships.

The path to Smuggler's Cove runs from the resort, through the jungle, clockwise around the lower slopes of the volcano, and then winds back down to the sea. Marked on the map are a number of scenic lookout points, and another path that branches off to a waterfall.

As well as maps, the guide book has numerous pictures of the native wildlife, mainly birds, insects and the various sea creatures that inhabit the lagoon. Luckily for the island's birdlife, rats and other predators like stoats, ferrets and snakes have never gained a foothold here. Nonetheless, thanks to man, a number of bird species, including three species of lorikeets, are listed as endangered.

Your other option is to head along the beach to the westernmost end of the island where the rocky point protrudes out to sea. This is the point that looked like the dolphin's nose from the plane, and is another prime spot for ships to run aground.

A hundred yards beyond the nose-shaped point, and submerged, except at low tide, are a jagged cluster of rocks. These rocks are marked on the map as a serious hazard to navigation. The guidebook explains how three boats have fallen victim to these rocks in recent years, two of them while sailing from New Caledonia to the Cook Islands, the other a small inter-island freighter whose skipper cut the corner too sharp in an effort to outrun a fast approaching storm.

If modern sailors have had problems navigating these waters, maybe the pirates of old did too. Could this be where the *Port-au-Prince* ran aground and floundered as it tried to find shelter from the storm?

You look across the lagoon. The point is way off in the distance where the western end of the reef meets the shore. Maybe snorkeling off the point would be the best way to find treasure.

After brief consideration, you decide to go overland to Smuggler's Cove. The day has barely begun and the temperature is already climbing. As the sun rises in the sky it will only get hotter. Walking under the jungle canopy will be much cooler. Maybe you'll even spot an endangered lorikeet or two on the way.

Tucking your guidebook into a side pocket of your daypack, you brush the sand off your shorts and turn inland. Weaving your way through the cluster of bungalows and resort outbuildings, you find a shell-covered path and enter the jungle. Within minutes, you are in a different world.

Under the canopy there is a faint but constant hum of insects. Swarms of midges fly in mini-tornadoes this way and that. A bright blue butterfly flits past followed by a red-winged dragonfly. You hear lots of birdsong, but so far have only seen mynas with their brown bodies, yellow eye patches and flashes of white on their wings. These bold birds are common in the South Pacific and you've seen quite a few around the resort already.

Leaves and twigs scrunch underfoot as you work your way uphill onto the lower slopes of the volcano. Flowering shrubs, vines and ferns crowd the path. Sturdy vines hang in tangles from trees.

When you see a flash of green above your head you stop and crane your neck upward hoping to see the bird again. You suspect it's a lorikeet. Then you see it swoop down onto a bush covered in pink flowers. The bird hops along a stem and sips nectar from the flower with its long tongue. As it drinks, you admire its beautiful colors. Its body is bright green. On its chest is a patch of red and there is a tuff of blue on top its head. It is a startling contrast to the more subdued colors of the birds back home.

As you watch the blue-crowned lorikeet move from flower to flower, you hear whispers and the snap of twigs on the path behind you. Turning in the direction of the sound, you see a brief flash of color through the foliage, first red, then yellow. Crouching down, you ease yourself back into a large fern, pulling one of the fronds down in front of your body to act as a shield.

"Where's he gone?" Jane mumbles as she approaches your hiding spot.

"He can't be too far in front," Adam replies. "I caught a glimpse of him a few minutes ago."

You pull the fern fond down a little more and keep as still as possible. A few seconds later you hear the footsteps pass your position and head further along the path.

Once the footsteps have disappeared, you ease yourself out of the fern. Walking as quietly as possible, you take off in pursuit, keeping a sharp lookout for flashes of color ahead of you.

Should you give them a fright for following you? Maybe you could pretend to be a dangerous animal and scare them away. You wonder if they've done much reading about the island's wildlife. Do they know that the most dangerous animal on the island is the wild pig … or is it the mosquito? You can't quite remember.

You are walking fast, trying to close the gap between you and the twins, when you see a flash of red in the distance. You cup your hands around your mouth and growl as loud as you can. You've been to the zoo plenty of times, and you're not sure your lion impression is that realistic, but you give it your best attempt.

When you hear a frightened squeal and then see the twins rise above the surrounding shrubs as they scurry up a tree, you smile.

"That seemed to work," you say to yourself.

You hide behind a tree trunk and try monkey sounds this time. "Oooh, oooh oooh!" you howl doing your best to sound like a chimpanzee. Surely they must know there aren't monkeys here on the island. "Oooh, oooh, oooh!"

The twins are still climbing. Then you see Jane stop and tilt her head. She says something to her brother then braces herself in the crook of the tree and starts scanning the area below her.

"Okay, who's making monkey sounds!" she yells. "Come on, I know you're out there!"

Sprung.

You come out from behind the tree and walk along the path. Thirty seconds later, you are standing at the foot of the tree, looking up at the twins.

"Why are you following me?" you ask.

Their faces are tinged with red as they start to climb down.

Jane is first to reach the ground. "Sorry. We just want some excitement."

"Yeah, the resort is boring," Adam says. "Besides, we can go wherever we want. You can't stop us."

You look from one twin to the other and think. Maybe you've been a little harsh. Maybe it would be fun to have some friends to go exploring with.

"Okay. You can come along on one condition."

"What's that?" Adam asks.

"I get to be expedition leader. After all, I'm the one who's done the research."

The twins nod eagerly, grins spreading across their faces.

"Okay, let's get moving, we've got a bit of ground to cover before we get to Smuggler's Cove."

The three of you follow the path in single file, with you in the lead. You can hear Jane humming softly behind you.

When you come to a fork in the path, you're not sure which way to go. Then Adam spots an old sign covered in vines. He pulls the greenery aside and reads the faded writing. "It says there's a waterfall off to the right. Smuggler's Cove is straight ahead."

"Let's go and check out the waterfall," Jane says. "I feel like a swim."

Adam shakes his head. "I think we should keep going and start hunting for treasure."

The twins look at you. You have the deciding vote. What should you do? It's hot and a swim would be nice. But then treasure is the reason you're here.

It is time to make a decision. Do you:

Go to the waterfall and have a swim? **P376**

Or

Go on to Smuggler's Cove? **P380**

Go to the waterfall and have a swim

"I like the idea of a swim too," you say. "The treasure's been around for 150 years. I don't think it's going anywhere."

Jane picks up her pack. "I bet I can hold my breath under water longer than you!"

You like Jane. She's so enthusiastic about everything.

"Let's get going," Adam says in a grump as he moves down the path. "We'll have a quick swim and then get back to the treasure hunt, okay?"

You nod and follow Adam. The path narrows and winds its way higher up the hillside. After a couple of zigzags, you can see over the trees back towards the coast, where waves crash white with foam on the reef. Tiny triangles of color, from the resort's fleet of sailing boats and wind surfers, dot the aqua water on the far side of the lagoon.

Before long, you see a swing bridge in the distance. The swing bridge is made from woven vines. Its deck is laid with arm-thick branches chopped from the jungle. The bridge crosses a swiftly moving creek that has cut a deep channel into the side of the hillside as it races to the sea.

Adam stops when he reaches the bridge and turns around. "Do you think this is safe?"

You have a closer look. "It looks pretty sturdy so it should be safe."

About ten vines have been woven together to form the main cables. You grab hold of the bridge's handrails, also made of woven vines, and take a step.

"It feels okay," you say to the other. "Look!" You jump up and down a couple times. "It's hardly moving."

Despite your confidence, the other two wait until you've reached the far side before venturing across. Jane is first. She comes across with no problems, but when Adam is half way across, Jane grabs one of the handrails and starts shaking it.

Adams face goes white. "Stop it, Jane!" he yells in a voice a little higher pitched than normal. "I swear I'll hit you!"

"Don't be such a baby," Jane says. "I'm just having a bit of fun. You're not going to fall."

Jane steps back and lets Adam wobble his way across. You can see the relief on his face when he reaches solid ground again.

"That wasn't funny. You know I hate heights."

Jane turns her back on Adam to head up the path, but not before you see a little grin cross her face.

Jane is trouble.

You hear the waterfall up ahead. It sounds like someone is running a bath, only louder. Then you feel moisture in the air as the wind-blown spray drifts into the jungle.

Jane is the first around the corner. "Wow! Look at that!"

You nearly bump into her as you take in the tumbling mass of white water.

The waterfall is about fifteen feet wide and thirty feet high. It pours over a lip of rock, straight out of the jungle into a shimmering pool below. Ferns and palms crowd the stream on both sides. Grey stones cover the bottom of the pool, and waves of bright green weed dance in the current.

"Last one in is a monkey's bum!" Jane yells as she runs down the path towards the pool.

Before you know it, Adam has scooted past you and is in hot pursuit of his sister. At the pool's edge Jane throws off her t-shirt and makes a running dive. Adam tosses his phone onto the pile and follows.

Adam is first to surface about half way across the expanse of water. Jane continues to swim underwater, the bright yellow of her swimsuit glowing under the water, until she is nearly under the cascade. When she surfaces, her teeth gleam white and her long hair plasters itself to her neck and shoulders.

"I win!" she yells as her fist pumps the air in triumph.

Not bothering to remove your t-shirt, you dive into the pool. The water is cool and refreshing. After paddling to where Jane and Adam are treading water you look down into the depths. "Amazing how clear the water is," you say.

You dive down to see if you can touch the bottom but you're forced to surface again before you get there.

"The water's a lot deeper than it looks," you tell the others when you surface. "I can't reach the bottom."

"Let me have a go," Jane says, before flipping over and kicking towards the bottom.

You and Adam watch as she pulls herself deeper and deeper. Before you know it, she's holding on to a clump of weed and looking around. After 20 seconds or so, slowly releasing air bubbles as she goes, she rises to the surface.

"Wow, you *are* good," you say when her head finally breaks the surface. "You were down there for ages."

Jane has a grin from ear to ear. "And look what I found."

Glinting in the palm of her hand is a small metal cross, like one you'd wear around your neck.

The three of you swim to the pond's edge and sit on a rock.

"It looks like silver," you say, giving the cross a polish on your shorts before having a closer look.

At the end of each arm is a small hollow. You suspect these would have held precious stones at one time. On the other side of the cross you see some tiny scratches, but then realize as you inspect them closer they are words etched into the metal. You tilt the cross so the light hits the surface and you can read the words.

"CAROLUS IIII D.G. 1805," you read. "That sounds vaguely familiar." You're sure you've read seem something similar in one of your treasure hunting books. You hand the cross back to Jane and try to remember what you've read.

You grab a towel from your daypack and dry your hair, still thinking hard as you do so. "Right, CAROLUS. If I remember correctly, that's Spanish for Charles."

Adam seems interested. “Do you think it came from the treasure ship that went down?”

“It’s certainly the right time,” you say. “The pirate ship we’re looking for was raiding the French and Spanish colonies along the South American coast, and then came to this part of the Pacific chasing whales to restock their supply of oil. I wonder if some of the treasure was salvaged from the wreck after all.”

“We could get some scuba gear from the resort and come back. Maybe there is more stuff at the bottom of the pool,” Jane says. “I got my dive ticket last summer in Hawaii.”

“That’s a good idea,” you say. I have my ticket too. We could dive together while Adam stays up top.”

You’ve got to admit that the bottom of a deep pool under a waterfall would be a great place to hide treasure.

“Or we could check out this Smuggler’s Cove place first and then decide,” Adam says. “It’s almost an hour back to the resort.”

Once again the twins look for you for a decision. The cross was a good find, and the date is certainly from the right era.

Should you check out Smuggler’s Cove before going all the way back for scuba gear? Or is the cross an indication that there is more treasure to be found?

It is time to make another decision. Do you:

Carry on to Smuggler’s Cove? **P380**

Or

Go back to resort for scuba gear? **P384**

Carry on to Smuggler's Cove

As the three of you make your way along the jungle path to Smuggler's Cove, the path twists and turns so much it's hard to know which direction you're heading. The canopy overhead is so dense that in places it feels like evening has come, even though your rumbling stomach tells you it is probably closer to lunchtime.

When you come to a large tree that's fallen across the path, you stop. "Anyone hungry?" you ask. "Maybe we should have lunch."

Jane and Adam nod their agreement, sit on the tree trunk and rummage through their daypacks.

"I've got a couple of apples and a chocolate energy bar," says Jane.

"Snap," you say, holding up a couple bars of your own. "I love chocolate."

Adam pulls out a bottle of water and packets of cheese and crackers. "I've got heaps of nuts too," he says waving a bulging zip-lock bag. "Sing out if you want some."

As the three of you have lunch, you discover that Adam and Jane's parents are both dentists. Jane tells you they're only happy when they're on vacation.

Adam nods. "Nobody is ever happy to see them at work. Their clients are either in pain or unhappy about how much it's going to cost. It's no wonder Mom and Dad are happy to get away from all the grumbling."

You'd never really thought much about the life of dentists. "Still, they can afford to buy you the latest phone and take you to nice places, so I bet you're not complaining."

Adam shrugs. "I'd rather they were happier sometimes. What's the use of money if you're miserable?"

Jane jumps up and starts closing her bag up. "Let's make them really happy and find some treasure. Then they can retire and be on vacation all the time."

"I'll go along with that," you say as you stand up and get ready to move off.

You and the twins have only gone on a hundred yards or so when a waist-high pile of stones appears about ten paces off the path.

"I wonder who made that cairn?" you say, pushing back fern fronds and making your way through the undergrowth.

The stones have been stacked with care and fit together snugly. On top of the pile is a large flat rock overgrown with lichen and moss. The moss is growing in a funny pattern.

You pull your pocket knife out and start scraping the growth off the stone. As you do so, letters are revealed.

"Wow, come look at this," you call out to the others.

Adam and Jane work their way through the greenery and peer down at the characters you've uncovered.

"Does that say 1806?" Jane asks.

The grooves in the rock are shallow. Wind, rain and plant life have pitted the surface over the years but you can still make them out.

"That's the year the ship went down!" you say.

Adams eyes widen. "So the rumors are true."

You can't believe what you're seeing. "It looks that way."

Jane steps back and gives the pile of rocks a quick once-over. "Do you think something is buried here? Treasure maybe?"

You shake your head. "Too obvious I would have thought." Then you have a thought. "Hey, Adam, help me lift the top stone, maybe the cairn is hollow."

You and Adam grab a side of the rock each and hoist it off the pile, flipping it onto the ground as you do so.

"Nope, not hollow," you say. Then you notice more writing on the underside of the rock.

"What's this?" you say, bending down and running your fingers over the surface. "Letters, but they're upside…"

Jane does an excited little hop and says, "*Port-au-Prince*! It says *Port-au-Prince*. Isn't that the ship you told us about?"

"The one and only," you say, unable to stop your face from

twisting up into a grin.

Adam bends down to stroke the rock. "So it did run aground here on the island."

"We're going to be rich!" Jane squeals.

"Not so fast," you say. "The treasure may be here on the island, but we still have to find it."

Adam scratches his head. "So what now?"

You're not quite sure what to do. Why would shipwrecked sailors build a cairn here in the jungle? And why would they put the date on one side and the name of their ship on the other? Could it be a hint as to where the treasure is hidden, or is it a memorial to those lost when the ship sank?

"I think we should carry on to Smuggler's Cove," you say.

With the cairn penciled onto your map, you rejoin the path. You've only walked another mile or so when you hear the faint sound of waves breaking. Minutes later, you come upon the rocky shore. To the east, about two hundred yards down the coast, is a small cove protected from the sea by a rocky arm that protrudes out into the ocean. To your surprise, there is a yacht anchored about thirty yards off shore. Sitting on the boat's deck are two men wearing straw hats and floral shirts.

Pulled up on the beach is a small rowboat.

"Get down," you whisper. "Someone's rowed their dinghy ashore, they must be nearby."

Jane's hand rests on your shoulder as she crouches down beside you. "Do you think they're looking for treasure too?" she whispers.

"Let's hope not. But if they are, we don't want them to know they have competition."

"So what do we do?" Adam asks quietly. "What if they don't want us here?"

"We can pretend we're tourists who've come for a swim," Jane says. "I doubt they'll worry about a bunch of kids."

"We *are* tourists, silly," Adam says with a hint of sarcasm in his voice. "We don't need to pretend."

"They won't know we're looking for treasure," Jane says. "And if they are, we might be able to get some valuable information from them."

Suddenly, the twins are both looking at you to make a decision. You're not sure what would be the best plan of action. The men on the yacht could be innocent tourists, or they could be up to something fishy.

What should you do? Do you:

Watch the yacht from the jungle? **P390**

Or

Pretend you're tourists going for a swim? **P393**

Go back to the resort for scuba gear

After finding the cross in the pool at the foot of the falls, you want to see if there is more treasure sitting on the bottom. Only Jane is a good enough swimmer to get to the bottom without scuba gear, and even she will tire quickly once she's swum to the bottom a few times.

"Okay, let's get back to the resort and get some gear," you say. "We'll be able to search the whole pool thoroughly that way. Where there's one artifact, there might be others."

Everyone has a bounce in their step and talks of what they'll spend their bounty on as the three of you head back to the resort.

The dive shop is tucked around the back and in the basement of the main building. You hire a small tank, regulator, and weight belt, and divide the equipment between you. Within fifteen minutes, you're trudging back into the jungle towards the waterfall.

The day is heating up and the jungle is humid. Sweat drips down your back. Half an hour later, just as you turn off the main path and head up towards the waterfall, a sudden flurry of wings and bright red bodies flash through the canopy overhead.

"Something's spooked the lorikeets," you say.

You are only a short way up the waterfall track when you hear heavy footsteps crashing through the undergrowth off to your left.

"Quiet, someone's coming," you whisper. "Quick, hide in the ferns. We don't want anyone to know we're here."

The three of you burrow into a mass of fronds beside the path and wait. The footsteps get closer and louder. Someone is breathing hard, like they've been running.

Then, through a gap in the ferns, you see a man carrying a wire cage full of lorikeets.

"Don't move," you whisper to the others.

When the sound of the man's footsteps has passed, you climb out of your hiding spot.

"Did you see the cage full of birds?" you ask Adam and Jane.

"He's been trapping. That'll be what scared the lorikeets a few moments ago."

Adam's face twists into a frown. "Surely that's illegal."

You leaf through your guidebook. "You're right, the book says the birds are protected."

"We need to do something," Jane says.

"But what?" you say. "This island's miles from anywhere."

Adam pulls out his cell phone. "We may not have a signal, but my phone still works as a camera. I should take some video so we have something to show the authorities."

Jane nods her agreement. "Let's leave the scuba gear here and follow him. If we get some pictures the police on the mainland might be able to identify them."

Their plan sounds dangerous, especially if the poachers see you taking photos. But you agree with the twins. You can't let some greedy idiot get away with poaching protected birds.

"Okay," you say. "But we'll need to be careful. Bird smuggling is big business and poachers are dangerous. Who knows what he'll do if he catches us spying. He might even be armed, so keep quiet and no talking."

That said, you push the scuba gear under a fern and break one of the fronds so you'll know where it is when you come back. Then you pick up your daypack and start moving down the track.

You are confident of catching up with the man carrying the heavy cage, so you don't rush. Instead you walk quietly and hope that you see him before he sees you.

When you get back to the junction where the waterfall track meets the main path, you stop.

"Which way?" Jane asks.

You think a moment. "I can't imagine him going towards the resort."

"I agree," Adam says. "He must be heading towards the cove."

It isn't long before you see a flash of color ahead of you.

You signal to the others and come to a stop. "There he is," you whisper. "Let's keep pace with him and see where he goes."

Fifteen minutes later, Jane tilts her head and cups a hand around an ear. "I think I hear the ocean. Maybe he has a boat."

"Okay, easy now," you say. "We don't want him to spot us."

As you move along the path, the sound of the waves gets louder. Coconut palms start to appear amongst the ferns and other broad-leafed plants, and after another fifty yards you see the ocean through a gap in the trees.

When you reach the edge of the jungle you stop. The man is walking along the shore towards a dinghy pulled up onto the rocky beach a hundred yards away. In the sparkling blue water of the cove, a single-masted yacht rocks gently at anchor. Two men sit on deck drinking beer.

"Welcome to Smuggler's Cove," you say.

"So what now?" Adam asks.

"Follow me," you say. "And keep low."

You step back into the jungle. Jane and Adam follow as you walk parallel to the beach in the direction of the yacht. The ground is sandy here and the shrubs and ferns less dense so the going is relatively easy while still giving you cover from the men on the boat.

When you think you've gone far enough, you creep back towards the beach along what looks like a natural watercourse. The twins follow close behind.

But just as the clear waters of Smuggler's Cove appear before you, your feet are whipped out from under you and you're hoisted into the air by a net.

"Yow!" Jane yelps in surprise.

"Ouch," Adam says. "Someone's squashing my legs."

The more you squirm, the tighter the net pulls around you, squashing the three of you together. Your arms are pressed to your body, and Adam's weight pins you against the mesh.

"What now?" Adam grunts. "Any other bright ideas from our

expedition leader?"

Jane's foot is pressed against the side of your face. You can see the ground about three feet below you. The net rocks back and forth like a hammock.

"I've got a knife in the side pouch of my daypack. Can anyone reach it?" you say.

"I think ... I think I can," Jane says, contorting limbs.

You hear Jane breathing hard with effort and then feel a tugging on your pack.

"Can you move to your right?" she asks.

"I'll try," you say, pressing hard with your elbows while rotating your body at the same time.

"Okay, that should do it."

With your face pressed hard to the mesh, you roll your eyes and try to see what is happening on the beach. Did the men on the boat hear the *twang* as the trap went off? Are they coming?

"Got it!" Jane says.

"Well, start cutting," you urge her. "Quickly, in case the men heard us."

"Watch it with that knife, Sis," Adam says. "You nearly got my leg there."

"Sorry," Jane says, hacking a little more carefully.

You can feel the net stretch as Jane cuts at it, and you sink closer and closer to the ground as each minute goes by. Then, like a zipper opening, the net splits in a rush and dumps you on the ground.

"Oooof!" you grunt as Adam lands on top of you.

Adam rolls away and you get onto your knees and look around. Two men in floral shirts are moving up the beach towards your position.

"They've seen us!" you say. "We need to get out of here."

"I'm still caught up!" Jane says, kicking her foot like she's trying to shake off her shoe.

You hear panic in her voice. When you look over, you see that a section of net has become entangled around her foot.

"Quick, give me the knife! Stay still." You start hacking at the strands holding her foot. "Get ready to run the moment you're free."

Adam has his camera out and is taking shots of the men coming towards you.

"Hey you!" one of the men shouts. "What are you doing?"

"Hurry up!" Adam says. "They're nearly here."

"Go," Jane says. "Save yourselves."

With one final slice of the net, Jane pulls her foot free and scrambles to her feet.

"Split up and run," you say, taking off back the way you came. "Meet you where we left the scuba gear."

With that, the three of you plunge into the jungle, running for all you're worth. You duck and weave around trees and shrubs, barging through clumps of fern and eventually come to rest at the base of a large tree. Breathing hard, you stop to catch your breath and listen for footsteps.

Then you hear Adam's voice. "Let me go!"

As you suck in air, your heart pounds. The men must have gone for Adam because he had the camera. You wonder if Jane got away or has suffered the same fate.

"If you kids tell anyone, your friend is toast!" one of the men yells into the jungle.

They sound so angry, but what can you do? Luckily, the contour of the land gives you a hint as to where you are. You head down a slight slope, hoping to cross the waterfall track, pulling the greenery back as you go. Every few minutes you stop, duck down and listen for footsteps. Finally, you find the track you're looking for, and a couple hundred meters up the trail, you see the broken fern frond.

You tuck yourself deep into the ferns and wait to see if Jane turns up. As you wait, you inspect the underside of the nearest frond. Two rows of little brown dots run in down each side of the leaf's finger-sized offshoots. These are the spores that will be blown into the wind and grow into more ferns when the conditions are right. You must remember to tell Adam all about them when you see him next. If you see him again, that is.

Fifteen minutes later, you hear the crunch of footsteps. You lean back deeper into the greenery and hope that it's Jane and not one of the men. Then you hear a voice.

"Helloooo. Anyone here?" It's Jane.

You crawl out from your hiding place and stand up, looking around as you do so. When you catch Jane's eye, you put one finger to your lips and wave her over. "Shush… The poachers might still be around."

Jane comes over and the two of you duck back under cover.

"Did you see them get Adam?" you whisper.

Jane shakes her head. "I heard him yell, but kept going. I didn't see any point in both of us getting caught."

"So what do we do now? Do we try and save Adam ourselves or go for help?"

"I don't know. I'm afraid they might hurt him."

"Don't worry, we'll work something out," you say.

You think hard. What should you do? Going back for help will take time. Do you have that luxury? What if the poachers take off with Adam in their boat? You may never see him again. But how can two kids handle evil poachers?

It is time to make an important decision. Do you:

Try to help Adam? **P410**

Or

Go back to the resort for help? **P422**

Watch the yacht from the jungle

The three of you sneak back to the cover of the jungle and creep silently towards the cove.

"Stay in single file," you whisper, "and watch where you step so we don't make too much noise."

Jane suppresses a giggle and falls in behind. "It's like we're ninja spies."

You carefully pull the shrubbery aside so it doesn't snap back in Jane's face and work your way closer to the yacht.

"I hope you know what you're doing," Adam whispers, bringing up the rear. "What if they catch us spying on them?"

You put your index finger up to your lip. "Quiet... If you guys keep talking, they'll hear us for sure."

The ground is sandy underfoot. Flowering shrubs crowd one another and the going is slow. Bees hum from flower to flower collecting nectar. After a few minutes, you've worked your way to a spot just inland from where the yacht is anchored. The beach slopes steeply towards the water and unlike the white sand, made from ground shells, on the lagoon side of the island, the sand here is coarse, dark and volcanic in origin. The men's voices can be heard talking and laughing over the slap of the waves.

You signal the others to get down and crawl towards the beach on hands and knees. From under a bush, you get a better view of what the men are doing. Jane and Adam follow your lead.

The three of you peer carefully through the lower branches. The men are close. The two on deck keep looking towards shore, obviously waiting for whoever is on shore to return.

"What are they doing?" Jane whispers close to your ear.

You look at her sternly and move your hand across your lips in a zipping motion. The last thing you want is for the men to hear you.

Black lettering graces the side of the boat's hull. *Moneymaker* it says. That sounds like the name of a treasure hunter's ship if ever you've heard one.

A moment later, there is whistling in the jungle behind you. You drop flat and hope whoever it is doesn't see you. The sound is ten yards to your right and moving towards the beach.

When you sneak a glance, you see a man with a cage full of brightly colored birds walking towards the dingy.

Holding the cage in one hand, the man drags the small boat into the water. He stows the cage in the front of the boat, climbs aboard and slots the oars into the rowlocks. His rowing technique is good. It doesn't take him long to cross the short distance to the yacht.

"Traps are working well," he calls up to the men on deck. "Here, grab this rope and get ready, I'll pass the cage up."

With a heave, the man raises the metal cage above his head, where it is grabbed by one of the men. The man on deck swings the cage over the railing and is about to lower it, when he screams out and drops the cage with a thump.

"Ouch! Filthy bird just took a hunk out of my hand!" he howls waving his hand in the air.

The other men laugh at their companion's misfortune. "I've told you before to watch out. Their beaks can take your finger right off if they get hold of it properly."

The hurt man tucks his injured hand under his armpit and paces around the deck for a moment, grumbling and cursing under his breath before coming back to kick the cage. "Watch it, you horrible birds. Next time I'll drop you overboard!"

"Horrible birds," a parrot mimics. "Horrible birds. Horrible birds."

The two men laugh again. "Those birds are smarter than you are, Jimmy. Maybe we should drop *you* overboard."

The man in the dinghy chuckles again and then grabs the railing and slides the dinghy through the water to the stern of the yacht. He climbs up a short ladder and secures the dinghy's rope to a cleat on deck.

"Another day, another dollar," one of the men says. "It always amazes me what people will pay for exotic birds."

As the men start preparing the yacht for departure, the man with the sore hand moves to the cockpit. He turns the key to start the diesel engine, and with a puff of smoke, the engine rumbles into life. The man checks that water is coming from the exhaust port in the back and then waits by the wheel. The other two go to the bow, ready to pull up the anchor. The man behind the wheel inches the yacht forward.

The men on the bow are talking, but the throb of the yacht's motor drowns out their voices.

"Poachers," you say to the twins. "The lowest of the low."

"Poor birds. What will happen to them?" Jane asks.

"Life in cages." Adam looks angry and starts to say something else, but then clamps his jaw closed and growls like a dog protecting his territory. His face is red and his clenched fists shake.

"Don't blow a foo-foo valve, little brother," Jane says. "Adam works at the animal shelter as a volunteer," she says to you. "He gets so angry when he sees animals being mistreated."

"With good reason," you say. "But what do we do about it?"

"We need to tell the authorities," Adam says. "That's what we do."

"But we're already here, so we may as well have a look around," Jane says. "The poachers are leaving. It will be a wasted trip otherwise."

The twins look to you. You could go back to the resort, but would the resort's management do anything? And Jane has a point about your trek being wasted if you go straight back to the resort.

It is time to make a decision. Do you:

Go back to the resort and report the poachers? **P398**

Or

Have a look around Smugglers Cove? **P404**

Pretend you are tourists going for a swim

"If we're going to do this," you say, "we've got to get our story straight."

Jane smiles at your decision. "I read somewhere that it's best to tell as much of the truth as possible when undercover. There's less things to remember that way."

"Okay, let's go for a swim and see if they approach us. If the men are tourists, they'll most likely say hello."

"And if not," Adam buts in, "they'll try to scare us off."

"Exactly!" Jane says.

"Whatever you do, don't mention treasure," you say. "If we ask too many questions they'll get suspicious."

With that, Jane pulls her towel out of her pack and walks calmly out of hiding and on to the stony beach. You and Adam, now committed to the plan, follow her lead.

You keep your head down, as if watching your step as you walk, but your eyes dart up every few seconds to see what the men's reaction is to your arrival. One of the men sees you and nudges the other with his foot. The other man is less subtle and stares a little too long, his smile turning down a little too quickly.

"They don't look pleased to see us," you whisper. "Keep moving, but get ready to scarper in a hurry."

Jane's acting skills are quite convincing. She skips on to the beach and, a short distance from the dingy, lays out her towel. "I'm going for a swim," she announces loud enough to carry to the men onboard the yacht."

You bend down to lay out your towel and whisper to Adam, "One of us should stay on the beach and keep an eye out for the shore party."

"I'm not a great swimmer," Adam says. "I don't mind staying."

"I might go for a quick snorkel and have a look around then," you say.

Jane hits the water then turns and calls out, "The water's so warm!"

With your mask and flippers in your hand you walk to the water's edge. After rinsing your mask, you slip the rubber strap over your head and sit in the coarse sand to put on your flippers. Then lifting your feet high, you walk backwards into the water.

Jane is right, the water is warm. You've only just started snorkeling when you hear Adam yell.

"Hey! What do you think you're doing?"

Jane has heard him too and is staring past you towards the beach.

You turn around to see what has got Adam so excited.

A man, carrying a cage of brightly colored birds has come out of the jungle and is making his way along the beach towards the dinghy.

By now, Jane is swimming back to shore. When she reaches your position, she says, "These guys are trapping birds. Adam's a fanatic when it comes to animal welfare. I hope he doesn't do something stupid."

"Me too."

By now, Adam is up off his towel and marching towards the man carrying the cage. The men on the yacht have seen him too.

"Quick," Jane says. "He's going to nut-off at this guy. We need to stop him."

"And fast," you say. "That man could get violent."

As the two of you race back to shore, you watch Adam. He's marching towards the man with the cages like a zealot on a mission, his vision focused straight ahead, his arms pumping.

The man sees Adam coming at him and puts his hands on his hips, seemingly unconcerned about the angry boy striding towards him.

You can't help admire Adam's courage as you hit the beach.

When Adam speaks, you can hear every word.

"These birds are protected, you brain-dead imbecile!" he yells. "Let them go or I'll report you to the authorities!"

"Subtle, your brother," you say to Jane.

Adam, although brave, is being guided by his heart and not his head. You're not quite sure what he expects to achieve. Does Adam really think this criminal is going to take any notice of a kid?

"Who are you to tell me what to do?" the man says. "You tourists think you run things now?"

But Adam isn't listening. He's had a rush of blood to his head, his face has gone scarlet in rage and he's not thinking straight.

"I'll see you in jail!" Adam yells, spittle flying. Then he looks over at the men on the yacht. "I'll see you all in jail!" Without warning, Adam runs at the man on the beach and pushes him hard in the chest.

The man, standing with feet spread in front of the cage, loses his balance and tumbles back, trips over the cage and falls awkwardly on the ground.

In a flash, Adam reaches down and unhooks the top of the cage. In a blur of color the dozen or so lorikeets fly off into the jungle.

"Why you little brat," the man growls from the ground. "Those birds were worth hundreds of dollars."

Thankfully, you and Jane have reached the scene.

"Adam, let's go." You grab Adam's arm but he stands fast. "Adam, I said it's time to go."

The man snarls like a wounded animal and lurches to his feet.

"Run, Adam!" Jane yells.

Adam sees the man coming at him with fists clenched and finally realizes how furious he is.

You hear splashes and cast a glance towards the boat. The two other men are swimming strongly towards the shore. They will be here in a moment.

Adam is too slow and the man's meaty hand clamps around his forearm.

"I'll teach you a lesson, you little rat bag!"

Jane takes a couple steps forward and kicks the man in the kneecap.

"Ouch!"

It's not a crippling blow, but it's enough of a distraction for Adam to break the man's grip.

"Run!" Jane yells again.

The other men have reached the beach and are sprinting towards you.

"Now!" you scream once more, tugging at Adam's arm.

Jane needs no prompting. In a flash, she heads back toward the pile of gear on the sand, scoops up her daypack and scurries into the jungle. You and Adam are twenty yards behind her.

As you hit the track leading inland, there is a thud and a grunt behind you. Without even turning, you know Adam has fallen. When you spin around for confirmation, you see one of the men from the yacht is nearly upon him.

"Go!" Adam says, his eyes pleading. "Go get help!"

You want to help, but it's too late. Adam is right. There is nothing to be gained by both of you being captured. You take off, casting a quick glance over your shoulder as you enter the jungle.

The man has hold of Adam's arm and is dragging him back towards the beach. Once you're twenty yards along the path and out of their view, you duck into some ferns and watch through the fronds. The second man from the boat is out of shape. The swim and the run have sapped his energy. When he sees that his friend has captured Adam, he bends over, puts his hands on his knees and gasps for air.

The man that Jane kicked in the knee is last to arrive. He hobbles over and glares at Adam, then yells into the jungle. "Hey brats, if you don't want your friend hurt, you'd better keep you're your mouths shut!"

And with that, two of the men force Adam into the dinghy and start rowing back towards their boat. The other picks up the empty cage and heads a hundred yards or so further down the beach and then turns and walks back into the jungle.

"Jane?" you call out. "Can you hear me?"

You climb out of your hiding spot and start down the path towards the resort, hoping to come across Jane. It isn't long before you hear a rustle of leaves in the canopy.

"Jane?"

Chimpanzee noises come from a tree branch above you and you catch a flash of yellow. "Jane, come down. They've got Adam."

Within thirty seconds, Jane is back on the ground. "Is he okay?"

"I don't know. Did you hear them yell out that we'd better keep quiet?"

Jane shakes her head. "What do we do?"

"We either try to help Adam, or go back to the resort I suppose." But you're not sure. What should you do?

It is time to make a decision. Do you:

Try to help Adam? **P410**

Or

Go back to the resort for help? **P422**

Go back to the resort and report the poachers

You can't help agreeing with Adam. Unless you report the poachers right away, they could disappear before the authorities have a chance to locate them. There are so many yachts cruising the South Pacific islands this time of year, a few hours could make all the difference.

"We'd better get back to the resort pronto," you say, doing some quick calculations in your head. "If we move fast, we'll be back in an hour. If that yacht is traveling at 8 knots, every hour that goes by the authorities will have another um … 250 square miles to search."

Jane looks surprised. "How did you figure that out so quickly?"

[If you are interested in finding out how the math works, go to **P461**. If not keep reading.]

You start down the path back towards the resort. You hear the twin's footsteps behind you. Jane mumbles numbers as you half walk, half jog through the jungle.

You've hardly had time to build up a sweat when you see something that looks like a thick spider's web off to your left. You signal a halt and point at whatever it is hanging in the trees. "What's that?"

Adam takes a step forward. "A bird net, I think. Those poachers must plan on coming back for more. I bet they anchor in the safety of the lagoon tonight and come back tomorrow."

You shrug. "It's possible, I suppose."

The net is positioned in such a way that that you hadn't noticed it before. The fine mesh, barely visible in the shade of the jungle canopy, stretches between two trees. The net hangs loose and there is already a parrot struggling in its mesh, squawking and flapping uselessly.

Adam is first to rush forward. "Have you got a knife?"

You think about Adam's comment about the poachers 'coming back' as you fish your pocket knife out of your daypack.

"Careful with the pressure you put on the net," Adam warns. "The fine bones in their wings are extremely fragile."

Adam holds the frightened bird still as you cut the strands of nylon holding it. The mesh, though fine, is as strong as fishing line. After a few minutes the last of the net falls away. Adam holds the bird in his outstretched arms and lets it go. With a squawk and a series of rapid wing beats the bird darts off to join his flock in the jungle.

"We should take the net back as evidence," Jane says. "The authorities may not believe us otherwise."

"Jane's right," you say. "I'll cut it down."

Five minutes later the net is bundled up in your daypack and the three of you are back on the path towards the resort.

"I wonder how many more of those awful nets they have strung up around the island," Adam says. "And how many poor birds they've captured."

"Don't worry, Adam," Jane says. "Once we report them, I'm sure the authorities will put an end to their operation."

"They'd better," Adam says. "Otherwise I'll sink their boat."

"How will you do that?" you ask. "Got a torpedo hidden in your luggage?"

"No, but I bet I can find a drill at the resort," Adam says, his voice sounding serious. "It doesn't take a very big leak to fill a boat with water."

Jane looks at her brother. "Let's hope it doesn't come to that."

"Enough talk about sinking boats," you say. "Save your breath for the trip back."

With that you start jogging. Within minutes, sweat is dripping from your forehead and down your back. The twins puff along behind you.

When the first of the resort's outbuildings appear, you slow to a walk and pull the water bottle out of your pack. Its contents are warm, but at least they're wet.

"So who do we report the poachers to?" Jane asks.

You turn your palms upward and shrug. "That's the problem, isn't it? Who can we trust?"

Jane gives you a curious look. "You don't trust the resort management? Do you think they're in on it?"

"They could be," Adam says. "It's hard to believe nobody's noticed nets before, but what choice do we have?"

"Adam's right," you say. "There aren't any police on the island, so management's the closest thing to authority there is around here."

"Unless we can contact the police directly," Jane says.

"How would we do that?" Adam says.

Jane gives her brother a cheeky grin. "Sneak into the office and use their phone. Who needs to know?"

Jane has a point. If someone at the resort is involved, telling them what you've discovered would only give the poachers time to retrieve their nets and flee. It could also be dangerous for you and the twins. Criminals don't like it when people interfere with their cash flow.

You're not sure Jane's plan is a good one. Adam's not looking too convinced either.

"Oh, come on, you two," Jane says. "Embrace your inner ninja!"

"Let's check the office before we make a decision," you say. "See if it's even possible."

Adam reluctantly agrees.

"Yippee, it's ninja spy time." Jane announces gleefully, about to set off.

"Wait," you say, grabbing her arm. "We need a plan, Miss Ninja."

After some discussion, the three of you decide that Jane, using her acting skills, will distract whoever is on the main desk, while you and Adam scope out the phone situation in the office next door.

"Right, can I go now?" Jane asks, keen to begin her role.

You look toward Adam, who nods his agreement. "Right," you say. "Let's do this."

Jane skips towards the main entrance and the reception desk beyond, while you and Adam walk around to the side door.

"Let's give Jane a minute before we go in," you say. "If we keep near the back wall of the lobby and walk quietly, we should be able to make it to the office without anyone at the main desk seeing us."

When you reach the side door, you can already hear Jane's voice. She's speaking to a middle-aged man in a floral shirt behind the desk.

"So what fishing charters do you offer?"

As the man lays a number of brochures on the counter and explains the times and costs of each option, Jane continues her act.

It's time for you and Adam to make your move.

When Jane sees you enter, she moves along the counter a little more, so that as the man follows her, his back is turned towards you and Adam.

It's only twenty paces to the office and you cover the ground quickly. Thankfully, the office door is open. You cross your fingers and hope it is empty, but unfortunately, as you get closer, you hear a man's voice.

"How many birds?" the voice in the office says. "Forty? Great."

You and Adam freeze, your backs to the wall next to the office door. You hear the crackle of a VHF radio and a male voice, but can't quite make out the words.

Then the man in the office speaks again. "Great … Yeah … I've got the buyer lined up."

"He must be talking to the poachers," you whisper in Adam's ear.

"Bring the yacht into the lagoon. Just make sure you keep the cages below deck so the tourists don't get a look."

Adam's jaw is clenched, his face turning red. You're afraid he's about to storm into the office, so you grab his arm and drag him back to the side door and out into the garden.

Once outside, you guide him onto a bench and sit down beside him. "Easy does it. You can't rush in there and confront the guy. You've got no proof, and no backup. What are you going to do, lock him in your family's bungalow until the police arrive? Duh, I don't think so."

"But…"

"Think," you say softly, hoping to calm Adam down. "We need a plan if we're going to stop these guys. You *do* want to stop them, don't you?"

"Sure, but…"

"Right then, let's use our heads and do this right. Too many crooks have gotten off because someone's gone off half-cocked and blown the investigation."

You can see the tension leaving Adam's face as he realizes you're on his side.

"Yeah, okay," he says. "I suppose you're right."

Moments later Jane arrives. "Why'd you come outside?"

You explain about the conversation you've overheard.

"So they *are* in on it," Jane says. "What now?"

"There are phones in the rooms," Adam says. "Let's use those."

You shake your head. "We can't. You've got to get reception to put you through to the number you want. They'll want to know why you're asking to be connected to the police or wildlife rangers. There must be another way."

Adam stands and places his hands on his hips. "If they're bringing their boat to the lagoon, I say we find a way to free the birds and sink it. That'll teach them a lesson."

"Yeah, let's sink their boat!" Jane says hopping up and down eagerly. "Underwater attack of the ninjas!"

"Are you serious?" you say, wondering what has gotten into these two. "Do you have any idea what would happen if we got caught?"

But Adam's eyes have glazed over. In his mind, he's already planning his assault.

You shake his arm. "Are you listening to me?"

Adam comes out of his trance and glares at you. "I'm going to do it with or without your help. I don't care if I get caught!"

"What do you suggest?" Jane asks, staring at you. "Got a better plan?"

There is nothing you'd like more than seeing the poachers' yacht on the bottom of the lagoon. It would certainly put a halt to their operation. But if you get caught, who knows what the poachers will do.

It's not an easy decision to make, but time is running out. Do you:

Try to sink the poachers' boat? **P448**

Or

Try to find some other way to contact the authorities? **P456**

Have a look around Smuggler's Cove

You've come this far so you don't see any harm in having a look around Smuggler's Cove while you're here. "A quick snorkel to see if it's worth coming back, then we'll go report the poachers. What do you say?"

The twins seem happy with this compromise.

The beach on this side of the island is steep, and the sand is dark from the island's many volcanic eruptions over the centuries, unlike the white sand of the lagoon beach. No reef means this part of the coast is open to whatever the Pacific throws at it. If it weren't for the cove being sheltered by a rocky point, snorkeling would be difficult except in the best of weather.

As the smuggler's yacht disappears around the point, the three of you come out of the jungle and make your way down to the water's edge. You stick in a toe. The water is warm and inviting.

You pull out your mask and flippers. "I'm going in."

The twins are quick to get their flippers on.

Within minutes, the three of you are floating on the surface looking down into a wonderland of gently swaying aquatic plants and interesting sea creatures.

You veer left to inspect the western side of the cove. This side is a little more exposed to the wind. You figure if something was to wash ashore, it's more likely to end up on this side of the cove.

At first the water in the cove is reasonably shallow. You can see the bottom as clear as if you were in a swimming pool. Blue fish dart left and right. Anemones, their tentacles waving, do their dance in the current.

You wonder if there are giant squid in these waters. Probably not you figure, they tend to hang around where waters are colder and deeper.

You are pleased the weather is calm and the waves slight. This coast would be treacherous in a storm. It's easy to imagine how a sailing ship could run aground in a spot like this.

As you kick your flippers, you glide along the surface and your head sweeps back and forth scanning the bottom for any sign of wreckage. Various corals, orange and purple starfish, sponges and crabs cover the rocky bottom along with a multitude of empty shells. Brightly colored fish dart this way and that.

When a large moray eel poke its head out of a crack in the rocks and stares up at you, his sharp teeth glistening in his partly open mouth, you kick a little harder. Morays are not a creature you want to tangle with, and this one looks hungry.

After about fifteen minutes, you stick your head out of the water. Where have the twins gone? At first you can't see them. Then there is a splash as Jane's head breaks the surface. Adam surfaces a split second later.

You pull off your mask and spit out your snorkel. "See anything?"

Both of them shake their heads.

"Okay, let's give it another few minutes and then head back."

The twins give you a thumbs-up and resume their search.

As you move further from shore, the water gets deeper and a sheer wall of rock plunges into the blue. On this wall grows an underwater jungle of marine life.

You feel the ocean swell lift you gently as you stare at the beauty below. When a big flash of silver appears out of nowhere, you jerk with fright, thinking it's a shark, but then the mass breaks up into thousands of smaller units and you realize it's only a school of fish.

Where did they come from? The rock wall looks solid all the way down, but there must be a passage or something you can't see from the surface. Once you heart rate returns to normal you take a deep breath and dive.

As you descend, you see the wall has an overhang. Below this protrusion, hidden from the surface, the dark mouth of a cave beckons. Thriving in the cracks around the entrance, are a number of red lobsters, their eyes moving back and forth at the end of spindly stalks as they watch your every move.

You grab the flashlight strapped to your leg and shine its narrow beam into the opening. The light only reaches about ten yards into the cave but it's enough for you to see an old anchor covered in barnacles up against one wall. Could this anchor be from the pirate ship that ran aground all those years ago?

In desperate need of air, you kick for the surface, angling out from under the overhand as you rise. When your head breaks the surface, you spit out your snorkel and suck in a deep breath of warm tropical air. Your heart jumps around in your chest. If there's an anchor here, maybe treasure isn't that far away.

You pull off your mask and look around for the others. When you see them off to your right, you wave and yell out. "Quick! Come over here!"

Jane reaches you first. "What is it?" she asks as she treads water beside you.

"There's an old anchor in a cave about ten feet down."

Adam's heard you too. "Could it be from the pirate ship?"

"It's looks about the right size and shape."

"We really need scuba gear if we're going to be exploring caves," Jane says.

"But how will we find the right place again?" Adam asks.

You look towards the beach and then out towards the point near the entrance to Smugglers Cove. "We need to find reference points and line them up," you say. "See that palm with the crooked trunk on the beach? We're in line with that and the top of the volcano behind it." You spin around and point towards the rocky coastline to the west. "And we're about thirty yards from shore. See that unusual rock with the narrow pointy top?"

"So," Jane says, "when we come back, we line up the funny palm tree, the volcano, and that pointy rock, and we'll be in the right spot?"

"Near enough," you say. "Shall we go get some tanks?"

"In a minute," Jane says. "I want to have a quick look first."

You pass your flashlight to Jane. "Here take this and be careful. I wouldn't recommend going inside. The currents are strong and unpredictable around here."

Jane takes a couple deep breaths, flips her feet into the air and dives headlong into the blue. You hold your mask to your face so you can watch as she kicks her way down.

Then with a big kick, the rest of her body disappears.

You lift you head out of the water and look towards Adam. "I hope that crazy sister of yours doesn't go inside."

Adam shrugs. "What can I say? She thinks she's bulletproof."

With a splash, your mask hits the water again. There is still no sign of Jane and it already feels like she's been down there for ages. Has she got stuck? Should you dive down to help?

You start taking a series of deep breaths in preparation to dive when a mop of blonde hair floats out from under the overhang. It's Jane and she's kicking hard for the surface.

Moments later she spits out her mouthpiece and takes a breath. You are about to tell her how reckless she's been when she holds out her hand. On her palm is a triangular wedge of silver.

You carefully pick up the piece and hold it closer to your face. "It's part of a coin," you tell the twins.

"Part of a coin?" Adam asks. "What happened to the rest of it?"

"In the old days, when they didn't have the right change, they'd chop coins into smaller pieces." You turn the piece over. Along one edge are three letters, a C, an A and an R. "I bet this once said Carolus. That's Charles in English. King Charles the Fourth ruled Spain in the late 1700s and early 1800s."

Jane's grin gets even bigger. "That date fits with your wreck, doesn't it?"

You nod. "Historians think the *Port-au-Prince* went down in the early 1800s, but coins last hundreds of years so this certainly could have come from the ship we're after. Fingers crossed we can find some more."

"I didn't go in very far," Jane says, "so I couldn't see much. But how could treasure have ended up in the cave?"

"Storms on an exposed coast like this can really toss things around."

Adam is listening intently to your exchange. "Let's go get some scuba gear so we can check it out."

The three of you are deep in thought as you make your way back to the beach. Within ten minutes, your gear has dried in the sun and you pack up and start back along the track to the resort.

By the time the first of the resort buildings comes into view, you've been walking for over an hour and your legs are tired.

The three of you sit on a low stone wall by the pool and discuss what to do next.

"I'm for getting back to the cove," Jane says. "I need treasure!"

"We *need* to report the poachers first," Adam says.

"But who can we trust?" Jane says. "What if the poachers are working with someone from the resort?"

Jane has a point. What if reporting the poachers to the management ends up warning them?

Maybe you should gather more evidence before you do anything. And, if you do decide to report them, what happens if the authorities stake out the cove? How will you secretly investigate the cave and find treasure with people lurking about?

Adam stands up. "I've been thinking on the walk back, and I reckon there's a good chance the poachers will sail in to the lagoon and anchor overnight. It's the only real anchorage on the island. When they do, I'm going to find some way to sink their boat."

"Brilliant," Jane says. "My brother the eco-warrior against three hardened criminals. Good luck with that, sport."

"But what if they don't come here?" you ask.

"I bet they do," Adam says with a serious look on his face. "In fact, I'll bet you ice cream for a week they do."

"If they do, and that's a big if," Jane says. "I think we should report them and then get back to treasure hunting."

You're not quite sure what you think. You'd love to sink the poachers' boat and put them out of action. But Jane has a point. Is it even your fight? And besides, what can three kids do against dangerous men?

Then you have an idea. "Maybe we can bypass the resort management and contact the authorities directly."

Adam frowns. "I'm waiting for the boat. I'll sink them even if I have to do it alone."

It's time to make a decision. Do you:

Agree with Adam and try to sink the poachers' boat if they turn up? **P448**

Or

Try to contact the authorities? **P456**

You have decided to try and help Adam

"Okay, let's see if we can find Adam," you say to Jane. "I don't think we have enough time to go all the way back to the resort for help."

Jane climbs out of the ferns. "So what do we do?"

"We'll have to be stealthy as ninjas, sneak up on them, free Adam, and then get away." You give Jane a big smile. "What could go wrong?"

Jane grins back. "I can think of a few things, but let's not worry about that now. Let's go get my brother."

"First, we'll need camouflage," you say. "Break off some fronds and tie them around your waist with vines. Have them pointing up like real ferns, that way when we stand still, we'll blend right in with the jungle."

"I've seen movies where commandos rub dirt on their faces," Jane says. "Maybe we should do that too?"

"Good idea," you say. You dig your fingers under the leaf litter at your feet. "The ground is damp under the leaves. Should smear just fine."

Despite the seriousness of the mission you are about to undertake, the two of you can't help laughing a little as you cover your arms, hair and faces. When the two of you have finished, you can barely recognize Jane. She looks half plant, half wild animal.

"Perfect," you say. "Let's go."

You take it slowly in case the poachers have posted a lookout. Every twenty yards or so you stop, stand perfectly still and listen for footsteps. When you see a flash of color, you stop so abruptly that Jane bumps into your back.

"Shhh… I see one of them."

"Where?" Jane whispers back.

You point to a spot 100 yards or so ahead. The man is leaning against a tree. He has a cigarette in one hand and a walkie-talkie in the other. As you stand there pretending to be a fern, you think about what should be your next step.

The man is too big. How can the two of you possibly subdue him?

You look around at your feet. "No rocks, the soil's soft here," you say. "We need a weapon of some sort."

Jane digs a hand into her pocket. "I have something that might help."

"What's that?"

She removes a bundle of nylon netting. All scrunched up, it looks quite small, but as she spreads the net out, your see it's bigger than you first thought. You stand on one side and give the net a sharp tug. The thin, clear filament is deceptively strong.

"I saw it lying just off the path a while ago and picked it up so some poor animal didn't get tangled up in it." Jane says.

"Good thing you did. At least now we've got something to work with."

After thinking for another few moments, you come up with a plan. "If we secure this piece of net between two trees, we might be able to get the man to run into it and tangle himself him up. Then we can pounce on him, tie him up with vines, and he'll be our prisoner."

"But how do we get him to run into the net?" Jane asks.

"Bait. Once we rig it up, you attract the poachers' attention and then lead him to our trap. Then we pounce."

Jane tilts her head to one side and then back to the other, considering what you've said. "Might work. But what then?"

"Prisoner exchange. We use his walkie-talkie to negotiate with the guys on the boat."

You know the plan has risks, but it's the only one you can think of. If Jane agrees, you'll need to set the trap fast. If the man leaves the jungle and goes back to the boat, your opportunity will be gone.

"Dealing with one man at a time is our only chance, Jane."

She exhales a long sigh, looks around the jungle as if she's trying to come up with an alternative, then turns back to you. "Okay, let's do it."

Thankfully, there are vines everywhere and your pocket knife is sharp. You and Jane move back along the path a bit and then work quickly, cutting lengths of vine and weaving them through the sides of the net.

Then the net is tied to saplings on either side of the track. These small trees should give way when the man's weight hits, bend inward and add to the tangle. Extra lassos of vine are piled up near the trap for quick use. As an added measure, another length of vine is strung across the path at ankle level, a yard or so before the net, to trip the man up and send him flying headlong into your trap. When you stand back to survey your handiwork, the trap is almost invisible.

"Okay," you say. "We've only got one chance at this. If the man looks like he's getting free, run for it. We'll meet back at the resort."

Jane gulps. You can see her hands are a little shaky. But then so are yours.

"Right, now we need to attract his attention. Take off your camouflage and stand on the far side of the net. Here, use some water from my drink bottle to wash some of that mud off you. Otherwise he'll think you're a member of some long lost tribe."

Jane takes your bottle and squirts water over her face and hair.

"Remember, keep the net between you and him at all times."

Jane wipes her face on her t-shirt. "Okay, got it."

As Jane stands in position, ready to act as decoy, you walk closer to where the man is standing and move a few steps off the path. Your camouflage gives you a view through its fronds. When you're near enough that you think the man will hear, you grab a dry branch and snap it sharply in two. The crack is like a rifle shot in the stillness of the jungle. When a flock of lorikeets takes off from the canopy above you, you duck down, hoping your camouflage is up to the task.

It isn't long before you hear footsteps. The man is coming to investigate. Then the footsteps speed up. He must have seen Jane further along.

You hear a yelp from Jane as she takes off, and then a yell from the man chasing her.

As soon as the man passes your position, you rip off your camouflage and race down the path after him.

A shout of alarm followed by a loud thump tells you the trap has worked. Around the next bend, you find the poacher lying on the path cursing and struggling in the net. The more he struggles, the more the nylon snags his feet and arms.

You grab a couple of loops from the pile you prepared earlier and slip the sturdy vines over his shoulders pulling them tight around his torso and tying knots to hold them in place.

Moments later Jane arrives back on the scene. She leaps into the air and body slams the man on the ground like she's a big-time wrestler.

"Oomph!" the man grunts as the air is forced from his lungs.

Jane jumps up and grabs some more vines, and between the two of you, the man is trussed up tight within minutes.

You pick up the walkie-talkie, and look down at him. "Well, well, what have we here?"

"You'd better let me—"

Jane kicks the man in the stomach. "You'd better hope my brother is okay, mister!"

This is a side of Jane you didn't expect. It's like she's taken the whole ninja thing to heart.

"Stop it, girly, or you'll be sorry."

Without hesitation, Jane kicks him even harder.

"Oomph!" the man grunts.

Jane glares down at him. "And don't call me girly, old man!"

As Jane and the man lock eyes, you hear the crackle of the walkie-talkie.

"Jimmy, are you there?" More static, then a click. "Come in, Jimmy. Can you hear me?"

You look at Jane and grin. "Let the negotiations begin."

"If you don't want another kick, you'd better stop staring at me!" Jane growls at the man.

You make a mental note never to piss Jane off, as you push the 'talk' button on the side of the transmitter. "Yeah, Jimmy can hear you."

"Who's that?"

"Never mind who this is," you say into the microphone. "We have Jimmy, and we want our friend back."

"You kids have Jimmy? Don't make me laugh. Come on, tell me. How'd you steal his transmitter?"

"We took it off him when we captured him. Now listen, we want you to let Adam go, or we're turning your friend into the authorities. Kidnapping is a serious offence."

"If you've got Jimmy, let me speak to him."

"He's a bit tied up at the moment," you say. "Do you want to deal, or do I go to the cops?"

There is silence for a minute. You suspect the two men are deciding what to do.

"We'll do nothing until you let us speak to Jimmy."

You hold the microphone near Jimmy's mouth and nod to Jane.

Jane gives him another solid kick.

"Oomph! Oh for Christ's sake, the brats have got me, alright! Do what they say and get me out of here while I still have some unbroken ribs."

You pull the transmitter away from Jimmy and speak clearly into it. "Here's what you're going to do. Bring Adam to the waterfall in exactly half an hour. That's where we'll do the exchange. If you don't show up, or if you show up early, we go to the authorities. Got it?"

Once again there is a brief silence before the man on the other end of the walkie-talkie comes back on. "Right. Half an hour."

"And Adam better be unhurt, or the deal's off!" you snarl before clicking off.

"Why the waterfall?" Jane asks.

You motion her out of Jimmy's earshot. "I have a cunning plan."

"How cunning?" Jane asks.

"Cunning as a fox." Then you explain.

As you talk, Jane's grin gets broader. "You are evil … but I like it."

"It should work, but we'll need to get moving to get in place before the men arrive. First, we'll need to get Jimmy to his feet and make it so he can walk."

Jimmy isn't a lightweight. By the time you roll him onto his back, cut some net away so he has limited movement and maneuver him to his feet, you and Jane are both sweating in the sticky jungle heat.

You give Jimmy a little shove along the path. "Right, Mister Poacher, get waddling."

Watching him walk is funny. Netting encases him from head to calf and his arms are bound tightly to his sides. He reminds you of a woman in a tight skirt as he takes small, awkward steps.

Whenever he slows down, you prod him with a stick.

"Stop poking me, brat, I'm going as fast as I can!"

The steep path leading up towards the waterfall doesn't help Jimmy's speed.

You wink at Jane. "Just keep it moving, mister."

When the three of you arrive at the waterfall, you stop, splash some cold water on your face and then pull out your map. You show Jane the path you spotted on it earlier.

"See just here." Your finger traces a line that runs from where you are standing, up and around the falls to the top of the cascade. "This is the path I was talking about. And here," you say, pointing to another line that leads from the top of the falls, around the far side of the volcano and back to the resort, "is our escape route."

"Perfect," Jane says.

You glance over at your captive. "Okay, Jimmy, time to do a little climbing."

Grabbing one of the vines tied around Jimmy's waist you lead him around the pond and up a narrow path. The track rises steeply. A couple of times, Jimmy stumbles and you have to help him back to his feet.

After ten minutes or so, the ground levels out and the trees and dense bush give way to flat slabs of rock. A rushing stream flows out of the jungle and thunders over the rocky ledge into the pond below.

Holding the vine around Jimmy's waist, you lead him to the edge of the rocky slab. Water rushes past beside you. When you peer over the edge, it is a straight drop to the water below, and because of the pool's clarity, you can see all the way to its bottom. "Whoa. That looks further than I expected."

Stepping back from the edge, you maneuver Jimmy so that he is visible from the path below and then stand slightly behind him holding tightly onto the vine so he doesn't trip and fall.

"Jane," you whisper, "can you go find our escape route?"

Jane nods then heads off, while you keep an eye out for the poachers.

A few minutes later Jane's back, she cups her hand to your ear. "Found it. The path looks in pretty good shape."

"Excellent."

"What now?" Jane asks.

"Now we get Adam back."

"My friends are going to make you brats pay," Jimmy snarls from his perch.

"You know, for a man standing on the edge of a waterfall with his hands tied behind his back, you're not very bright are you?" You nudge Jimmy a little closer to the edge with the stick. "You sure you want to piss me off right now?"

Jimmy peers over the edge and swallows. "Sorry, kid. Don't do anything crazy now."

"That's better," you say, pulling him back a bit. "Now keep your trap shut."

It's Jane's keen sense of hearing that alerts you to the sound of approaching footsteps.

"That's far enough!" you yell to the men when they reach the edge of the pool.

The men shield their eyes from the glaring sun as they look up at you. They have tied Adam's wrists but he looks okay.

"Untie Adam and we'll let your guy go," you say. "Adam, when they untie you, run up the path to the right of the falls as quickly as possible."

You see a tiny smile pass between the two men. You can tell they've got something planned … but then so do you.

"Okay, we're untying him now."

As soon as Adam's wrists are free, he does as instructed and sprints off up the path.

"Okay, and here's your guy. You'd better get him before he drowns." And with that, you shove Jimmy over the edge. "Bye bye, jerk."

"Nooooooooooo!" Jimmy yells.

The splash sends a tower of water flying up.

"What the heck?" one of the men says as he dives into the water after Jimmy. The other man is about to run after Adam when his friend yells out. "Get in here. I can't hold him up on my own, moron!"

The second man dives into the water. When he surfaces, the two of them are holding Jimmy's head above water and slowly dogpaddling back to a spot where they can get out of the water.

Jimmy is okay, but none too happy. "Just wait until I get my hands on those brats!" he splutters.

Moments later, Adam arrives.

"Okay, time to get moving," you say.

"Hey, thanks, you two, good work," Adam says.

"Let's get out of here," Jane says. "We can congratulate ourselves once we're back at the resort."

Without any more mucking around, the three of you scurry off into the jungle. You keep up a good pace, but you're pretty sure your plan has worked and the poachers will try to leave the island quickly.

According to the map, the path you're on curves in a big arc around the slopes of the volcano. Being at a slightly higher altitude, this part of the mountain is covered in trees and broad-leafed shrubs, but every now and then you come across a patch of stunted growth trying to gain a foothold on top of an old lava flow.

At one such flow, a pair of gray-brown birds with unusually large feet and orange legs are digging a burrow in the warm volcanic soil.

"Look, megapodes!" you say.

"Kwway-kwe-kerrr," the male bird sings.

"Kirrrr," the female replies.

"Funny looking things," Jane says. "What happened to the feathers on their throats?"

Below the bird's orange beaks is a sparse patch where the feathers look like they've been plucked.

"I think that's natural. I read these birds bury their eggs and then let the heat in the soil do the incubation."

"What? They just lay them and leave them?" Jane asks.

You nod. "I think so."

"Doesn't podes mean feet?" Adam asks.

"Yes," you say. "And mega mean really big."

"So we've discovered Big Foot?" Jane says, making a face of exaggerated astonishment.

Adam raises his eyes to the sky and sighs. "A big-footed chicken maybe."

You laugh at Adam's joke. "Hey you two, we've made good time. Let's take a minute and grab a bite and something to drink. It's important to keep hydrated in these hot climates."

You pull out your drink bottle and an energy bar and watch the birds as you eat, glancing occasionally back along the track in case the poachers appear.

When you've finished, you re-shoulder your pack. "Okay, break's over, we'd better get moving." You start along the track again. "I hate to think what Jimmy would do to us given the opportunity, especially after his belly flop off the cliff."

The twins don't need much convincing.

After crossing the old lava flow, the three of you re-enter the forest and continue your loop around the mountain towards the resort. Small streams cut their way down the rocky slope, and higher up the mountain, large birds soar as they pick up thermals near the volcano's summit.

You are just starting to cross a tricky part of the track, where heavy rain has washed some of it away, when you hear a low rumble from deep underground.

Just as Jane swings her head around looking for the source of the noise, the earth starts shaking and the rumbling gets louder.

"It's an eruption!" Adam yells. "The mountain's going to blow!"

And here you were thinking the volcano was safe. But then as quickly as the noise started, the rumbling stops.

You wipe the sweat off your forehead. "Phew! False alarm."

"Or prelude," Adam says.

You are about to move off, when you hear a strange clacking sound … and it's getting louder. When you look up the slope in the direction of the noise you see rocks and boulders tumbling down the mountainside.

"Rock fall!" you shout. "Run for it!"

The three of you scramble over the wash-out and hit the track sprinting. Thankfully the track is reasonably clear and without too many tree roots to trip you up. When the rocks hit the bush line, you hear the cracking of branches in the jungle behind you. Then a tortured creaking as the trees struggle to hold back the weight of the larger rocks. Then, once again, there's an eerie silence.

"Oh boy, that was close," Jane says.

"Not wrong there," you say with hands on knees sucking in deep breaths of air.

"This island is a death trap," Adam says. "Poachers, volcanoes, boulders bouncing down the mountainside. What next?"

Having caught your breath, you walk over and slap Adam on the back. "Don't worry," you say. "At least we haven't had a tsunami."

"Yet," Adam says, trying to smile. "You do know eruptions cause tsunamis, eh?"

"Oh, stop being a worry wart," Jane says. "We're ninja spies on a great adventure. Nothing can harm us."

You like Jane's optimism, but you also know that it's foolish not to have a healthy respect for nature. "Let's just keep moving and watch out for potential hazards. Even ninja spies aren't boulder proof."

A few minutes later, when the ground starts shaking a second time, you suspect the volcano is only warming up. You grab the nearest tree and hang on. After a minute's vibration, the mountain once again goes silent.

"I think its practicing for the main show," Adam says. "Let's just hope it doesn't do a Krakatoa on us."

Jane's brow creases. "Krakatoa?"

"You know, the Indonesian volcano that blew up and wiped out over 30,000 people," Adam says. "That eruption caused a huge tsunami that wiped out whole towns."

Jane raises her eyebrows. "But were any ninjas hurt?"

Adam mutters under his breath and rolls his eyes skyward.

Jane makes a face at her brother. "I didn't think so!"

"Well I don't know much about volcanoes," you say, "except that I don't want to be on them when they go off." And with that said, you take off down the path again.

"I'm with you," Adam says falling in behind.

"Ninja spies, evacuate the mountain!" Jane says as she jogs past the two of you. "Last one to the resort is a monkey's bum."

"See what I have to put up with?" Adam says.

Adam may find his sister a pain at times, but he follows her lead and increases his pace.

It's only another half an hour before the track cuts through a forest of pandanus palms, with their narrow spiny leaves and their strange stilted roots that look like mini teepees holding the main trunk clear of the ground.

When you come to a junction, you stop and pull out your map. Adam and Jane look over your shoulder.

You point to a spot where two tracks meet. "We're just here I reckon."

"This track along the beach looks longer," Jane says tracing her finger along the line that runs along the coast.

"Yes, it's longer to the resort that way, but it's further from the volcano," Adam says. "The further we are from the mountain, the better."

"But what if the poachers are following us?" Jane says. "They could take the shorter track around the volcano and cut us off before we get to the resort."

The twins look at you, expecting a decision. Do you:

Take the beach track? **P429**

Or

Take the shorter jungle track? **P438**

Go back to the resort for help

You can't see any other alternative other than going back to the resort to get help. What are two kids supposed to do against three criminals?

"They said they'd hurt Adam if we said anything," Jane says. "Do you think they're telling the truth?"

You look at Jane's worried expression. "They could be bluffing."

"But how do we know?" Jane asks. "And what if they're not?"

Adam's capture is certainly a dilemma. It will take time to get back to the resort, even if you jog the whole way. The men on the yacht could be long gone by the time you get help from the resort.

You sit down, lean back against a coconut palm and think.

"Maybe you're right, Jane. What if they're not bluffing? They could dump Adam out at sea and deny ever having seen him. It would be their word against ours. Could we even identify them properly? Remember if they've got Adam, they've got Adam's camera too."

Jane, normally so self-assured, is looking shaky. "But what—what can we do?"

"I'm not sure, but I think we need to try. Let's sneak back and see what they're up to eh? We might think of something."

Jane nods and then clenches her jaw in an attempt to look determined, but you see through her act. She's scared, and with good reason. Her brother is in danger and you may not be able to help him.

You step off the path and lead Jane into the jungle. "Hunters usually set their traps on paths."

"So that's why you're going off trail?" Jane asks.

"Yep. I'll lead us back to the cove cross-country, it may be harder going but we're less likely to run into trouble that way. You never know what booby traps the poachers have set up."

As the two of you work your way through the dense undergrowth, you hear the chatter of birds above you. You wonder if the birds are calling out a warning because you're in their territory, or just going about their normal business.

You figure you're about half way back to the cove when you see a thick length of black rubber stretching between two trees off to your left. The rubber is about eight inches wide and ten feet long. Interested, you veer towards it.

As you get closer you see fine mesh hanging below the rubber. "It's a net."

The rubber is suspended just above head level with the net hanging to the ground below.

"Why rubber?" Jane asks. "How does that help them catch birds?"

You have a look at the set up. "I don't think it is for catching birds."

Jane goes pale "Wha—what do you mean? Is it for ca—catching people?"

"Wild pigs more likely," you say with a grin. "The rubber will give some flex and stop the net ripping when one runs into it. See over there." You point to a pile of husked coconuts, their fibrous outer covering removed, leaving only the brown hard nut. "Whoever set this up has been collecting coconuts too. More likely locals than poachers."

"They sure got a lot of them," Jane says.

Then an idea hits you. "Of course! Coconuts!"

Jane gives you a funny look. "Huh?"

"What's the same size as a coconut and used to be fired by pirate ships?"

"What? Pirate ships?"

"Cannon balls!" you say. "Coconuts are like cannon balls!"

"But we don't have a cannon," Jane says.

"But we do have the makings of a slingshot."

"We do?" Jane says.

You point to the thick band of rubber stretched between the two trees. "Yes. A big one."

A smile of understanding flashes across Jane's face as she sees where you're going. "So, your plan is to tie the rubber between two trees near the cove and fire coconuts at the yacht?"

You nod. "Exactly."

"But won't the poachers just pull up their anchor and sail off?"

"They might if they can get to the bow of their boat without getting knocked out. Our job will be to stop that happening."

"You are evil," Jane says. "I like it."

"Right, let's get this thing down."

You climb up one tree and get to work untying the rubber. Jane climbs up the other. Once back on the ground you stand on one end and try pulling the strip of rubber up with your arms. The band is incredibly strong. With your knife, you cut a coconut-sized section of net to use as your slingshot's pouch and attach it to the rubber. Then you take off your day-pack and fill it with as many coconuts as it will carry. Jane does the same.

You shoulder your pack. "Right, bombardier, to the beach!"

Jane winks. "Aar, me hearty. Let's sink these buccaneers."

The two of you make a cautious approach to the beach, in case the poachers have posted a lookout.

"Look for two trees about six feet apart," you say as you scout around.

Jane spots a couple up ahead. "How about these two?"

You inspect the trees, and then walk in a straight line back from the beach to check the firing line. The angle seems good. And there's a bonus. The trees she's pointed out have a row of low shrubs between them and the water. These shrubs will give you cover while you set up and, with a bit of luck, hide your position for a time while the poachers figure out where the flying coconuts are coming from.

"Perfect," you say. "Let's get set up."

Setting up the slingshot is a simple matter. You take a double loop of rubber around each tree at about shoulder height and tie a knot. Then you clear a path, so you can stretch the rubber back as far as possible before shooting.

"These guys are going to freak!" Jane says with a grin.

After a final check that all is right, you look over at Jane. "Ready for action, bombardier?"

"Aye aye, Captain."

"Load coconut," you say as you slip the first coconut into the pouch.

"St—retch," Jane says as the two of you grab the pouch and pull back as hard as you can.

"Elevation," you say kneeling down and angling your shot upward so it will have some distance to it.

"Three, two, one, FIRE!" you yell in unison.

With a *twang* the coconut flies in a parabolic arc towards the yacht.

"It's a hit!" Jane exclaims as the rock-hard nut crashes into the side of the boat, leaving a small dent in the fiberglass.

"Load!" you yell.

The two of you quickly repeat the process.

"FIRE!"

The next impact has the men scrambling up from below.

"Can you see Adam?" Jane says.

One of the men is standing on the cabin top, looking your way.

"Quick, let's get him!"

"FIRE!"

The coconut lands in the cockpit only feet away.

"Someone's shooting at us," the man calls to his companion. "Let's get out of here."

A man comes up from below and moves towards the bow.

"Let's get him!" Jane calls.

"Load!"

"FIRE!"

The coconut hits the deck a few feet from where the man is fiddling with the anchor rope. The shot's a miss, but it's close enough to give the man a fright and he scurries back to the relative safety of the cockpit.

"FIRE!"

This nut crashes through one of the yacht's side windows. There's more shouting from below.

Another man comes on deck with a pair of binoculars and scans the shore. The way he is sweeping back and forth means he hasn't spotted your position.

"Load," you whisper.

The two of you stretch back the slingshot. You take half a step to the right and aim at the man with the binoculars.

"Down a bit more," you say.

"Fire!"

The coconut screams out of the jungle. It is nearly upon him before he drops the binoculars and reacts.

Unfortunately for him, he's too slow. The coconut doubles him over as it smacks into his pot belly. Then he staggers back and falls over the railing and splashes into the sea.

"Got him!" you say.

Jane points. "There's Adam."

The distraction you've created has allowed Adam time to open the front hatch and climb onto the bow.

His hands are tied, but he steps over the railing and jumps into the water anyway.

"Give me your knife. I'm going to help," Jane says.

You reach in your pocket and hand it over.

"Cover me." And with that Jane streaks out of the jungle, runs down the beach and plunges into the water.

You load another coconut and pull back. Without Jane's help, you really have to dig deep to pull the rubber back far enough, and you can't hold it long or do much aiming before having to let go. But still, you manage to fire three more nuts off in quick succession.

Thankfully, the men are too busy dodging coconuts and helping their friend get back on board to notice that Adam has jumped ship.

Adam floats on his back, slowly kicking his way to shore. As you fire another nut, you see Jane has nearly reached him.

She cuts the rope binding Adam's wrists.

Another nut hits the cabin top just as the men pull their friend aboard.

One of the men yells out. "The boy!"

"Fire!" you yell, sending another nut flying through the air.

This one shatters a tray of food and drinks sitting in the cockpit. Glass goes flying.

"Let's get out of here," The injured man says as he drips on deck. "Get that anchor up!"

Jane and Adam are running up the beach. Soon you'll have a full crew of gunners again.

"Load!" Jane says as she grabs another coconut. "Let's teach these guys a lesson!"

With three of you, the firing is much faster. Nuts zip through the air every fifteen seconds or so. Adam scouts around for more nuts, but after another five minutes you've exhausted your ammo.

"We'd better get out of here before they come ashore," you say.

"They'd better put the fire out before their boat burns you mean," Adam says.

You look at Adam. "What did you say?"

"Before I escaped I found a lighter and set the bunk in the front cabin on fire. It's polyurethane foam so it should burn like crazy."

"Holy moly!" Jane says with a grin. "My brother the arsonist."

Now that Adam's mentioned it, you can see a few wisps of smoke coming from the front hatch. The men have seen it too. One of them grabs a fire extinguisher from the cockpit and disappears below.

"Let's get out of here," Jane says. "I've had enough adventure for one day."

You look at the twins and smile. "There's always tomorrow, me hearties."

Congratulations, this part of your story is over. You've saved Adam, and put a serious dent in the poachers' operation. Maybe in another path you'll find some treasure.

428

It is time to make a decision. Do you:

Go back to the beginning of the story and try another path? **P365**

Or

Go to the Big List of Choices and start reading from another part of the story? **P536**

Take the longer beach track

"I think the volcano's going to blow," you say. "We'd better stick to the coast."

The twins follow as you veer left and head down the slope towards the sparkling water of the Pacific Ocean rather than carry on around the higher loop track.

Ten minutes later, when you feel another rumble beneath your feet, you're sure you've made the right decision.

Higher up the mountain, you hear rocks tumbling downhill and crashing into trees.

"I wouldn't want to be up there," Adam says, picking up the pace. "This mountain is angry about something."

As if to confirm Adam's point, a blast of ash and rock shoots out of the crater, peppering the upper slopes with rocks. The resulting tremor nearly knocks you off your feet.

"Crikey!" Jane cries out, in a poor imitation of an Australian accent. "Ground's jumping round like a kangaroo being chased by a pack of dingoes."

This time both you and Adam roll your eyes. But Jane's not wrong about the volcano. The mountain's definitely working up a head of steam.

The three of you keep up the pace, eager to get as far away from the eruption as possible, and it isn't long before the track begins to level out. More ferns appear and you can see the tops of the coconut palms in the distance. The ground under your feet is less rocky and the sound of waves breaking creates a gentle background to the chirping of the birds.

You're only half a mile from the coast, when you hear an explosion of some magnitude behind you.

"Holy moly," Jane exclaims. "The mountain's bleeding."

You look up through a gap in the trees. Near the top of the cone, blood-red lava flows out from vents in the volcano's flanks. Rivers of red run down the mountain, consuming everything in their path. Dense smoke billows into the air, and with each explosion, more rocks and debris are ejected high into the air.

A flock of lorikeets skim the treetops as they flee the upper slopes and you hear a loud crashing through the undergrowth that you suspect is a wild pig frightened by the rumbling.

"I wonder what's happening on the other side of the island," Adam says. "Do you think the lava will threaten the resort?"

You scratch your head. "It's possible. We'll find out soon enough, I suppose."

When you come out of the bush onto the coast and look in the direction of the resort, you see a curtain of smoke rising in front of you.

Jane grabs your arm. "What's that?"

"I hope I'm wrong, but I think one of the lava flows has made it all the way to the sea."

Jane frowns. "You mean we're cut off?"

You wave the twins forward. "I'm not sure. Let's check it out."

It takes about ten minutes to reach the lava flow. Its acidic smoke makes you cough. Thankfully, a sea breeze is blowing most of the smoke is up the slope.

Only the lushness of the green tropical plants stops the fire spreading wildly across the island. Were it the dry season, heaven knows what sort of fires the lava flow would have started.

"It's wiped out the track," Adam says.

He's right. Although the lava is beginning to crust over, cracks show the fiery red, still fluid, lava running beneath.

You shake your head. "No way across that. We'd end up looking like overcooked marshmallows."

Adam looks nervous. "What now?" he asks.

"Goodness … gracious … great balls of fire," Jane sings in her best rock and roll voice.

Eyes roll.

While Jane tries to make light of your situation, you think hard about how to get out of this predicament. But then Jane surprises you with a suggestion.

"I've seen documentaries on TV. When lava flows into the ocean it makes lots of steam, but the water always wins in the end and cools the lava down. Couldn't we just swim around it?"

"I'm not that great a swimmer, remember," Adam says.

But what Jane has said makes perfect sense.

"Let's go to the beach and check it out," you say. "We can always put some coconuts in our day packs for buoyancy."

"Okay," Adam says. "Anything's better than being captured."

"Or toasted," Jane says.

Where the lava meets the sea is a battleground. Hot lava flows forward and waves crashing on the shore put up a defense. Steam is everywhere. The lava crackles and pops as it is doused with cold seawater, but still it keeps coming.

"How wide is the flow do you think?" you ask the twins.

"Two hundred yards maybe," Adam replies.

"Easy-peasy," Jane says. "We can swim that no problem."

You put your pack on the ground and look around. "Okay let's gather some coconuts. And make it quick, this mountain isn't getting any friendlier."

If there is one thing this island isn't short of, it's coconuts. Within a couple minutes your packs are full to bursting.

"These are heavy. You sure they'll float?" Adam asks.

You raise your eyebrows at Adam. "Coconuts float all over the Pacific silly. Is your pack lighter than it would be if it was filled with water?"

Adam lifts his pack by its straps. "Yeah, I suppose…"

"Anything lighter than water will float. There's lots of air trapped by the coconut's husk. Believe me, they'll float just fine." You lift your pack and sling it over your shoulder. "Come on, let's go."

There is no protective lagoon on this part of the coast. You'll have to enter the water from the rocks. You find an area where an old lava flow protrudes into the sea and walk out onto it.

"Time your leap so you get sucked out by a retreating wave," you say. "And don't lose hold of your pack."

Adam looks nervous.

"I'll go first," Jane says. "I'm the strongest swimmer. Once I'm in the water, I can help if one of you gets has problems."

Again, Jane is making a lot of sense. You nod and watch as she shifts her pack onto her chest and puts her arms through the straps.

"Look guys, I'm the hunch stomach of Notre Dame."

Your eyes roll. "Enough with the jokes already," you say, but secretly you're pleased that Jane has a sense of humor. It will make things easier for Adam when it's his turn to jump.

Jane moves further out onto the rock and gets ready to leap. As a wave breaks, the white foam rushes up around her ankles, then as the water surges back, she takes two quick steps, leaps in, and is sucked out with the retreating wave.

She paddles out beyond the next wave and then turns back toward shore. Her day pack holds her upper body well above the water. "See, I told you. Easy-peasy."

You and Adam repeat the exercise without any drama, and start swimming out around the lava flow. You're pleased you took your face mask out of your pack and put it in a side pouch. The sight below is spectacular.

Lava, red and burning, like an undersea river, flows out along the sea bed. Tiny bubbles rise from the boiling water where the lava touches the ocean. You can feel the heat radiating from the lava flow and are careful not to stray too close.

Then suddenly there is a silver flash beneath you. Then another. Your heart races, thinking that sharks have surrounded you, but then a dolphin jumps out of the water and twirls in the air before splashing down.

"Dolphins!" Jane yells. "Hundreds of them."

"I wonder if they're attracted by the heat of the lava?" Adam says.

More and more dolphins join in the fun as they leap over you, around you, and swim under you.

"So cute!" Jane squeals as a young dolphin comes up to investigate these new creatures that have invaded her territory.

Then after a series of gravity defying leaps, each more spectacular than the previous, the pod swims west and the dolphins disappear.

"Wow that was amazing," Jane says.

The dolphins have taken your mind off things, and before you know it, you have reached a spot where it's safe to come ashore. The place you've chosen isn't so much a beach as a channel in the rock between two old lava flows. Seaweed clogs the sides of the channel, but there looks to be a clear run up the center into shore.

You put your face down in the water, and kick your feet. Fish are everywhere. Sea urchins and hermit crabs crowd the bottom. It's like looking into an aquarium.

One type of coral looks like miniature red trees that have lost their leaves. Another resembles a pale blue brain. Anemones wave their tentacles and seaweeds of yellow and green sway gently in the tide. Electric-blue fish swim lazily by, while schools of red, white and orange striped fish move as one in shoals of a hundred or so. A bright yellow fish the size of a dinner plate nibbles at something on a lump of pale white coral, and orange sea stars move slowly across the rocky bottom looking for shellfish to eat.

You're only twenty yards from shore when you see something sparkle. You stop kicking and float in place. Then you see it again.

You lift your face out of the water. "Stop, I see something on the bottom." You pass your sodden daypack to Jane. "Can you hold this please? I'm going to take a closer look."

After a deep breath, you kick for the bottom. Once there you hold onto a piece of kelp to keep from floating up. Now where was that…

And then you see them. A trail of gold coins running along the eastern side of the channel.

In need of air, you shoot to the surface. "Coins on the bottom," you tell the others when your head breaks the surface. "Heaps of them!"

"Holy moly," Jane says with a big toothy grin. "We're gonna be rich."

Jane passes Adam the two packs and you and she dive again. This time you manage to pick up half a dozen coins before having to resurface. With each dive, you find a few more coins, but it becomes obvious fairly quickly that this isn't the mother lode.

"How many coins have we got altogether?" you ask Adam who has been looking after the coins as you and Jane do the diving.

Adam does a quick count. "Twenty-seven. What's the price of gold?"

You try to remember what you saw online before you left for your vacation. "About 1200 U.S. an ounce, I think."

It's time for some quick calculations. You decide to multiply 30 times 1200 and then subtract 3 times 1200 to make it easy.

"Let see, 3 times 12 is 36. Put the three 0's back on and that's 36,000. Less 3 times 1200 which is 3600. That means we've got 36,000 less 3600. Or 32,400 dollars worth."

"Crikey!" Jane says. "That'll buy a few kangaroo burgers."

The three of you are congratulating each other when you hear a male voice nearby.

"There those brats are!"

You look towards land, but see nothing. Then you hear the low rumble of a diesel engine.

"The poachers aren't chasing us by foot," Jane says. "They've come by boat."

"They must be trying to beat us back to the resort," Adam says.

"No time to wait," you say, retrieving your pack from Adam and kicking towards shore. "Let's get out of here before they launch their dinghy."

Scrambling up the rocky beach, the three of you dump your

coconuts and rejoin the coastal path. The men motor just off shore, watching you as you go.

"How are we going to shake them?" Jane asks.

"That's a good question, sis," Adam says before turning to you. "How are we going to shake them?"

"Let's just keep going. What can they do once we're back at the resort?" you say.

Your eyes follow the yacht as you walk quickly along the path. The volcano is still spewing ash and lava, and every now and then you feel the ground shaking.

Then a violent jolt knocks you off your feet.

"Holy moly," Jane says picking herself up. "That was the strongest one yet."

"Too big for comfort," you say. "I'm not liking this."

As you start moving again, you notice the sea receding. Where once there was water, now you can see fish flopping about. "That's odd," you say.

"Not odd," Adam says. "It's a tsunami!"

You look out to sea. A wall of white water is heading towards shore. "Run!"

The three of you drop your packs and move quickly away from the beach. "Keep running for high ground," Adam yells. "Who know how far it will come inland."

As you dodge trees and palms and head further inland the ground gradually rises. With the volcano still erupting you don't really want to climb too high, but then you don't want to get caught by the incoming wave either. Then you hit an old lava flow where the ground rises steeply. You take a narrow path up the side of the flow, pumping your legs for all they're worth.

By the time you get to the ridge, you figure you're far enough from the beach to be safe. You breathe hard and watch the wave approaching the yacht.

"They've seen it coming," Adam says. "They're trying to turn their bow into the wave."

The three of you watch, spellbound by the sight unfolding before you.

As the wave rushes in, the bow of the yacht rises, and rises. It looks as though it's going to make it over, but then the sheer force of the water forces the yacht back. When the bow drops, and the boat turns side on to the wave, you know the boat is doomed.

As the seabed shallows near the shore, the wave rises, and rises, and rises.

"Holy moly!" you say, stealing Jane's favorite expression. "Look at it go!"

The yacht is on its side, mast down in the water. You can see the men hanging on for dear life as the wave pushes the boat towards the land. The suddenly the yacht capsizes, the mast snaps, and the men are tossed in the water.

"I don't like their chances," Adam says as the wave rushes to shore.

Soon after the yacht is smashed on the rocks, the wave retreats. This is as bad as its arrival. Everything and everyone is sucked back out to sea.

Once the wave has gone, the three of you walk down to the water, amazed at how the area has been stripped clean of vegetation, and anything else the wave could take with it. Much debris floats offshore.

"Our packs are gone," you say. "And the gold."

"And the poachers by the looks of it," Adam says. "Unless they managed to grab something to keep afloat."

You walk to the water's edge, searching for survivors. There is no sign of the men. Then as you're looking around, you see a glint of something in a tidal pool. You hop over a couple rocks and bend down to investigate.

It's a gold coin. Then you see another. "Hey look," you say, holding the coin up between your thumb and index finger. "Gold!"

"There's a couple over here too," Jane says, picking up a coin. Then she does a little dance and twirls. "There're all over the place!"

And she's right. The tsunami has picked up coins from the seabed and thrown them up onto the shore. The gold, being so heavy, got trapped in the cracks in the rocks and was left behind when the wave retreated.

As the three of you spend the next ten minutes searching, you wonder if this is the *Port-au-Prince's* treasure that the wave has picked up on its rush to shore.

"We could spend the rest of the day hunting for coins," you say, "but we should probably get back to the resort and see how things are. People could be hurt. If things are okay, we can come back tomorrow. Besides," you say, pulling a handful of coins from your pocket. "We've got plenty already."

So that's what you do. Half an hour later, as you round a protective headland, you see that the resort survived the tsunami and everyone is fine. Even the volcano has gone back to sleep.

After reporting what happened to the yacht and answering a few questions over the phone with the police back in the capital, the three of you sit on the beach with a cold soda and watch the reds and oranges of the tropical sunset.

"Looks like we're coin collecting tomorrow," you say to the twins.

Adam gives you the thumbs up. "Meet by the pool after breakfast?"

"Sounds like a plan," you say.

"Crikey," Jane says as the last of the sun dips below the horizon. "We're gonna be rich!"

Congratulations, you've reached the end of this part of the story. You've survived a volcanic eruption, tsunami and being chased by poachers. Well done!

Now it's time to make another decision. Do you:

Go back to the beginning of the story and try another path? **P365**

Or

Go to the List of Choices and read another part of the story? **P536**

Take the jungle track

The mountain is quiet again, so you decide to take the much shorter jungle track to the resort.

"I think speed is the critical factor here," you tell the twins. "The sooner we get back to the resort, the better."

"I'm with you," Jane says.

As you proceed along the path, overhanging tree branches block out the sky and the jungle is eerily quiet.

"This place is spooky," Jane says, sticking close to you and Adam.

About a quarter of a mile along, you come to a fast-moving stream that has cut a deep chasm down the side of the mountain in its rush to get to the sea. From a rocky ledge at the chasm's lip, you look down. A narrow track zigs down, crosses the stream at the bottom, and then zags back up and out the other side.

"Watch your step, these rocks might be loose," you warn the twins as you carefully take your first step down the steep bank.

When you reach the bottom, you wait for the others. Adam is first to arrive.

"That rock looks slippery," he says, pointing down at the smooth basalt on the bottom of the stream bed. "Maybe we should lock arms as we cross so we don't fall over."

The stream is only calf deep, but the water is rushing past at quite a pace. Below, in the darkness of the chasm, you hear the sound of tumbling water, a waterfall perhaps, so keeping your footing is important.

The three of you link arms and take small tentative steps as you start across.

"You're right about the rock being slick," Jane says, tightening her grip on your arm.

The crossing is only ten or twelve steps, and you're nearly there when you and the twins are knocked off your feet by another big quake.

With a splash, you find yourself sitting in water up to your waist and sliding down the smooth rock deeper into the chasm.

"Hang on!" you yell. "Keep your feet below you for protection!"

The three of you, with arms still linked, are pushed at an ever increasing speed down the natural waterslide worn into the rock. There is nothing to grab onto and no place to get out. All you can do is go with the flow.

"Yikes!" Jane screams as the three of you go flying over an eight-foot waterfall.

Thankfully the pool is deep enough that you don't hit bottom when you splash down, but you've barely had time to get over the shock of the drop and catch your breath before the power of the water whisks you downstream into the next half-pipe.

"Keep our arms linked," you tell the others, knowing you've got a better chance of survival if you stick together.

The deeper you slide into the chasm, the darker it gets.

When the gradient suddenly steepens to almost vertical and you see a tunnel entrance coming up. There is nothing you can do.

"We're going underground!" you yell.

Instantly it's so dark you can't even see the twins.

Adam's been quiet so far, apart from the odd grunt as he's struggled to keep his head above water, but now that you've gone underground you can hear him whimpering. Or is that you?

If this slide had been at a fun park, you'd be having the time of your life, but not knowing what is coming up next in the total darkness makes this the scariest thing you've ever experienced.

The slide seems to go on forever. It twists and turns, dips and dives. At times you hear a drop coming up, and at others you just plunge into space not knowing how far you'll fall before you hit whatever's at the bottom.

Even though you're sliding quickly, time seems to move very slowly. It's like your brain has switched to survival mode. Adrenaline surges through you.

After what seems like ages, you feel Jane's arm tighten on yours.

"Is that light I see?" she says.

You realize you've had your eyes screwed tight. Sure enough, there is a faint light coming from cracks in the rocky roof of the tunnel.

Then there's another drop of about six feet, and you're deposited into an underground pool almost as large as the swimming pool at the resort.

Soft light filters down from above, giving the cave a ghostly feel.

"The water tastes salty," Jane says. "This pool must join up to the ocean."

What Jane says makes sense. Water always runs downhill towards the ocean. You must have slid through an old volcanic vent worn smooth by hundreds if not hundreds of thousands of years of water running through it to the sea.

The cracks in the rock above must be the result of tremors and erosion.

"Now we just need to find a way out," Adam says, not sounding all that confident.

"I've got my waterproof flashlight," you say, rummaging in your backpack. You breathe a sigh of relief when it still works.

The narrow beam shows a low roof of hardened lava.

"If the sea is getting in," Adam says, "there must be an opening somewhere. We just need to find it."

"I'm the best swimmer," Jane says. "Give me the flashlight and I'll see if I can find one."

With flashlight in hand, Jane takes a deep breath and dives. You and Adam follow her progress as the light moves along the bottom of the pool, sweeping back and forth as Jane searches. About twenty yards away, she comes up for air and then dives again.

It isn't until her third dive that she pops up with news. "I've found a passage!"

"Can we get through?" you ask.

"Fish are swimming in and out so we should be able to as well."

You and Adam dogpaddle over to where Jane is treading water. After taking a deep breath you dive down to check out the passage Jane has found. It's about fifteen yards long with faint light at the end of it. It looks plenty big enough to swim through.

You've just surfaced, when you feel a surge of water come pouring into the cave through the passage. The roof of the cave gets closer as all the extra water comes streaming in. Then as the water rushes out again, it's about all you can do to keep from getting sucked out with it.

"Man, that tidal surge is strong," you say. "If we're going to get out of here we'll have to time our exit carefully."

Adam, being the weakest swimmer, looks petrified.

Jane sees her brother's nervousness. "Adam and I can link arms and go together."

The look of relief on Adam's face is immediate. "Yeah, that way we'll have twice the kicking power."

You could mention that they'll also have twice the bulk to move through the water, but there is no point in undermining his confidence. "Okay," you say. "That's a good idea. Do you want the flashlight?"

"Nah," Jane says shaking her head. There's plenty of light coming from the other end. We'll be fine." Jane looks at her brother. "You ready?"

Adam swallows loudly and nods.

"Okay, here comes the next wave," Jane says. "As soon as it starts going out, dive and kick like crazy."

The siblings link arms and tread water waiting for the water to start its outward journey.

"Three, two, one go!" says Jane, taking a deep breath and diving.

You watch nervously as the twins disappear into the underwater tunnel, especially as it's your turn next. You put your flashlight back in the side pocket of your daypack and get ready to dive. You have time for three deep breaths before you feel the water in the cave begin to rise.

As the water starts to surge out, you take one last breath and dive. At first the pull of the water is slight, but as you enter the passage and the volume of water is restricted, the pull is stronger and you barely need to kick. Most of your efforts are around trying not to scrape along the rough sides of the tunnel. The last thing you want is to end up in the sea with cuts bleeding into the water. Sharks might think you're lunch.

You forget about sharks as you spot an old anchor leaning against one wall of the tunnel. You wonder briefly if it might be from a pirate ship, but then before you know it, you see sunlight streaming down from above and you kick hard for the light.

When your head breaks the surface, you look for Jane and Adam.

"Pssst!"

You look around for the noise.

"Pssst! Over here."

You turn to your right and see Jane and Adam hiding behind a rock. Then you see the poachers' yacht bobbing gently in the cove between you and the beach.

You can't believe your eyes. You've been washed down the mountain all the way back to Smugglers Cove!

"Get over here before they see you," Adam whispers, signaling you over.

Thankfully, the men on deck have their backs to you.

You dive down and swim underwater towards the rock where Adam and Jane are hiding.

"We've ended up back where we started," you whisper. "This is one crazy island."

"And those horrible poachers are still here," Adam says softly, careful not to let the men hear him.

You look around for a solution, but the rock you're hiding behind is about twenty yards from any other cover. If you try to swim to shore, the poachers could see you.

"We might have to hang here until nightfall," you say.

Then you hear a loud voice drift over the water from the yacht. It's Jimmy berating his friends.

"Why don't you lazy sods give me a hand with the last couple of traps, then we can get out of here," he says. "I've had a hard day."

The two men laugh.

One of the men slaps Jimmy on the back. "At least if you decide to give up poaching, you can always take up cliff diving!"

"Shut up, you drongo!" Jimmy growls. "That fall almost killed me!"

The two men laugh again.

"Okay, we'll help," the other man says once he's stopped laughing. "I don't want to be hanging around here when the authorities arrive."

The three men finish their drinks, climb down into the dinghy and start rowing away from you towards the shore.

You look at Adam and then at Jane. "Are you thinking what I'm thinking?"

Jane smiles. "A spot of piracy perhaps?"

"You got it."

"Those poachers will kill us," Adam says.

"Only if we get caught," Jane says. "And ninjas never get caught."

"It's worth the risk," you say. "If we hijack their boat, the only way they can get off the island is to come back to the resort. By then, we'll have the authorities waiting for them."

You look towards shore. The men are about half way to the beach.

"Once they've gone into the jungle we'll need to move fast. Who knows how long they'll be gone," you say.

It isn't long before Jimmy and the other two men drag the dinghy above the tide and march off into the jungle with their cages. As soon as they've disappeared, you and the twins start swimming towards the yacht.

"Ever driven a boat before?" Jane asks as she dogpaddles beside you.

You shake your head.

"I've done a bit," Adam says. "My friend's father has a boat, how different can it be?"

"About thirty feet, I reckon," Jane says.

The ladder at the back of the yacht comes right down to water level so it's easy for you and the twins to climb aboard. When you reach the cockpit, you're pleased to see the key is in the ignition.

Adam has a look around and takes the role of captain. "We need to get the motor running and motor over the anchor to unhook it from the bottom. Then once we pull the anchor up, off we go."

Never having done much boating, you take Adam's word for it. "Jane and I can pull up the anchor."

Adam puts the gear lever on 'N' for neutral and turns the key. There is an immediate puff of black smoke from the back of the boat, and a satisfying rumble of the diesel motor as it comes to life. Water from the exhaust pours from a hole in the stern.

"Right," Adam says. "I'm going to ease us forward over the anchor, so you two get hauling on that rope."

At first the rope refuses to budge, but then as the boat moves forward and the angle of the rope through the water changes, you feel movement.

"It's coming!" you yell back at Adam.

You and Jane coil the anchor rope on the deck as you pull. Just as the anchor comes out of the water you hear someone yelling from shore.

"Hey! What do you think you're doing?"

The men climb into the dinghy and one of them grabs the oars and frantically rows towards the yacht.

"Time to get out of Dodge, partner," Jane says in her best cowgirl accent. "Those pesky rustlers are back."

There is a surge of white water at the back of the boat as Adam pushes the throttle forward and the yacht picks up speed. For a brief moment, Adam points the yacht out to sea but then he spins the wheel and brings the yacht back around.

"What are you doing?" you say. "Escape is the other way."

Adam pushes the throttle even further forward. The diesel engine is really racing now. The boat's speed increases.

You look at the indicator on the control panel. The yacht is doing nearly 11 knots.

You look at Adam. His face is wild. "I said, what are you doing?"

"Tidying up," Adam says, turning the wheel a bit to starboard and pointing the bow of the yacht directly at the men in the dinghy.

"Holy moly!" Jane says. "You're going to ram them!"

The men are quick to realize what Adam is up to as well. The rower has turned the dinghy around and is now frantically trying to get back to shore. Unfortunately for the poachers, panic and good rowing technique don't usually go together. Within ten seconds the men realize the yacht is going to collide with the much smaller dinghy and they leap into the water.

Adam, showing skills you never expected, steers the boat until it is nearly upon the dinghy and then pulls back the throttle a little and spins the wheel hard to the left, swerving the yacht at the last moment.

"Take the wheel and point her out to sea," Adams says to you as he grabs a boathook and leans over the side. With a sweep of the hook, Adam snags the abandoned dinghy's painter and pulls the rope aboard. Then with a couple of loops and a half hitch around a cleat on deck, the dingy is secured and the three of you are heading back out to sea with the dingy in tow.

"Good skills, Captain Hook," you say to Adam. "That was one slick maneuver."

By the time you're out of the cove, the bedraggled men are arguing with each other back on the beach.

A few hundred yards off shore, Adam turns the yacht to the southeast.

"Right, to the lagoon," Adam says pushing the throttle slowly forward until the rev counter hits 2200 rpm. "Now we just have to find the gap in the reef and we're home sweet home."

"Gap in the reef?" Jane asks.

"Yeah, when we get close, one of you will have to climb up in the rigging so you can guide me through the passage into the lagoon. You can't see the coral from deck level. The light's all wrong."

Adam picks up the radio in the wheelhouse and flips on the power. "*Moneymaker* calling maritime radio, *Moneymaker* calling maritime radio, please come in, maritime radio, this is urgent."

The radio crackles. "This is maritime radio, *Moneymaker*, what is the nature of your emergency?"

Adam explains the situation and then hangs up the hand piece. "That should do the trick."

"What do we do with all the birds below? Should we release them?" Jane asks.

"Better keep them for the time being. The authorities will need them for evidence," Adam says. "They'll let them go once they've taken photos, I'm sure."

An hour and a half later, as the yacht rounds the headland and the first resort buildings appear, Adam points to the southwest. "Nearly there. One of you'd better get up the mast as far as the first set of spreaders."

"Spreaders?" Jane says.

"Those metal cross-members sticking out from the mast that are holding the rigging in place," Adam says.

"Oh, okay," Jane says crossing the deck and putting her foot in the first of the aluminum steps attached to the mast. "Arrr, this should be fun, me hearties." And with that, she scampers up the mast like she's been at sea all her life.

"I'll cruise along the reef, you tell me when you see a gap big enough for the boat to fit though," Adam yells up to his sister.

Jane throws one leg over the spreader like it's a horizontal bar in gym class, wraps her arm around the mast and concentrates on the reef. A few minutes later she calls out. "Gap ho!"

Jane points to a spot on the reef where the water is calmer.

"Okay," Adam says swinging the bow around towards the gap. "I see it. Yell out if I get off course."

"Aye aye, Captain Hook."

Within minutes the boat is inside the reef and you're dropping the anchor. Tourists watch from the beach. A float plane sits by the wooden jetty. Two of the people on the beach are in uniform.

When the anchor is on the bottom, Adam tells you to pay out a bit of extra rope and then tie off to the sturdy post near the boat's bow. Then he puts the motor in reverse and digs in the anchor before turning off the engine. "Welcome to paradise," he says with a smile. "The dinghy will be leaving for shore in exactly one minute."

"Aye aye," you and Jane say in unison.

"Hey," Jane says. "Before we go ashore, look what I found below." Jane shows you a small canvas bag filled with American dollars.

"Wow," you say, with eyes agog. "Where did you find that?"

"In the main cabin, under some socks."

"So what do we do with it?" Adam asks. "Turn it in?"

You look at Adam and smile. "Why don't we discuss that as we row ashore?"

Congratulations, this part of your story is over. You've made it safely back to the lagoon, survived an eruption and foiled the plans of the lorikeet poachers. Well done!

Now it is time for another decision. Do you:

Go to the beginning of the book and try another path? **P365**

Or

Go to the List of Choices and start reading from another part of the story? **P536**

Try to sink the poachers' boat

Adam seems determined to sink the poachers' boat with or without your help. On his own, he's bound to let emotion get the better of him and end up in trouble. You decide that it's better if you and Jane help. With three of you, at least there is a chance of success.

"Okay, I'll help," you say. "But only if we make a plan and stick to it. No crazy stuff, okay?"

"Glug, glug, glug," Jane says with a glint in her eye.

Adam gives his sister a smile then turns back to you. "What plan did you have in mind?"

Your left hand strokes your chin as you think. "Let's check in with our families and then meet up at the beach. We can plan our attack while we keep a lookout for the yacht."

The twins agree and head off towards their bungalow. As you walk through the compound, you wonder what you've got yourself in to. Poachers are dangerous.

You think of all the things you'll need to do for the operation to be successful. You'll need to get onto their boat, release the birds, open a valve or drill some holes in the hull to let the water in, and then get away unseen. And what happens if one or more of the men stay on board to guard the yacht?

After checking in with your family, you grab a couple more energy bars and head for the beach. Adam and Jane are already there when you arrive. Adam is fiddling with something under his beach towel.

"What have you got there?" you ask as you toss them each an energy bar.

Adam hefts the object. "When we were walking back to our room, I noticed one of the maintenance men working in one of the bungalows. His toolbox was on the verandah outside so I asked him if I could borrow a drill for a couple of hours."

"To drill holes in coconuts," Jane adds, "for drinking the milk. He believed us."

Adam lifts the corner of his towel and shows you a hand drill complete with a chunky half-inch wood bit. "A few holes with this bad boy should do the trick."

You run your finger over the edge of the drill bit. "Whoa, that's sharp."

Adam gives you an evil looking grin. "I drilled a hole in a fence post outside our bungalow. Like hot steel through butter."

Jane giggles. She's enjoying the intrigue far more than she should be. "I can't wait to start."

"Let's not get ahead of ourselves," you say. "We have a few things to figure out first."

You sit in the sand next to the twins and start discussing possibilities. Nearly an hour has gone by when you see the yacht come around the headland in the distance.

"Here they come," you say. "The wind direction is coming off the beach so they'll need to drop their sail and turn on the motor before they can come into the lagoon."

As the yacht gets nearer they drop the mainsail.

"Why have they got a man up in the rigging?" you say.

"He'll be there to spot the gap in the reef and guide the boat through," Adam answers. "There will be too much reflection off the water to see the reef from deck level."

Ten minutes later, the yacht is 100 yards off the beach and the men have dropped anchor. The yacht rocks gently in the light chop.

The men waste no time. One of them climbs down the stern ladder towards the dinghy floating at the end of its rope.

"Fingers crossed they all come ashore," you say.

Jane stands up. "I'll grab a surf board." Without waiting for comment, she runs over towards a collection of boards leaning against a tree for use by the resort's guests.

Unfortunately, only two of the men climb into the dinghy. The third unties the dinghy's painter from the cleat on the deck and tosses it to the men in the small boat. Then he passes them a set of oars.

"Get some pictures as they come ashore," you say to Adam. "We need all the evidence we can get."

Jane lays the surfboard down in the sand and sits back down. "You never know. It might come in handy eh?"

"So what now?" Adam asks. "How are we going to do anything when they've still got a guy onboard?"

You shrug and go back to thinking.

A few minutes later, it's Jane that speaks up. "What if I pretend to be drowning? Do you think he'd leave the boat to save me?"

Her idea is a good one and it makes you think. What sort of men are the poachers? Surely he wouldn't let a young girl drown. Even criminals have kids.

Adam looks doubtful. "But will that give us enough time?"

"It might, if Jane gets him to bring her in to shore and not back to the yacht," you say.

Then you explain the rest of your plan.

"You are evil," Jane says. "I like it."

Adam still looks unsure. "Jane would have to be pretty convincing."

"Do ya'll doubt my acting ability?" Jane drawls in a mock Southern accent, her hands clenched to her chest, eyelids fluttering. "I'll have ya'll know I'm a fine actor."

"Swoon all you like, sis, we're talking about criminals here. Who knows what they'll do."

Trying not to laugh at Jane's performance, you give a brief nod towards Adam. "Your brother's right, Jane, we need a plan B in case plan A goes wrong. Think, you guys. What do we do if the guy stays on the boat?"

By now, the two men from the yacht are dragging the dinghy up onto the sand. The one in charge tells the other to stay by the boat and marches up the sand towards the resort.

Adam watches as the man passes the surfboards and disappears into the resort. "He may not be gone very long. I don't think we have time for a plan B."

Having seen the man's urgency as he walked past, Adam may well be right. "Okay. Adam, grab the drill and let's go. Jane, give us a few minutes to get in to position before you hit the water."

"Ya'll come back now," Jane says, fluttering her eyelids once more.

You pick up the surf board and carry it to the water. It's one of those old long boards so both you and he have no problem fitting on it.

Paddling in a wide arc, you come at the yacht from the seaward side. The man on deck has his back to you as he watches the activity on the beach. Then you see Jane swimming towards the yacht, her strokes strong and steady.

About twenty yards short of the boat, she starts splashing and yelling. The man on the yacht stands up.

"Help!" Jane cries out. "My legs have got cramp."

To add effect, Jane sinks below the water briefly before clawing her way back to the surface and repeating her plea.

The man on deck is torn. You can almost see his mind working as he decides what to do. Your entire plan depends on the next few moments. He paces up and down the deck of the yacht. No doubt he's been told to stay on board by the boss man. But he's unsure.

When Jane goes under for a second time, the man takes off his shirt and shoes.

"He's going to save her," you whisper to Adam. "Come on, mister, dive in."

For a third time, Jane splutters and sinks below the waves and finally, the man steps over the railing and dives into the water.

When the man reaches Jane, he flips her onto her back and starts side-stroking back to the boat.

Jane, realizing where he's taking her, starts to struggle. "No, take me to my Dad on the beach, please."

For a moment, the poacher hesitates, but then stops. Maybe he's just remembered he's got birds onboard.

Again, Jane cries out to be taken to the beach. She becomes a dead weight, slides out of his grasp and sinks below the water.

The man gives up and does what she asks. Jane floats, allowing herself to be towed to the beach. The 80 or so yards should take them a few minutes. You just hope it's enough.

"Go," you say.

You and Adam paddle flat out towards the yacht. When you reach the stern, you take the surfboard's leg strap and loop it around a rung of the ladder to keep it from floating away, and scamper aboard.

The companionway hatch is open. Down four steps and you're in the saloon. On the floor sits two cages, each holding twenty or so lorikeets.

"Let's get these cages on deck," you say.

The wire cages are awkward. The birds start making a racket when they see you.

Carrying an end each, you and Adam maneuver the cages up onto the deck. The birds are loud, but thankfully the wind is blowing out to sea so most of the sound is carried away from the beach.

You take a quick look shoreward. Jane and the man are only thirty yards from the beach. "I'll let the birds out, you get drilling."

Adam heads below while you open the cages. The lorikeets waste no time in flying off.

After throwing the cages overboard, you stick you head through the companionway and look for Adam. You hear sounds coming from one of the cabins. "Drill quickly, because as soon as Jane hits the beach we're out of here."

Keeping low behind the cabin tops, you watch Jane's progress. As she and the man near the beach she starts struggling again. You can hear her cries of panic as she twists in the man's grasp. Finally, when the man can touch bottom, he picks Jane up, throws her over his shoulder and marches to where his companion is waiting beside the dinghy.

Jane pretends to be in distress, arm flapping, coughing and gasping for breath. Her rescuer moves Jane into the recovery position and hovers over her until one of the staff from the resort comes over to see what is going on.

"Okay, time to go!" you yell down to Adam.

Adam appears from the depths of the boat. "The water's not coming in fast enough!"

"Well we can't stay here any longer!"

Then Adam sees something in the galley that attracts his attention. He grabs a bottle of methylated spirits and starts pouring it all over the seat cushions.

"Hey," you yell, "this isn't part of the plan!"

"It's the new plan B," Adam says, striking a lighter he's found by the stove and setting fire to one of the seats in the saloon. "Let's hope these cushions are polypropylene. Burns like crazy, that stuff."

Smoke begins to fill the cabin.

"Adam, we've got to go now!"

The two of you rush to the stern and leap into the water. You untie the leg rope, climb on the surfboard and start paddling like crazy, not towards the beach, but parallel to it away from the yacht.

"The poachers haven't seen the smoke yet," you say to Adam as you look over towards the beach. "Correction, they've just spotted it."

The two men are frantically dragging the dingy into the water. The larger of the two grabs the oars and starts rowing as fast as he can.

The men don't notice as you and Adam join another group of people mucking around on surfboards and wind surfers in the lagoon.

"I think we've done it," Adam says.

Adam was right about the polypropylene. Thick smoke billows from the yacht. By the time the men in the dinghy reach the boat, the flames are too intense for them to get aboard. When a series of loud bangs start popping, you can only assume ammunition of some sort is going off inside the boat.

"It's a lost cause!" the man with the oars yells as he starts rowing back to shore.

By now, there is a crowd on the beach. It includes the head poacher who is waving his arms and talking to a male staff member.

"See the guy on the beach with the poacher dude?" you say to Adam. "He must be their contact. We must get a picture of him when we get ashore."

"The boss man doesn't look too happy," Adam says.

You and Adam reach the beach at about the same time as the two men in the dinghy.

As you join the other tourists watching the burning boat, you edge closer to where the poachers are standing. The head poacher is cursing at his companions as if the fire were their fault.

Jane, now fully recovered, sees that the two of you are back on the beach and comes over to join you. "Good skills," she says. "Ninjas one, poachers nil."

Adam unzips a pocket in his shorts and pulls out three items about the size of small candy bars. "Wrong again, Sis. Ninjas three, poachers nil." And with that he drops a gold bar into each of your hands. "One each … just don't let the poachers see them."

"Where did you get these?" you say, turning your back to the poachers.

Jane's eyes are bulging, but she wastes no time slotting her bar into the pocket of her shorts.

"When I opened a floor panel to drill a hole, they were just lying there. I didn't see any point in leaving them behind."

You have a closer look at the ingot and read the small writing stamped into it. "One Ounce 99.9 per cent pure."

"What's that worth, I wonder?" Jane says

"Last I heard gold was over twelve hundred US dollars an ounce," you say.

"Wow," Jane says. "Being a ninja pays pretty good."

Adam puts his bar back in his pocket. "I'm going to donate mine to the Animal Rescue people."

You think for a moment at what you'll do with your share, but then realize you've got pretty much everything you need. You're on vacation on a beautiful island. You've got friends. Hey what else do you need?

You pass your ingot back to Adam. "Here, give them mine too. I'll just blow it otherwise. It may as well do some good."

Jane shakes her head. "But, I need shoes and dresses and—and... Just joking," she says, handing her ingot back to Adam. "I wouldn't feel right spending ill-gotten gold on myself anyway."

Adam tucks the gold away. "Thanks, you two. This will make a big difference."

You shrug. "It's only money."

As the three of you watch the last of the boat disappear, you notice the sun is dipping below the horizon. Reds, fiery oranges and every color in between contrast with the sparkling blue of the lagoon. The rocky point, shaped like the dolphin's nose at the far end of the lagoon is just a silhouette.

"So what adventure are we having tomorrow?" Jane asks.

"We've still got treasure to find, remember?" you say. "Meet you here on the beach after breakfast?"

"Arrr me hearty," Jane says in her best pirate accent.

"Arrr," Adam says joining in the fun.

And with that, the three of you head back to your families, excited at what tomorrow may bring.

Congratulations, you've finished this part of your story. You have successfully stopped the poachers and found some gold which will go to a good cause. Well done!

Now it is time to make another decision. Do you:

Go back to the beginning of the story and follow another path? **P365**

Or

Go to the Big List of Choices and start reading from another part of the story? **P536**

Contact the authorities

"Let's not do anything radical," you say. "Better we find a way to contact the authorities without anyone from the resort finding out, and let them deal with the poachers. Using the resort's phones is out because of the calls having to go through reception, that's going to limit our options."

The three of you are silent a moment, as you each try to come up with a solution.

"I've got it," Jane says. "Boats have radios, right?"

"Yes…" you say hesitantly wondering where Jane is going with this.

"And the police have radios?"

"Yeah, sure."

"There must be at least three boats in the lagoon. Surely one of them has a radio we can use." Jane looks like she's just eaten the last chocolate in the box.

"But the poachers have a boat too, sis," Adam says, countering her argument. "And if they hear our transmission, they'll scarper. Then your whole plan goes down the gurgler."

Jane frowns. "Hmm … I didn't think of that."

"But what if they didn't hear the transmission?" Adam says. "What if their radio antennae were out of order?"

You give Adam a questioning look. "And how do you plan on achieving that?"

"Well," Adam says. "I've done a fair bit of fishing with my friend and his dad. I can cast a lure pretty much wherever I want."

"Okay," you say. "But how's catching fish going to help?"

"If I cast a wire trace, with a big lure on it, over the yacht's antennae, and then start reeling in, I might be able to rip it off."

"You really think that will work?" you ask.

"I really think we should give it a go. What have we got to lose?"

"I'll admit, little bro's pretty good with a rod," Jane says. "Streuth, she's worth a crack!"

Two sets of eyes roll at the return of Jane's Aussie accent, but after some further discussion, the three of you decide to try out Adam's plan.

"Right," Adam says. "Jane and I will rent one of the resort's small motor boats. Then we'll drop you off near one of the larger boats moored in the bay so you can get to their radio. Then, with Jane steering, I'll hook the poachers' antennae and then we'll motor off at top speed and do our best to rip it off their mast."

"Sounds like something out of a movie," you say, wondering if the scheme will work.

"I'm not so sure. Fishing ninjas doesn't quite have the same ring to it." Jane says with a giggle.

After renting the strongest pole and tackle he can find, Adam rigs up a line. Then the three of you climb aboard the runabout you've rented.

"Which boat should we try?" Adam asks.

You look at your choices. "That marlin boat's pretty flash. It's bound to have reliable VHF."

Adam turns the key to start the runabout. "The marlin boat it is then."

Jane grabs your arm. "There they are, right on schedule!"

You and Adam turn your gaze towards the reef. Sure enough, the poachers' boat is heading into the lagoon.

Your runabout starts first pop. Jane unties the bowline from the jetty and Adam pushes the throttle forward. As he points the bow towards the reef, Adam yells over the roar of the 25hp outboard. "We'll do a loop and approach the marlin boat from behind so nobody from shore sees what we're up to. You'll have to jump overboard and swim the last 10 yards or so."

You swallow, and try to steady your nerves. "Just what I always wanted to do while on vacation, jump from a speeding boat."

Jane laughs. "Think of it as walking the plank. At least it's better than being keel-hauled."

You're getting close to the marlin boat.

"Okay, get ready to jump," Adam says. "I'll slow down the boat, but only for a moment. Oh, and don't forget to use channel 16, that's the emergency channel."

Thirty seconds later, Adam throttles down, and you leap over the side. Immediately, he's back on the gas and bouncing away over the slight chop in the lagoon.

Thankfully, the marlin boat has a ladder on its stern. You make your way into the wheelhouse and look for the switch to power up the radio.

After turning on the radio, you look at the screen and see the radio is already set on the right channel. There is a crackle of static and you hear brief conversations come over the speaker. You lift the handset out of its cradle and get ready to transmit.

Meanwhile, Adam has swung the runabout in a lazy arc and is heading to where the yacht is busy dropping anchor. Jane takes the controls as Adam lines up his cast.

The poachers' antennae is a slim rod sticking up from a bracket near the top of the mast next to a wind speed indicator, radar reflector, and navigation light. You can't believe he really thinks he has a chance of snagging such a small target.

Adam stands in the back of the runabout, his backside pressed against the transom for stability. The long pole is upright. As you watch, Adam practices his casting by flicking the pole back and forth, trying to get a feel for it.

As the runabout nears the yacht, one of the men is busy securing the anchor, while another is preparing the dinghy to come ashore. Then two of the men climb down into the dinghy and start to head towards shore.

Jane turns the runabout and goes around for another pass.

By the time Jane lines up for the next pass, the men and their dinghy are halfway to the beach. Jane throttles back just as Adam whips the pole forwards, sending the lure flying high in the air. The heavy lure passes clean over the bracket holding the antennae and Adam starts reeling for all he's worth. As Adam reels in, the lure stops midflight, drops and then hooks itself around the bracket. Adam fist pumps the air and then puts the pole into a special hole in the aluminum hull of the runabout designed to keep rods from falling overboard when fishing.

Jane lets out a rebel yell and steers the boat towards the yacht. When she's ten yards from colliding with the yacht, she swings the runabout into a sharp turn and puts on more power.

As the runabout streaks away from the yacht, the line tightens. At first the yacht's mast tilts towards the fleeing runabout and you're sure the line will break. But leverage is a wonderful thing and the line is stronger than you imagined. It holds as the yacht tilts further and further over.

The remaining man on deck trips and nearly falls over the side as the deck beneath his feet is suddenly no longer level. Then there is a wrenching sound as the bracket is ripped off the mast.

This time, as the deck tilts quickly back the opposite way, the man on deck is caught off balance again and goes flying over the rail.

You click the transmit button. "Maritime radio, maritime radio, maritime radio," you repeat three times as instructed by Adam. "Mayday. Come in, maritime radio."

"This is maritime radio, what is the nature of your emergency?"

It takes you a few moments to explain the situation, but the operator agrees to call the police and pass on your message.

The man on the yacht is climbing up the ladder as Jane and Adam motor toward your boat. You give them the thumbs up, switch off the radio and dive overboard. A minute later, Adam helps you out of the water and onto the runabout.

"Did you get through?" he asks.

"Ninjas one, poachers nil," you say. "The police are on their way."

"Yippee!" Jane yells.

You look over at the yacht and see the man looking around, still wondering what hit him and how he got tipped into the drink on a perfectly flat lagoon.

"Let's hope he doesn't notice the missing aerial before the police arrive," you say to the twins. "What did you do with the antennae you caught?"

Adam points to the middle of the lagoon. "It's now a dive feature over there at the bottom of the lagoon."

After dropping off the runabout, returning the fishing gear, minus some trace and a lure, and grabbing some cold drinks, the three of you go and sit on the beach to wait for the police to show up.

As you wait, the two poachers and a man from the resort walk down the beach and climb into the dinghy.

"They'll be off to do the deal for the birds no doubt," Adam says.

You cross your fingers. "I just hope the cops show up soon."

Jane takes a long sip of her soda. "Looks like we'll have to find the treasure tomorrow."

"We've got all week," you say. "The treasure's been here for 150 years. I don't think it's going anywhere this afternoon."

"Unlike our poacher friends," Adam says, pointing to the gray patrol boat entering the lagoon. "It's going to be interesting to see how they explain all the birds on board."

Congratulations, this part of your story is over. You've done well. But have you tried all the possible path the story takes?

It is time to make another decision. Do you:

Go back to the beginning of the story and try another path? **P365**

Or

Go to the Big List of Choices and start reading from another part of the story? **P536**

It's all about the math

"How did you do that so quickly in your head?" Jane asks.

By now, Adam is listening too.

"It's not exact," you say, trying to think of an easy way to explain it. "But the yacht can go in pretty much any direction, right?"

The twins nod.

"A knot is 1.15 miles. So 8 knots is a fraction over 9 miles. That means there will be a circular search area with a radius of 9 miles, minus a little bit of land, right? Imagine a big circle with a dot in its center. The dot is the yacht and the rest of the circle is a place the yacht could be, apart from the small bit of land that makes up the island, of course."

Jane and Adam seem to be following your explanation, so you continue.

"To calculate the area of a circle you square the radius, squaring means multiplying the radius by itself, and then we multiply that answer by pi or 3.14."

"What a radius?" Jane asks.

"It's the distance from the dot in the middle of the circle to the outer edge of the circle. Like the spoke of a bike wheel."

"So the radius squared is 9 times 9 which is 81, and then we multiply 81 times 3.14?" Jane asks.

"That's right," you say. "I made it easier by working out what 3 times 81 was first. 3 times 80 is 240 and 3 times 1 is 3."

Jane's got the hang of it now. "So that's 240 plus 3 which equals 243."

You nod. "Then I take .14 and multiply that times 81. This is a bit trickier but when you realize .14 is the same as 14 per cent, it's easy. To get 10 percent of 81 you move the decimal point one place to the left or 8.1 … let's call it 8 for simplicity. Then we take 4 percent of 81 which is a bit less than half of 10 percent … so let's just estimate it and call it 3."

462

"So we have 243 plus 8 plus 3 which is 254," Jane says.

You smile. "That's right. Then we just need to take off a bit for the land area. Like I said, it's not exact but it's near enough."

"It like working out a puzzle," Jane says. "Kind of fun when you think of it that way."

"Yep," you say. "And the more you learn the better the puzzles get. Math is full of sneaky tricks. It's just a matter of knowing them."

Without any further explanation, you turn and start down the path back towards the resort. You hear the twins' footsteps behind you. Jane mumbles numbers as you half walk, half jog through the jungle.

Go back to the story **P398**

Dolphin Island FAQs

Q. Is Dolphin Island a real place?

A. No, Dolphin Island is fictional island. However there are many islands in the South Pacific that are similar to what has been described in this story. Polynesia means 'many islands'. If you are interested in the area where this story is set, try looking up and reading about Tonga or Samoa.

Q. Was the *Port-au-Prince* a real ship?

A. Yes. The *Port-au-Prince* was a tall ship of 500 tons that carried 24 cannon. The ship was built in France before being captured by the British. It then became a privateer (legal pirate by license from the British government) and was sent to raid Spanish ships off the South American coast. After some raiding the *Port-au-Prince* sailed to the South Pacific to hunt whales for their oil. Sometime in 1806, while in the Ha'apai island group in the Kingdom of Tonga, she was attacked by the locals and is presumed to have sunk somewhere nearby. It was never discovered how successful the ship had been in her raiding, as all her treasure is presumed to have gone down with the ship. Many experts believe remnants of *Port-au-Prince* were found in 2012 off Foa Island in Tonga.

Q. Are megapodes real?

A. Yes. Megapodes are real birds that bury their eggs in the warm volcanic soil to act as an incubator. There are many interesting birds in the South Pacific region.

Q. What happened at Krakatoa?

A. Krakatoa is a volcanic island between Java and Sumatra in Indonesia. It exploded in 1883, killing somewhere between 36,000 and 120,000 people (depending on how the statistics were calculated). The bangs from the huge explosions (4 in total) were heard over 3,000 miles away in Australia. Now that is some bang. The area is still very actice..

IN THE MAGICIAN'S HOUSE

By DM Potter

In your turret

You can't remember a time before you lived in the Magician's house. There are many rooms, but finding them is not always easy. The house is cloaked in mystery, and you explore it every day.

You find the kitchen most mornings. You follow the lovely smells and don't think too hard about it. Perhaps your recent dreams help you get to breakfast without much trouble. More likely, it's because the Magician wants his breakfast.

You can find a lot of places in the house and, for this reason, you're often asked to fetch things. The other servants get lost more often than you do. Sometimes you find them in the corners of rooms and give them a friendly pat to bring them out of a 'drawing room dream'. That is what the cook, Mrs. Noogles, calls them.

Dreams swirl around in the Magician's house like dust in the corners of other houses. Little stories get stuck in the crannies. Just for a moment, while you are sweeping a corner, you can find yourself running across a green field, speaking to a great crowd, steering an iron horse through twisty roads, or picking ripe strawberries in a bright warm field. The dreams are quickly over, but other times you are transported to different places. So you watch where you step.

It is very early in the morning, and you wake up in your turret. It is your own tower with a winding staircase down to the house.

Something lands on your pillow and rolls against your cheek, cold and small. You put your hand out. It's that red frog again. It stares at you, unblinking. You put it carefully with your other treasures and oddities.

The sky is dark purple, with one last star valiantly blinking as the sun turns your corner of the world into day. You love looking out of your tower window and catching the day starting like this—in this moment the whole world is magic, not just the place you live.

Down the spiral staircase, on the next floor, you wash the sleep from your eyes and put on fresh clothes. A noise like a marble falling down the stairs becomes the sound of a rubber ball until the red frog appears with a final splat. He takes a quick dip in the big jug of water you keep for him there. When he jumps out, he doesn't leave any wet marks on the flagstone floor. He seems to absorb moisture. The jug is now only half full.

By the window, a row of ants are marching across the floor. The frog jumps over to the row of insects and whips out his tongue to catch ant after ant until the column is gone. If only getting *your* breakfast was that easy.

Outside the window, you can see the buildings of London—St. Paul's cathedral is a beautiful dome by the river Thames. Horses and carts make their deliveries down the twisty lanes. Much of London is still sleeping, but servants are stirring to light the fires and make their master's breakfast. You must tend to your master too.

You wonder which room your tower will join with today. Sometimes it will deliver you to a hallway that easily gets you to the servant's staircase and down to the kitchen, but often there is another destination at the foot of the stairs. Things are seldom as they appear. You have learned to be cautious in case you step in a lily pond in the wide conservatory or walk into the shiny suit of armor that appears in different places each day.

The stairs wind down until you meet up with the rest of the house. Here is where you are usually faced with your first choice for the day. This morning, a wide corridor with arched ceilings stretches off to the left and right. Embroidered tapestries hang along the oak paneled walls.

To your left, the corridor ends abruptly. A suit of armor stands at the dead end, its bright metallic form leans slightly forward, its gauntlet holding up the edge of the last tapestry. Behind it, you glimpse the corner of a small door. You wouldn't expect a kitchen behind there.

To your right, the corridor is blocked by an impassable hole in the floor with a ladder poking out. The carpet is ripped and torn around the hole as though a bomb has gone off in the night. That's weird. You didn't hear an explosion. You're not confident the kitchen would be down there either.

There are no other options. It's time to make your first decision of the day. Do you:

Climb down into the hole? **P491**

Or

Look behind the secret door? **P468**

Take the secret door behind the suit of armor

The Magician doesn't leave notes, but he does leave signs. The door behind the tapestry seems like an invitation, and you've decided to take it. You take a good look at the tapestry before you go behind it. You want to remember the picture so you can recognize it again. The picture isn't one of the most interesting in the Magician's house—many are embroidered with scenes of fantastic creatures, but this is just a rather dense forest with the roof of a tower peeking out of it.

The armor appears in different places in the Magician's house all the time. You bumped into it last week when you were carrying a large flower display. It was standing in the middle of the ballroom as if it were about to dance. Another time, you found it in the garden under a tree. You've looked before, but there's nobody inside.

Today, the armor has a leather pouch swinging from one gauntlet, offering it to you. You take a look inside the pouch and find a jar. There's a faint yellow swirl moving inside. The glass is warm in your hand, and a faded handwritten label reads: *sunshine*. You decide to take the jar with you.

Now you examine the door.

The door behind the tapestry is set into the wall, so when the cloth covered it, there were no bumps that would have made you think something was behind it. The door creaks as it opens stiffly inwards. Inside there is a dark passage. It probably travels between other rooms in the house and was designed as a servants' passage—big old houses have them so guests can move about in the grand spaces and servants can bustle about without disturbing them. Who knows, maybe you have found a speedier way to the kitchen?

You take a step inside. As you do, you hear a plop. The red frog lands in front of you.

"Coming along to explore, are you?"

The red frog looks up at you with big eyes. It can probably see quite well in the dark, but you can't.

Fearing you will tread on the little amphibian, you bend and scoop it up. It feels warm in your hand. It makes a couple of leaps up your arm and then snuggles itself on your shoulder. Together, you begin to step down the hidden passage.

You treat a new part of the Magician's house like you're walking on thin ice. You keep your back foot ready to take your weight should reality give way. The Magician's house swirls with dreams that pool in corners of rooms and cluster on carpets like other houses attract dust. It's not the usual way for a house to behave.

Behind you, the door clicks shut, and it is suddenly dark. You hear clanking as the suit of armor resumes its position in front of the tapestry and drops the tapestry back over the doorway. Oh well, it isn't as if anyone would come looking for you anyway. You shudder when you think about being trapped in here forever. Don't be stupid, you remind yourself. You know better than to get frightened in this passage. You might as well feel like that in the whole house!

Now, where are we going?

As your eyes try to make sense of the darkness, your feet slowly feel their way forward. You can smell dust in the air, but there doesn't seem to be anything to trip on. The leather pouch, slung over your shoulder, feels warm. You take another peek inside the pouch and realize the jar is quite visible. Sunshine, eh? You take out the jar and unscrew the lid a tiny bit. Soft yellow light swirls out like smoke. As the light spreads, you can see more and more of the passage. Not knowing how much light you have, or how much you'll need, you put the lid back on. Now you can see quite well and resume cautious exploration.

A cool draft to your right draws your eye to a part of the wall where the paneling is different. At eye level is a piece of board about the size of a large book with a hinge at one end. It's a little window of some sort. You open it and find yourself staring into a room you've seen before. It's the Magician's drawing room and has high ceilings and long portraits hanging from every wall.

470

It is time to make a decision. Do you:

Investigate the drawing room? **P471**

Or

Go down the secret passage? **P474**

Investigate the Magician's drawing room

The drawing room is octagonal. It has a carved door in one wall and paintings on all the rest. The paintings all show the Magician. The one closest to the door shows him performing in a theatre. He is dressed in purple robes and a pointy hat and is making a great glass orb float in the air. The next painting shows the Magician sawing a long box in half—there is a person's head at one end and their feet at the other. Another painting shows the Magician making potions, and in another he wears shiny armor and stands next to a dragon.

The pictures are bemusing. Although you recognize the Magician in each picture, you can't recall what he looks like when you look away. You never seem to be able to remember exactly what the Magician looks like, even though you have breakfast with him most mornings. It's the same with these paintings. You can remember details like the clothes he is wearing and other people and things in the pictures, but when you look away you can't bring the Magician's face to your mind.

The red frog climbs up from your shoulder and jumps on your head. It is looking too.

There is a table in the center of the room. On top of the table is a round woven basket shaped almost like a ball. The basket has a woven lid. As you watch it, the basket gives an almost imperceptible shudder. You wonder what is inside. The frog on your head gives a little twitch, perhaps wanting you to move on. Then the basket gives a little twitch too. What is in there?

By the light of the sunshine jar, you see a catch in the wall. You lift the catch, and a panel swings open. You step inside the room, curious about what is inside the basket.

You cross the room and take a quick peek out of the far door. Hooray! The kitchen door is only a short distance down the hallway. You put the frog down and leave the door open so the way to the kitchen will be more likely to stay put. You'll only be a minute and then you can get straight to breakfast.

Now, back to the basket. What could be making it move? It shudders and shakes as you get nearer and then, as you reach out, goes perfectly still. You'll open and shut the lid fast to see what is inside. You'll just take a quick peek.

You count out loud: "One, two, three!"

The snake in the basket is very fast. Before you blink, it has sunk its fangs into your wrist and then disappeared back into the basket. The lid drops back on the top. A cold heaviness spreads up your arm from the bite. You watch as your hand and arm turn to stone as the poison spreads further. Before you can run to the door, your whole body becomes heavy and everything slows down.

Staring across the room, you see another picture of the Magician. He has a flute and is charming a snake out of a basket, the same basket that is on the table, the same snake that bit you. The Magician's eyes are laughing.

Sometime later, you hear people coming into the room. Being a statue, you can't turn to see who is there, and the voices are muffled. The snake's bite has dulled your senses. Eventually, the gardeners arrive and tip you up into a wheelbarrow. They move you outside by the topiary and fountains. You watch the moon getting full and then turning into a small crescent again. Some nights, strange creatures come into the Magician's garden. If you ever change back, you'd like to find out more about them. There is a lot of time to think. What would have happened if you hadn't opened the basket but had turned back and kept going down the passage? If you ever come back to life, you'd like to find out. From time to time, the red frog comes and sits beside you.

You finally come back to life during a lightning storm. Wet and cold, you head indoors and find your way back to your room in the turret. Maybe someone else will have moved in? To your relief, it still looks like your room. In the morning, you are incredibly hungry and vow to yourself NOT to get distracted on the way to breakfast in the future.

At breakfast, everyone greets you like a long-lost friend and asks what it was like to be turned to stone.

After breakfast, you go out to see where you had been standing in the garden and see that your footprints are still clearly visible on the ground. You must have been standing there for months.

It is time to make a decision. Do you

Return to your room in the turret and start over again? **P465**

Or

Go back to the secret passage? **P474**

Go down the secret passage

A faint breeze alerts you to the possibility of another door in the passage. On one side of the hall, the wall is made of blackboard canvas with upside down writing and numbers on it and some sort of map. Why is the writing upside down? Hang on—some of this writing is familiar. This is the back of the big roller blackboard in the Magician's classroom.

The schoolroom must be on the other side of the wall. When the board is rolled forward, the writing on this side will be upside down.

Yesterday, in the schoolroom, you were asking how long it took to sail to the other side of the world. Miss Eleanor Spurlock, the teacher, drew a quick map of Australia as she answered the question. You remember her drawing the southern continent now. That island you are looking at is Australia, but you didn't recognize it upside down.

The giant blackboard takes up half of one of the schoolroom walls. There is a rope and pulley to turn the blackboard—when you pull the rope, the whole board rotates like a giant flat wheel, revealing a new expanse of board for Miss Spurlock to draw on.

Sometimes she asks you or one of your classmates to turn the board. Turning the crank is fun, but what is also interesting are the pictures that are sometimes revealed in a new stretch of blackboard canvas.

Once, a large portrait of a tiger appeared and nobody had the heart to erase it, so everything was written around it that day. Later, when you looked for the tiger again, it wasn't there.

Another time, a large sailing ship was revealed with a sailor leaning over the side to see a mermaid. Again, everyone agreed to leave the picture, and next time it came around, you saw that the ship was leaving. The man now had a tail, and he was swimming off with the mermaid.

Further down the secret passage, you hear someone crying through the walls. You recognize the back of a large painting with a spy hole within it. You open the sunshine jar a tiny bit so you have more light. This section of the passage is quite different from the rest. It is all made of wood, and parts almost look as if it has grown here rather than been built.

The back of the picture seems very organic. It has a glossy wooden frame, which seems odd considering this is the back of the picture and nobody would be viewing it from this side.

When you slide the panel open, you are looking into a circular room a little bigger than your own turret. There is a wooden bed with blue and green embroidered sheets and coverlet. It looks somehow as if it grew in the room as the base of the bed seems to have roots that sink into the wooden floor. A girl is thumping the pillows on the bed. A mirror leaning against one wall reflects the picture you stand behind. It is a picture of Medusa—the woman who had snakes instead of hair. You have seen her in a book about mythology. The rest of the room contains a chest and a small bookcase and a table and chair. There is an ornate window with a seat built under it and some sort of weaving frame.

The crying girl rolls across the bed and then pushes herself up and over to the dressing table. She is wearing a green velvet dress. Her long black hair is arranged in raven ringlets. She angrily wipes her eyes and reaches for a book. You see she has a stack of them. You love books, and you peer to see what kind they are, but the next thing you see is that she hurls the top one against the window. You brace yourself, thinking the window will smash, but the book just bounces off it and slaps to the floor. She sighs and opens another one up and starts reading.

She seems so despondent.

You let more sunshine out of the jar to see the picture you stand behind. You see it is in fact a door set into the wall. There is a wooden handle on the picture and, just like the bed, the handle seems to have grown there like a branch.

Should you open the door or continue down the passage?

476

It is time to make a decision. Do you:

Continue down the secret passage? **P477**

Or

Open the door? **P481**

Continue down the passageway

You have a nagging feeling you missed out on something, but breakfast is the most important thing on your mind. You head on down the corridor, and soon there is another little door just like the first one you entered. Hopefully, the kitchen is on the other side.

The passage door opens into a large pot cupboard and, with a clatter, you crawl out through pans and tins into the kitchen. As you open the door, you smell reassuring breakfast smells. Your homing instincts have done it again.

The kitchen is the anchor of the whole house. It is more solid and reliable and, of course, it is where the food is. To call it simply 'the kitchen' just doesn't do it justice. It is a vast area with three different fireplaces, multiple ovens, and work tables. Over to the right are two wooden doors which lead to the pantries and the herbarium. They are always there—they don't move around. Over to the left, a door takes you to the sun room and on to the cook's quarters. The sun room looks out to the garden and even when it's night time it looks like day through its windows. The gardeners sit there in the evenings sometimes to look for slugs with their slug nets.

The floor is made of flagstones. They are great grey slabs of stone sunk into the ground. They were once flat but over time they have acquired slight dips where they have been smoothed by many feet. The passage of time has served to form comforting paths that ease the way for someone burdened by a tray of empty glasses or piping hot pies.

The kitchen is a deep room—the walls either side of the cupboard you crawled out of are covered in shelves and more cupboards containing plates and pots and saucepans of burnished copper.

The other side of the kitchen is set with benches running from one end to the other. The wall immediately above the benches is set with a crazy collection of different tiles—yellow and cerulean and violet and black and white with blue pictures. Above those are wide windows that go to the ceiling. From wherever you are in the kitchens, you can look out to the gardens. Above your head hangs a jungle of herbs, strings of onions, and braids of garlic. There are hooks holding jugs and copper pots. Sometimes, a pair of eyes peeks from a pot.

The kitchen is warm when snow covers the garden outside and cool when summer is at its height. At the stove, your friend Henry is frying bacon and sausages. Mrs. Noogles turns to you and smiles.

"You've made good time this morning—come and help with these potato cakes."

You make haste to help her at the griddle, and when they are all cooked and piled in a golden pyramid, you take them to the table. The rest of the household are turning up now—some come through doors and others in stranger ways than you arrived. Scarlet, the housemaid, marches up from steps that materialize from a large flag stone in the floor. The librarian reads herself in, nose in a cookbook.

Last to arrive is the Magician. He folds himself into the room and smiles at everyone in morning greeting. The gardeners lift their caps to him, and Scarlet makes a quick bob. You are putting the last of the cutlery on the table, so you nod and he nods right back.

"Get yourselves seated!" commands Mrs. Noogles, and everybody does. You know that in most great houses the master would eat on his own—never with the servants, and never in the kitchen. But the Magician is not like most masters.

Everyone makes quick work of breakfast. You eat heartily and, like most of your colleagues, you put a few snacks aside for later. If you have trouble finding the kitchen, you won't go hungry.

Henry, your friend, has found a strange boy called Charlie in the house. Mrs. Noogles cleaned him up and invited him to breakfast, and the Magician seems to have taken a shine to him. He invites him to join you all. You're pleased—Charlie seems like fun. He's heading out to grab his gear and asks if you want to go with him. You're considering whether you will when Mrs. Noogles says you only have two options:

Do a few tasks in the herb room and then get to school, or polish the suit of armor—which might take a while.

It is time to make a decision. Do you:

Help with the herbs? **P502**

Or

Polish the armor? **P480**

Polish the armor

Mrs. Noogles shows you to the armory. You had no idea there was an armory. She taps on a flagstone, and the stone rumbles beneath the rest of the floor to form a first step. Down forty more steps you find a large bench set up with clothes and oil and screwdrivers and hammers. There is not one but three suits of armor waiting patiently by the bench as if they were queuing to get their library books issued, or to buy something in a shop. So that's why you see the suit of armor everywhere—there are lots!

"Goodness! It's been a while since we did some polishing. Looks like the job has been piling up," says Mrs. Noogles.

She points out what needs to be done. Each suit must be dismantled and each piece polished and oiled. You'll be lucky to be out of here by dinner. Oh well, you think, better get started, it's not always an exciting day in the Magician's house.

You have just finished the first one when you look up and find a fourth has arrived. This could be a really long day.

It's time to make a decision. Do you:

See Mrs. Noogles about another task instead? **P502**

Or

Start at the beginning of the story and try another path? **P465**

Open the door

The picture door creaks open stiffly. As you step into the room, you smell clean fresh air and the scent of pine trees. The girl whirls towards you in surprise. She grabs a book as if she will throw it at you, and you duck in case she does. Then she puts down the book and smiles as she works out you aren't a threat.

You introduce yourself. As you do, the red frog jumps down to the floor with a plop.

"Nice frog. Is it enchanted? What can it do?"

Now that she mentions it, you suppose the frog probably *is* enchanted in some way, but you explain you have never seen it do anything useful or even interesting. It's just a frog.

"Have you tried kissing it? They do that in stories, you know."

You both look at the frog, but neither of you think this is a good time to try kissing it. The girl introduces herself as Devorah. You decide to ask what the problem is—you explain how you accidentally ended up spying on her on your way to breakfast.

"It wasn't on purpose—I was on my way to the kitchen, and I found the secret passage and then…"

Devorah cuts your apology off:

"It's perfectly fine. I'm so happy to have someone to talk to! Perhaps this means I can get out of the passage too!"

While she's talking, you look around the room. It's high up in a tower and much bigger than your own turret. There is no staircase, so you wonder how Devorah gets outside. Her home is less like a building and more like being inside a giant tree. Near the picture doorway you entered is a large balcony. The view is completely different from your bedroom. Instead of seeing London, a great forest stretches out as far as you can see. You are far from the Magician's house. At the foot of the tower, great roots anchor it to the forest floor as though it grew there. It's a dizzyingly long way down, and the surrounding trees are not close enough to jump to. You can see a rough road starts at the foot of the tower and disappears into the forest. Here and there, the road appears again on the hills off in the distance. At the top of one hill, you see a small thatched hut. Other than that, the tower is alone in a sea of trees.

Devorah calls you back into the room.

"Be careful out there—she might see you!"

"Who?"

"The witch, Baba Yaga."

"What a funny name," you say. "I've never heard of Baba Yaga."

"How can you not know her? She torments the country."

"I'm not from this country. I am from a magic house, though."

Devorah nods and doesn't seem too surprised.

"Your Magician's house has connected to a very different part of the world."

Devorah explains she has been imprisoned in this tower for months.

"It was wintertime when I came here, and now it's nearly winter again. My father, the king, stood up to Baba Yaga. She arrived in her house that moves on chicken feet, and she took me away. I thought she would eat me, but she locked me up here. I suppose my father will do what she wants with me imprisoned. And worse, when she visits me she talks about her son all the time. I think she wants me to marry him."

Devorah shudders, thinking about Baba Yaga's son. Then she grins in a brave way and leans in to whisper, "I've been trying to steal a little of her magic each time she visits—just a tiny amount when she climbs in the window and won't notice. Her magic is very strong. I'm using it to try to escape using the picture you came through."

Devorah has only recently been able to come through the picture doorway but hasn't yet been able to cross over to the Magician's house.

You ask why the witch climbs in the window and doesn't use the door.

"There is no door. This is an enchanted tower." Devorah looks at you like you don't know anything. You don't know much, but this story is reminding you of a tale about a girl with long, long hair. Maybe that's where this witch, Baba Yaga, got the idea from.

"How do you steal her magic?" you ask.

Devorah looks ashamed. "I know it's not very nice to use other people's magic, but I need to get out of here. I thought if I made a magical door, I might be able to escape."

Devorah tells you she steals magic from the witch by plucking one of her hairs as she helps haul her in the window.

"That's very clever," you say, and Devorah smiles.

"I learned a little magic from my great-great-aunt who lives outside my father's castle. She taught me how to weave rogue magic, and that's what I've done."

Devorah shows you a fine thread of plaited hair surrounding the picture. In this way, she's charmed the picture to become a portal. You tell her you think she's been very clever.

"I've added some charms of protection as you would to a door. I was hoping it would start to act like a door, and it has! I just felt for other magic and tried to connect to it. So far, I've only managed to get a little way down the passage. You coming through might have helped strengthen the connection, I'm sure, but I think I'm going to need a little more magic to get myself through."

Devorah is keen to try to get through the passage again and into the safety of the Magician's house. You both step through the picture door and close it behind you. Back inside the corridor, you open the sunshine jar again. You head to the door you thought would take you to the kitchen.

At the end of the passage, there is a door exactly like the one you entered this morning—you have travelled in a circle and are back where you started. When you open the door, the suit of armor stands there holding the tapestry up. You walk through all right, but something is wrong—Devorah can't come through. It's as though there is a wall for her that you can't see.

"My spell isn't strong enough. I can't get through the door. You've been able to visit me, but I need a bit more magic to get through. I'll have to wait for the witch and risk taking a tiny bit more of her power."

You are nervous of Devorah getting caught by the witch stealing more magic. Maybe you could do something to help.

"Have you tried signaling to that hut you can see from your tower?" you ask.

Devorah looks alarmed.

"Hut? You saw a hut? But that's her! She travels in a hut on chicken legs. There isn't anyone else on that road and no other dwelling. That means she's coming. I have to get back before she finds what I've been doing."

Devorah hastens back down the passage to her prison. What should you do?

It is time to make a decision. Do you:

Go for help? **P489**

Or

Return with Devorah to her tower? **P485**

Return with Devorah to her tower

You follow Devorah down the passage. Behind you, the door shuts, and now the passage is in near darkness. The sunshine jar is empty.

The tower must be close by on your right. You bump into Devorah, who must be searching too, and then retch as you smell something rotten like dead meat. Devorah is trembling—she leans close and holds a finger to your lips. You don't need her to tell you that the witch is here.

The sound of the witch's voice makes your blood run cold.

"That's right, my pretty, keep quiet and let me listen to your heart, beating fast like a trapped little bird. Two trapped birds. Mmmmm, someone smells delicious. It seems you've found yourself some tasty company."

The witch is very close. You step backwards softly, wishing frantically that the Magician's house would play a trick on her so you can escape. You put your hand out to feel the wall, but instead you feel trees! Underfoot, the ground is suddenly rough, and you realize the witch has transported you both back to her forest. It is dark and terrifying.

The red frog tickles at your neck. You didn't even know it was still with you. You carefully gather it and crouch down to feel for a safe place on the ground for it to sit. You might be going to meet a sticky end, but there's no need for the frog to join you. It feels very warm, perhaps trying to give you a little courage. When you stand up again, Devorah feels for your hand. You stand still and listen for the witch's approach. You can't run because you would just hit a tree in the thick forest.

Just then, Devorah taps you, and you wonder why. Then you see a red glow on the ground that is steadily getting bigger and brighter. The frog is giving off light and getting larger! It is now the size of a cat. As the light gets brighter, you start to see the shapes of trees and the forest floor—ahead you see the looming form of the tower that

Devorah has spent so long trapped inside. At the base of the tower stands Baba Yaga. She is a black malevolent shape that reeks of carrion. Perhaps the frog wants to help so you can make a run for it?

Baba Yaga steps forward.

"What's this? You've found a new pet."

She looks at the frog as it glows and grows. She appears about to kick your little friend, so you throw the empty jar of sunshine at her. The witch doesn't even flinch, but she doesn't hurt the frog. Instead, she turns her gaze to look at you. Her eyes are black and merciless, and the light from the frog reveals a strangely distorted face with a wide mouth and sharp, pointed teeth.

She licks her lips, and her face twists into a horrible smile. Then she says, "Let's get the oven stoked."

She makes a cackling bird call. There is scrabbling and creaking as her enchanted hut comes into the clearing. It moves on four giant chicken legs with a drunken dancing step. The hut turns so the front door is facing you. The door opens, and you see an oven with a raging fire inside.

"Crebbit!"

The frog makes the first sound you have ever heard from it. It is now the size of a lion. It jumps between you and the house as if to say "Don't try it."

The witch laughs, and then several things happen at once. She raises her hands to throw a spell, and the frog opens its mouth. She opens her own mouth but nothing comes out because the frog's long tongue has shot out and wrapped around her, and she is being dragged into its mouth. There is a gulp from the frog, and then its stomach glows an especially bright red like a furnace. You imagine you can hear the witch screaming, but you aren't sure because there is suddenly so much more noise. The witch's house is disintegrating, and four ordinary-looking chickens fly free from the spell that has made them carry her home. They head off into the night, squawking and flying about erratically into the forest. The tower, Devorah's prison, begins to creak and change too. The witch's magic is fading rapidly.

The picture of Medusa, which Devorah made into a door, lands near you with a thud. It is propped against the trunk of what was once the tower but now is a very tall, but ordinary-looking, tree. Light is now coming from the sky, and you can see the forest around you.

Devorah walks toward the painting. After meeting the witch, the picture of Medusa with snakes for hair doesn't seem too bad. You catch yourself thinking she might have been a very lonely person if everyone she met turned to stone. Devorah tries the door. Luckily it is still working.

"Quick! You had better return before the magic is gone," she says.

You try to convince her to come with you, but she shakes her head and points up the dirt road. There, in the distance, you see horses and riders approaching. Devorah waves to them.

"It's my father's men—they will take me home. This place has been hidden to them by magic, but now they've found me."

The riders carry banners and wear old-fashioned chainmail and leather helms. Large dogs run alongside the horses. You're glad they are apparently friends of hers.

Devorah throws her arms around you in a hug and then pushes you through the painting door with the red frog following. It shuts with a clang, and you know it will never open again. You start to fumble your way along in the passage. There is a loud plopping sound, and then you see a slight red glow ahead at your feet. The red frog is still glowing, and it helps you find a door.

You fall out of the passage and bang into the suit of armor, which clatters to the floor of the kitchen. Most of the household are eating at the long kitchen table. Mrs. Noogles tells you that you can clean up that suit of armor as soon as you've had something to eat. Then she sees the red frog. It is the size of a very large dog.

"What have you been feeding that frog?"

In a normal house, people might have been asking where you have been all this time, but this is the Magician's house, and people know bizarre things happen. You bet your weird morning was one of the oddest, though. The red frog hops over to the door to the garden and looks up at the door knob. You open the door and watch it hop off toward the water fountain. You wonder if you will find it back in your tower tomorrow.

Mrs. Noogles calls you to the table, and you realize you are famished. You sit down and listen to the others talking. The Magician looks over to you and smiles, and you grin back.

You have reached the end of this part of the story.

Now you have another decision to make. Do you:

Start the story over again and try other paths? **P465**

Or

Consult the list of choices to find somewhere you haven't been yet? **P537**

Go for help

You watch Devorah run back to her prison. There must be something you can do. You don't think the hole in the ground will help. You need to find the Magician or someone else who knows magic. You look behind another tapestry and find a door that leads you to a balcony. There is a clanking beside you, and you turn to see the suit of armor now standing to attention at the start of an ornate flight of stairs.

You know these stairs very well. If you run down the middle, you'll take twice as long to get down them as it would if you skip down the sides. There is a party in the middle of the stairs—or the house is keeping the memory of one. If you go down the center, all you'll do is end up saying "excuse me" and "pardon me" and "it's just down the hall" to a host of tittering ladies and mustachioed men and avoiding waiters carrying trays with precariously balanced glasses.

You want to go down fast. You leap down the stairs, hugging the wall, and then hear banging and crashing in a nearby room, but you can't spare time to investigate. It can't be Devorah because she can't get through. At last, you see the kitchen door.

You burst through and find most of the household eating their breakfast. The Magician is there too making short work of a plate of sausages and other good breakfast fare. The cook, Mrs. Noogles, starts to tell you off for being so late. It's your job to help. At the same time, you are blurting your story to everyone and repeating the message that there is a girl trapped in a tower by a witch.

"Interesting," says the Magician.

"Appalling," says Mrs. Noogles.

One of the garden boys hesitantly asks whether Devorah is good-looking. You scowl at him and yell in frustration:

"I need some help here!"

There is silence after you yell, and then you hear a croaking from a pot cupboard. Mrs. Noogles opens the cupboard door, and out squeezes the red frog. Everyone stares. It is now the size of a large dog. It also seems to be giving off heat and belching. The smell is not pleasant. The frog looks at you, and then hops to the garden door. It looks up at the door knob expectantly. You start to let it out when the Magician calls out, "Wait!" He crosses over and takes a good look at the frog. He opens its mouth and peers in. It doesn't smell good.

The Magician announces the frog has recently eaten something or someone particularly malevolent.

"Was the frog with you at this tree tower?"

You nod yes.

"Well, I suspect your new friend won't be having any more trouble from her witch. This frog is attracted to bad, and it's had a bellyful today."

The Magician turns to the cheeky gardener.

"You'd better fetch a shovel. What goes in must come out, and we'll need a pit digging for this lot. Still, it might be just the thing to start a nice crop of rhubarb."

The Magician lets the frog outside, and together you head back to the tapestry where you found the passage. There is no door anymore. How will you know for sure that Devorah is all right? Wait. The picture on the tapestry no longer shows a tower in a forest.

You look at the new scene depicted on the fabric. Between the forest's trees is a road. A group of riders is heading off down its path. All but one of the riders wears armor. She has long raven hair, and has half turned back on her horse and waves at you. It is Devorah. She is going home.

She probably can't see, but, just in case, you wave back.

You have reached the end of this part of the story. Do you:

Return to the beginning of this story and try another path? **P465**

Or

Go to the list of choices and choose somewhere else to start reading from? **P537**

Go down the ladder into the hole

You hold onto the smooth wooden ends of the ladder that poke out above the floor and swing yourself onto its rungs. Clambering downwards, you hope you'll soon smell frying bacon.

You want to go to the kitchen, but you know that you can't always predict where things will be in the Magician's house. The kitchen could be found upstairs or down. There is no sense to it. In fact, most people who live in the Magician's house keep a sandwich or an apple in their pocket in case they don't see the kitchen for a while. As you think about food your stomach growls, anticipating one of Mrs. Noogles' breakfasts.

Mrs. Noogles is the cook in the house, and she never wanders far from her domain. She says she has lost patience with the rest of the house. Her quarters are at the back of the kitchen. She has a sunny room with a view of the garden, a fireplace and an easy chair. You have never seen her in the chair, as she is usually bustling about.

The ladder is sturdy and well-secured so it doesn't wobble. The hole above you gets smaller as you climb downward. Tiny glow worms give enough light for you to make out what sort of a hole you've entered. You put out your hand and touch smooth cold rock and moss. In one place, there are so many glow worms that you can make out mushrooms growing on a ledge beside a cave. The cave would be great to explore when you've done your work and had breakfast. That's assuming you ever see it again.

As you climb further down the hole, the light dims. Your eyes are open wide and straining to see between the rungs of the ladder. Suddenly, another pair of eyes opens right in front of you.

You freeze. The eyes look at you, and you look at the eyes. You hear your heart thump loudly and then, even louder, you hear the noise of your rumbling stomach. The rumble echoes through the hole. The owner of the eyes lets out a deep chuckle, and you relax at once. You are just about to ask the owner of the eyes if they think the kitchen is near when they surprise you again. Whoever it is reaches between the rungs of the ladder and pushes you off! You lose your grip

and

fall.

You flail uselessly but can't grip on to anything to stop your fall. But as you reach about, you realize you aren't falling that fast. It is like falling through treacle or custard. The air seems thicker than usual. You relax a little and enjoy falling for a while, there isn't anything you can really do about it, and at this speed you don't think you'll get hurt.

Just as you are starting to really enjoy the ride, it changes: you fall faster, and light rushes up underneath you. Before you can panic, you arrive with a thump that knocks the breath out of you. When you come to your senses, you see you are back on your bed in your turret room. Above, you can see a hole in the arched ceiling, except instead of seeing the morning sun through the hole, you just see darkness. You hear that chuckle again, and a face pushes into your room as if parting black clouds. You recognize the large eyes, which you now see are bright green. The rest of its face is a velvety black so it is hard to see a mouth or nose or eyebrows, but it is the face of a large shaggy cat. It grins to show an impressive number of teeth.

"Hey—why did you push me?" you ask the cat creature, not really expecting a reply. It grins again and then replies:

"To get you where you were going faster!"

The cat face disappears but then pops back a moment later.

"Don't suppose you could throw a few mice in the hole sometime? I'm getting bored with catching bats."

You stare at the hole a bit longer, but the creature has gone.

A plunking noise alerts you to the red frog. It is springing up the wall. Its little suckered feet allow it to stick where gravity wouldn't usually allow, but it's a difficult task. It hurls itself toward the hole in the ceiling, but, with each jump, gravity takes its toll, and twice it falls, morphing into something made of rubber that sends it bouncing a little higher up the wall to try again. Finally, it lands just next to the hole and catches one side of it with a foot before losing its grip and landing beside you. One edge of the hole peels off the ceiling, like a pancake you once flipped too high. The frog hurls itself up the wall again and pulls another section of the hole away.

On its next attempt, the frog manages to wriggle underneath a section of the hole, which finally detaches it from the ceiling. It falls like a leaf and covers most of your bed.

The other side of the hole isn't a hole at all. The frog sits on top of it. You touch it cautiously. It is soft as silk. You fold it up so the hole is on the inside, and soon it's not much bigger than a handkerchief. Thinking this hole might come in handy, you carefully put it in your pocket before you and the frog head back down the stairs.

This time when you head down the stairs, the hole has gone because it's in your pocket. You can still go behind the tapestry that the suit of armor is showing you, or you can head down a green carpeted hallway.

Which way should you go?

It is time to make a decision. Do you:

Go down the hallway? **P494**

Or

Go through the secret door behind the suit of armor? **P468**

Go down the hallway

You step carefully, hoping to find your way to breakfast. You treat the ground as if it is an icy surface—keeping your back foot ready to take your weight should reality slip away.

The Magician's house swirls with dreams that pool in corners of rooms and cluster on carpets like other houses attract dust. Although you can't remember living any other way, you know it's not a usual way for a house to behave.

Mrs. Noogles has had quite enough of the rest of the house. She is the cook and she never wanders far from her kitchen—partly that's because she is always busy concocting food and partly because she long ago lost patience with the rest of the house. She has burnt the dinner too many times being caught out in a 'dining room dream' as she calls it. She can reliably find her quarters through a door at the back of the kitchen—a large sunny room with a view of the garden, a fireplace and an easy chair. She also has an area of the garden where she directs the growing of herbs and vegetables and fruit and a room where she dries herbs and stores her preserves and jams.

Actually, you quite like some of the dreams you have found in the house—but you have learned to watch your footing so you don't have to see a dream through if you don't want to. They aren't all pleasant. Finding your way through the dreams doesn't seem to be something everyone in the house can do. Mrs. Noogles looked at you strangely when you once described your 'back-foot' technique to her.

The grand staircase appears, and you nimbly miss the third step down. Treading on the third step transforms the quiet house to a crowded party with a ball going on and a host of masked people leaping about making noise, clinking glasses and talking about ridiculous things. It was good the first few times you experienced it, but it makes going down the stairs very slow because of all the times you need to say "excuse me" as you pass people and "no, thank you" as you are offered drinks and "just down the hall on the left" for the people looking for a powder room. If you do go down through the party, it all disappears when you hit the last stair.

If you are hungry, you can pick up little pies from the silver trays as they are offered around. Unfortunately, it is the sort of party where all the food is very small and you are expected to take only one thing from a tray at a time, so really it is better to push on and look for the kitchen.

You slide down the last half of the banister, feeling pretty pleased with your start to the day. Ahead, the kitchen door is open at the end of the corridor, and there are pleasant cooking smells wafting toward you. You veer to the left to avoid a dream of walking through a summer field after a sun shower. It is always annoying to get wet feet. You are just passing the last door when you hear a huge thump and somebody cries out.

You are so close to breakfast!

What do you do? Do you:

Find out what made the noise behind the door? **P496**

Or

Ignore the noise and head down the passageway? **P477**

Find out what made the noise behind the door

You open the door cautiously and immediately let out a sneeze. The room is swirling with soot from the chimney. A small person sits near the hearth, rubbing their head. They are so covered in soot that they are almost completely black—except for the whites of their eyes, which look up at you in fear. It's a chimney sweep. You have seen them before on London's streets, making their way through the city. You've never seen one up close before, though.

"Please, I lost my way, and I'm in ever so much trouble. I didn't mean to cause a mess."

The sweep seems so scared, and you wonder if he is hurt. You can't imagine how he could have been cleaning in the Magician's chimneys. You know for a fact the Magician sends a pair of enchanted squirrels through there every second Wednesday, so he doesn't need a sweep.

"Cheer up. You won't be in trouble," you say. "I was just about to get some breakfast. Are you peckish? If you want to eat, come with me. I can help you find the front door after that if you like."

The sweep smiles and nods. He looks down at himself and is clearly wondering how he should proceed because with every step he will make a sooty footprint.

"Don't worry," you say, "there're a lot of cleaners here." You don't mention you haven't seen them yourself, but someone or something straightens up round here all the time. "We'll get you seen to."

You step back in the hall, and he follows. You have just shut the door when the sweep suddenly exclaims:

"My brush!"

He opens the door again and stops stock still. The room is completely clean—the only evidence he has ever been there is his brush sitting at attention by the fireplace.

"See," you say, "they're very fast. Now let's make haste before we miss breakfast."

The sweep is astounded that a sooty room with no other door has been cleaned so fast, and he enters the room cautiously to collect his brush. As he leaves, he bends to look under the furniture as if maids with dusters and brooms might be hiding there. You take his hand and carefully negotiate the last few steps to the kitchen.

When the sweep sees the kitchen, he stops and stares. The kitchen is like the anchor of the whole house. Somehow it is more solid and reliable and, of course, it is where the food is. To call it simply the kitchen just doesn't do it justice. It is a vast area with three different fireplaces, multiple ovens, and work tables. To the right are two wooden doors that lead to the cool store and the herbarium. To the left, a door takes you to the sun room and on to Mrs. Noogles' quarters. The sun room is sunny and you can see the garden as if it's day, even when it's night, through its windows.

The kitchen floor is made of flagstones, great squares of stone that remind you of a giant's chess board. They were once probably flat, but over time they have acquired slight dips and been smoothed by many feet.

The walls are covered in shelves containing plates and pots and saucepans of burnished copper. The other side of the kitchen has a bench running from one end to the other. The wall above the bench is set with a crazy collection of different tiles—yellow and cerulean and violet and black and white with blue pictures. Above the rows of tiles are wide windows that go all the way to the ceiling. From wherever you are in the kitchens, you can look out to the gardens.

Your friend Henry is frying bacon and sausages. He grins at you and nods to the sweep and then gets back to his task.

"What manner of mess do we have here?" Mrs. Noogles says as she emerges from the cool store. She sets down the potatoes she was fetching, puts out a grater and a bowl and points at you.

Mmmm, potato cakes, you think. You know what to do and set to grating the potatoes. Mrs. Noogles takes charge of the sweep.

"We'll need hot water and soap."

From above her head, she reaches for a large tin tub. At that moment, Scarlet, the housemaid, comes into the room. She is yawning and stretching and about to start her day too. Mrs. Noogles sends her up to the servants' wardrobe to find some clothes for the sweep and then sets the tub into an alcove. She bustles about fetching kettles of hot water and raps on the window to attract the attention of a passing gardener. He comes in with more water from the pump, which she adds to the steaming bath.

The sweep stands about surveying the kitchen and being careful not to let soot fall in the way. He eyes the bath warily but is clearly interested in the food you are preparing. Lastly, Mrs. Noogles directs you to fetch a screen from the storeroom, and then she and the sweep disappear behind it, and there is a splashing sound as the sweep is immersed in water and given a good soaping. Mrs. Noogles lets out a steady stream of instructions to you and Henry from behind the screen.

You put the potato cakes onto the griddle and start making the toast. The sweep keeps up his chatter.

"I won't half be in trouble, Mrs. Noogles, if I don't get out and find my boss."

You think he is probably relishing the chance to get clean and looking forward to the prospect of a hot breakfast.

Scarlet returns with towels, britches, a shirt, and some shoes. There are all sorts in the storerooms, including fancy dress. You are fairly sure Scarlett was wearing a different pair of shoes earlier. Mrs. Noogles comes from behind the screen and gathers them up and then leaves the sweep to get dressed. She plunges herself into plating up bacon and sausages and the potato cakes you and Henry have prepared. You have buttered the toast, and now you set about wiping down the table and setting out places for everyone in the household.

"I think Himself will be coming for his breakfast this morning, so let's lay a few extra places."

How Mrs. Noogles knows this, you can't guess. 'Himself' is the name she uses for the Magician. You know from talking to other servants in the alley that it isn't usual for a master to eat with the household staff, but the Magician isn't usual and neither is the house. It isn't usual for the staff to go to school, but a schoolroom presents itself from time to time, and no matter how much you've tried to avoid it, the doors all seem to open onto lessons in a determined way.

The sweep rounds the screen and looks a perfectly ordinary person now he is not covered in soot. You are about to usher him to the table when every door to the kitchen opens at once—two gardeners enter from outside, stamping their feet to avoid dirt coming onto the floor, Murphy the butler arrives from another door, and the teacher comes through a cupboard door. The Magician arrives at the table without the need of a door. One moment he wasn't there, and the next he sort of folds himself into the space.

"A particularly fine morning, Mrs. Noogles," says the Magician. "Sit, lad."

He points the sweep to a seat at the long table. The gardeners don't need telling and sit themselves down as fast as if they were playing musical chairs. Soon everyone except Mrs. Noogles and you are seated as you plunk down plates and knives and forks and toast before helping to carry over platters of potato cakes and bacon and a great dish of scrambled eggs and fried tomatoes. As soon as the Magician raises a fork to his mouth, everyone else follows.

"I think we'd like to know your name, young man," states the Magician.

"Mmmf, mmmfh, I'm Charlie," says the sweep through a mouthful of food.

"He came down the chimney," you add, though you suspect the Magician knows this already. He knows most things that happen in the house.

The Magician nods and continues to ask Charlie questions. Charlie explains that his father earned less money than his family spent.

"The result of earning *more* than you spend is happiness, but the result of earning *less* than you spend is ruin," Charlie says. "Well, that's what my muvver said when they were taking all our furniture away."

Now Charlie's family is in debtor's prison, and he works in a blacking factory.

"I glue the labels on the pots. Night times, I stay in an attic with other boys like me. One of them told me about sweeping. I thought it might be better than gluing. It's not, though. I got turned around in the dark and was lost. I fell and I heard them on the rooftops looking for me. I called out, and the guv'ner said I was lost too far down and just to leave me. And that's what they did."

You shudder at the cruelty of leaving Charlie like that.

"What are you going to do now?" you ask.

"Tomorrow, I'm going back to the blacking factory. It pays my way. Maybe soon my father will be out of prison, and I can go back to school."

"You like school?" The Magician perks up. You aren't so excited by this topic. You were hoping the events of this morning might delay school.

"Charlie," says the Magician, "how would you like to work for me for a while? I could use another assistant at the theatre where I work. You can room here with the other staff and, if you'd like, you can attend the schoolroom with the others."

Charlie grins and nods and thanks the Magician for his offer. He turns and grins at you.

"Thank you so much for bringing me here!"

You are a little embarrassed because you have only brought him a few doors down the corridor, but you can see your actions have perhaps changed his life for the better, and that makes you feel really good.

Charlie will be fun to have around, and maybe you'll get to go with him to the theatre. You've been once or twice to deliver the Magician's equipment and to guard it from prying eyes.

Charlie needs to go and get his things from the attic where he stays. He asks if you want to tag along.

501

It is time to make a decision. Do you:

Go with Charlie to get his things? **P514**

Or

Don't go with Charlie? **P502**

Suddenly, Mrs. Noogles is calling.

Mrs. Noogles is calling. She wants you to clean up after breakfast.

You take the scraps out to the hen house, and when you return Henry is whistling as he washes the dishes. You join him drying the plates, and then Mrs. Noogles gets you to work on her herbs. This is something you really like doing. Mrs. Noogles has all sorts of dried plants that she uses for cooking and medicine. You are gradually learning a lot about the process. This morning, there are herbs to hang up to dry and others to take down. Sometimes, your job is wrapping muslin over flower heads to collect the seeds. Every job has a different smell to it. You package up mustard seeds set aside from the other day and offer to take them back into the storeroom before you head to the library.

The storeroom is one of your favorite rooms. It smells of thyme and cumin and paprika and other good things for cooking. At the back of the room are shelves of jams and pickles, and once you found a whole tin of jam tarts and you went back to the kitchen with one less in the tin. You look at the shelves now and notice a little tube with writing on it. *Hope.*

You have to reach high up to store the mustard seeds and, unbeknownst to you, the little tube falls in your pocket.

The library is another of your favorite rooms, and it's where you left your homework yesterday. That's your next destination. You've discovered a pretty good way to get there: carry a book. You learned the trick from Hannah, one of the librarians, who you noticed takes a book with her whenever she returns there. It isn't unusual for a librarian to carry a book, but the way she carried it was unusual. It was like an explorer with a compass. The rooms of the house are never short of books. The kitchen has cookery books, of course, but you wouldn't want to take one of those and get Mrs. Noogles annoyed. But over at the end of the benches is a room between the kitchen and the greenhouse. It is a small sunny space where the gardeners sometimes meet and talk. Mrs. Noogles can pass them a plate of biscuits and they can hand over bunches of carrots or new potatoes without taking off their boots. It's called the mud room because it's often filled with muddy boots, but that's only one side. There's also a wooden table and old comfy chairs and the thing you've come for, a bookshelf.

You don't need to read the book that will help get you to the library, but you can't help scanning the titles. There is one about the history of roses—hmm, clearly a gardener's choice, and so are many of the others, but this one seems out of place: *A Baroness Instructs the Genteel Art of Dance*. Huh! Nobody is going to miss that. You pull it out and cross through the kitchen. You don't think too hard about the library but step out into the corridor holding the book out a little ahead and let it make the choices about the direction you take.

The first room you enter is the ballroom. You step round a corner and there it is, and when you turn back, the way you came has gone. In fact, you are now standing in the middle of the ballroom. Arriving like this makes some people dizzy, but you've had it happen before so you stay on your feet.

The last time you were in the ballroom, you were helping at the Magician's winter solstice ball. It was a strange and wonderful affair. Guests were arriving for days, and the Magician erected extra towers in the garden for them to stay in—rather like some people put up tents. It was hard to know the difference between guests and entertainers, as many of the Magician's friends are also entertainers.

There were jugglers and lion tamers and trapeze artists and illusionists. There were also a couple from America who were crack shots with pistols and a number of fortune tellers and musicians. The days before they arrived were spent dusting the dreams from the house—Scarlet, Henry and you were set to work using brooms with pillowcases tied onto their ends herding them into wardrobes and placing signs on their doors such as 'do not enter'—but still some people did. Some went inside for fun (the picking strawberries dream in winter was quite entertaining), while others went in because they did not seem to think the signs applied to them.

The pistol shooting man didn't think signs were meant for him. His name was Wild Bill, and he strode into a cupboard on the first day he arrived and did not come out again until three days later. His partner didn't seem to mind and spent most of her time with a snake charmer who could tell the most entertaining stories. When the pistol shooter returned, she had already developed a new act with snakes. She claimed they were good to work with because they were deaf, unlike the other animals they'd tried to work with over the years who were unnerved by pistol shots and whip cracks.

The last night of the get-together was solstice night—the longest night of winter. The Magician said it was the night winter cracked and spring got in under ice and snow and began to send out green shoots and warmth under the earth. There was feasting and merriment and lots of dancing. The Magician had walked out onto the ballroom floor first with Mrs. Noogles. She wore a dress with the colors of autumn leaves, and as she danced the dress became the colors of spring.

The ballroom is deserted now after the hectic days and nights of the solstice ball, and your feet echo as you cross the parquet floor made from small blocks of wood laid in an intricate scene. Without people all over it, you can see it is a mosaic of a forest. There are trees all around the outside of the room, and in the middle there is a party going on with tall regal people and other creatures—half men and half goats—dancing and playing flutes. There are a group of girls dancing in a circle with the goat men. At the edge of the party, looking quite out of place, you see what looks like one of the young gardeners who works for the Magician. Come to think of it, you haven't seen him since the solstice party. You stare at the picture on the floor. Is the gardener trapped in the mosaic? Is the picture somehow real?

In your hand, the book seems to gently tug at you, and you remember you were heading to the library. You feel strange walking over the floor. It's like the feeling you have in a graveyard where you don't need to be told to keep to the path. You take care not to tread on the animals and people as you make your way across the room. There are several doors in the far wall—all big and imposing. The book tugs you toward the one on the left. The suit of armor is standing beside it. Was it there before? You were quite busy looking at the floor, so you can't say for sure.

You open the door and have a moment of pride. The book has acted like a compass steering you toward the mass of books and manuscripts the Magician has stored. On the other side of the door is the library. It is a cavernous expanse of tables and shelves and cabinets with treasures from the Magician's travels.

"Don't shut that door!" a voice calls out from behind stacks of books on a table.

Then out from behind the stack comes Hannah, the librarian.

"From the sound of your footsteps, you were on a flat wooden floor. Leave the door open so I can move some of these books out to be sorted. That door has opened straight onto a flight of stairs for two days, which was absolutely useless for sorting!"

You hold open the door as the librarian bustles over and wedges a wooden triangle underneath it. Then she pulls a velvet curtain rope from her pocket and secures the door handle to a hook at the end of a shelf for good measure.

Looking up, she explains. "I wouldn't want to lose my new stock somewhere in the house if the door shut. You never know when the house is going to shuffle around."

You nod in agreement and are about to go and grab your homework when you wonder if Hannah will know whether the gardener is in any trouble. You offer to push the trolley of books she is now loading up from the table. When you get closer, you notice they smell vaguely of smoke and one or two are singed at the edges.

Hannah sees you pick one up and sniff it and offers up an explanation: "Fire rescue. There are some rare volumes here. I want to air them out and check them over for my catalogue."

Hannah goes back for more books. She returns pushing another trolley. The smell of smoke is profound even in the large ball room. You look down at the floor to find the gardener—he isn't where you remember him. There is still a party scene with music and dancing and strange creatures, half goats and half men. You can't be sure if they have moved. Hannah notices you staring at the floor and comes over to take a look.

"Those are satyrs," she says.

"The picture on the floor has changed," you tell her. You explain how earlier you saw the gardener and now you don't.

Hannah is instantly interested. She studies the floor more intently and, like you, takes care not to walk on the creatures beneath your feet.

Suddenly, she calls out. "Is this your man?"

"That's him," you reply.

The gardener has climbed a tree. You notice something else. A wolf. You are sure you didn't see it before, and it is approaching the reveling group. A long tongue lolls from its mouth, and it appears to be very large.

Hannah springs into action and races back inside the library declaring: "We must rescue him at once!"

She returns wearing a cape with a hood, carrying a woven basket.

"Well," she says, "are you coming?"

You wonder how you'll enter the floor scene and how you'll rescue the gardener, but you follow Hannah as she begins a circuitous sort of half dance, gesturing to you to do the same. As you follow her path, it begins to make some sense. Her footsteps wind between the trees and other motifs set into the floor. In time, the ballroom floor softens between your feet, you begin to scuff up dirt, then leaves and small twigs. Looking up, you see that the ballroom walls are now decorated with a forest scene on the wallpaper. The smell of burnt books gradually fades and is replaced by the pleasant smell of damp earth after it has rained.

Before long, you duck to avoid a branch, and when you look around, there is no sign of the ballroom at all. Hannah moves along stealthily. From her basket she draws a dagger and tucks it into her belt. She also brings out a bar of chocolate and breaks a piece off.

"While we are down here it would be best if you don't eat anything from this forest—do you understand? This type of enchantment often works by binding you with food and drink."

You nod and start to think back on the breakfast chats where the librarians have been describing their acquisition activities. You'd assumed they would be (you blush a little) boring. But the way Hannah has jumped into this mission makes you think you have completely underrated her job. Just then, you hear a howl in the distance. Hannah slows and cocks her head to listen. She signals for you to hold still. Slowly, she takes off her cloak and turns it around—inside, it is the color of blood.

"I'm going to scout ahead. Walk toward the sound of music and keep out of sight. See if you can find the gardener. You'll see my cloak when I want you to."

"But won't the wolf see you?"

"Wolves are colorblind, but they smell and hear better than we do. Anyway, I'm not convinced that the wolf is our greatest enemy here. I'll be back soon."

She flips the hood of her cloak over her head and vanishes, apart from her basket, which winks out of sight as it disappears under the folds of the cloak.

You head on through the woods, scrunching leaves underfoot as you move between the trees. You don't know if you are following a path or just places where the trees are not too close together. You come to a clearing and notice a strange thing. Over to your right, a tree is bursting into pink and white spring buds, but the path by which you entered the glade is covered in orange, brown and red fallen leaves. There are patches of snow to your left, but ahead the trees hold ripe summer fruit. This place has all the seasons going on at once. You walk across the clearing to a peach tree laden with perfect golden fruit. The air, as you get closer, is heavy with the sweet fruity scent. You are about to reach out and pick one when a voice from above calls out.

"I wouldn't if I were you!"

Up in another tree is the gardener. His smile broadens in recognition when he sees you, and he jumps down to clap your back and jump around.

"You've come from the Magician's house!"

You tell him how you saw him in the floor and followed a path till it turned into the forest. You ask his name, and he tells you he is Ted. As soon as Ted speaks his name, you remember him clearly, which makes you worry there might be some sort of forgetting spell involved in this adventure.

"How long have I been down here?" Ted asks. "Is the solstice party still going?"

You explain it's been quite a while since the Magician's annual party. And then you wonder:

"Have you eaten anything?"

Ted shakes his head. "I'm not sure, but places like this usually have enchanted food. Look around, its summer and winter and spring all at once. Whatever grows here is grown with the aid of magic. The Magician has rules for us gardeners: we grow things in season, and there's only a little magic around the edges—keeping the bugs away and helping plants find the light and grow deep roots, but the food we eat is nourished by the land and not magic. This here is something different."

Then the gardener looks at you expectantly. "I don't suppose you brought any food, did you?"

In fact, you do have something you saved from breakfast—everyone keeps a snack in their pocket if they work in the Magician's house. You pull out a crumbling piece of toast, and the gardener looks at it as though it is a three course meal on silver trays. He is about to take a corner before asking:

"Do you know how to get out of here?"

You tell him you don't know, but before he can be too

disappointed, you tell him about the librarian. "She'll know what to do or else there will be three of us missing, and surely the Magician will come looking with three staff lost in the house!"

Ted nods. Just then, a howl sounds very close by, and Ted invites you to climb up into the tree he came down from. You find he has made a platform up there—a number of slender branches and stems have been woven across some central ones to form something like a large hammock. He has other things up there too, and he's also woven a set of stairs to a higher platform.

You have only just climbed up when you hear paws padding into the glade, and you know the wolf is below. There is a sniffing and snuffling under your tree. The wolf must have followed your scent. You wonder if it will leave or stay and what has happened to Hannah.

Just then, a whistle sounds and the wolf crashes off. There is another whistle, closer this time, and then the wolf comes racing back to sniff at your tree and then tears back off across the glen in another direction. Someone else enters the clearing, and you and Ted look at each other trying to work out if you should call out or not. Hannah's voice interrupts your silent debate:

"Well, is anyone going to invite me into the tree?"

Ted lowers down his hand, and Hannah, ignoring it, climbs up like a monkey. You think of all those ladders in the library and wonder if that is how she got to be such a climber.

"Right," she says, very business-like. "Looks like we've got ourselves a typical enchanted forest situation. A few ways in, but, as yet, no discernible way out. A fly trap of sorts. There's a big doggie out there with sharp teeth, but he likes to play fetch. Not really a problem." She looks at Ted. "You been here long?"

Ted tells Hannah his story. Blushing, he tells her that there were some beautiful girls he'd seen heading off each night, as if to a ball, and he'd wanted to dance with one of them. He'd followed them the first night and had seen them enter the ballroom and start dancing. Before long, they had disappeared from sight, and he'd felt sure if he knew the steps, he could dance his way into the heart of the last dancer.

"Hmmm," says Hannah. "So you weren't meant to land in this trap—you've just come in the back door. I was hoping we wouldn't have to go talk to the satyrs, but we may need to find out how to get back to the house from them. They aren't always friendly. Still, we might have something we can trade."

The drumming of hooves can be heard in the distance—you look down below in time to see the wolf, who had been curled up at the foot of the tree, prick his ears and listen intently. He wags his tail and retreats into denser forest a short distance away. You can see him crouching. It isn't long before three brown pigs appear. They have long tusks and are covered in shaggy hair. They begin to root about under the peach tree. One of them runs at the tree and bangs it with his head. A few ripe peaches fall to the floor, and the pigs begin to snarl and fight over them. While they are battling for the peaches, the wolf leaps out and rushes toward them. The pigs race off, and the wolf gives chase.

"I think we should join the party," says Hannah. She climbs down from the tree and starts walking. Ted follows, and you climb cautiously down too. As you walk, you ask Ted if he's spoken to the satyrs before.

"Oh yes. After I was lost here, I asked them if they knew the way for me to get back home, but they answered me in riddles and taunted me. The librarian is right, they aren't very nice. The pigs are their pets, and they aren't very nice either. "

You head on through the trees, which seem to go on forever. This world had seemed so small from above on the tiled floor of the ballroom, but it is so much bigger here. The librarian produces another round of chocolate from her basket, and Ted's eyes light up.

"Have you got a lot of food in that basket?" he asks.

"I've got one or two goodies."

She smiles at Ted, but you think she isn't quite as confident as she was at first. The terrain around you is changing. The trees are thinning out and the seasonal changes that could be seen from a short distance—ice and snow in patches among summer greens are less evident. The wood gives way to scrub, and then the dirt starts to kick up dryly as you tread. It is desolate.

"If I had to guess, I'd say someone doesn't want us to come this way," says Hannah.

"I haven't seen this part of the woods before," says Ted.

He sounds uncertain. You wish you could do something to help. You put your hands in your pockets and check to see if there's anything useful. There's the hole—but you can't imagine that would be useful right now. And what's this? You pull out the tube you'd seen earlier today in the storeroom.

"What's that?" asks Hannah.

You hand her the tube marked 'hope', and she smiles broadly.

"I'd say this is very handy."

She breaks off the end, and you see that the tube contains doughnut-shaped lozenges. Hannah hands them around and pops one in her mouth. Ted, as always, is eager for any 'real' food.

You put the hope into your mouth and feel a rush of zingy citrus. "Lemon!" you say just as Ted calls out "Strawberry!"

"Mine is raspberry," says Hannah. "Hope must taste differently to different people. Huh? Did anyone see that building there before?"

Not too far away, a wooden building stands on its own. It has large windows at the front and a double width door. Above the door is a sign which clearly states 'Library'.

"Well, that's just dandy," exclaims Hannah. "Now we just need to enquire about returns."

She sets off again, and you and Ted follow, looking at one another and laughing. You can't believe things seemed so grim before. You head towards the building. As you do, the ground changes, becoming a little flatter and with a tile here and there, a wooden one. Around the building, the ground is different, and it starts to change underfoot as you near it. Before long, the floor resembles that of the ballroom floor earlier this morning, except instead of seeing a forest floor and satyrs and wolves and trees, you see some of the people who live in the Magician's house and even the Magician himself standing with his hands on his hips looking up at you.

Just as you are about to get to the library, there is the sound of angry squealing in the distance, and the pigs race up in a cloud of dust. The satyrs are close behind, and they laugh at you menacingly. The pigs start to blow at the library, and the building begins to buckle and sway. You pick up speed to try and get to it before it disappears. Hannah lets out a whistle, and the wolf appears and starts snarling and snapping at the pigs. They stop blowing as the wolf harasses them. The library is within reach. Ted opens the door and holds out his hand to you and tosses you inside. Then he reaches for Hannah, who is still encouraging the wolf. The satyrs have begun to angrily kick at the wolf, which dodges them as it continues to keep the pigs from destroying the library.

At last, Ted grabs on to Hannah and pulls her into the library. He is about to slam the door when Hannah grabs it and lets out a low whistle. The wolf leaps inside too as she slams the door on the angry pigs and satyrs outside. The library begins to move as if it has been picked up by a tornado. Books explode from shelves and whirl around. The wolf leans into Hannah and whines in fear. Ted steadies Hannah, but she doesn't seem to need any help that you can see. At last, the wind dies down. Hannah opens the door with the wolf beside her. She steps out, and you see you are entering the Magician's library.

Across the room, you see the door Hannah propped open earlier and beyond that … a great big hole in the ballroom floor. The Magician is standing next to it as though he is preparing to cast a spell. He waves and doesn't seem too concerned about the mess.

You are the last person to step out of the strange library. The building melts back into the library wall, leaving a door that is framed with intricate carvings of leaves and vines and little pigs and satyrs.

Congratulations, you've reached the end of this part of your story.

What would you like to do now? Do you:

Go back to the beginning of this story? **P465**

Or

Check the list of choices to read from somewhere else? **P537**

Go with Charlie to get his things

It is still pretty early in the morning. Along the road, deliveries are being made in the neighborhood: bread and vegetables and meat and coal. As you round the corner of your street, Charlie exclaims and says "But that's the house we were cleaning over there. How did I end up in your master's roof? How very strange!"

If Charlie is going to be living at the Magician's house, he'll learn pretty quickly that 'strange' is an everyday event—but he's had a frightening time lately and you don't want him scared. Instead, you ask him about his family. Charlie chats about growing up outside of London in the country, the school he went to and the books he read. He might like the Magician's schoolroom—people turn up and teach and the lessons have a way of coming in handy later on, but each time you stumble upon the schoolroom it seems entirely accidental.

As you talk, the streets narrow and get busier. Charlie points at a large stone building.

"That's where my family are."

A sign outside reads *King's Bench.*

"Do you think the Magician would let me take them some scraps sometimes? They have poor food there. It's a bleak house."

You nod. Mrs. Noogles often gives away food to people who come around the back. No doubt she will find some food for Charlie's family. It does strike you as odd that someone should be imprisoned for not paying their debts—how would they ever get out? How could they work? Charlie explains that often relations pool together to pay debts. He is hopeful a family cousin will help them.

Down a small alleyway, you come to the house of the bailiff who has taken in the sons of the debtors. It is part a string of rickety houses built into the side of the prison's brick wall—the only straight part of the buildings.

The bailiff's house is four rickety stories high, and patched up here and there like a quilt with spare boards. Like the rest of the street, there is an air of dilapidation and squalor. You follow Charlie through a faded red door. Inside, the building smells of boiled cabbage and sweaty socks.

"The first floor is the bailiff's rooms," says Charlie.

As he starts up the stairs, a woman with a baby steps into the hallway and waves to him. "Home early, Charlie? Everything all right?"

"Yes, Mrs. Winch—everything's roses! I've found a man's going to put me up and give me a job and he has a schoolroom! I'm going back to school! I'm just getting my things."

Mrs. Winch reminds him about the rent that is due, and Charlie says he will be back to pay the balance. He springs up the stairs, beckoning you to follow. The next floor is rented out by the room to families and couples and smells of double cabbage and socks. You wonder what the next floor will smell like as you start up the next set of stairs. Unlike the Magician's house, you don't have to be careful of slipping into dreams, but there is a real danger of slipping through the floorboards as they are buckling and broken and patched.

The last floor is a converted attic. You needn't have worried about the smell because the draft carries it all away. It's cold and grim.

Charlie moves to a small pile of rags and boxes in the corner, and gathers his few things. You see his treasures are books and papers and his coat and hat. Here and there in the attic are other piles of belongings that must correspond to other boys. Charlie explains they are all children of debtors and the bailiff's family is very good to keep them. They are able to pay a small rent and also make some payment toward their family's debt. Suddenly, Charlie looks stricken.

"Do you think the Magician will pay me?"

Charlie glances around the attic, and you know he is thinking that if he can't be paid he really should stay in the grim position he was just happily leaving. You reassure him that the Magician is a strange fellow but also a fair one, and if he needs money you are sure it will be provided, especially if Charlie is helping at the theatre, because this is how the Magician earns his living. Charlie grins and looks very happy.

At the bottom of the stairs, the bailiff's wife is waiting with a baby on her hip. She puts a finger up to her lips to tell you to keep quiet. She points to her front room and then retreats to the back of the house. At her warning, you both slow down and hear gruff voices.

"You owe me a boy! That latest one didn't show this morning. I heard he was doing chimneys. I pay you good money to find me kids for the factory. Pay me back or give me another boy!"

Charlie's eyes go wide—there's obviously some arrangement about his job at the blacking factory. You both try to make your way cautiously outside to the street. Just as you are at the front door, there is a banging at it. You and Charlie scarper back up the stairs and crouch down to listen from the second floor. Charlie whispers that when the coast is clear you should both run out.

Heavy steps are heard in the front passage and someone opens the front door. Peering round the banister, you see the back of a big man with a heavy belt filling the doorway. A set of large keys hangs off his wide belt. This must be Mr. Winch, the bailiff. He is talking to another man who sounds just as angry as the one in the front parlor. It is the chimney sweep, and he is complaining that he lost the new sweep straight off and he wants some money back.

The bailiff isn't quite so kind after all. He is organizing children of debtors to be used as factory workers and chimney sweeps. He is taking money from the other men and he is getting rent from the children.

"Now see here!" he is telling the chimney sweep. "It's not my problem if you lose your workers down chimneys—you got to train them proper! I might find you another boy for the same arrangement, but I don't owe you nothing!"

"You owe me something, though, Winch." It is the man from the factory.

"You guaranteed me that boy for nine months of gluing. Assured me, you did! Then he's hopped off to the sweep, and he's lost him! You lost me my worker, and he was a good one too—he could read!

He never glued the labels upside down!"

The three men continue to argue. You feel a squeeze from Charlie. He signals you to follow him down the hall, holding his fingers to his lips to say to keep quiet.

Singing in a room off the hallway draws your attention to a doorway. Perhaps it would be a good idea to ask one of the people living on this floor to shelter you for a while? On the other hand, you and Charlie have done nothing wrong. The bailiff might be making money from other people's misfortune, but he has made his own trouble, he really doesn't own you. Maybe you should both just head through their argument and step out the front door?

It is time to make a decision. Do you:

Ask the singer if you can shelter with them? **P518**

Or

Try and run out of the house? **P529**

Ask the singer if you can shelter with them

You decide to wait it out until the men have gone from downstairs. Charlie knocks gently on the door next to you in the hallway. The singing stops and a woman's voice can be heard asking who is there. Charlie opens the door and steps inside with you following closely. If the person inside gives you up, you will be trapped.

The room inside faces the sun. The brightness momentarily blinds you after the dark dinginess of the rest of the house. You also notice with relief that you have left the smell of cabbage and dampness that overpowers the rest of the house. Instead, the air is filled with a very pleasant mix of flowers and perfumes. In the middle of the room, a worktable holds all sorts of jars and bottles. Closer to the window, there are potted leafy plants with pink and white and purple flowers. This is more like a room you might find in the Magician's house, not a poor London tenement building.

"What do you two want?" The voice is frail and delicate like lace and has a French accent. In amongst the clutter of bottles and beakers, you finally locate the room's occupant. She is an old woman with a grey smock over her voluminous skirts. She is carefully pouring liquid from a large container into several small bottles.

"Pardon, Madame, je suis Charles."

Charlie introduces himself in French and then asks if you can both shelter for a short while. Surely, he must be the only French-speaking chimney sweep in London! The little old woman is impressed too. She asks him questions and then, realizing you are not following the conversation, politely continues in English.

She laughs wryly when she hears that Charlie's labor has been sold to both the blacking factory and the sweep.

"That rogue! You were right to be careful, Charlie. He won't want you knowing what he's up to. He may lose his job at the prison if it's known he is profiteering. You must wait here until it is safe to leave."

Just then, you hear heavy footsteps out in the corridor as the three men head up to the attic. There is a splintering sound and loud cursing as it seems one of them has met with a rotten step. You wonder if the bailiff will realize that Charlie's things are gone. You don't have to wonder for long—his voice belts out to his wife through the house.

"Myra! You seen that Charlie today? His things ain't here!"

Mrs. Winch yells back that the boy came earlier with another kid to fetch his things—she says she reminded him about the rent. The bailiff's footsteps come back down He is telling the sweep and the blacking factory manager not to worry, now there's two kids, one for each of them … as soon as he finds them.

"I'll let that Charlie know there'll be trouble for his family if he doesn't get back to work. That'll fix him. The other one's probably a stray you can put down your chimneys and nobody will miss them."

Footsteps on the landing seem to be coming closer. There is a knock on the door and the door knob begins to turn.

You shudder to think of going down a small dark chimney and look pleadingly at your host, hoping she will not give you away. She looks very angry at what she is hearing and beckons you both to step inside a wardrobe in one corner of her room by her bed. Would that be a good place to hide?

Quick! Make a decision! Where are you and Charlie going to hide? Do you:

Hide in the wardrobe? **P525**

Or

Dive under the bed? **P520**

Dive under the bed

The bailiff's feet appear on the floor just inches from you. He asks your host if she has seen two kids.

"No, monsieur."

"Well, you won't mind me having a little look around then, will you?"

His feet return to the bed, and in seconds he has grabbed both you and Charlie and is dragging you out. He hauls you both down the stairs and triumphantly presents you to the sweep and the factory manager.

"There you go, one for each of you. You'll have to lock 'em up when you aren't using them. This one knows it's a longer lag for his dad if he don't work, and no doubt this one can be convinced to do their duty too. A bit of hunger will work wonders."

The sweep looks at you with disgust. "This one doesn't seem small enough for chimneys, but since Charlie managed to wiggle out before, I'll take him again."

The blacking factory owner grabs you by the back of your shirt. "This one doesn't seem to cough. I lose them to the black lung after six months of stirring the pots. Give me a rope."

While the bailiff goes for a rope, you struggle to get free of the factory manager's arms. Meanwhile, Charlie's face is twisted in anguish. He looks terrified to be going back to the dark chimneys. His predicament might be worse than your own.

You have an idea and look at the sweep. "My master sent me back here to get your name. You left your boy in his chimney, and he wants you to pay for the damage he caused."

The sweep looks cautious. "Now, steady on here—a boy getting stuck isn't my fault."

The greedy factory manager recognizes an opportunity and turns to the sweep. "Tell you what, since you can't have him running around ruining your good name, how about you give that one to me as well and I'll keep him secure."

The sweep nods and starts deliberating about money with the bailiff, as he feels he has paid for something he didn't get. Mr. Winch ends up agreeing to give him some coins and then ties both of you up.

Charlie doesn't look much happier, but you think if you're both together you might be able to find a way back to the Magician's house. You try to give him a reassuring look.

The blacking factory man whistles out the front door to where another man in a horse and cart is waiting. He jumps down from his seat and comes inside to help your captor. The two men toss you on the back of the cart with a rag tied over your mouth to keep you from yelling out. In this part of London, you doubt anyone would come to your aid anyway. A smelly tarpaulin is thrown over you. There is just enough light to see Charlie's frightened eyes as the cart starts moving down the lane.

You have only travelled a few streets before the cart stops once more. There are voices. Then the tarp is moved, and you are hoisted over the back of a man and taken inside a building you guess must be the blacking factory. You are taken down some stairs and dumped on a pile of sacks. Charlie lands with a woof of dust beside you. The manager addresses him:

"Well, Charlie, you've lost me a good day's work, if not more. The rest of the boys have probably been slacking off while I've been out chasing you. It's not good for business, boy. From now on, you'll be staying here with your friend, and we can take what you owe me out of your wages. I've half a mind to beat you black and blue, but that will probably just make you slower. Starting tomorrow, I want you two working. Tonight, you'll sleep down here with the rats—that will give you a taste of what it's like to cross me. It's just a taste, mind. You don't want to go doing that regular."

He picks up a stick and tosses it towards you both.

"This should give you a fighting chance against being bitten. With any luck, you'll clear a few rats out for me."

With that, he loosens the ropes around Charlie's arms, and heads back up the cellar stairs. You hear a deadbolt slide home on the other side of the door. There is faint light coming from under the door and a little more shows between the floorboards over your head. You hear Charlie moving around getting untied. He isn't the only one rustling. Rats are coming out of the corners to see what might be worth picking over.

Once Charlie has freed himself, he helps you too. The two of you stand up, rubbing the places where the ropes had rubbed at your wrists, and look at your prison.

"I've lost my books," says Charlie, and a few tears start to leak from his grimy face.

You look at him and laugh. "Charlie, we're locked in a cellar with the light fading and a horde of rats about to bite us, and *you* are crying about books."

Charlie smiles and awkwardly wipes the tears away. He starts apologizing to you for the trouble you are in. You hush him quiet and are about to tell him not to worry when a rat makes a dash across Charlie's boot and bites at his shoe lace. He shoos the rat away by stamping and picks up the stick.

"I have an idea about the rats," you say. "Did you happen to put anything from breakfast in your pocket?"

Shamefacedly, Charlie nods. From his trouser pocket, he pulls a rather mangled piece of toast, and from your own pocket you pull out the hole you folded up and tucked away this morning. Charlie watches, astonished, as you lay it out on the floor like a carpet. As soon as the hole is laid down, the ladder appears—inviting you in.

"Are we going down there?" asks Charlie.

"I'm not sure," you say, "but hopefully the rats are."

You sprinkle a line of crumbs close to the hole and carefully sprinkle some more down the sides. You both stand back to watch.

Before long, the boldest rats are scampering toward the hole and munching on the crumbs. Others follow, not wanting to miss out. Thinking there is a feast inside, they swarm down the sides—you count at least fifty. You hope the creature inside enjoys them as much as mice.

Now that the rat problem is over, you look around the cellar to see if there is any way out. It's built of stone blocks, and the walls are very solid. You walk to the back behind barrels of foul-smelling stuff and more piles of sacks, but find the cellar has no other way out.

Charlie has been searching too. He comes down the cellar stairs from where he has been checking the door and peers into the hole. "Where does that go?"

"I don't know." You explain that you think there will be an opening down the ladder, but you have no idea where.

Charlie asks if he has heard correctly and that when you first explored the hole its bottom was on the ceiling. You nod. Charlie looks around and finds half a brick. He leans over the hole and drops it in. You both listen. Splash! Wherever the hole ends up, it's a wet ending. Then you hear a yell, and Charlie says he thinks it's a boy who works stirring the blacking pot upstairs. The hole might come out right over the boiling cauldron. You certainly don't want to end up in that.

A big cat face emerges from the hole. "Thanks for the rats, my friend, but luckily I missed the brick." It looks around. "This isn't the Magician's house, is it?"

"Sorry about the brick," Charlie stammers. "We are attempting to escape from this cellar, and I was trying to determine where the hole would lead us."

The black cat eyes him and evidently decides to forgive him for chucking the brick down its hole. "Then I suggest the hole be repositioned somewhere which would allow you both an alternative exit."

After the cat disappears, you pick up the portable hole and think about where it might be best to put it next.

Charlie, though, is way ahead of you. "If we put it on the floor and it comes out in the ceiling of the room above, it might follow that if we put it against the far wall we might get out of the front door!"

524

He's really quite clever and completely wasted putting labels on jars, you think. The two of you take hold of the hole and then cast it like a fishing net at the back wall of the cellar, hoping it will form a tunnel rather than a hole.

It works.

When it lands this time, there is no ladder, and you can just walk inside. Near the entrance of the hole, there are glow worms to light the path, but just as before they soon give way to darkness. You are out in front and, before long, your foot finds the end of the path and a custardy nothing beyond it.

"Jump, kittens!" You hear the cat say. So taking each other's hand you both leap. The two of you fall in slow motion. Eventually, you land on a heap of sacks by the front door of the factory beside a black tunnel that looks like it was blasted into the brick wall of the factory.

Quickly, you roll up the hole and stuff it back in your pocket. In moments, you are both running towards the Magician's house and clapping each other on the back, congratulating each other on your escape.

Congratulations, you've reached the end of this part of your story.

What would you like to do now? Do you:

Go back to the beginning of this story? **P465**

Or

Check the List of Choices to read from somewhere else? **P537**

Hide in the wardrobe

Just as the wardrobe door shuts, the bailiff enters the room.

Through the keyhole, you see a barrel-chested man with long greasy hair tied up at his neck. A leather belt stretches around his waist from which jangles a bundle of large keys. He asks the French lady if she has seen two runaway kids.

"Their parents are debtors."

She says she hasn't seen you, but he strides into the room and looks around anyway. She asks him to leave, saying he will damage her things, but he ignores her. He crouches low and looks under the bed you nearly hid under. He takes another look around and then leaves. The lady puts her fingers to her lips and gestures for you to stay put. Next to you, Charlie is fidgeting.

"Is he gone?" he whispers.

"Shhhh," you hiss.

The bailiff heads back downstairs. You listen to muffled talking from the three men. Then there is one, then two, and a short while later, a third bang of the front door. All this time the lady has been patiently working with her bottles. When the last man leaves, she gets up and beckons you both out of the wardrobe. You both thank her for hiding you. Your rescuer introduces herself as Mignette.

"I'm happy to have helped, children. I know what it's like to be hunted. I escaped from Paris during the revolution. You never knew if you would be next to be imprisoned or worse. So I packed what I could of my business and came by boat to London."

"What is your business, Madame Mignette?" you ask.

"Why, perfume, of course! All the rich ladies need perfume, so they do not have to smell the filth of the streets and to make the men think they are like flowers themselves!"

Mignette points to the row of little bottles she is filling and offers you a sniff. The delicate scent of flowers wafts from each small vial. You watch Mignette place a small cork stopper in each and then melt wax around the cork to keep it secure. Lastly, she reaches for glue and labels, but Charlie stops her:

"I know the drill, madame," he declares and deftly adds a label to each perfume bottle while Mignette goes on to fill another batch. Having watched the process, you help with the corks and wax, and the three of you complete her work.

After a while, Mignette suggests you are both probably safe to leave. "If they were watching the building, they have probably gone." She hands you both a small bottle of perfume as thanks for the morning's work. You thank her again and warily head out of her apartment.

Outside, you keep a sharp eye out as you head back to the Magician's house. Before long, you are entering the servants' entrance and looking at the disapproving face of Mrs. Noogles. You have been away all morning and haven't been any help in the kitchen. Lunch looks to be almost prepared. Charlie hands her his bottle of perfume and says you both stopped to earn a gift for her. Mrs. Noogles breaks into a grin and tells you that you deserved some time off.

"Now get your young selves off to the schoolroom, and I'll see you when it's time to eat again."

With a sinking feeling, you realize you haven't done your homework. Maybe a new pupil will distract Miss Spurlock. You glance at Charlie and see he is giddy with excitement at the prospect of schooling. You have to smile—school can be a chore but you know it would beat working in the blacking factory or cleaning chimneys any day. You show him to the door that you hope will lead you to the schoolroom. As you head down the corridor, you resume your careful walking and explain to Charlie that this house has its own equivalent of faulty floorboards. Charlie is disbelieving until you both wander into a patch of carpet that acts like sand and causes you to drag your feet and hear gulls in the distance. You take his hand and guide him to the wall where your footing is surer, and before long you are entering the schoolroom.

Miss Spurlock looks up from a book she is reading the class as you both enter the classroom. She smiles at Charlie and says she has been expecting a new student today. She asks Charlie about his education, and he chatters about books he has read.

"You like stories, Charlie?"

"Very much, Miss."

Miss Spurlock says she'd like him to write her a story so she can get an idea of his education so far. She hands him paper and ink. Then she hands you a list of mathematical problems to practice.

The thing about Miss Spurlock is she always comes up with fascinating math problems. The first one is about calculating how many cream cakes you would have to eat if you were trapped in a pile of them and the way out was a trapdoor in the floor. Her instructions always say *show your workings.* Miss Spurlock says the workings are more important than the answer when you are learning to reckon. You know there may not be a perfect answer, but it is fun to consider. You sit down and think about what you know, and soon your mind is deep in numbers and their logic. Charlie scrawls furiously beside you. When Miss Spurlock sends you out to help with lunch, he is still scribbling.

Back in the kitchen with Mrs. Noogles, you set out the dinner plates, and she again tells you the Magician will join you all for the meal. You are slicing tomatoes for the salad when everyone else arrives to eat. Miss Spurlock is looking very happy. When the Magician arrives, she suggests to him that Charlie reads his story to everybody. The gardeners look a little uncomfortable at this, and you can tell they think the story will be boring and might interfere with the Victoria sponge cake Mrs. Noogles has ready for dessert.

Charlie looks nervous, but the Magician says it is a magnificent idea and he would love to hear it. So Charlie stands up and begins his tale.

You can't believe it! He has taken your adventures this morning and dressed them up. He describes Mignette and her escape from France with so much more detail. The maids and gardeners gasp and worry if she will make it to safety. Charlie stops just as all seems to be lost:

"Should I keep reading, or am I keeping us from cake?" he asks with the knowing smile of a born performer.

"Keep reading! Keep reading!" everyone cries.

Then Charlie describes fisticuffs between the bailiff and the chimney sweep and finally the hero—Charlie Dickens—is saved with his friend (you!) and is able to attend a fine classroom and eat first-rate food. Everybody cheers at the end, and Miss Spurlock tells him he has a talent for telling stories.

"You should keep it up."

Congratulations, you've reached the end of this part of your story.

What would you like to do now? Do you:

Go back to the beginning of this story? **P465**

Or

Check the List of Choices to read from somewhere else? **P537**

Try to run out of the house

Halfway down the stairs, Mr. Winch steps out above you and the factory manager steps out below.

You both try to get to the door but it's useless, and the two men overpower you and truss you up like a chicken for the roasting pan. You are gagged and put into big sacks and thrown on the back of a cart. In no time, you are carried into the blacking factory where Charlie worked before he became a chimney sweep.

The factory manager throws you both into a room with jars and labels and says just three words:

"Get to work!"

He closes the door, and you hear a bolt being slid on the other side, locking you in.

"I'm so sorry," says Charlie. A tear escapes down his cheek.

"Don't worry," you say.

You've remembered the hole in your pocket. Charlie watches as you place it on the floor. The ladder appears, and Charlie follows you down.

"Where does this go?" asks Charlie. You have to tell him you don't know, but it seems like a good way to get out of the factory. After a while, you hear the voice of the factory manager above. He's discovered the hole, and it sounds as if he's following you down.

"Jump," you tell Charlie, and you pull him loose from the ladder. Your fall is slow, like moving through custard. When you land, you recognize the foot of the grand stairs—you are back in the Magician's house.

"Step exactly where I step," you tell Charlie and head up the stairs. About half way up, there is a bit of a trap for the unwary traveler. If you head up the middle, you'll end up in the middle of a party crowded with people. You know how to avoid it, though, by skipping up the side. Charlie follows, and you are nearly at the top of the stairs when the factory manager comes out of the hole. He is only slightly surprised to find himself in a grand house and immediately leaps up the stairs to catch you both.

Charlie moves as if to run, but you tell him to wait. As you expected, the manager disappears into a crowd of people. He's now trapped in the party. You and Charlie slide down the banister and nearly bump into the Magician.

"Have you been bringing vermin into the house?" he asks you.

"Sorry, sir, we had to, we were being chased," says Charlie.

The factory manager has just made it out of the party. He looks very confused but still very, very angry.

"Don't worry, lad," says the Magician, and he snaps his fingers. The factory manager turns into a fat black rat. The rat sees your hole in the ground and runs down it.

A few seconds later, there is a squeak and a purring voice from the hole speaks up, "Delicious!"

"Right, you two, off to the schoolroom," says the Magician.

Congratulations, you've reached the end of this part of your story.

What would you like to do now? Do you:

Go back to the beginning of this story? P465

Or

Check the List of Choices to read from somewhere else? P537

Big List of Choices

DEADLINE DELIVERY

STRANDED STARSHIP

MYSTIC PORTAL

DANGER ON DOLPHIN ISLAND

IN THE MAGICIAN'S HOUSE

Please Review This Book

If you enjoyed this book, please review it on Amazon. This not only helps the authors, it also helps readers decide if the book is right for them.

Thanks, and may your life be full of wonderful choices,

The team at the Fairytale Factory

YouSayWhichWay.com